D0344541

A Paris Apartment

A Paris Apartment

Michelle Gable

THOMAS DUNNE BOOKS
St. Martin's Press
New York

THOMAS DUNNE BOOKS.
An imprint of St. Martin's Press.

Printed in the United States of America. For information, address St. Martin's Press, 175 Fifth Avenue, New York, N.Y. 10010.

www.thomasdunnebooks.com
www.stmartinspress.com

Design by Kathryn Parise

The Library of Congress Cataloging-in-Publication Data is available upon request.

ISBN 978-1-250-04873-8 (hardcover)
ISBN 978-1-4668-4962-4 (e-book)

St. Martin's Press books may be purchased for educational, business, or promotional use. For information on bulk purchases, please contact Macmillan Corporate and Premium Sales Department at 1-800-221-7945, extension 5442, or write specialmarkets@macmillan.com.

10 9 8 7 6 5 4

For Dennis.

For everything.

Part Un

Chapitre I

She only wanted to get out of town.

When her boss sidled up and said the words "apartment," "ninth arrondissement," and "a ton of nineteenth-century crap," April instantly thought: vacation. There would be work involved, but no matter, she was going to Paris. As every writer, poet, painter, and, yes, furniture assessor knew, it was the perfect place for escape.

The Paris team was already there. Olivier was in charge. April pictured him right then winding through the apartment, tablet in hand, scratching out notes with bony, crooked fingers. He'd called in reinforcements from New York because they needed another appraiser, specifically a furniture expert, to bolster their shoddy credentials in that area. According to April's boss the seven-room apartment held "enough pieces to outfit twelve upmarket bordellos." Peter's expectations were low. April's were high, but for a different reason. In the end they were both wrong.

Chapitre II

While her husband tightened his bow tie and straightened both sleeves, tucking and pulling to make his appearance ever more immaculate, April packed for her redeye to Charles de Gaulle. She was normally an efficient and well-honed traveler, but the thirty-day trip was screwing with her luggage ratios. April was never gone more than a week but, apparently, sometime in the two hours between "ton of crap" and before the issuance of a plane ticket, someone must've tipped Peter off that this was not your average find. Stay as long as you need, he said. We can extend the ticket.

April would remind him of this later.

"What's the problem?" Troy asked, noticing his wife's pinched forehead. He yanked his shirt straight.

"Packing. I'm not sure I have enough. Thirty days. In Paris. In June. Which means the temperature can shift sixty degrees in any given twenty-four-hour period. As they say, you don't go to Paris for the weather."

April looked up, eyes zeroing in on Troy's left cuff link as it caught the light from the overhead chandelier. It was an irrepressible habit, "assessing" things, and April had to stop her brain from calculating how much that speck of onyx and platinum might go for at auction. It wasn't that she longed for her husband's sudden demise; not as a matter of course, anyway, and never as a means to obtain wealth. Rather, her mental appraisals were a by-product of working for the world's largest auction house.

"What's with the glare?" Troy asked, chuckling slightly. "Wrong links for this get-up?"

"No. They're great. Perfect."

April looked away, relieved she did not specialize in trinkets passed down from grouchy wrinkled coots and therefore lacked the education to size up her husband's accoutrements. She did, however, have a hard-won de facto master's degree when it came to assessing Troy Vogt. That alone told April the cuff links, the ones her husband earmarked for specific work events, were inestimable, at least to him. What it said about who might be in attendance April did not want to consider.

"I'm overwhelmed." April shook her head, staring at her suitcase but not speaking strictly of sweaters and scarves.

"Pack light," Troy said. "You can always buy more once you're there. It is Paris, you know."

April smiled. "That's your answer to everything, isn't it? Buy more."

"And that's a bad thing?" Troy said with a wink as he moved toward the full-length mirror, gently patting April's backside as he squeezed past. "You are a rare wife indeed."

A rare "wife." The word startled April but shouldn't have. It had a new meaning now. Wife. *Wife*.

"Not that anyone's keeping track," Troy went on, "except for all of Wall Street, but my 'buy more' philosophy is why the recession was the best thing to happen to my firm and our investors."

"What a charming attitude," April said, trying to joke. There'd been painfully little humor in their home of late. The whole thing felt creaky, rusted out. "Who doesn't love the perspective of a smug Wall Street guy to really drive the point home?"

Troy laughed and slipped on his tuxedo jacket. He continued staring into the mirror, chortling to himself, as April sneaked one last pair of ballet flats into her hard-backed suitcase.

"Well, speaking of smug Wall Street guys," Troy said with manufactured cheer, "it seems you lucked out once again."

"Lucked out?" April steadied herself against the chest of drawers (*George III, mahogany bow-fronted, circa 1790*) as she eyed her suitcase, sizing up its potential weight. "In what way?"

It didn't look that heavy.

April inhaled. Forever imagining her shoulders wide and strong like an Olympic swimmer's instead of the slight, refined ones she really possessed, April heaved the bulging suitcase off the bed. It promptly thumped onto the floor, one-half centimeter away from shattering the bones in her left foot.

"Lucked out in avoiding another packing injury, for one," Troy said. "You realize that thing is bigger than you are, right? Sweetheart, you already have the fortuitous plane ticket. You don't need to break your foot to avoid going to one of my miserable work events."

"Oh, they're not that bad." April wiped her brow, then tilted the suitcase on its side.

" 'Not that bad'? They're awful and you know it. The other wives will be downright envious."

The other wives. And what of them, April wondered? What did they think when they pictured Troy? When they pictured her?

"You are my lucky girl," Troy went on. "Paris will save you. It will save you from yet another dreary evening in a roomful of capitalist drones."

"Oh, yes, those wretched capitalists." April rolled her eyes and continued in a poorly played British accent. "Sooo fortunate to avoid that ilk. Their vulgar obsession with monetary gain! They've no class *a'tall*."

April hoped she'd adequately blanketed the sadness with her lame attempts at humor. She did feel fortunate. However, it was not because she got to bypass a swanky work event and tête-à-têtes with the brightest (and most insufferable) on Wall Street.

No, April could hang with the best of them, despite not knowing what happened in Asian markets that morning. She could even tolerate the scene's newest trophy wife, who would inevitably overindulge in the champagne and spend half the night marveling at April's various graduate degrees, ultimately screeching to those within booze-spilling range, "Troy's wife majored in furniture!"

But April couldn't remember the last time her PhD in Art History was mistaken for showroom salesmanship. Troy almost never asked her along these days. He was forever "just popping by" events that were "no-spouses" or otherwise "too boring" for April to attend. That was the problem. Troy called her lucky, he called her saved, but April couldn't very well feel grateful to avoid a situation she'd never been expected to attend. Or worse, one where her company wasn't even desired.

Troy stopped bringing her when things between them had been relatively good. Now, who knew? Was she even supposed to go? In the end

April did feel "lucky" and "saved" because with a ticket to Paris in hand, she didn't have to contemplate that night's noninvitation. She did not have to wonder if it was by design.

"The accent needs work," Troy said as he moved to her side.

"For the record"—April batted away Troy's arm as he tried to help with the luggage—"I enjoy your events. The people are interesting. The conversation lively."

"Liar."

He turned back toward the mirror and gave himself a smoldering stare. April never knew if Troy did this because he suspected she was looking or because he thought she wasn't.

"What's so important that you need to ship out tonight anyway?" he asked, the forced casualness in his voice indicative of a certain level of suspicion.

"You know how these things go." April wondered if he'd cop to his own wariness. "Furniture emergencies. Have to get in there before the competition catches wind of the sale."

"But you're not usually gone more than a week, ten days max, and never with so little notice. It's somewhat disconcerting to get an 'I have to go out of town' text and then come home to find one's wife packing for a month."

Is it? April wanted to say. Are you really all that bothered?

Under normal circumstances she might joke about *him* being the lucky one now, wife out of town and all that. But the figurative cuts and bruises were too fresh, their long-term prognosis unclear.

"I was surprised by the urgency, too," April said. And she was surprised, but also grateful. "According to the guys in Paris, it's a remarkable find. A woman died in the South of France but had an apartment in Pigalle that's been in the family for over a century. They never owned the apartment, but leased it for a hundred years."

As she spoke, her shoulders began to loosen, her jaw started to unclench. This was a place April still knew how to navigate.

"The woman," she said, "the deceased, hadn't been inside since 1940. No one has. I keep thinking the information must be wrong. Maybe the actual dates were lost in translation and it's only been shuttered since an ugly divorce sometime in the late nineties."

April felt herself cringe at the word "divorce" but it was too late. The word was already out. And she'd been so careful to avoid it.

"Seventy years!" she chirped, her voice climbing toward the thirteen-foot ceilings. "Unimaginable!"

"I don't know," Troy said and shrugged, betraying nothing with his stern, stone face. "Same thing probably happens in Manhattan all the time. Places stay locked up while estate lawyers and trusts cut automatic checks each month, no one bothering to question a thing."

"Not if it was anything like this apartment. Evidently it's crammed to the ceiling with furniture and paintings and basically every item that came into the family's possession prior to World War II."

"Anything good?"

"Olivier seems to believe so, or I wouldn't be going. If nothing else, it's all fresh to market. Not even the Germans got in there." April shook her head in amazement. "You'd think at least one errant, gambling-addicted, drugged-up family member would have wanted to get his hands on the stuff somewhere along the way."

"Unless it's shit." Troy picked up his phone and tapped out a message. His formerly smooth brow bunched up. "A Parisian hoarder," he continued, though he was now most of the way checked out of their conversation.

April sighed.

"Ah, hon, I'm just kidding," he said, always quick with the necessary retraction, like a reflex. "It sounds very cool. Really."

The sigh? She hadn't meant it like that.

"Yes. Cool." April waved her hand around as if clearing the air. The gesture was haphazard but enough to pull Troy temporarily from his phone.

"Your rings," he said, staring at her hand and frowning slightly. "They're in the safe?"

April nodded and looked down at her bare finger. No one wore their good jewelry in Europe, right? This wasn't about their marriage, it was about her job. Biting her lip, April blinked away the sudden sting in her eyes.

"Troy, listen—" April started, but he was already back to punching at his phone.

Suddenly April's own phone rang. The car was downstairs. She looked over at her handsome husband and around at their handsome home and thought how happy she had been. For a time her life was bright and shining. *Her* apartment held everything she always wanted. Seventy years? She'd hoped to stay longer. Forever.

"I'll miss you," Troy said, appearing at April's side as she tucked her phone into the leather tote she'd packed for the plane.

As he wrapped her in a hug, his perfectly masculine Troy scent filling every pocket of air around them, April tried to take him in. She tried not to contemplate when or if she'd have this five-senses feel of him again.

Troy gently kissed the top of her head.

"I don't want you to leave," he said, sighing loudly. "Maybe you can wait. A few days?"

He sounded so sincere.

"Oh, don't worry," April said and pulled away. "I'll be back soon."

Chapitre III

April would never forget the smell of that apartment.

Seventy years seemed like nothing once she stepped into the Parisian flat. The stench was closer to one thousand, if smells had age. April inhaled the most negligible of breaths and instantly the taste of dust and perfume filled her eyes, her nose, her mouth. The scratchy sweetness would stay in the back of her throat for months. The sight would stay with her for longer.

The flat was in the Ninth Arrondissement, on the Right Bank, near the

Opéra Garnier, the Folies Bergère, and the Pigalle red-light district. This was your colorful Paris, your Paris of writers and artists and filmmakers. April suspected the home had been colorful once, too, before time covered it in dust and neglect.

On the flight across the Atlantic, April relentlessly tore through the material Sotheby's had compiled for her. The apartment had seven rooms: an antechamber, a drawing room, a dining room, two bedrooms, one bathroom, and a kitchen. In the photographs the flat was not large but the opulence apparent: high wood ceilings, pink damask wallpaper, gilded moldings.

But the glossy prints did little to convey the reality. Now, standing in the stifling air, it was overwhelming. All that stuff, rooms and rooms full of stuff. Troy was right, April thought with a smile: This woman was a hoarder. A rich and seemingly flashy hoarder, but a hoarder nonetheless. For the first time in her career April wondered if she had the chops to pull it off.

Walking gingerly through the maze of furniture, April heard voices in the rear of the flat. She was anxious to see Olivier and get up to speed, and while her legs so badly wanted to run, April remained almost on her tiptoes, maneuvering the small footpaths that wound through the seemingly infinite collection of mirrors and armchairs and propped-up artwork, to say nothing of the taxidermied mammals and birds. The mental inventorying started immediately.

Ten cautious steps and five feet later, April spied a Louis XVI gilt-metal bureau plat, a pair of George III mahogany armchairs, a Charles X Savonnerie carpet, and one unbelievable mid-eighteenth-century gold girandole. All gnarled and viney, the piece had a life of its own. It looked as if it wanted to unwind itself and stab someone.

Every turn brought another surprise. Alongside items that would have easily been considered antiques a hundred years ago, April found a six-foot-tall stuffed ostrich and a Mickey Mouse doll slumped in the corner behind it. Spying her colleagues though a cracked doorway, April skipped around a stunning black-and-gold japanned bureau-cabinet and almost bumped into a drab, utilitarian bookshelf piled with papers.

"Ah, Madame Vogt," said a voice. "Welcome to Paris. You missed the rains."

April scooted through the door to find Olivier standing with two other men. One fellow she'd seen before in New York at an auction. He worked for Sotheby's in some capacity, and she remembered his sloppy drunkenness followed by multiple attempts at pawing her assistant. Then again, perhaps April had her Frenchmen confused.

"Bonjour," she said. "So pleased to see you again, Olivier."

"Bonjour, Madame Vogt!" said the weaselly Frenchman. "How are things in New York? I've been trying to make it back for months."

Ah, that's right, she remembered him now. His name was Marc, and he was the one who nearly tackled her assistant, Birdie. April tried to hold back her sneer, politely kissing both cheeks and mumbling the usual French niceties under her breath, hoping her disdain came across as good old-fashioned Parisian aloofness.

Beside Olivier and Marc stood a lanky man with floppy black hair and a lavender dress shirt. April's eyes could not help but follow the elegant seams of the shirt as it tucked precisely, straightly into pinstriped slacks. She gawked a little at his enviable hips and torso, which jutted forward in such a manner as to convey assertiveness or cockiness or something she couldn't quite name. April was already starting to redden when she noticed the cigarette dangling from his mouth.

"You can't smoke in here!" April screeched. The smallest spark could well incinerate the entire flat, anyone could see that. "Out! Put it out!"

The man chortled, dropped his cigarette, and pressed it into the floorboards with a buffed and shiny loafer. Before she had time to reconsider, April crouched and plucked it from the ground. She waved it through the air to ensure full extinguishment.

"You are a dedicated antitobacconist," the man noted with a smirk as April shuttled the butt into her pocket.

"She's with us," Olivier said by way of explanation, or apology. "This is April Vogt. She is our Continental furniture specialist."

"Ah," the no-longer-smoking interloper said in his heavy French accent. "L'Américaine."

"April Vogt." She extended a hand. He smirked again, nodded, and then pulled her in for a double-kiss salutation. He smelled like expensive cigarettes and even more expensive cologne. April found herself off-kilter from the traditional but unavoidably personal gesture.

"This is Luc Thébault," Olivier said. "He's Madame Quatremer's solicitor."

"Madame Quatremer?"

"The deceased. This was her apartment."

"That is not exactly accurate," Luc said and rested his arm against a chair. April shuddered as she watched the price depreciate beneath his careless, untrained touch. "Technically I represent not Madame Quatremer but the estate. Generally they don't allow dead people to hire attorneys. In any case, this was her grandmother's flat. Madame Quatremer resided in Sarlat and never made it up this way, as you might've surmised given the condition of the interior."

"And Monsieur Thébault is the one who called us about the items," Olivier explained. "For which we are quite grateful."

"You should be." Luc turned to April. "You"—he said and scanned her from head to toe— "could almost pass for French. I was not expecting . . . that."

April smiled weakly. Years ago, after she managed to snag the curator position at an eighteenth-century Paris furniture museum (now defunct), she read up on how to look Parisian. Or, rather, how not to look quite so American. Dress in smart, dark, tailored items, the literature told her; things easy to put together, to match, to throw on and look as if you'd hardly done anything at all. And that, April thought, was more or less how *she* was thrown together. Straight, dark, and tailored, made entirely of clean lines. The hair, the eyes, the nose: all casually assembled; unobjectionable basic pieces. To stand out all she needed was a jaunty scarf and a Bréton top, which was Impersonating-the-French Rule Number Two.

"No response, Madame Vogt?" Luc said. "Not so garrulous as you should be. I thought these Americans, they jibber-jabber all the time."

He moved his hand like a quacking duck.

"We choose our words more carefully than most, it seems." April lifted her chin, then turned. "So, Olivier. It looks like we have a bit of work to do."

She glanced over his shoulder and spied a Louis-Philippe malachite table butted up against a glorious Louis XVI walnut canapé. Her eyes bugged. The treasures seemed to multiply before her.

"Some of these pieces—they're unbelievable." Her voice came out reverential and yet also sad.

April thought of the failed furniture museum and frowned. What if it hadn't gone under? What if she had stayed in Paris one more month? Two months? She met Troy at Charles de Gaulle on her way out of the city. He took a seat across from her in the Air France lounge, a chance meeting, as she'd never been in a business-class lounge before, much less allowed herself to be chatted up by some random guy in one. At the time April figured if you were leaving town in shame you might as well do it in style. Inexplicably, Troy found her appealing and remained undeterred by this dark-haired woman sucking in tears, trying to let go of the first adult dream she ever had.

"No need to cry over it, Madame Vogt," Luc said. "It's only furniture."

"I wasn't crying," she snapped. "And 'only furniture'? Please! You could fill an entire museum with only the pieces in this room."

"Never mind the settees and bureaus, Madame Vogt," Olivier said, snapping his fingers and startling April to attention. He pointed to the spot in front of him. "Do you see this? The painting?"

April made a wide arc around Luc and walked toward Olivier. Before him, against a wall, rested a portrait of a woman. The painting was almost as tall as April, and though the woman herself was in profile she was unquestionably stunning.

Leaning on a mauve daybed, the subject stared away from the portraitist. Her hair was brown, mussed, pulled back so loosely it was really more out than up. Her dress was pink, frothy, and magnificent, whipping around her bottom half like a mermaid's tail. Despite the grandeur of her gown, the woman's jewelry was spartan, spare, and her face the very clearest sort of beauty.

"She is gorgeous," April said, mind still picking through the furniture but eyes fixed on this. "Simply gorgeous."

"Gorgeous. Yes. But do you see it? Do you see what this is?"

April moved closer and straight into a bath of sunlight.

"Please close the shutters," she said and futilely held her tote up to the light bursting through the glass. "We need to be careful with the items in here."

"The lady," Olivier urged. "Madame Vogt. The painting."

April stopped. She looked, harder this time, again noticing the woman's minimal jewelry (a small strand of pearls, one ring for each hand) and also her downright aggressive décolletage. If the painting were a modern-day photograph someone would enlarge it to catch a glimpse of nipple.

Then she saw it. The color. The brushstrokes. The unmistakable *swish*.

"Oh my god," April said and tucked both hands under her armpits. She wanted to touch the painting. She wanted to touch it badly. It was half the reason she had been drawn to the industry in the first place. There were things she got to put her hands on that the general public did not.

"What do you think of her?" Olivier asked. It was a challenge, not a question. He wanted specifics. He wanted to compare notes.

"Boldini," she whispered. "I think it's a Boldini. But that can't be. Is it?"

"Yes!" Olivier clapped his hands together, nearly singing with satisfaction. He'd found both the portrait and the right person to do the job. He turned to Marc. "See? This is what I told you. You said to me, 'Non, c'est impossible!' But Madame Vogt sees it too."

"I thought she did furniture," Marc pointed out.

Luc snorted. April shot him an unintentional scowl.

"Yes, well, I know a few other things too," she said.

Indeed, one did not spend years chasing multiple Art History degrees, or living in Paris for that matter, without the ability to recognize a little Giovanni Boldini. The "Master of Swish" was once the most famous portrait artist in the world. In the late nineteenth and early twentieth centuries you weren't anyone unless Boldini painted you. This woman was someone.

"I don't remember this one," April said. "Portrait of Madame Juilliard, Lady Colin Campbell, the Duchess of Marlborough, several of Donna Franca Florio. But not her."

April's heart was racing now. She liked Boldini. She liked him fine. One could not dispute his mastery of portraiture. But although she'd seen a dozen or more of his paintings in person, April had never felt like this. The woman was beautiful, yes. But she was more than that. She was a presence.

"I cannot believe this," April whispered.

"As far as I know, this is not in his repertoire," Olivier said. "Could it be a fake?"

No. Not a fake. April understood this already.

"A damn good one if that's the case," she said. "On the other hand—" April paused for a moment and pretended to contemplate the possibility. "Who'd lock a Boldini up all these years? He didn't have to die to become famous. He was already known. Who would do this? Why?"

"Who's Boldini?" Luc asked as he lit another cigarette.

"Can you put that out?" April snapped. "I don't want the odor attached to everything in the place."

Luc cackled something to Olivier. April opened her mouth to remind them she was fluent enough to understand the French equivalent of "uptight." That's when she noticed, pushed up against the wall, the mauve daybed from the picture. April's breath caught. All at once she could see this woman sitting on that piece of furniture. She could see her at the dressing table, writing letters on the bureau plat, gazing at herself in any one of a hundred looking glasses. A room that was dead ten minutes ago suddenly felt very much alive.

Chapitre IV

April had overseen hundreds of auctions in her career. The spoils usually came from different versions of the same place: grandmother's manse or father's country house or a penthouse having just gone on the market. Unlike the contemporary-art world, where pieces now traded like stocks, for sport and for gain, April still procured her assets from three D's: debt, divorce, or death. The pieces before her were from a dead woman's apartment, yes, but more than that, they were from the past. Countless museum-quality objects, untouched, curated only by spiders and ghosts.

April slipped on her gloves and approached the daybed.

"Madame Vogt?" Olivier said. "Madame Vogt, are you listening?"

"Oh, what? Sorry, I was just . . ."

She'd nearly forgotten her colleagues were still present.

"We're going to step outside for chat and a smoke. For your benefit, bien sûr."

"Merci."

"I'd invite you along but presume you're disinterested in such an arrangement."

"Please, go ahead. I'll stay behind and begin a plan for the sorting and inventorying of the items. So much to do!"

April tried to contain her glee. Yes, *bons messieurs*, please leave. She wanted to be alone with this woman and her things.

"Ah. The famous American work ethic on full display," Luc said. "Très bien!"

"Well, I'm here to do a job."

Together the men, inexplicably, laughed.

"Don't start calculating the premiums without us!" Olivier called before the three slipped out of the flat.

April nodded and forced a smile. The door clicked. She shot across the room to the bookcase near the doorway.

It was the bookcase she had almost knocked over on her way in. She did not care for the piece. Though old, it felt more late-century college-dorm room than upscale bordello, and would not fetch much at auction. But its shelves were crammed with papers, which she'd spied during her labyrinthine walk over. On every conceivable surface sat a stack, on every stack, five more stacks. The resident of the apartment was either a prolific writer or the nemesis of every bill collector in Paris.

It was not snooping, April told herself. Not really. It was provenance. The documents would aid with provenance. Maybe they'd mention the painting. Unlikely, but a good-enough excuse.

April picked up one stack, and then another, and then a third, releasing each from its seventy-year slumber. The documents were bound with faded ribbons: green and pink and light blue. The papers themselves were yellowed, worn down to the weight of the cobwebs around her. The writing was faint, at times illegible, but as April leafed through the pages, the words seemed to brighten, the sentences perked up.

Papers in hand, April crept toward the window. She looked down to the street, where Olivier, Marc, and Luc were yukking it up on the curb, the lead glass no match for their voices. She had some time. April knew from experience that once Olivier got going he was difficult to shut up.

She sat down on the very chair she'd previously shooed Luc away from. With the first stack on her lap, April cautiously untied the celery-colored ribbon. As she separated each sheet from its neighbor, April flipped through the documents. Bills. Letters. Diary entries. Her heart galloped.

The numbers did not seem right. Madame Quatremer sealed the apartment in 1940. Boldini, if the painting *was* a Boldini, died in 1931. But these dates? They could not be correct.

Then again, if they were—if on the off chance these dates were valid and not falsified by Madame Quatremer or her shifty solicitor, Luc—then the story was not an amazing 1940 plus seventy years. The tale was older than that.

The page April held read in tight, neat script: "2 July 1898." It was not from the last century but the one before it. She glanced at the bookcase. How far back did this go?

April scanned the letters, biting back a smile. This woman, the writer, she was brave, unfettered, and damn funny. Her penmanship was impeccable, even when writing words like “flatulist,” “manhood,” and “nipples.” If these letters were real—and of course April knew they were—if these entries were real, the author had guts. She was unafraid. Then again, she was also unaware. Never could she have envisioned an American pawing through her belongings a century in arrears.

Guilt creeping in, April retied the stacks. The documents weren’t part of the Quatremer estate, at least not as it related to the auction house. Exposed skin and gastrointestinal problems would not establish provenance no matter how much April wished it so.

As she looped the ribbon around itself, a single sentence caught April’s eye. Her first thought was, thank god, I’m not completely invading someone’s privacy.

Her second was: holy crap. We were right. That painting is a Boldini.

Chapitre V

Paris, 20 July 1898

I sat for Boldini today. Again.

Only a few more sketches and all will be right, he promises. A few more sketches? That man and his incessant scribbling will drive me straight into an idiot’s asylum! Truth be told, it would prove welcome relief. At last I would finally be done with this godforsaken portrait. A veritable fool’s errand it is. He has yet to pick up a brush! Let this be a warning to all women: A celebrated, handsome artist intent on re-creating your likeness is not so romantic a scenario.

Turn this way, turn that way, he says. Frowns, furrowed brows, salty language, and much crumpled paper. Then we start the whole thing over. Did I mention it is hot? Murderously hot? Between the heat and the fumes I expected to keel over at any second. I would be offended if the rigmarole was not so very Giovanni. He has done this before.

"You are meant to be a painter," I said to him. "Not a cartoonist!"

He did not appreciate the inference, but, truly, there is perfectionism and there is dementia, and he is teetering dangerously close to the latter. "Master of Swish," indeed. It would behoove him to swish a little less.

Marguérite came with me the last time. She told me I do not make it easy on him, at which I had to laugh. Has she ever known me to make it easy on any man? No, in fact mostly I aim to do the opposite. Either way M. Boldini absolutely deserves it. I do tease him. I do warn him against repeating his forebear's succès de scandale. God help me if a strap falls off my shoulder and I become the next Madame Gautreau.

But it is all in good fun. He knows this and, further, would never repeat Sargent's artistic miscalculations no matter how many (many, many) times I say he is in danger of doing exactly that. Unlike Sargent, Giovanni will take caution. He values commerce as much as art and has no desire for *la vie de bohème*. In that way we are quite the same.

I suppose I could let up a little, but what I did not tell Marguérite—nay, what I did not tell Giovanni himself—is that it is not merely my impatience driving me to niggle. There is a certain deadline we are working against. If Madame Gautreau's errant strap threatened to destroy multiple reputations, I cannot fathom what would happen at next year's salon if Boldini displayed a painting of a woman ripe with pregnancy. An unmarried woman, no less! Mon Dieu!

It is easy enough to hide, but a time will come when I must confess to Giovanni, to Marguérite, to all of Paris! For now, I will delay the inevitable as long as possible. I have not yet decided what to tell Boldini. Will I say the baby is his? Will I say it is someone else's? Lying to this man does not sit well with me, especially with all the lies and secrets kept about my own lineage. However, a woman cannot live on good intentions alone. Sometimes you have to tell a lie to live the truth.

Chapitre VI

Paris, 1 August 1898

Boldini, the bastard! His latest sketch is beyond unacceptable. And he intends to use it! The situation is disastrous. He is such a *merde*!

The sketch was only practice, he said. I should have known better, and in fact the minute he picked up a pencil I objected. I was in no form for immortalization, having just been *très horizontale* with him on my purple lounging chair.

"You look sublime," he said, when in fact I did not. I had only just sat up. My eyes were slits, my hair tousled and out of its form. I had lost a bracelet in the sheets, and my whitening powder was almost completely rubbed off.

And my dress! I can hardly stand to discuss the state of my gown. Dear God: crunched-up sleeves, wrinkled bodice, and not even laced all the way closed! It is a dress I hate, no less. One I never meant to buy! I will have to write about the dress. I should have known the blasted pink frock would prove my downfall. Now if Boldini has his way the wretched gown will outlive me!

"Unless you want me to break your sketching hand," I warned when he did not stop his scribbling. "Please release the writing implement."

"I told you, it is simply practice," he promised. "You look so beautiful I must capture it."

"You are quite the snake charmer. But I am no snake, thus not to be charmed."

"Not to worry," he said, the hint of smile dancing on his lips. "It is just for me, for my private use. Trust me, my sweet, you have never looked so exquisite. I want to remember this."

How could I possibly object to the sentiment? My shoulders relaxed. I no longer glanced around trying to locate a pistol.

Stupid, stupid woman am I.

For a moment the process was not untenable. It was enjoyable, even, a wonder to see Giovanni actually *smile* when he worked instead of grimace and shriek and act like the petulant child he is. He called me beautiful and perfect, and as anyone familiar with Giovanni knows, these are weighty words for that man.

Eventually he finished. As I rose to my feet, he continued to sit at his drawing table, grinning like a madman, pencil clenched in his fist. I said the only thing I could: "Merde."

Laughing maniacally, Giovanni threw his pencil to the ground, clapped his hands together, and deemed this the portrait he would paint! Not the one we'd been working on for the devil knows how many weeks. Not the one of the carefully selected frock, proper jewels, and head tilted just so. Donna Franca Florio herself (spit, hack) could never look so good. No, he wanted this, sketched in haste, painted in cruelty!

"Off to Monte Carlo!" he then said.

Monte Carlo! For a month! I wanted to lock him in a stranglehold, but even that seemed too generous a treatment.

"Mon Dieu!" I said.

He laughed.

"Never speak to me again!" I said.

He laughed.

Stupid, awful, deplorable man. You can't pry a blasted smile from beneath his mustache for months on end, and suddenly he was giddy as a loon.

"I hope your genitals rot and fall off!"

And then I told him.

Of course I had to tell him. I planned to all along, but his indecorous behavior hastened the news. As it turned out he had recognized the changes in me. He took note of the extra roundness in my stomach and bosom. It was easy enough to hide on the street and in company, but one cannot wear a corset at all times. Well, *some* people are fond of such arrangements, but not M. Boldini.

"I did wonder," he said once all was done, once the confession fell from my mouth and we both said things we already regretted. "That you could not get back into that dress."

The nerve!

I wanted to scream, remind him there were certain considerate gentlemen in this city who employed coiffeurs and chambermaids during the four-to-five for any ladies who might find themselves a touch unkempt after a visit. A tightening here, a bustle there, hair fixed, shipshape back to one's rightful state! What M. Boldini failed to comprehend was that not everyone suffered the indignity of sneaking back home with a whalebone corset sequestered beneath her cloak!

"You are not exempted from aiding me in these matters," I told him. "This gown will not lace itself."

"Not unless," he said, "it has very big hands."

The gown! The dratted gown! I hated it the minute I laid eyes on it! And now it was to be immortalized in a picture, by the very hand of the Master of Swish.

Alas. I must write about the gown.

Earlier in the week Doucet, my preferred atelier, sent over a woman and three dresses. The model was instantly familiar. She put on the first dress. I said no. She put on the second. Again I said no. All the while my brain tried to place her. When she put on the third, a translucent pink gown with deep décolletage and sleeves the size of tents, the recollection hit. I stifled a giggle because at our last meeting the young lady was in a most indelicate position indeed!

It goes back to Marguérite, which is almost always the case. She is my closest friend, indeed, "friend" is not strong enough a word. As delightful as she may be, one must temper the information one provides sweet Marguérite. Several months past I elected to share with her my most prized beautification secret. She agonizes endlessly over her (lack of) clear skin and (lack of) sweet breath. I prescribed a daily enema as a solution but neglected to add it should be done in private. With Marguérite these things must be spelled out!

When I went to call on her the next day, there she was, leaning against the mantle, her *robe d'intérieur* hiked up around her waist and a chambermaid administering the very treatment I ordained. No fewer than four Arab servants looked on with eyes popping out of their skulls. Oh, Marguérite!

So on that day, when the model stood before me in a pink dress much the same color as Marguerite's undercarriage, the memory clicked into place. Here was the former chambermaid, the enema giver! A smart woman, she. It did not take her long to seek alternate employ. And really, she was too pretty a creature to tussle with Marguérite's backside.

"Well, you have certainly moved up in the world," I said with a laugh.

"Beg pardon?" The woman turned to better display the frock.

"No need to be coy," I said. "I do not blame you for leaving Marguérite's home. Let me apologize for my friend. Her enthusiasm for new beauty regimes often obfuscates her sense of decorum. I would have been in Doucet's begging for a job, too!"

"I have no idea of what you speak," the woman replied, lips quivering.

"You were a chambermaid with my dear friend Marguérite. I saw you assisting in certain matters."

"I am going to change," she said. "Please consider these dresses, and inform M. Doucet if you plan to purchase one."

She scuttled out of the room so quickly I did not have a moment to provide assurance that Marguérite was the one to be embarrassed, not her.

In the end I felt obligated to purchase the pink gown, and further obligated to wear it at least once. If I had not cared so little for the dress I wouldn't have been so careless in Giovanni's studio! You see? As I said, it always goes back to Marguérite.

Dear God, Giovanni is going to paint the dress.

Dear God, what did I tell Giovanni?

Giovanni. The baby. I need to address that particular fiasco. Now is not the time. As they say: *J'ai d'autres chats à fouetter.* Plus I've lost the mood to write. All this talk of Marguérite and I cannot stop seeing her up against the fireplace, flesh displayed like a ham hock at the market, coils and coils of tubes dropping from her nancy. And, I must add, a nancy not so pert and fresh as it once was!

Chapitre VII

"Reading private correspondence, Madame Vogt?"

April jumped. The pages tumbled out of her hands and she caught them between both knees. Skin throbbing, April looked up at the faces of the three men, their expressions ranging from amusement to scorn.

"Oh, hello there, I was just—"

Luc reached down. He patted her thigh.

"Allons-y!" He tapped her again. "Open up."

April separated her legs an inch and let the papers fall into his hands. The day was cool, but sweat collected along her hairline and on the back of her neck. She did not need a mirror to acknowledge the round tomato redness of her face.

"I thought you were a furniture specialist," Luc said as he thumbed through the pages. "Olivier did not tell me of your expertise in manuscripts. I will have to confirm whether the beneficiary of Madame Quatremer's estate wants these papers assessed as well. Until then they are not for public consumption."

"It's not exactly public consumption," April said, nausea snaking up through her insides. She'd been in Paris sixty minutes and already pissed off the client. He could easily have another house conduct the auction.

The premiums on the take would be stratospheric, and her job gone within thirty seconds of losing the deal.

"Madame Vogt—" Olivier started.

"These documents will help with provenance," she said quickly. April cleared her throat and glanced toward the painting. "In fact, you were correct, Olivier. What an eye you have! The portrait *is* a Boldini. I believe we've found the journals of the very woman in the painting!"

"Really?" Olivier raised an eyebrow. "Alone not five minutes and you've already authenticated the piece? Monsieur Thébault, please return the journals to April so she can show the group the relevant entry."

Luc smirked, apparently the one expression he most often used, and passed the papers April's way. Not once did he take his eyes off hers, not once did he soften the look on his face.

"Merci beaucoup. Let's see . . . here it is! July twentieth, 1898. 'I sat for Boldini today,' " she read.

"Hmm . . . ," Marc said. "I suppose that's a start."

"Our authoress also goes on to call him 'Master of Swish.' She even mentions the pink dress."

April pointed to the painting, to the very frock the woman despised. She suppressed a grin, thinking of Marguérite and her *nancy*.

"Something amusing, Madame Vogt?"

"Yes, well. The woman has a way with words. She's fascinating, really, and I've only read a few pages. According to the entry, she was pregnant at the time of the portrait, a child possibly even fathered by Boldini himself."

This was no small thing: a mother-to-be rendered by the most famous portraitist of the Belle Époque. Why hadn't Madame Quatremer wanted the painting? April had begged her father for one measly photograph of her own mother while pregnant, it didn't even matter the baby inside. Her brother, her—April would've taken either one. She only wanted to see her mom as exactly that: a mom. Maternal. At the start of her life instead of in the hopeless half-state in which she toiled out her final days.

Sorry, kiddo, your mother and me, we're not packrats. We were never big on photography. All we ever needed were the memories.

Fat lot of good that did everyone.

"A bastard child," Marc clucked. "Quite interesting."

"I'm not one of your so-called furniture experts," Luc said as Marc flicked through the pages. "But a dead woman's sexual . . . proclivities hardly seem relevant to the appraisal of furniture."

"Unfathomable," Marc said, scanning the entry a second and third time. "It is a Boldini."

"Well, we shall need a touch more to authenticate the piece," Olivier said. "But this is a good start. Thank you, April, for taking care of things while we stepped out."

April nodded and tried to avoid Luc's serpentlike, lingering gaze hovering somewhere on her periphery. Beneath her suit trickles of sweat continued to roll down her back. If only he'd stop staring this would all go away.

"Look at this entry," Marc said. "Someone's a *sniffeur*?"

"Our lady enjoyed the cocaine?" Olivier said with a chuckle. "That could explain the mess in this home."

"Hold on just a minute!" Luc lunged forward and reclaimed the diaries. "These are private documents, and you've not been granted permission to rifle through them."

Luc grabbed a box from the corner, a box so old and worn it could've been how the journals arrived in the first place. Perhaps the woman ordered them shipped to her home in bulk, a whole pallet full, enough to put down any word that floated into her brain, any feeling that surged through her body.

"Would you like to borrow a pair of gloves to handle those?" April had to ask.

"No need."

"Where do you plan to take them?" April said and looked toward her colleagues. "Will they be somewhere we can access for research? It's possible I might need them for provenance."

"Yes, Madame Vogt is correct," Olivier said. "Perhaps you can leave them with us, to aid with valuation."

"Non. I'll return them to the beneficiary of Madame Quatremer's estate," Luc said as he transferred ribbon-wound stacks of paper from bookshelf to box. "She can decide how to dispose of them."

"Dispose?" April said with a gulp.

"You have no need of them here."

Wincing at his gross mishandling of the papers, April felt an unexpected sting somewhere in the middle of her chest. She wanted more. She wanted to know about the pregnancy, about Boldini's reaction, and, God help her, she wanted to know more about Marguérite's tawdry behavior.

"If I may, who is the beneficiary?" April asked.

"It hardly matters."

"You said Madame Quatremer's grandmother rented this flat. Is the woman in the painting the grandmother? Was she pregnant with . . ." She tried to do the math. "Was she pregnant with Madame Quatremer's mother? Does that pan out?"

"None of that is necessary to your appraisal," Luc said as he flung the last stacks of papers into the box. "It's gossip, nothing more."

"Actually," Olivier started. "If we have more color as to the background of the furnishings, we can elicit a higher price at auction. People like pieces with a bit of history, a story to tell."

"We are done here," Luc snapped. "My client cares not of maximum dollars."

"Doesn't everyone care of maximum dollars?" April said, trying for a joke. "That's what they teach us in America."

Luc rolled his eyes and chucked a few more books and documents on top of the diaries. April turned away from him and stared at the woman in pink, as if she were physically in the apartment, too. With a sudden feeling of responsibility for her voice and legacy, April mouthed a quick apology of regret.

"Gentlemen, if you'll excuse me," April said, her breath tangled up somewhere in her ribs.

She shouldn't care that Luc was manhandling the documents but April cared more than was appropriate. It was easy, sometimes, in her line of work to picture only things and not the people who once owned them. April would not make that mistake now.

"I'm going to start on the furniture. Snap a few photos. Get straight to work." Her voice cracked, and cracked again. April forced a cough to cover it all up. It was dusty. A good-enough excuse. "Monsieur Thébault, nice to meet you."

She shook his hand and quickly skittered out of the room, leaving the men to discuss contracts and timelines.

As she walked down the hallway, April imagined the dark-haired, full-bodied woman moving, dancing, floating through the flat. She tried to picture her own mother too, once dark-haired and full-bodied herself, yet somehow less real than the woman in the painting. There were no portraits, no pieces of furniture, nothing to anchor her mom to the world. April squeezed her eyes closed but, like trying to grab a sunset, she saw flashes of color but could not hold on.

Chapitre VIII

In the antechamber April busied herself with a blue-and-gold lacquer armchair and a Tabriz meditation carpet from Persia, which, though not Continental by origin, *was* by purchase. In other words, exactly the kind of thing you'd find in a wealthy European's nineteenth-century apartment.

As she picked through the items, April tried not to think of the Boldini, or the woman in the painting. Sorting it all would prove challenge enough. Emotions had no room to hang out.

April stepped behind the armchair to inspect a mahogany writing desk. It was perfect and simple, this piece, though not insignificant. She ran her fingers across its surface, clearing the dust to reveal two stamps bearing the name "JH RIESENER."

"Jean-Henri Riesener," she whispered in awe.

Riesener was the favorite cabinetmaker of Marie Antoinette. Even this basic unadorned writing desk had almost incalculable value.

"Who *were* you, Madame?" she said. "Who *were* you?"

Atop the Riesener sat two carved ivory figures of Jeanne d'Arc. Behind the Jeannes stood a thick jade vase etched with a battle scene. Unable to reach it, April stepped on a nearby trunk, treading carefully on its steel hinges so as not to damage the piece. April stretched toward the vase to check for the artist's markings but found the object too weighty for her thrilled and shaky hands. As she pushed it fully back onto the shelf, goose bumps tickled the back of her neck.

"Madame Vogt."

"Mon Dieu!"

She leaped from the trunk but misjudged the floor's traction. Slipping on her slick-bottomed flats, April tumbled backward, nearly impaling her upper left hamstring on a fireplace poker, though ultimately finding herself in a far more precarious position: cheek smack against Luc's chest. He looped an arm around her back.

"Tout va bien?"

"Merde."

"Oh là là! I did not expect this language from such a nice American!" Luc said, with what was becoming a trademark smirk.

"I'm not that nice." April pushed away momentarily but had not regained her footing. She grabbed for Luc again, choosing to decimate her pride instead of the eight-foot-tall glass butterfly behind her. "I apologize if I offended you, but you snuck up on me."

"Je suis désolé," Luc said, grinning, no hint of apology anywhere near those pointy teeth. He tightened his arm around her shoulders. "The salty language is unexpected but, yes, this hug. It is very American."

"It's not a hug."

April tried to jerk her body away but had not an inch to move.

"Careful." Luc released April from his hold, but she continued to feel every part of him. That was his hip, non? It was merely his hipbone.

"I'm nothing if not careful," April muttered.

"Tell me, Madame Vogt, are you staying nearby?"

"They've rented a flat for me on the rue Fontaine," April said absently. "In the Ninth."

Usually she would not divulge such details to a strange man in a foreign city, but April was still trying to work out how to stop touching him in this packed and delicate space.

"Are you familiar with Le Café Zéphyr? It is also in the Ninth." Luc held tight to April's gaze and remained entirely unbothered by her squirmy panic. Could he feel the sweat on her? she wondered.

"Never heard of it."

April wiggled to the left, but it came across as more of a snuggling-in than an attempt to escape. She could nearly hear the woman in the portrait tittering in amusement. This wasn't a publicly attended enema but humiliating all the same.

"Do not look so worried, Madame Vogt," Luc said with a chortle. "I am not trying to . . . what do they call it in America? Oh, yes, I am not trying to *sexually badger* you."

The image of a sexual badger popped into April's mind, a furry varmint with oversize teeth, gold chains, and a silk smoking jacket. She laughed in spite of herself, in spite of Luc Thébault and this ridiculous situation she found herself in.

"It's 'harass,'" April said and pursed her lips. "Not 'badger.' You're not sexually harassing."

"I'm glad you concur," Luc said, pleased, as he (finally!) stepped out of April's way. A pocket of cool air whooshed through the space.

"I don't . . . I don't not concur." April shook her head, confused. "Sorry. Jet-lagged. Not thinking clearly. So you want to meet. When? Why?"

"It seems you have questions, so many questions," he said. "The first of these about the woman in the painting, non?"

April nodded, curious but also wary.

"I can answer your questions, Madame Vogt. At least some of them. If you are willing to meet for le café with a sexual badger, that is."

April hesitated. It didn't seem right to discuss business over coffee without Olivier and Marc present, especially given the annoyingly flirtatious mannerisms and French swagger of this particular individual. April thought of Troy, of his ceaseless client lunches and dinners. Because it was scandalous once didn't mean it had to be every time. Anyway, at least one of them was capable of a little restraint.

"I suppose," she said at last. "What time?"

"Three o'clock," he said. "Café Zéphyr. I will be on the patio. Waiting."

Chapitre IX

Hazy and hollowed out from lack of sleep and food, April plunked down on the apartment building's cold marble staircase. Thirty minutes until her meeting with Luc. Not enough time to work, but enough time to do what she had to. It was a task April looked forward to and dreaded in equal measure.

Twenty-six minutes remained. Twenty-three. April wavered. Three months ago she'd already have dialed Troy's number. Now, phone in hand, April ran the expected script through her brain.

First Troy would inquire about Paris. Fine. Lovely. A lot to do. April might ask about the previous night's soiree, though she'd already received a partial report via text from a grad-school friend who secured overpriced artwork for the folks in Troy's sphere. "Some chick was all over your husband," Melanie wrote. It was the first thing April saw when she stepped off the plane in Paris.

Yet. Troy was still her husband. Gossipy text or no, April had to call. She would say some things. He would say other things. All these things would be dwarfed by what they didn't say.

It was eight-thirty in the morning in New York, which was the best time to reach Troy if one wanted to reach him at all. Much past nine o'clock and everyone already had their claws into him. As April punched in his number, her hands felt clammy, her heart noisy. Maybe she should call later, when he'd be too busy to talk. There really was no winning, only lesser degrees of loss.

"Troy Vogt's office," said a cheery voice.

Troy's assistant. Sweet. Upbeat. Perhaps in possession of inside information.

"Hi, Kimberly, it's me."

A pause. April imagined all he might've said to her. Troy was tight-lipped, taciturn, only ever showing the best side of himself. Still, sometimes there were certain explanations required, directives to make: You can put the calls through. Don't worry, April is no longer in the house.

"Oh! April! Hi!" Kimberly chirped. April tried not to assess the degree of effort she put into her greeting. "How's Paris? God, you are the luckiest person in the world! Paris. Jeez. I picked the wrong career path."

"Well, I've only been gone about eight hours, so there's little Paris so far. Only a dusty, abandoned flat and some surly Frenchmen."

"The apartment sounds dismal, but I'd take the Frenchmen."

"Trust me when I say the flat is the better deal," April said. "So, is Troy in? Or is he already unreachable?"

April was hoping, a little bit.

"For you he's always available."

Sarcasm? Smirking? April shook her head. Jesus, Vogt, get a grip.

"If he's not around, I can call back—"

"No. He's around. Hold on a sec, I think someone is standing in his doorway."

"Really, it's fine. I'll try later."

"Nope! Give me one little minute! I'm going to put you on hold."

Click.

April exhaled. Instead of the standard office-line Muzak, she listened as a pretty, tinkly voice updated her on the latest machinations of the capital markets. It was funny, her career versus his. The value of April's work hinged entirely on history, on provenance. In Troy's no one cared unless it happened in the last quarter or had some chance of happening in the next three to five years at a 20-plus percent return.

"April!"

She jumped.

"I didn't think I'd hear from you," he said.

"You didn't think you'd hear from me?" April tried a giggle. As she had never been a giggler, the whole thing came out sounding like someone stepped on a chipmunk.

"I mean . . . um . . . I only meant I didn't expect to hear from you so soon."

"I had a break between meetings," she said. "So, uh . . ."

Wrong. It felt wrong. This was her husband, but everything was off.

"So, yeah," she said. "Thought I'd . . . well . . . give you a ring."

As she spoke April looked down at her hands. She tried to picture the antique platinum band now in its safe, and the three-carat yellow diamond engagement ring Troy offered when he proposed at some muckety-muck private club in Pittsburgh. She'd already been in town for work, staying up the street at an Omni when Troy materialized by surprise, via private jet. He whisked April away from chain-hotel ordinariness to the secret parts of a city she'd never seen.

"Well, I am honored," Troy said. "This is a great way to start the morning. So, how is springtime in Paris? The old broad a hoarder like I said?"

"Actually. . . . yes. Sort of." April shook her head, and smiled. "But this is the good kind of hoarding. Not like the people on television with decades-old pizza boxes and seventy-two piles of terrier crap in their living rooms. This is high-class hoarding. If everyone hoarded like this my job would be a lot easier."

"Details, Vogt. Give me the details. What did you find?"

"What did I find?"

April could've told him about the girandole or the mounted rhinoceros horn or the bronze bathtub, but all she wanted to talk about was Boldini. Boldini and the woman in pink.

"I found the Belle Époque," she said. "This flat, it's not a mere *house*. It's a time period. God, I can't help but think of my old museum. If we'd been able to procure any of these items—it never would've closed."

But then April wouldn't have met Troy, she realized too late, the words already out of her mouth.

"If only," Troy said as he clacked out something on his keyboard. "So, which is your favorite piece?"

"Favorite piece?" April said and feigned a gasp. "Troy Edward Vogt, I can't believe you'd ask such a thing! I love all my furniture equally."

This was not true, of course. She already had a favorite, the Boldini, a piece not even in her purview.

"Come on," Troy said. "It's like children. You might not have a favorite overall but you have a favorite *today*."

"All right, well . . ."

April thought again of the Boldini, not that she'd ever really stopped. She opened her mouth to tell Troy, but as the words started to form, April held them back. All of a sudden she felt protective, selfish almost, of the woman in pink. For now it was the two of them. April wasn't ready to share her with another man.

"Well." She cleared her throat. "The last thing I saw was a Louis XV ormolu porcelain mantel clock, circa 1750-something. It's in perfect condition and will easily go for over a hundred thousand. But you should see it! If I were describing it to my father, I'd call it a dog clock. Porcelain pugs and roses. Gaudy as hell but such a rare find."

"A dog clock for a hundred grand. Sometimes I wonder about other people."

"I also found a positively shocking pair of painted ostrich eggs sequestered aux chiottes."

"What?" Troy barked out a laugh. "My French is a little rusty, but did the well-mannered, sweet April Vogt just tell me there were ostrich eggs hidden in the *shitter*?"

"Non! I would never use such foul language." April grinned. It felt good to smile with Troy even if she could not see his face. "You misheard. Alas, yes, the eggs were in the lavatory. One pair of gorgeously painted eggs with the most intricate chinoiserie imaginable."

"Chinoiserie. Sounds like something you're not supposed to say in polite company."

"Please. Nothing so scandalous, really. It's a painting style, Asian-inspired vignettes. On the eggs there's a woman carrying a lamp, a man with an umbrella, monkeys waving a flag, you know, the basic hallmarks of the style."

"Monkeys," Troy said. "Now you're talking."

"They're mounted on these incredible bronze stands," April said, immune to her husband's teasing. She closed her eyes and pictured the gilded legs with their pineapples and branches and serpents. Catalog copy started to form in her head. "The stands themselves are works of art. And the eggs, they're in perfect condition. An amazing find on their own, but a drop in the bucket, a miniscule speck in the universe that is this person's home. By the by, there is also a formerly living Malayan tiger, now stuffed and lying on his side in the hallway."

"The whole thing sounds wild."

"Exactly. Wild. It's incomprehensible that someone knew about this apartment and didn't touch a thing."

April thought of the people then: the daughter, the granddaughter, the other bodies who must've come into and out of their lives. The word in April's head was "legacy." Why did someone board up a legacy? The rhinoceros horns, mounted butterflies, and fancy pianos were merely the start.

"How long do you think you'll be away?" Troy asked.

"I'm scheduled for a month," April reminded him, insides churning as she tried not to contemplate the real reason he might want a firm date. Her flight to JFK was not the only return trip in question.

"A month?"

"It could be less," April added quickly. "The Paris office can help out on the furniture side. On the other hand, it could also be longer. A lot longer. I can't even estimate how many pieces we have."

"So, what? Two weeks? Six months? In between?"

April forced a smile. "Trying to get an exact date out of me, Monsieur Vogt?"

Other wives might joke about a fictional girlfriend at a time like this. But not April. Definitely not April.

"Just anxious for you to come back to the States," Troy said. "That's all."

His face moved over the line. He frowned. Or grimaced. Troy enacted some kind of facial shift that caused his rough and stubbled skin to sandpaper against the mouthpiece. Whatever the case, he sounded sincere. April understood at least that much.

"I'll let you know as soon as I do," she said.

That Troy seemed anxious for her to return only made April's stomach knot further. Was it longing and desire, or eagerness to finally take their marriage out of limbo? Was it possible to serve divorce papers to someone in France?

"Listen, we should talk about—"

"So how was your dinner last night?" April asked, unprepared to grapple with the topic of her questionable return. "I heard it was quite the event!"

"You heard? From whom?"

"No one. I mean. Well. Melanie—the one from grad school?"

April hated that her words came out like questions.

"Oh yeah? And what did this Melissa person say?"

"It's Melanie. Not Melissa. She said it was glitzy. Lots of diamonds. Spectacular food. Tout à fait délicieux! You know, the usual. Anyway, I'll let you go."

"April—"

"Seriously." April jumped to her feet and started cramming papers into her tote. "I have a meeting. I really should be off. Au 'voir."

"Hold on a minute! Are you okay?"

"Okay? Of course I'm okay. Who wouldn't be okay in Paris?"

"Well, you sound like you've had a few too many cafés. I know you. You do this when you're nervous. Or upset. Did Melissa say something?"

"*Melanie*. And no, she didn't say anything. Forget I mentioned it. Do you hear me now? I'm talking normally." This was going even worse than she'd feared.

"I think I know what this is about," Troy said and sighed. "So let's put it on the table."

"There's no table. Nothing to put on it."

A lie. A flagrant, screaming, bloodred lie.

"Susannah was at the gala last night."

April almost laughed. That was Troy's big revelation? Susannah was there? With Troy? April had a thousand concerns when it came to her husband, but his ex-wife wasn't one of them.

"Great," April said, and meant it. "Terrific. Hope you two got to catch up. I'm sure she and Armand have a wonderful summer planned for the girls. And, for the record, Melanie didn't mention Susannah at all."

"Perhaps not. But Susannah was up to her usual tricks. You'd think over a dozen years of separation and a subsequent marriage to an arms dealer would eliminate her desire to bad-mouth me."

"Armand is not an arms dealer."

"Right." Troy snorted. "So they insist. Anyway, Susannah was at it again last night, worse than usual. Her looks may have faded but not her ability to be a bitch."

"Okay, that's rude, not to mention untrue. About her looks, anyway."

"And that was just during cocktail hour," Troy went on. "She was hammered. And acting horrible, even by Susannah standards. I'm not sure if this Melanie person ran into her or one of her cohorts—"

"Enough about Melanie, all right? She didn't say a peep about your ex-wife. And, by the way, you could stand to be a little less haughty. You're not exactly free and clear of the bad-mouthing of ex-spouses bit."

This was old hat. Susannah was known to slander Troy, and he was known to bite back. She started it, yes. But of the two of them, Susannah was the one who stuck closest to the truth.

Okay, so maybe April had one teensy problem with the ex-wife. It wasn't about the gossip, either. Nor was it about Susannah's looks (prettier, if not older) or that she birthed Troy's two daughters. No one could compete with the warm bath of postbaby love into which every couple dunked, however briefly, however shitty the marriage. April had no ambitions to unseat the mother hen and could suffer steely Nordic looks and lithe, beautiful teens all day long. But April could not stand feeling dumb.

Susannah didn't have a better degree from a better college or a superior job—or even a job at all—but what Susannah had was "knowledge." She'd left. Moved on. Seen Troy for who he was. April was the blind and doltish second wife. There were entire sitcoms based on the likes of her.

"I'm not bad-mouthing Susannah," Troy insisted. "I only mentioned her name because you brought up this friend of yours."

"All I said was Melanie was there. You took it to some other place."

Poor Melanie. One semidrunken text and she'd fallen smack in the middle of marital unrest. April pictured court documents with her friend's name in them, subpoenas of old grad-school friends.

"All right," Troy said. "You insist on avoiding this. Avoid it, then. Forever. I give up."

"You give up. Fantastic. Glad I'm in the loop."

"I don't mean it like *that*. You know I don't." He made a choking sound. "I have to go. I can't have this conversation right now."

"Fine." April knew she sounded petulant, but it was the only way to maintain a semblance of dignity. Any softness would've sent her straight into wrecked sobs. She'd seen him with his daughters. Troy had no patience for tears.

"For the record, April, in case you *were* wondering. Willow was also there. Okay? She was at the dinner-gala thing—"

There it was. The word April was waiting for. *Willow*. A punch to the gut.

"Troy, really. I have to go."

"April. Listen. We need to talk about this. Willow was there."

Another punch, harder this time. It was as if he were hitting her on purpose.

"Enough."

"And because Susannah was also there," he continued, "she was positively thrilled to assemble all the random pieces and form some kind of sordid story."

"It's an old story," April grumbled. "Already been told."

"I avoided Willow as best as I could, I promise. If we hadn't been in public, I would have physically tossed her into the coat check. But I had to at least be civil for work's sake, and she used every opportunity to make it as uncomfortable as possible. It probably looked disastrous. Willow can be so—"

"Can you stop saying her name?"

April hated that godforsaken name. It was a ridiculous moniker, probably not even real. In April's head she was only ever the Consultant or, alternately, Get out of my brain you horrible slut.

The Consultant was a renowned "environmentalist" (please!), with long, scraggly hair and big saucer eyes and the proclivity to sit cross-legged when interviewed on national television. Willow freaking Weintraub. Or, more likely, Jennifer or Debbie Weintraub. Debbie Weintraub could never be a renowned environmentalist with fluttering Bambi eyes, but Willow Weintraub was a name destined for morning talk shows and glossy magazines.

For the last six months (of a twelve-month contract) she consulted on Troy's version of the ubiquitous "green fund" at a rate of $375 per hour. Ms. Weintraub was contractually in bed with Stanhope Capital. And on one infamous occasion, also with April's husband.

"Okay," Troy said. "I'll stop saying her name if you tell me what I should say."

"Nothing, all right? I'm done talking about this. It sucks, but there's nothing to discuss. It's over. I'm over it."

"Are you sure?" Troy asked. "Because you keep saying you're fine, but sometimes I have to wonder."

She was mad, but Troy was right. April kept saying she was fine, but like Troy, she also wondered. It was half the reason she'd leaped at the opportunity to go to Paris. The departure was sudden, but they'd been tiptoeing around each other for months. April needed to leave, find some other place to figure things out. She was pretty sure Troy thought she should go, too. He'd never be so rude as to say "get out," given that he was universally At Fault, but they'd been in love, were maybe in love still, which meant April could read his thoughts.

From the few friends who knew about the mistake, the unanimous wisdom was that Troy should pack up and hit the bricks. But April understood the uncertainty in their marriage had little to do with whether or not *Troy* wanted to stay in their apartment or in their marriage. It was *April* who needed to leave. It was *April* who needed to give herself the space to decide whether or not to come back. Of course the problem with space was now Troy had it, too. Maybe he'd decide his transgression wasn't a onetime blunder but the symptom of a larger problem.

Honesty was the best policy. But honestly? Some part of April wished Troy had never confessed. If he hadn't, April could go on believing the life she saw before her: a funny, charming husband, two beautiful stepdaughters on Wednesdays and alternate weekends, a lovely apartment, and an occupation that was less like a job and closer to a hobby.

It was a onetime indiscretion, happening in some foreign country. A mistake. Troy was not caught but turned himself in. He didn't have to tell her. Why, it was gallant, almost! Thanks for nothing, April sometimes thought. At least one of them could now sleep at night.

"April? Are you still there?"

Eyes closed, April held her breath for several moments, the sudden constriction of her jacket a comfort, almost like a hug.

"I told you, I'm fine," she said. "But you're right. I don't really know."

Two long beats.

"All right," he said at last. "Fair enough."

April could nearly see the pinch of his lips.

"I really have to go," she said. For once not an excuse. "I'm actually very late for a meeting."

"Yes, me too. One more thing. Your father called looking for you last night."

"Oh, god, you didn't tell him anything, did you?"

"At this point *is* there anything to tell? But no, I didn't say a word. We didn't even talk. He left a message."

"I left him a message, too, telling him I was headed out of the country. I guess he still hasn't figured out how to work voicemail."

April checked her watch. Seven after three; officially more than a few minutes late. She hustled out the door and onto the street, tote slung over a shoulder, papers jammed beneath her arm.

"I love you, April," Troy said. "No matter what happens, I hope you know that."

What could April say? Nothing. This was both a literal and a figurative truth. She was clutching a phone between chin and shoulder while simultaneously trying to navigate Parisian cobblestones as well as the future of her marriage. Opening her mouth would send the phone crashing to the street, perhaps also the same fate her marriage might suffer if she said what she truly wanted to.

But April's lips, her brain—everything—felt gummed up. So instead of good-bye she gave a polite "Mm-hmm" and pressed the Off button with her ear even as she understood Troy was already gone.

Chapitre X

Luc was where he said he'd be, reclining casually on the patio of the Café Zéphyr, smoking a cigarette.

He nodded when April walked up and then stood to pull out a chair, the cigarette barely hanging on between both lips. April mumbled a thank-you and sat.

"I'm pleased you could join me," he said. "I took the liberty of ordering a plate of bread. I know you Americans like your snacks."

April rolled her eyes.

"I'm glad my countrymen can be so predictable. It's like we're all the same person! You don't even have to consider how to handle us individually."

Warmed by her hurried walk to the café, April shrugged off her jacket and settled into the chair. Around them voices purred and dishes clinked. Cars and scooters whipped around the corner, screeching and honking their clownlike horns.

"So, are you enjoying your stay in Paris so far, Madame Vogt?" Luc asked and took a drag of his cigarette.

"Yes, it's lovely. And please, call me April."

"Ah, Avril, like the month. This is the perfect season for you. Your parents loved the springtime, non?"

"I think they only liked the name." She pulled a pen and notepad from her tote bag. "All right, so I'm ready to discuss the apartment."

"I'm curious. You do not wear a ring, but Olivier says there is a husband. Are you married, Avril?"

April suppressed a snort. Was she married? That was the question, wasn't it?

"Oui." It was the legally accurate statement, absent ring notwithstanding. "So, about your client—"

"Your husband, what does he do?"

"He works in finance," April said, exasperation inching up her spine. "Je suis désolée, Monsieur Thébault, but I do not have a lot of time. I hate to rush this meeting, but I assume you are billing someone by the hour, so it behooves us both to address the topic at hand."

Luc chuckled. "You really are worried about succumbing to my charms, aren't you?"

"Not at this time. So let's discuss the apartment." April scribbled senseless notes on the pad to give her hands something to do. "I'm ready to listen to whatever you have to say about the woman in the painting."

"You despise questions, non?"

"Questions are fantastic. I love questions. I have about a million of them for *you*."

"Très bien. Then tell me, Madame Vogt—Avril—why *are* you so interested in the woman in the painting?"

"If it's a Boldini we have a rather significant find. That portrait alone could go for a million euros or more. It'd make international news. 'Continental furniture' doesn't usually make such waves. Lord knows it's not one of the major grossing departments, or even a moderately grossing one."

"I did not ask why you were interested in the *painting*. I asked why you were interested in the *woman*."

"I'm only interested inasmuch as she's related to the painting and the furniture in the flat."

"Uh-huh. Then it makes perfect sense you'd read her private diaries."

"As Marc and Olivier told you themselves," April said and glanced around for a waiter. Luc sipped espresso, but it was obvious she was going to require something stronger. "The diaries will help with provenance, which will boost value. Buyers love a good story. You've seen the apartment and all the things in it. It's extraordinary. I merely want to understand the history of the assets as well as why someone left them behind."

"What does abandoning the flat have to do with value?"

"Valuable items, economically or emotionally, tend to stay in families. They are usually passed on."

Usually, but not always, as April knew all too well.

"You want to know history from a purely academic standpoint," Luc said, skeptical. "Vraiment?"

"Yes. Really." Where was that damn waiter?

"Well, you were correct in your assumption about the family lineage. The woman in the painting was Lisette Quatremer's grand-mère."

"Really?" April's eyes went wide. The waiter appeared behind her. Suddenly she wanted him to go away.

"Madame?"

"Uh, yes, hello. Bonjour, je voudrais du vin." She pointed to the menu.

"Entre-Deux-Mers?"

"Oui. S'il vous plaît."

"I thought Americans didn't consume alcohol during daylight hours," Luc said. "Your kind, a bit of teetotalers, non?"

"Non. Most *definitely* non."

Suddenly ravenous, April reached for a piece of bread and spared no caution in slathering it with a thick coat of butter. She'd just proved Luc's theory, that Americans loved their snacking, but April didn't much care. It was worth it. Along with her memories of every café, every midnight dinner, the thousands of glasses of wine, April remembered the butter. It was creamier in Paris, saltier.

"Tell me more about the grand-mère," April said and sat on her hands so she couldn't physically take another bite. The thought of leaning over and lapping her baguette and beurre cat-style briefly occurred to her.

Everyone knew Americans were animals anyway. "Are you certain it's the woman in the painting?"

"Yes, quite. She's very beautiful, non?"

"Amazing. She actually reminds me of . . . someone I know. Anyway, do you know her name?"

The waiter reappeared over Luc's left shoulder. April exhaled. Oh, thank god. The wine was finally here.

"According to Lisette Quatremer's family, her name was Marthe de Florian," Luc said.

"Family? Madame Quatremer had a family?"

"Well, in a manner of speaking. But not in the manner you are thinking." Luc sipped from his espresso, the tiny cup looking ridiculous in his big hands.

"Marthe de Florian." April let the name settle on her tongue. *Marthe.* Or *Mart,* as one would say in English. "Who was she? Obviously someone important, given that Boldini painted her, not to mention the opulence and value of everything I've seen in her flat so far. Who was her family? Her husband?"

"Not married," Luc said and winked. "Quite the contrary, as a matter of fact. Madame de Florian was a well-known demimondaine."

"Demimondaine?" April's forehead lifted up into her hairline. "Madame de Florian was a courtesan?"

This was worthy of a drink for sure, and April removed her hands from under her legs in order to grasp the stem of her glass.

"Oui," Luc said. "An impressive apartment for a prostitute, non?"

"Demimondaines were no mere prostitutes," April said and took another long sip of her wine. "In Madame de Florian's time there were certainly common streetwalkers. Filles soumises, literally translated as 'submissive whores.' Above them were les grisettes, usually working women, dressmakers and such, who used sex to supplement their incomes. Yet another level up were les lorettes. And then there were les demimondaines, a very singular breed."

"But still a prostitute."

"Technically speaking. But les demimondaines were quite fashionable. The highest members of society mimicked their dress and hairstyles but could not possibly keep up. Even the wealthiest matron had only one husband lining her pocketbook, demimondaines had many. Why settle for a single man's largesse when you can curry the favor of five or more? Her occupation makes sense, really, given the pieces in the apartment."

"Fascinating," Luc said with a grin. "I admire your deep knowledge of hookers."

"Demimondaines," April corrected him, grinning back. "They were a fascinating group of women. It wasn't merely sleeping around, either. They had societal duties and even career obligations. And the general consensus was that a cocotte had not arrived unless she'd inspired four duels, a suicide, and had at least one déniaisé."

"Ah, déniaiser," Luc said. "To fuck your lover's oldest son."

April coughed, choking on her last sip of wine as Luc signaled the waiter for two more glasses. This discussion called for reinforcements, it seemed.

"I'm sorry," he said. "Have I offended your sensibilities?"

"Yes. Tremendously so. You know how delicate we Americans are."

Luc paused, obtaining license to unsubtly look April up and down; as if needing to verify her Americaness. She tried to muster a little outrage. This was smarmy, non? He did just spell out the particulars of an incestuous ménage à trois in the same breath used to order wine, and was now clearly performing a mental appraisal of her physical attributes (*Face of piece slightly tired, veneer worn down; given lack of size and visual interest, bosom assumed original*). But despite her best intentions, April couldn't feel disgusted. She would've with anyone else and was surprised to find herself giving Luc this pass.

"You can stop gawking," she mumbled. "You'll find nothing out of the ordinary in terms of my Americanism."

"It's curious," he said as the waiter approached. "Though you are very tan, you don't look American."

Luc plucked their new glasses from the waiter's service tray—placing one in front of April and the other at his side. It should've seemed impatient or arrogant, how he usurped the server's duty without permission. Instead April felt flattered, much to her irritation. It was as if Luc couldn't trust anyone else with the task and wanted deliver the glass to April personally.

Composing herself, she replied.

"Olive-skinned. Not tan."

"Still, not American."

"Yes, you mentioned something along those lines earlier when inspecting my attire."

"I meant it entirely as a compliment," he said.

"Well, I left my sweatpants and sneakers at home, so I understand the confusion. It's an utter shame, of course. I don't want people to think I'm not from the good old U.S. of A."

Luc laughed and ground his cigarette into the ashtray.

"I think you will be an interesting diversion."

"I'm here to work, not divert," April said quickly, trying not to think too hard about what he meant. "Tell me, what else do you know about Marthe de Florian? About the painting?"

"All right," Luc said and shook his head, smiling, as he sucked the wine through his teeth. "Back to business. After a quick perusing of some of her journals, we know a few things about Marthe de Florian. Of course this assumes what I've read so far is accurate."

"Why wouldn't it be accurate? She wrote them!"

"The woman was known to exaggerate. Or so I'm told. But if Boldini did in fact paint her in 1898, she was twenty-four at the time."

"Twenty-four and also pregnant."

"So it would seem. Lisette Quatremer's mother was born in 1899, so it could make sense."

"What happened to Lisette's mother?"

He shrugged. "Don't know. Though I gather her maman died at a young age."

"And why did Lisette leave Paris in the first place?"

"Je ne sais pas. Given she departed in 1940, it was likely related to the war."

"But she never returned. How could she abandon all her family's things? How could she leave *Paris* and not come back?"

"You *do* like questions."

"And how come Lisette's heirs are selling *everything* before seeing a single piece?"

Luc shrugged again. "There is only one heir. And I don't have the answer for you."

April tried not to let the irritation show on her face. Luc promised answers yet all he'd really provided was a name, occupation, and year of birth, all things April could've gleaned on her own. She didn't know if he was endeavoring to be a pain in the ass or if it was merely a by-product of his personality. He was, after all, an attorney, and Parisian—and Luc.

"Do you have any other information about the painting?" April asked, her voice nearing desperation. "About Marthe de Florian? Perhaps your client might allow us to read the journals?"

"You are quite anxious about the diaries, non?"

" 'Anxious' isn't the word. However, I believe—"

"Auctioneers," he said and turned to reach for the leather portfolio he'd placed on the café table earlier. "Such an urgent breed."

"Technically, I'm an auction house expert," April said, then cringed.

The title was said with no degree of pomp. When bandied about the office, it was like calling someone a human resources specialist or revenue accountant, the word "expert" almost commoditized. But said to people outside the auction world it sounded downright haughty.

"Or 'auctioneer,' " April said. "Whichever you prefer. Anyway, I'm only trying to do my job. This will help your client's estate."

"Yes. I know. Provenance."

Luc was so fatigued by the excuse April didn't bother to respond or make eye contact at all. She'd already grown tired of being the butt of his jokes. However, if April had bothered to look up instead of staring morosely into her wine, she would've seen in his eyes the playful spark she'd already come to understand was Luc's way of showing . . . something. And she wouldn't have been so startled by the thud on the tabletop.

"What the—" April grabbed her glass as if to save the wine from spilling.

She spotted four blue-ribboned stacks of paper on the table between them.

"Are those—"

"Her diaries? Yes, some of them," Luc said. "I've rifled through them a bit since I last saw you."

"Rifled?" April gulped.

"Skimmed. I've only read a few but I believe the first one is dated 1891. That's where you should begin. Maybe, if you're good, I'll let you see the rest."

If she was good.

April's heart sang. She reached for the diaries and thanked Luc, this time looking him straight in the eyes. Perhaps she'd misjudged the man, written him off as a roadblock when instead he could prove an ally. Of course he was still churlish and crusty, but it was a start. Maybe he'd give April what she wanted. She promised herself that no matter how aggravating Luc would get—and she already sensed he would prove quite so—she would at least give him a chance.

Chapitre XI

Paris, 24 April 1891

Well, today was the day. The glorious Jeanne Hugo finally married Léon Daudet, allegedly merging two celebrated republican dynasties into one. What utter mayhem. The crowds! The trumpets! The constant dowry speculation! All for France's *Jeanne au pain sec*: Jeanne with toast. That this was Victor Hugo's nickname for his cherished granddaughter tells you a little something about the girl. The man was famous for his skill with words, and this is his chosen description? Jeanne with toast? I prefer Jeanne *or* toast, in which case I pick the toast.

Who in this country does not know of Jeanne Hugo-now-Daudet? Yet what does anyone really know? She is beautiful. This is her raison d'être but ultimately not a compliment in the slightest. Instead it is the one positive thing anyone can say about her, and even the word as applied is debatable. I once saw a circus nudist who bore more than a passing resemblance to our fair *Jeanne au pain sec*. In fact the horse upon which she rode called to mind Madame Daudet's bone structure. In fairness to the equine, he did not sport the same ungainly fine black mustache. In fairness to the bareback rider, her personality was far more alluring!

Having been raised in a convent, I should endeavor to be more gracious. The nuns certainly taught me better. But Jeanne's physical unsightliness is a fact. Allow not your heart to weep on her behalf. Our new Madame Daudet is not a pitiable, gangly-faced thing unable to stop her nose from crooking or teeth from jutting. She is ugly because of what's inside, because of the things she's done. Jeanne herself has allowed the gradual blackening from the inside out. Most people do not understand this of her. To the public she is a silly girl sipping Pernod and buying the dearest gowns because she can. I, of course, know better. My connection runs deeper.

Nonetheless I feel some modicum of remorse for my uncharitable thoughts. I picture Sœur Marie and see her sour displeasure. Of course this would not be the nun's only quibble with me. That I stole from her is the reason I'm in Paris at all. Alas, *nous sommes qui nous sommes.*

We are who we are. Ironic when you are speaking of Jeanne Hugo. Ironic when you are speaking of me.

In the end my distaste for the bride could not keep me from witnessing the biggest wedding of my lifetime. Along with the throngs of thousands (someone said the number was closer to a million!), I squeezed myself onto the rue de la Pompe to view her marital procession. I needed to see the spectacle up close. I wanted to witness Jeanne and this new husband, a man so lauded even his reputed flatulence could not keep him from society's upper echelons. But the crowd was too thick, and the only piece of supposed dynasty I saw was Jeanne's pale, corpulent brother. Georges was barely able to stand upright, as is customary. I am surprised he would venture out in public, given his gambling debts. He is fortunate no one stabbed him.

The atmosphere was festive, I will allow Jeanne that much. People spoke to strangers, exchanged embraces, and beamed at one another as the Daudet carriage passed. For a moment we were one expansive, all-encompassing Parisian family.

My own streetside neighbors included an elderly couple and their grown children as well as a thin, shaky girl vagabond. She said her name was Marguérite, and though she claimed to be fifteen I would place her closer to twelve. I am not sure where she lives, and she was very clearly not there to see the bride but instead to pick pockets. Nonetheless I liked her immediately, no doubt because the first thing she said to me was, "Is there anyone more loathsome than Jeanne Hugo?"

I laughed and said I felt much the same.

Though the fledgling pickpocket probably despises Jeanne for her wealth, this is not what bothers me. It is not what Jeanne *has* that I find so disagreeable, but who she *is*. Not just now, but before. Forever. I cannot help but feel she stole a piece of me, even if she refuses to acknowledge it.

Chapitre XII

"Ça va, Avril?"

April shook her head.

"Yes? Okay? What?"

"You didn't answer my question."

She placed the journals on the table and laid both hands over the tops, as if to protect them.

"Your question?" she said. "I'm sorry. I missed it. I was engrossed in the diary."

"Yes, I know. It's quite compelling, isn't it?"

"Incredibly compelling. Do you think I might meet with your client? Between the journals and a brief interview, I could quickly get all the background required to complete my work."

"Ah, so hungry la jolie fille, and you only just ate." He nodded toward the journals as his eyes skipped over to the mangled piece of bread.

"Well, to establish provenance it'd be quite helpful—"

"You and your provenance. I've already grown tired of the word."

"Shall I use the phrase 'more money' instead?" she asked. "Because that's really what we're talking about."

"Mo' money, mo' problems."

"Excuse me?" April barked out a laugh, startled by the unexpected phrase. She couldn't decide if Luc was trying to amuse her or whether he was simply funny without the effort.

"Is that not what they say in the United States?"

"Well, if you're a rapper, I suppose," April said, still laughing. "Though the French accent adds a unique dimension."

"It always does, Madame Vogt," Luc replied, with just enough confidence to make April blush. "As charmingly as you demand your journals and your provenance-gathering interviews, unfortunately my response must be no."

"To which part? Because if I only had a moment with—"

"The heir does not wish to meet with any curious auctioneers. Oh, my apologies, that is not the correct term. What was it? 'Auction expert'?" Luc wiggled his brows.

" 'Auctioneer' is fine," April said quickly. "And I understand completely. I don't mean to intrude. Surely she is grieving now, but if she happens to change her mind—"

"I did not say the heir is female. And a change of mind is not anticipated."

"Very well then," April said. "The journals should be enough."

She glanced down at the stack of documents, skimming their lines, trying to catch another word, another phrase, any reference to the Hugo family or to anyone else.

"You can hardly stop reading," Luc said with a wink. "I've never had to compete with a moldy stack of paper to secure the attentions of a woman."

April bristled. Mo' problems indeed. What was Luc trying to prove? That he could discombobulate the fairer sex with his innate charisma and rakish good looks? Well, mission accomplished. This Luc Thébault character gave Frenchmen a worse name than they already had. Perhaps she'd been too charitable. His penchant for aggravating her would not be easy to ignore.

"Seems odd you'd be trying to secure my attentions in the first place," she said.

"Ah, funny Avril. I'm only, how do they say it in America? I'm only joshing you."

" 'Joshing' me? They do not say that. They do not say that at all."

He laughed. Again. It was as though he was almost always laughing (with, at, about). And that damn smirk, forever lingering as if she'd caught him approaching a smile or at the tail end of one. It left April feeling itchy and impatient, wanting in on the joke but also hoping to catch him outside the smirk.

"You are an interesting woman, Madame Vogt."

"I respectfully disagree," April said. "Regardless, thank you for use of the diaries."

April half rose to her feet and reached across the table.

"Where are the rest?" she said, stretching, grabbing. "There were a lot more in the flat."

"Not so fast, Avril." Luc himself stood and gently pressed April back into her seat. She curled her hands into her lap, chagrined. "My client wants to see them first—naturally the discovery is news to them as well. You will receive the documents piecemeal, after my client finishes them. Is this acceptable? Or will it hamper your furniture appraisals?"

"No, I don't believe it will," April said, quietly, and with thanks. "Tell whomever it is thank-you. We greatly appreciate the cooperation."

Suddenly a man and his dog paused on the sidewalk beside their table. While the man squawked into his mobile, the dog squatted into position, looked defiantly at April, and relieved his bowels. The owner shouted something into the phone, yanked the leash, and continued on, hardly missing a beat.

"Merde," April said under her breath.

"You don't like dog shit, Madame Vogt? Perhaps Paris is not the city for you."

"Some streets around here are more shit than sidewalk," April murmured. "If that guy was in New York and didn't pick up after his dog, he'd have a medium-size mob chasing after him. Paris is an amazing city, but you can hardly enjoy the view. You have to keep your eyes plastered on the sidewalk, forever on the hunt for merde, lest it end up on your big, fat American shoes."

"Hmm. Well, I do not find it particularly odd that a person might not want to hold a steaming pile of shit in his hand, nothing but a thin barrier of plastic protecting his skin."

"If you want a dog, it's the price you pay," April said.

"Speaking of paying the price, tell me about le mari."

"My husband?" April did not miss the irony, that a conversation about shit quickly dovetailed into one about marriage. "How does that relate to paying a price?"

The question was rhetorical; April already knew the answer.

"I am only joshing," Luc said, doing his best to keep a straight face. "Tell me about your husband."

"I'm not sure what to say."

"Not sure? This is a normal query, non? Regular chitchat between colleagues?"

"Well, his name is Troy." April inhaled. Only the facts. "We've been married seven years. He is a smart man and a tremendous father."

"Father? You have children?" Luc's brows jumped so high they almost left his face entirely.

"Well, no, technically they're h-h-his," she stuttered. "But mine, too. Stepdaughters. They're teenagers."

"Ah, evil stepmother," Luc said. "I like it. I like it very much. You said your husband was in finance. What does he do?"

"Runs an LBO fund." April peeked into the breadbasket and snatched away one final piece. "He does big deals."

"Wall Street?"

"Oui." April blushed. Wall was not the Street it once was. Instead of connoting money and power it now called to mind shysters and deadbeats. Not that Troy technically worked on Wall Street, but April felt the need to explain that her husband was not a Ponzi schemer, inside trader, or any other kind of financial pariah. He simply bought and sold companies using leverage and cash.

"My brother is also a solicitor," Luc said. "He works with corporations, doing big deals, as you say. Perhaps I know of your husband's company."

"You might. They've had a few transactions in France and throughout Europe," April said, stopping herself from launching into a full résumé of the Stanhope Group. She wouldn't have been surprised to find a connection or two between Luc and Troy, but it wasn't a connection April wanted established. "Your brother would probably recognize the name, they're fairly well known."

"Notorious?"

"No. Well known. Respected."

"It's great to be well known," Luc said and threw a fistful of euros onto the table. "Shall we depart? I'll pick up the tab. You can get us next time."

"Oh. Okay." April blinked.

"Are you going to . . ." he nodded toward the papers sitting beneath April's napkin. "The journals?"

"Right. I guess the family hasn't had a chance to read these yet," April said, realizing she had to give them up.

"Actually," Luc said and paused. "Why don't you take them? I'm not due back in Sarlat for a few days. It's fine for you to hold on to them in the interim. I'll let my client know. You seem very conscientious. Doubtless they are in great hands."

"Oui! I will take excellent care. My entire career is based on taking excellent care. Thank you," April said, extending her arm for a departing handshake. "Again."

Luc reached for her arm, and much like their first meeting, pulled her closer.

"Thank you for a delightful meeting, Avril," he said, politely kissing each cheek, this time, though, lingering a moment longer than he had earlier in the day. His scent was still smoky and perfumed, but now also tinged with the smell of the wine they shared. "I'll be in touch."

April watched him walk away. To any outside observer she appeared obvious and gawping. April knew this, yet could not stop herself from staring, nor could she stop the feeling that was right then crawling through her gut, a result of the wine, no doubt, and access to the journals. Yes, it had to be those things. There was no other explanation that was acceptable, or that April could afford to entertain.

Chapitre XIII

April's flat was no match for Marthe de Florian's.

The buildings shared the same Haussmann facade, the utterly Parisian look with its height and horizontal lines and scrolled wrought-iron balconies. That's where the similarities ended, though. Where Marthe had seven rooms, April had only three. Marthe's flat was so thick with museum-quality furnishings one could hardly walk through without stumbling. April's flat was so sparse she wondered if there were enough places to rest both her backside and her computer simultaneously. It was a pity, she thought, to throw such a thirdhand jumble of self-assembled furniture into a quintessential Haussmann, even if it was a rental property.

Despite its lack of decorative charm, April loved the place upon sight. She loved the location, its original thick-plank wood floors, and how one side of the living room was more windows than wall. April imagined herself leaning against the panes at night, a glass of wine in hand, the city twinkling before her. The apartment did not show all it had to offer, but it still showed Paris.

After checking her e-mail (no impending crises so far), April thumped her tote and BlackBerry onto the white-lacquered dining table, though "dining table" was a rather grandiose term for something that could hold, at most, two dinner plates—or in April's case, serve as combination computer desk and makeup vanity. She could not imagine an instance requiring multiple dishes.

All the table-plate contemplation made April's stomach rumble, though it was not food she wanted to consume first. She was hungry again, despite the bread-scarfing during her meeting with Luc, but instead of trying to find something to eat she reached for the white protective gloves in her leather tote.

"Oh, be quiet," April said to her still-roaring stomach as she gently removed Marthe's journal entries from her purse. Hunger was fierce but the pull of the diaries stronger.

April's plan was to spread the pages on the kitchen counter and read them quickly, fast-food style, standing up with her shoes still on. But the language appeared suddenly blurry, smudged, indecipherable. It was as though April had lost the entirety of her French skills in the hour since she last used them. Perhaps it was due to jet lag, or maybe because her only sustenance over the last two days was in the form of wine, bread, and enormous slabs of butter.

"Food," April said aloud to no one, a wicked headache spreading across her brain. "I need food."

Light-headed and unable to muster the energy to leave the flat, April fished around in her tote for the pack of cashews she had stashed from the flight. Her BlackBerry buzzed from beneath her purse.

"Dammit," she groused. "It's like people want me to work or something. Hello, this is April Vogt."

April kicked off both shoes and plunged an arm deeper into her bag.

"It's me. Why do you never check Caller ID before picking up? I mean, like ever? Even once in your lifetime?"

"Oh, Birdie, hey. Sorry. I'm in the middle of a deep investigation." April found two squares of airline chocolate melted onto the back of a hairbrush. "What's going on?"

"I just sent over some files for you to review ASAP," Birdie said. "We're supposed to have twenty-five lots coming out of this office a day. We're, like, way behind."

"Yes. Sure. I'll read them shortly. I need to take care of a few things first. Then I'll get right on it."

April peeled a piece of chocolate off her brush and popped it into her mouth, too ravenous to feel embarrassed about the state of her culinary sampling in Paris thus far.

"I drafted up the descriptions," Birdie said. "I think they're in pretty good shape, if I do say so myself. But Peter needs your sign-off. Also, check numbers three, forty-six, and two-twelve. Your original notes were a little hard to decipher, and some of the descriptions don't seem to match the time period. Your handwriting is atrocious, by the way."

"So they say. I'll take a look. Thanks for putting it together. I'm sure you did an excellent job."

Birdie always did an excellent job. Sometimes April wondered if she should work for Birdie instead of the other way around. Of course anyone who took borderline illegible notes and forgot to eat would make a crappy assistant indeed.

"I can always send them to Peter," Birdie said. "If you're too busy with the apartment."

"No, it's fine. I'm happy to look them over."

Happy to look them over was the truth, thanks to Birdie's always-stellar work product. Normally jet lag, lack of food, and two glasses of wine would make April unable to wax poetic about commodes. But if Birdie had done the heavy lifting, then April could easily correct the grammar and review factual details. She could change the number eight back into a nine.

"Think you can get it to me by COB today?" Birdie asked. "New York time?"

"That shouldn't be a problem."

"Perfect. Thanks."

April heard much shuffling and bumping then, followed by the inevitable flurry of curse words.

"Goddamn bastard!"

"You okay, Birds?"

"Jesus fuck! I stubbed my toe!"

"You really need to be more careful," April said with a yawn. "You make me nervous."

Birdie was a walking worker's comp liability. She was forever banging knees, jamming toes, and stapling scarves to photo decks. Although, April supposed, if you barely reached five feet and moved like a hummingbird (her nickname was no coincidence), the margin for error was slim. It was easy to smash into windshields or twist yourself up in branches.

"It's the layout around here," Birdie said. "It's an accident waiting to happen."

"Yes. Yes, you are."

Unsatisfied by her purse chocolate, April wandered into the kitchen, hoping the previous occupants left something behind. A stale piece of bread, an old jar of olives—she would take anything.

"Perhaps if you moved at a more reasonable pace," April said and popped open the cabinet. "You wouldn't have to worry about dry-cleaning bills, excessive bandage consumption, or the fact you look like a battered woman when you wear a tank top."

"It's the price I pay for efficiency, Madame."

"Not sure it's a trade-off our insurance carrier would approve," April said. "Anything else?"

"No."

"All right then, I'll talk to you—"

"Wait. April. Real quick." Birdie inhaled. "So. Um. Daniel's mom? She's on the board of the Columbia Cancer Center?"

"How lovely for your mother-in-law. Birds—"

"She's not my mother-in-law. Not yet, anyway! So. Yeah. Daniel and I went with them to the gala the other night?"

April closed her eyes. That she might keel over did not seem out of the question. Who would find her? She could be on that floor for days before someone realized she was gone.

"And you saw Troy," April finished so Birdie wouldn't have to. "He didn't mention he ran into you, but he already told me all about it. And I do mean *all.* I know Susannah was running her mouth and that people were talking. I know *she* was there, too. So, enough."

"Fine. Whatever." Birdie sounded a little short, her feathers plucked. "I'm not trying to make you mad."

"I know. And I'm not even mad. Honestly, I'm tired of discussing it. I'm tired of thinking about it. You're trying to help and support me, and I appreciate that." April's eyes were still closed. "I think, maybe, at least while I'm here in Paris . . . Unless it's something you think I'd stake my marriage on—I'd rather not know any more. It's not going to change what's already happened. I need to start thinking about how to move on."

April should never've told her. With Birdie it was easy to open up. She invited that kind of emotional connection. April hadn't planned to grow so tight with her assistant, but neither had she planned to end up in a fourth-floor conference room relaying the details of her husband's treachery to said assistant while hiccupping through a snotty, slobbery mess.

"Okay," Birdie said. "Understood. And I'm sorry."

"No apology necessary, promise."

"Okay. Good."

April opened her eyes again. She turned back toward the counter. That's when she saw it, sitting on the little blue tiles beside the coffeemaker: a bottle of wine with an envelope propped against it.

"Oh my god!" April grabbed the bottle and held it to her chest. "The owners of the apartment left me wine. And, a note. A note on linen stationery!"

"Oh. Linen. Why didn't you say so? Sounds thrilling." Birdie's sarcasm ran a close second to her penchant for clumsiness.

April tore into the envelope. The owner's funny, squiggly handwriting lifted off the page. April scanned the note, picking up only the key words. *Bonjour. Opéra. Métro. Fermez la porte.* And then the most important sentence of all: *Fromage dans le frigo.*

Cheese was in the fridge.

"I have to go," April said. "Emergency."

"I'll get my catalog copy tonight, yes?"

"Oui. Good-bye, Birdie. I'll ring you later."

April clicked off the phone.

Carefully, she stepped across the kitchen floor, the bottle of wine still clutched to her chest. April swung open the door of the stainless-steel refrigerator. Though it was approximately one-half the width of even the most basic Costco model, it had all April needed inside, specifically, a glorious selection of *fromages*, not to mention truffled pâté de foie gras and several other delicacies the likes of which she'd not seen since last leaving the city. April almost sobbed with these strangers' generosity. Or maybe it was only her blood sugar.

Displaying all the couth of a grizzly bear, April ripped off a hunk of Ossau-Iraty, put the bottle under her arm, and marched back into the living room. Gloves back on, she grabbed the diaries from the table. Then, only as an afterthought, April tracked down a corkscrew and glass, though the latter was not strictly necessary.

Slogging to the bedroom, April nearly tripped over her suitcase. She should unpack, and typically April was a put-stuff-away-first kind of person. But there was unpacking on the one hand and wine, cheese, and Marthe on the other. Organization would have to wait.

Still in her charcoal pants and a top she suspected was more polyester than the silk promised by the tag, April slid into the formerly made-up bed, uncorked the wine, and started to read.

Chapitre XIV

Paris, 5 May 1891

It's been nearly two weeks since the glorious nuptials of *Jeanne au pain sec* and still people cannot stop speaking of the event.

The newspapers hit the street corners each morning, and I find myself unable to walk past. Instead I stop and pull a knife from the pocket at the hem of my dress. When no one's looking, or no one's paying attention, I slice through the twine and lift a newspaper from the top of the stack. Paper hidden beneath my coat, I scurry back to the *hôtel* to read the latest of Jeanne's treasures.

It should've abated by now, a fortnight having passed. Yet each morning there it is, another enumeration of the wedding gifts bestowed upon Jeanne Daudet née Hugo. It's as though every Frenchman squandered his life's savings for the chance to purchase the couple an overpriced, impractical marital prize. It's rumored she's hired four people solely to unwrap gifts. Indeed there are not enough minutes in a lifetime to get through them all.

If only I had people throwing presents my way! It would solve my every problem. The paltry sum I lifted from Sœur Marie is almost gone. I've been frugal with money, even though it means staying in this dodgy *hôtel des femmes* from which I write. Montmartre is not the place for young girls raised in convents. The cabarets! The debauchery! The lawlessness! I have only participated a time or two.

With my ever-dwindling funds the *hôtel* has turned from sacrifice to luxury. At least the weather's warming, and the rotten place is not quite so rotten. The water stopped freezing in the basin. I no longer sleep with every piece of clothing I own piled on top of me. This residence was all I could afford when I stole into the city three months ago. I cannot afford it anymore.

Several of my *hôtel*-mates work in nearby textile factories. They are forever trying to secure me a job. Alas, the wages are small and the penalties high. The girls have bleeding hands, rough complexions. The ones who are twenty look like they're forty. The ones who are thirty look most of the way to dead.

One girl earns wages transporting materials from the windmills to the factories. Though a better option than working in the factories themselves, she is rather starting to look like the mule she is. Whenever I am tempted to take up a similar form of employ I ask myself what do we women have but our looks? Our charms, yes, but it's difficult to charm after a twelve-hour shift.

In the *hôtel* we also have many of the girls, *les filles soumises*, who work on the rue Le Peletier. They say the money comes easily, this trading skin for coins. Well, of course it comes easily! They are paid a pittance. The men spend more on drink!

Though I find this gamut of options most unappealing, I would be lying to say I have not considered each of them. In the end it is all too little money for too much suffering. Though suffer I will soon as well. If only I could bring myself to work in a factory or a *maison de tolerance*, I would not be in my current financial straits.

I have one week to devise a solution, a week if I eat sparsely and flirt with the *hôtel* manager. He is not so much a man as a gnome, but I am quite adept at looking the other way. My rent can perhaps be a few days late if I say the right words. The manager is lenient when someone makes him feel important, I suppose the same as most.

Now I will close this book and find more ways to watch my francs until something comes along to pull me from this mess. I came to Paris for a better life, and a better life I shall have!

Chapitre XV

Paris, 12 May 1891

Oh, *Jeanne au pain sec! Ma chérie*, you did help me after all!

These past few days have been murderous, simply murderous. The clouds, the sky, the air—they all pushed down on me with such force I could scarcely breathe. The reckoning was at hand, my final days as a Parisienne.

To make matters worse, the *hôtel* manager fled town on some unnamed and reportedly scandalous jaunt. He left operations to his old crone of a mother. Perhaps she is his wife. In either case, unlike her predecessor she refuses to take partial payment in batted eyelashes and flirtatious exchanges.

"If you don't remit your weekly fee in the next eight hours," she told me, "you are out on the street. There are others who want your room."

This was no idle threat. Despite the absolute filth of the place, people were anxious to get a room. When Blanche succumbed to tuberculosis, two girls fought over her bed-sit before the coroner had even removed her body from the room.

"Eight hours?" I said, my voice like a frog's. "But can't I possibly have—"

"Eight hours!" she screeched, baring those brown-gray teeth of hers.

Nodding, I turned and staggered down the front steps.

Walking the boulevard, I sucked back the tears. Sœur Marie told me never to cry. It shows weakness. There is nothing worse than weakness.

So I walked. And I walked. The sun poured over me. I do not possess proper clothing for the weather or this city, the whole of my wardrobe appropriate for dank convents, certainly not Parisian streets in the springtime.

As the sun raged on and the outdoor cafés filled with smoke and happiness, perspiration ran down my forehead and neck. If I glanced in a window, which I did not dare, doubtless I would've seen my face scarlet and shiny. People looked my way askance. They stepped into the street to avoid me. One bicyclist almost mowed me down, perhaps on purpose. At the corner I stopped to reclaim my composure.

Sometimes catching your breath is the best thing to do.

I leaned against the railing of a café and dropped my head onto my chest. The patio was packed with men, smoking and drinking and swapping tales of the cabarets, the cancan girls, the pantomime shows. Cabarets, I thought. I could learn the cancan. Indeed, it was better than working in a factory or receiving chicken feed for opening my legs.

At once the wave of panic and self-pity began to recede. I lifted my head, and that's when I saw it, tacked to the café window, a sign the (literal) color of a sunset. The woman on the poster smiled at me. She lifted her yellow skirts to display the round, smooth tops of her thighs. A feather popped up from the back of her head. She was beautiful, grand, even.

"Folies Bergère," the sign read. The most renowned cabaret in the city. Even I, a convent girl, had heard of it. There were worse ways to earn money, I thought. Much worse.

After ripping the poster from the glass, I immediately proceeded to the dance hall, located just below Montmartre, in the Ninth. My feet ached by the time I reached 32 rue Richer, but I wasted not a moment to compose myself. If I waited too long I would almost certainly reconsider.

When I walked into the hall dozens of bodies hummed around me, all of them setting up for the evening's festivities. A lithe woman hung from the ceiling as she changed a light in the chandelier. A short man with a long nose coaxed an elephant through a doorway. I saw three ladies dressed like men, two acrobats, and seven parrots bushwhacking the place-setters. It was a circus, and the show hadn't even begun.

"Excuse me," I said to the first person who acknowledged my presence. "May I speak to the man in charge?"

He nodded toward the bar, then promptly moved on to other things.

Beside the bar stood a gentleman nearly six feet tall with black, curled hair and a black, curled beard. He wore rings on every finger and a floor-length red velveteen coat lined with fur. Not one for subtlety, I thought. Like the rest of the place, he was a performance of his own.

"Bonjour," I said and marched to his side. I was still sweating, overheating. Staring at his coat offered no favors. I felt as though I, too, was covered in fur. "I would like a job as a cancan dancer in your establishment."

I expected an assessment of my physique, perhaps a request to lift my skirt, which I was fully prepared to do. Instead he responded to my query with laughter. Really, it was more of a guffaw. My cheeks blazed. I did not know it was possible to be inappropriate in a cabaret.

"I'm sorry, Mademoiselle," he said. "This is a professional establishment. No filles soumises at the Folies Bergère."

"Filles soumises?"

The voice of Sœur Marie rang in my ears. Marthe, you must think before you speak. Always ask yourself if there is a gentler way to express your feelings. Alas, I was not in the domain of Sœur Marie any longer, and the Folies Bergère was no convent.

"Félicitations, Monsieur!" I sang as a most disingenuous smile stretched across my face. "You are the very first person to call me a submissive whore. To my face, anyway."

"You're the one looking for work," he replied, smirking.

"If you care to learn the truth, I was raised by nuns, so am actually quite the opposite. But I understand your confusion. Since you are so accustomed to seeing whores it must be difficult to distinguish a respectable woman from a fille soumise. How sad for you!"

"Mademoiselle, such insolent talk is not advisable when trying to secure a job," he said, knitting together his brows while a small smile dropped from the side of his mouth. "What did you say your name was?"

"I didn't. It's Marthe," I told him.

"Marthe? Just Marthe? Do you have a surname?"

Like any good orphan I did not. I knew I had to create something fancy, a name with flourish. I thought of the *hôtel grisettes* and their own pseudonyms. The girls always added a "de" before whatever whimsical surname they devised. This small word gave a woman countenance, they said, it gave her a history. *De* meant you were from somewhere instead of, like most of us, being from nowhere at all.

"De Florian," I said. "Marthe de Florian."

"Pleased to meet you, Mademoiselle de Florian. While I appreciate your inquiry, this is a prestigious establishment and not a place for wide-eyed villagers bumbling up from the countryside."

"I'm have more savvy than you think," I told him.

"I don't doubt it. The point is, Mademoiselle de Florian, my girls are skilled dancers and performers." He pointed to a poster on the wall, the same one that was right then folded up in my palm. "These girls have careers. They bring with them names we can use in advertisements, names that draw a crowd. You, my dear, are strong in beauty but lacking in name."

"If you let me dance," I told him. "The crowds will come."

He shook his head. "I'm sorry, but I cannot allow it. It would hardly be fair."

"Fair?" I started. "Let me tell you about fair."

Suddenly I caught sight of a large brass clock hanging from the far wall. The minutes were disappearing. I would be out of the *hôtel* by nightfall.

"You have to help me," I said, lips quivering. "I've nowhere else to go."

A woman walked up then. A tall woman with cherry hair and the loveliest gown I'd seen up close. The bodice was made of the thickest, finest black satin, a dozen or more buttons running up the front. She'd tucked peonies into her décolletage. A wide gray skirt spilled out behind her.

"Bonjour, Gérard," she said and placed her satchel on the counter. She removed a cigarette and lit it with one of the still-flickering candles. "Good night last night?"

"Terrific, yes."

"I see Monsieur l'Éléphant is uncooperative as ever." She exhaled one long stream of smoke in my direction. I tried not to blink. "And who is this?"

"Émilie, this is Marthe de Florian. Mademoiselle de Florian, this is Émilie."

"Is she the new barmaid?" Émilie inquired. "Finally you listen to my pleas! You cannot run a cabaret on dancers alone."

"Oh, no," he said. "She's merely—"

"Yes!" I sang before I could think better of it. "I am the new barmaid!"

"Pardon me?" Gérard said, eyes bulging.

"Very pleased to meet you." I shot a hand toward this Émilie, Gérard scowling somewhere over my left shoulder.

"Thank god," Émilie said and mashed her cigarette into a stool. "We need much help around here. And you're pretty to boot. When can you start?"

"Right now, of course!" I whopped my purse onto the bar beside Émilie's. "I'd like to request a small paycheck advance."

"Paycheck advance? Mademoiselle, if you want to be a barmaid you need to wear the dress." Gérard pointed at Émilie. "And if you want to wear the dress you'll need to remit fifty francs."

"Fifty francs?" I choked. I didn't even have the five francs needed to pay off the craggy old landlady. "Is that negotiable?"

Émilie chuckled.

"Absolutely not," Gérard growled.

"Well, that's just not feasible," I said. I was done with. It was to the brothels or the gypsum mines for me.

Suddenly a verbal sparring broke out several tables away. One man tried to clean while a patron batted him away with a cane. Instantly I knew the assailant. He was the same puffy, sweaty man known to the entire city.

"Is that—?" I started.

"Yes, Georges Hugo," Émilie said. "We let him stay all day. He really has nowhere else to go. It's safer for him here."

"Safer for Paris, too," Gérard grumbled. "His day is incomplete unless he's challenged at least three different people to a duel."

M. Hugo had several packages by his feet, seven or eight at least. I could not keep my eyes from them. I stared. I daresay I ogled.

Émilie did not miss it.

"Presents for his sister, no doubt. La princesse." She rolled her eyes. "He can hardly walk a step without someone thrusting one in his direction."

"Wedding gifts," I gasped. "For Jeanne."

My mind flashed back to Madame Daudet's wedding procession, to standing on that street, the waif by my side and the crowd pushing at my back. I'd thought then if I could get my hands on a gift or two all my problems would be solved.

"Gérard, is it?" I said, turning back to the red-coated man. "I will pay your unseemly dress fee, but please let me work first. It is a long way to my apartment, and I want to get started right away."

He showed reluctance, unsurprising given that I'd already shown my hand, namely that I had nothing in it.

"Oh, ease up, Gérard," Émilie said. "I'll show the new girl around. There's a dress left over from the last woman. They're about the same size. Marthe, come with me into the back. We can get things started. I'm so pleased you're here."

Émilie did not give her boss a chance to say no. I will remember this: Do not give them a chance to say no.

And that, dear journal, is how I started my first day of work at the Folies Bergère. Not as a cancan dancer but a barmaid. Alas, the day did not end when I left 32 rue Richer. In fact it continues on! Here I sit in my bed, in the *hôtel* I can now afford, with Jeanne Hugo's brother snoring beside me.

It is not what you think!

He's starting to rustle. It is, as they say, to be continued.

Chapitre XVI

If not for an early sunrise and lackluster window treatments, April might have missed the workday completely.

When the sun exploded across her face, she sprang to sitting. She was disoriented, her head full of cancan dancers and elephants. She half-expected to see a fleshy, sweaty man snoring beside her. It took April several minutes to remember her name and what country she was in. She'd blame the jet lag, but it was really more the fault of a good French burgundy, plus a healthy dose of Marthe.

Groaning, April swung her legs off the side of the bed, recoiling as her feet touched the brisk wood floors. Her stomach rumbled, or maybe it hadn't stopped. A glance in the mirror revealed haggard-beast hair, purple-tinged teeth, and crumpled clothes she first put on two days ago on some other continent.

"Working on a few things from home," April texted to Olivier as she wriggled out of her suit. "Home." It was a curious word for a place she'd only entered a few hours ago. Still, it was more home to her than the apartment in Manhattan, the one with her name on the deed. "Will be at the flat later this morning, between nine and ten."

April chucked her phone on the dresser and slid into the shower, if it could be called that. She'd had more satisfying personal space and water pressure in her junior-high locker room. The stall was narrow; the knobs required great force to turn. A metal spigot dangled overhead, barely spitting out drops of tepid water. April spun around, futilely trying to wet every inch of her body. Historical buildings could have dodgy bathroom situations, but this was ridiculous. Jeanne Hugo probably had better accommodations a hundred years ago. Of course she was Jeanne Hugo. *Jeanne au pain sec* could've asked for a shower given by elephants, and the city would've immediately marched twenty-five of them through her front door.

Jeanne Hugo, April thought. What was her real story? Or, rather, what was the deal with Jeanne and Marthe?

It was funny, this centuries-long obsession with celebrities and their offspring. Hugo, Kennedy, Windsor—not much had changed other than the form of media covering them. April's father called it the "lucky sperm club," and indeed it seemed that Jeanne accomplished little aside from being born into the right family. Despite Marthe's grumblings, it wasn't exactly newsworthy. Even Jesus Christ got street cred for the whole son-of-God business.

April was not exactly up on pop culture. Celebrity references went almost entirely over her head. But Victor Hugo? April would've stood next to Marthe and all manner of street urchins to catch a glimpse of the Hugo-Daudet marital procession. She was a theater dork, according to Troy anyway, but Victor Hugo meant something to April. Unbeknownst to Hugo or his family or anyone who ever knew him, the man was part of April's own (admittedly inferior) provenance.

The musical adaptation of Hugo's brilliant novel *Les Misérables* was the first Broadway show April ever saw, even though technically she saw it in Los Angeles. She went with her dad, on a Sunday, two weeks after she turned fifteen. A couple of women beside them clucked and grinned at the father-daughter outing: What a sweet dad! What a delightful young lady! In fact her dad *was* sweet. April was, if not delightful, at least not horrible, as far as teenage girls went.

But what "Frick and Frack" (Dad's words) did not understand was that only four hours earlier, April's father, the kind and paunchy dad smiling beside them, had given up. In a breath, or so it seemed to April, her mother's illness had surpassed her father's ability to take care of her. Sometime in the early-morning hours Sandra Potter was transferred from their home to a nearby nursing facility. April woke to find her mother gone, two theater tickets in her place. *Les Miz* was her mom's favorite play.

"Your mom is very sick," April's dad told her.

It was the first and last reference he ever made to the illness. Later he used words like "comfortable" and "easier" and "for the best," but he never again said the word "sick." April had to get the real story from her brother. Her brother got his information from pestering the doctors.

That day, though, April asked no questions. She sought no information. Instead she shrugged, fished a pair of white, midheel pumps from the bottom of her mother's closet, and concentrated on which *Les Miz* T-shirt to buy. Baggy or fitted? Did Cosette's flowing hair draw undue attention to April's flat chest? Ultimately she chose the gray one, size extra-large despite her extra-small frame.

April ended up leaving the T-shirt, still in its bag, on the floor beneath her seat. She did not expect to like the performance and viewed the entire outing as a favor to her father instead of the other way around. But when the lights hit the stage, the revolutionaries fought, and Valjean and Fantine sang, April was entranced. She did not consider herself a sap, but during the performance her eyes were wet most of the time. Only as an adult did she realize the tears were probably less about the play and more about the morning's events.

Her father returned to Los Angeles the next day to fetch the abandoned shirt. It was the last errand he ever ran for his kids, other than shuttling them to the hospital or to church. Once April's mother was spirited out of the home, his attentions went along with her. He could focus only on his wife's sad, slow decline.

In hindsight it was sweet. At the time, though, it seemed grossly unfair. So while her father was at the hospital, or at church, or doing whatever it was he did to pay the bills, April played her *Les Miz* soundtrack on repeat and at high volume most waking hours. Though it annoyed her brother, it transported April and, more important, drowned out the deep boom of silence their mother left behind. Within a week even the neighbor's dog could've barked "Do You Hear the People Sing?"

As she finished trying to wring the shampoo out of her hair, April quietly sang a few verses of "Master of the House." It wasn't until she reached "kidney of a horse, liver of a cat (filling up the sausages with this and that)" that April realized she had tears in her eyes. How was it that she'd gone farther from home yet suddenly felt closer than ever? Like Marthe, April blamed Jeanne Hugo.

After cleansing herself of airplane and shuttered-apartment stink, April grabbed a washcloth-sized towel from the rack. She checked her phone and frowned. No messages. Not that Troy was required to call, but April wouldn't have minded.

As she toweled off and planned her non-American outfit for the day, April checked her phone another thirty-seven or thirty-eight times. It remained so quiet it hurt her ears.

April threw on jeans, a light sweater, and an Hermès scarf she purchased in her barely surviving museum curating days. It was an investment, April figured back then. Sort of like Marthe's barmaid dress. Of course April was never in danger of losing her home, at least not when she bought the scarf.

Outside the air was cool. The fog hung low, turning the sky navy blue. Because it was still relatively early, the streets were quiet save for a smattering of delivery people, cleaning crews, and a few revelers trudging home from a night out. This was not the neighborhood for ambitious office workers, which endeared it to April even more.

After greeting several garbagemen with what Luc Thébault would surely've described as typical American verve, April stepped into the *boulangerie* across the street. A bell tinkled overhead. Though the smell was intoxicating enough to make even the pickiest of Parisians fret with indecisiveness, April knew exactly what she wanted. She tiptoed to the glass case.

Bonjour, les chouquettes, I've missed you.

Chouquettes. The perfect pastry. Puffed up. Light. They came in two versions, dusted with sugar granules or chocolate chips. April elected the *sucre perlé*. If you were in Paris your food might as well glitter.

After purchasing exactly one dozen of them, several times making blithe reference to a large family back in the flat, April requested a to-go cup of coffee. Opening her purse to pay the vendor, she couldn't resist peeking at her BlackBerry once again. No new messages.

With sugar and caffeine as consolation, April scurried back to her apartment, where she estimated there was enough time to gorge herself on at least six or seven *chouquettes* while engaging in a little "research."

She told Olivier she planned to work from home, and Marthe's diaries legitimately qualified as "work." Plus April was in no hurry to trot them out beneath the curious eyes of her Parisian cohorts. The documents were a find, and April didn't care to answer questions about how she got them, when she got them, or why she was suddenly the estate attorney's primary contact. It all felt too precarious, delicate, as if one misstep might break the whole thing.

Chapitre XVII

Paris, 13 May 1891

I brought Georges Hugo and his packages back to my bed-sit, oh, yes I did! He only just left. Not to worry, the only *packages* I touched were the ones wrapped in paper. *Mon dieu!*

Many times I've heard my sweet *hôtel* neighbor Aimée complain about the effects of drink on men. Though I cannot speak from experience, it is, according to her, quite the softening agent. Evidently some men become so inebriated the only way to consummate the act would be to tie his member to a shoehorn and slide it in like a foot into a shoe! Aimée likened it to a damp stocking. It all sounds positively dreadful. Dressing will never be the same.

What young Aimée did not tell me, but what I already know, is that drink also makes people forget. Though I've not had to tussle with any drunken, flaccid men, my convent was famous for its wine production, and Sœur Marie did not hesitate to partake. We had multihour conversations she later forgot in their entirety.

"What were you up to last night, Marthe?" she would ask. "I didn't see you the whole evening!"

Never mind she'd spent three hours regaling me with stories of her younger days (she was not always a woman of the Lord!) and that I often helped her change and get into bed. Once or twice I even assisted her on the toilet!

So when Georges Hugo came back to my bed-sit expecting a host of pleasures, I understood I only needed to *tell* him what happened. It didn't actually *have* to happen. By the time we returned to the *hôtel* he was stupid with drink and quite near passing out. To hasten his slumber, I paid Aimée my last three francs to hit him in the back of the skull with an iron. Not to worry, she took care not to permanently injure the man! She has done this before.

Georges woke in the morning groggy and with the start of a headache. Aimée sat in for me and explained, in great detail, the acts "we" performed. I figured it was best for her to impersonate me. The things she told him I've never heard of! Apparently men like accessing women at multiple points of entry. And Aimée can fit a penis all the way down her throat!

Aimée spun a good (and sufficiently raunchy) tale, Georges none the wiser. Even if he could not remember doing *those* things with *that* woman, a man of his stature would never admit it! Pleased with the reports of his sexual prowess, he nodded along and ultimately smacked Aimée on the backside before reaching for his billfold. He remitted a tidy sum and shuffled out of the *hôtel*, whistling as he went.

I split the fee with Aimée, who was pleased to earn something for her artifice. She was quite grateful for a full 50 percent considering she didn't have to perform on the implied sexual contract. For my part, I didn't mind sharing because the money was not why I brought Georges back to my room in the first place.

It was about the presents, of course! The wedding gifts of Madame Daudet née Hugo. In the end the poor fellow's load was much heavier when he entered the building versus when he left. Sadly, there will be at least a few *cadeaux de Jeanne* that won't make it into the newspaper registries. There will, however, be quite a number of exquisite wedding gifts featured in any one of the Montmartre pawnbrokerages! There will also be, among other things, a new barmaid's gown for me.

Merci, ma chérie! Merci!

Things might work out after all.

Chapitre XVIII

Paris, 18 June 1891

The Folies Bergère is a sight! Even after a month of employment I cannot get over the spectacle. It's an assault on the senses. Everywhere there are lights and mirrors and luxurious fabrics, to speak nothing of the luxurious women! "Overflowing" is the word. Everything is overflowing. Even the fountains in the garden! You cannot walk past without drenching the lower half of your skirt.

Each evening brings a steady wave of people, both men and women. The guests sweep through the front doors and take a seat wherever they please. Some promenade the galleries while animals and humans perform on stage. Already I've written about the elephant. Gérard still cannot get him to bend to his wishes and, even worse, the beast has helped himself to a seat upon many a *habitué*.

We have other animals, though. Animals that are a touch more compliant! There are monkeys and horses and even a tiger. It is not as dangerous as it sounds. Though Gérard claims otherwise, I am certain he drugs the cat. Instead of roaring ferociously the poor creature stumbles around the stage and nine times out of ten falls into the orchestra.

In addition to the animal shows, on any given night patrons can witness ballet, operetta, or acrobatics with special effects. More than one person has caught fire. And last night—last night! The scene almost defies description.

Imagine this: A glass chandelier dangles over the audience. It is massive, three tiers tall and bigger than most carriages. Now picture yourself sitting below this magnificent chandelier, the light dancing on your gloves and skirt. It's a hallmark of the Folies, everyone has heard of the famous chandelier. Customers come to expect this display: the glittering lights, the dancing reflections, the polished crystal. It is so magical, so transcendent; depending on the dancer it can be the best part of the show.

Suppose you were one of our patrons last night. You sit down and notice there is something different about your skirt. It looks, somehow, less luminous. Its threads do not dance. Then you realize: the chandelier! *Mon dieu!* They forgot to light it! You glance up. You gasp! Because instead of rows of glass and lights you see rows of women—nude women. A chandelier of nipples and flesh!

The performers stayed like that for three hours, smiles plastered on their faces, dark, prominent nipples unfailingly erect, pointed outward. Some of our most famous cancan dancers were up there. It made me quite glad to be a barmaid. I enjoyed the sight but do not have the fortitude. Or the lack of modesty!

Aside from naked ladies hoisted in the sky, I've met many interesting people at my post—more interesting than if I'd been hanging nude from a lighting fixture, that's for certain. There are, of course, the various Hugo relations. Thankfully Georges shows no sign of recognition when he and I interact. I also meet painters and poets and writers, even pseudowriters such as that gossipmonger Marcel Proust. He thinks himself a master of words when he does nothing more than write a society column. What a bore he is!

A fellow named Robert de Montesquiou pays me quite a lot of attention. He is supposedly a poet of some sort, though I've never heard of him. He certainly dresses poetically enough, his favorite a pistachio-colored suit with a white velvet waistcoat. Often he wears flowers in place of a necktie and he always sports a ring the size of an egg, inside which he claims to keep human tears. He is quite fond of the boys but once tried to woo Émilie with a bedpan. It belonged to Napoleon in his Waterloo days but nonetheless was still a bedpan. He is dangerously handsome but I don't know what to make of him.

Despite the frequent amusements, my job can prove quite boring at times. It's rather plebeian, and by the end of the day my hands are sore and my feet swollen. Don't misunderstand! I mean not to complain. For the most part I enjoy it. I love looking at the dresses coming in, the dresses going out, the dresses coming off. Indeed, they come off!

Though I was being mouthy at the time, my assessment on that first day was not far off the mark. While the girls at the Folies Bergère are hardly the sickly creatures creeping out of the rue Le Peletier brothels on a nightly basis (God bless you, Aimée, *Je t'adore*!), they are not exactly virginal. There are special rooms. There are special women. There are not-so-special men who go with these women into these rooms and come out looking rather pleased.

I asked Émilie about this once. She demurred and pretended to not know. After baiting her multiple times (the dresses, they cannot afford those dresses on their wages, and what about the jewels? The rubies, the pearls, the diamonds!), she finally told me they were not prostitutes but instead demimondaines. *Les demimondaine*s. I am not sure precisely what this means but I aim to find out. It is a rather lovely word, isn't it? *Demimondaine*. It sounds almost regal.

Part Deux

Chapitre XIX

Though April knew she was running late, she was still surprised to find Olivier already at the apartment. In Paris, New York City, and many less glamorous locales, April was always the first one in the office. Not that Marthe's was merely a place of *business*, but April was a first-to-arrive-last-to-leave kind of person. Then again, it was rare for her to have jet lag, a mild hangover, and a century-old journal on loan so maybe these were somewhat extenuating circumstances.

"Bonjour," April said as she tottered in on too-high heels. Given her questionable physical state and the jittery sugar rush, April should've stuck with her trusty flats. "How is everyone this morning?"

April extracted a napkin from her bag and set it, and her third coffee of the morning, atop the least-special-looking table in the room.

"Bonjour, Madame Vogt," Olivier said. "Comment allez-vous?"

"Bien, et vous?"

"Bien."

April glanced around and somehow, in the light of a different day, with a full night's sleep behind her, the apartment appeared even more unwieldy. Yesterday April saw boundless treasures. She still saw the treasures, but they were mired in an impossible amount of work. Marthe must've quickly learned what a demimondaine was and put the knowledge to good use. April was not standing in the apartment of a barmaid.

"You look alarmed, Madame Vogt."

"April. Please. Alarmed, no. It's all a bit overwhelming, though."

"Yes," Olivier said. "We have a lot to accomplish."

"To say the least. When do you plan to transfer the items to your office?" April flipped open her notepad. "What delivery service do you use? There's one I used years ago; they were top-notch. I'll have to see if they're still around."

Olivier shook his head.

"We won't move anything until just prior to the viewings. We haven't the room. Quite an astronomical number of things have come in over the past few months, and we don't have space for Madame Quatremer's belongings, too."

Marthe's belongings, April wanted to say. These were Marthe's things. Madame Quatremer never wanted them, not for a single moment in all of seventy years.

"All right," April said, unsure if this was good news or bad. "I guess we work here."

The flat was beautiful, but haunting, inspiring, yet distracting. April was probably better off in the basement of an auction house, a place that did not have chandeliers upon which her brain might project areolas. Still, inefficiencies notwithstanding, April found she wanted to stay in the apartment as long as she could.

"If we've not expressed it before," Olivier said. "We are quite grateful you made the journey over. We value your help. You certainly understand Continental furniture better than anyone in our office."

"Merci beaucoup." April said. "I'm glad to be here."

Despite the compliment, April frowned. Distraction whirred around her head like crickets. Something was off. April's brain felt thick, muddled, confused.

"Is it just me," she started. "Or is the flat weird in some way . . ."

April looked over her shoulder and realized the problem with a jolt. The Boldini. It was missing.

"Where's the painting?!" she gasped. "What happened to it?"

Olivier shrugged. "*That* we took back to the offices for assessment."

April clutched her stomach, her body swayed. The thought of not seeing the portrait again made her downright sick. It was only the *chouquettes*, she told herself. Consumption of ten pastries in a one-hour span was inadvisable no matter how strong one's constitution.

"But it's not yet been authenticated," April said, her breathing labored, as if all the dust from the apartment was now inside her lungs. "We need a plan to determine provenance before we start staging. I have some documents loaned to us by the estate that may help in this regard."

Bring her back. Bring the damn painting back.

"Ne vous inquiétez pas," Olivier said. "It's all but taken care of. As it turns out Boldini's wife wrote a biography that was never published. In it, she mentions the portrait. Sounds as though we have provenance fairly well settled."

"Wow," April said. "Okay. That's great news. About the verification. Terrific. Lucky."

It was all these things: great, terrific, lucky. Still, April felt as if she was lying. So that was it then? No more Folies Bergère or demimondaines or nipple chandeliers? It was good news for the auction, not so good for Luc's so-called curious auctioneer.

"Madame Vogt," Olivier said. "Is everything all right? Vous-êtes stressée."

"No. Not stressed."

Except *very* stressed. She wanted the portrait. April wanted the room to stay exactly as it had been the day before.

"Madame Vogt?"

"I'm . . . uh . . . I'm thinking about the auction itself. Do you have a preliminary timetable? We need to calendar it soon."

Schedules. Calendars. These were the things April was supposed to worry about—not courtesans, frothy gowns, or the swindling of prominent republican family members. But Marthe deserved to be on the calendar too. She *was* the schedule. That this was a Boldini meant thousands would see Marthe's face. April wanted them to see the rest of her too.

"This has the opportunity to be a very special auction," April continued, ideas coalescing in her mind.

Maybe they could build something around Marthe de Florian herself, lend the woman a certain kind of posthumous fame, notoriety comparable to Jeanne Hugo's—preferably exceeding Jeanne's—April thought with a smirk.

"I'm envisioning a multiday exhibit," she said. "The history is quite rich. Though the woman is unknown, even to us auction-house types, she consorted with Proust and Montesquiou and even the Hugo family. And of course Boldini himself! Think of the stories our pieces could tell."

"Ah! Quite clever you are," Olivier said.

April started to beam.

"Alas. Non," he said. "It is already decided."

"Decided . . ."

"Most of the assets will go into 'Important French Furniture, Sculptures, and Works of Art' in September. The rest shall fit with 'Important European Silver, Gold Boxes, and Vertu.' Which is"—he checked his phone—"in October."

"What? That can't be right?" April said, confused. "Filler pieces? That doesn't make sense."

"We were a little lacking this upcoming season, to be honest. So these items will round everything out quite nicely."

At once April's hopes for the auction were pummeled. Marthe had been locked up and stashed away for over seventy years. They'd made this tremendous discovery but once her pieces were broken up and scattered amongst other half-baked lots, it'd be like they never found her in the first place.

"You look a little peaked," Olivier noted. "Do you need to sit down? It can get quite stuffy in here."

"Olivier." April inhaled deeply. "I implore you to reconsider. You flew me to Paris for my expertise and—"

"Indeed we did," he said. "Alas, it's been decided. I think it's for the best. So, shall we get to work?"

Without waiting for an answer, Olivier turned and strode toward the kitchen, leaving April slack-jawed and staggering in the hallway. They couldn't do this to Marthe. If she showed Olivier the journals, perhaps he'd change his mind. Or, worse, perhaps he wouldn't.

"This is not happening," April said as she hugged her purse to her chest, feeling the weight of Marthe's journals through the leather. "You're getting your own auction. Important French Furniture? C'est merdique."

Strong words but the right ones. *C'est merdique*: It was shitty indeed.

Chapitre XX

April hunted Olivier down an hour later, which felt like the minimum length of time before she could reasonably accost him again. In the fifty-seven minutes (fifty-eight, fifty-nine) since Olivier dismissed her auction ideas, April had accomplished little, her brain too congested with frustration, with the goddamn furniture and vertu.

"Important European Silver." That's what you called a random piece from a random home you didn't know what to do with, a piece whose catalog copy was uninspired, untied to something greater. Or as Birdie once joked upon trying to describe a mangled fork from a crumbling British castle, "It's silver, dude, and from a castle, isn't that enough?"

"Olivier," April said. "Can we chat?"

She approached the kitchen, where he stood, back toward the doorway and looking through a crate of sealed wine.

"Bonjour, April," he said without turning around. "How's it coming with the furniture? Not sure any of this wine is auctionable—"

"We need to discuss the apartment."

"L'appartement?" He turned to face her. "What is there to discuss? It is a rental, non? It does not get transferred with the estate."

"I don't mean the apartment itself," April said, trying to settle the pitch in her voice. "These aren't filler pieces, Olivier. You can't cram them into other auctions."

He shrugged. "I disagree."

"What about the Boldini? You can't possibly—"

"The Impressionist and Modern Art Auction. A perfect fit."

"Impressionist and Modern Art," April repeated, dazed. "You can't do that."

Marc's head popped around the corner.

"Ça va?" he said. "Is there a problem in here?"

"Yes, there's a problem!" April said in anguish.

She suddenly pictured the two men running around the Paris auction house, sticking pieces of Marthe's life into the empty, awkward spaces of other peoples' broken estates. Together Madame de Florian's things told a story, with the gilt and ostriches and all of it.

"This is not filler," she said again, helplessly gesturing around the room, as if she'd known these belongings for decades instead of hours. "You can't do this."

Maybe if she said it enough times they'd agree.

"We see no reason to conduct an entirely different auction," Olivier said. "It's cost-prohibitive. Think of the catalogs and the dinners. We'd never make any money if we gave every interesting find its own auction. You know this, April. You've been in the business for years. This is not Contemporary Art." He made a face. "It's much more economical to place these assets with other properties."

Properties, assets—that's all the pieces represented to them, goods to be collected and monetized. It was, of course, the whole point to Sotheby's, though not necessarily to April, at least not then.

"Olivier, Marc, I fully appreciate the need for conservatism," she said. "But hear me out. I'm a little surprised you did not consult me, but it's your office and I understand the dynamics. As you said, I've been in the business long enough, and I truly feel we're being shortsighted. There are intangibles to realize. Together these pieces have that extra something, the provenance that made Rockefeller's Rothko go for $73 million instead of $30 million, that je ne sais quoi that fetched several hundred thousand dollars for Jackie O's fake plastic pearls."

"Elisabetta Quatremer was no Jacqueline Onassis." Olivier chuckled. "Unless you have an iconic photograph of Sean-Sean wrapping her belongings around his chin."

"John-John." April shook her head wearily. "Not Sean-Sean."

"This is what I said, non? Either way, unless Madame Quatremer has progeny considered so-called American royalty, or is a long-lost Rockefeller, her name would not draw people to a separate auction. It'd be one more event, tens of thousands of euros wasted. It's far easier to put her with the regularly scheduled auctions."

"It's Marthe de Florian who has the intrigue," April said, picturing what was sure to be the catalog description—"Private Collection, Paris"—instead of what it should've said. Instead of Marthe's full name in print. "It's the woman in the Boldini people will care about, not Madame Quatremer."

God, she'd have to show them the diaries sooner rather than later, wouldn't she? April bristled at the thought.

"My research is only very preliminary," she continued. "But based on what I've read, I truly believe if we marketed her auction in the right way we'd more than recoup the cost. If people came to know the woman in the painting, the lots would have the dual benefit of being a Boldini *and* featuring the artist's lover, a woman with a fascinating background of her own. This goodwill would extend to the other objects, and raise the value across all and in total."

"April—"

She was too far gone now to be stopped.

"Our entire job is to get bidders to see the value of the pieces beyond their physical description. The story we could tell with Marthe would net us at least double. I'm sure of it."

" 'Marthe,' is it?" Olivier smirked. "On a first-name basis?"

"Yes, as a matter of fact, and if we play this wisely the entire art world will be on a first-name basis with her, too."

"You pose a very convincing argument, but it's too risky. I don't know that I can line up enough buyers for this type of sale."

"But these pieces themselves! Forget Marthe's story. Every asset here is fresh to market! That's its own selling point."

"Ah, well. Blame the economy. And the department. This is what the team has decided. Je suis désolé. I'm sorry we did not include you in the discussions."

"Oh it's . . ." April mumbled. "Unnecessary."

She was, after all, merely the American hired to look under desks and at the backsides of rugs.

April wondered if she could go above their heads. Marthe deserved her own spotlight even if, like everything else in this world, it boiled down to economics. Not much had changed. A hundred years ago Marthe didn't have enough name to get her own show at the Folies. Instead Gérard relegated her to the bar, filling in where Émilie could not. April said it before and she'd say it again: Marthe was not filler.

"I do not mean to disappoint you," Olivier said. He frowned almost imperceptibly, and for a second April believed him. "But I am glad you understand. In any case, it is time for me to go. I have a meeting in the office. Do you need anything before I leave?"

"I think I'm fine here. I'll be working in the master bedroom today. I'll ring your mobile later with an update."

"Very well. We'll speak this afternoon. Au 'voir, April."

"Au 'voir."

April pivoted on her heels and shuffled to the back of the flat, eyes hot with the threat of tears. Marthe de Florian. She was almost already gone.

Furniture, she reminded herself. You're here for the furniture.

Olivier was right. This was business, and she would do well to treat it like the series of economic transactions it would soon become. No use getting attached to a woman in a painting. What did April care for a Belle Époque prostitute? It had nothing to do with walnut bookcases or mauve settees.

Unfortunately it was impossible to weed through Marthe's boudoir without seeing the woman in it. Though the room was as jumbled as the rest of the flat, at the center was an imposing mahogany-and-gilt-bronze mounted *Aux Nénuphars* bed. It had a towering headboard sprung with golden cobras. Matching cobra-legged tables, also with the water lily motif, sat nearby. It was not enough to say the pieces were extravagant. A similar set was on display in the Musée d'Orsay.

Though April was there for the furniture (as she reminded herself six, seven, a dozen times), what she really wanted was the journals. Upstanding, bookish Continental furniture expert April Vogt was far more interested in what happened *on* the bed than who made it and in what year. This was a first.

Gloves on, April lifted the diaries from their folder. She poked her head around the wall to where Olivier and Marc stood squabbling in French about where to order sandwiches for their afternoon meeting. She had time for a few pages. It was the least April could do for the woman who once lived there, a woman whose life would soon be parceled off and sold to the highest bidder.

Chapitre XXI

Paris, 22 September 1891

I've found you can acquire things from the male species, valuable things. A little flirtation and they are aflutter, tripping over themselves to compliment and dole out the treasures. *Vous-êtes plus belle que les étoiles!* More beautiful than the stars? Hardly, but I will take your candlesticks and lacquered boxes. *Merci, Georges Hugo.*

Thus far I've acquired: four gowns, two necklaces, one painting, and countless francs tucked into pockets and sleeves. I've already run out of room in my bed-sit and therefore have three pairs of candlesticks living with Aimée. She will likely sell them and claim theft. I don't mind. It gives me an excuse to acquire something new!

Have I relinquished a few things to secure these spoils? Well, yes, but not *the* thing, though not for lack of trying on the part of these so-called gentlemen! What Aimée and Louise and the other girls in the *hôtel* do not realize is that *the* thing isn't even necessary. Why drop your drawers for every man with a few francs when you can instead offer a sweet, coy romance? I brush up against him in a certain way, protest only meekly when a hand wiggles down the front of my dress. They're only nipples but can elicit such excitement, such largesse!

Sometimes I let my fingers slide down the front of *his* pants. Sœur Marie would fall to the convent floor if she heard such a thing! *C'est pas si mal.* This is not so bad. Really, such fondling is more scientific experiment than anything else. Indeed, after my first handling of a man I was more amazed than the first time I set foot in the Folies. The object no less garish!

Needless to say Sœur Marie did not prepare me for the aggressiveness with which a man's lower half would come alive with a few touches. Goodness, I have to stop myself from laughing. It is really quite ridiculous, this creature, like one from the bottom of the ocean. I can scarcely hold this pen, I'm laughing so hard. Of course the pen itself calls to mind the width of a few less fortunate fellows. *Mon dieu!*

Thank heavens I'm a woman.

Now that I've composed myself I must say this. Dear journal, lest you think I'm a gal about town like our precious Aimée, I must immediately disabuse you of the notion. The difference between her and me, other than the obvious, *le grand acte*, is that I deal in romance. My dalliances last longer than one night! Is there anything wrong with being in love? Or at least pretending to be? No matter the size of a man's fortune (or of his member!), he is like every other man, every other human being, as a matter of fact. We all, every last one of us, we only want to be loved.

A new gentleman came to my station last evening. It's as though he knew I'd recently become unattached, my most recent paramour having left the country due to a political obligation abroad (his wife the politics, her pregnancy the obligation). This new fellow was a curious-looking man, short of stature and with piles of brown-gray curls whipping around the tops of his ears. He was portly in a way suggesting love of good food and not of booze or sloth. In other words he was a happy fat. And unlike most Parisians he did not have a beard. The smoothness of his skin was almost disconcerting.

"What can I get for you this evening?" I asked.

He ordered a scotch, then wondered aloud why I was behind the bar and not onstage. I pointed an empty glass in his direction and chastised (smiling, winking) the lack of originality. I'd heard the same comment three times that day. And it'd been a slow day.

The man blushed, which pulled a smile from my own mouth. His was not a line but the only thing he could think to say. He was new to the Folies, it seemed. I liked him immediately.

"To tell you the truth." I leaned across the bar, dipping my chest dramatically. "Behind the bar is the best place to be."

A lie, this. One I tell the men, one I tell myself. Everyone wants her own show.

"It's far safer," I went on. "Plus I'm able to chat with all the handsome customers, such as yourself. I prefer a good conversation to hours of ogling."

"Ah," he said, still blushing. "Understood."

"What's your name?" I asked as I buffed the glass.

"Burée. Pierre Burée."

"What brings you to Folies Bergère, Monsieur Burée?" I began to pour. "Are you from Paris? Or are you just passing through?"

"I was born here, but have not been back in years. I live in South America."

I cocked an eyebrow. It is a common boast these days, but almost never true.

"South America, you say? What part?"

"Argentina," he responded without hesitation.

"Where in Argentina?"

"The southernmost tip. Near Santa Cruz. Are you familiar with the area, Mademoiselle . . . ?"

"De Florian. Marthe de Florian."

"So you've been to South America, Mademoiselle de Florian? You do look rather Latin: the dark hair, the dark eyes, the olive skin."

Though M. Burée would later say he meant it as a compliment, his words made me bridle. I am already self-conscious about my so-called olive skin. Pierre thought I resemble a Latin woman, but according to Émilie and Gérard the coloring is closer to Gypsy. Émilie is forever trying to pass her whitewash formula off on me, the alabaster skin tone being de rigueur, and Émilie's particular brand of paleness the envy of many a dancer. I, too, could have her porcelain skin if only I lathered the thick paste on my face thrice daily. And so I've commenced the regimen. It burns, this formula, but only a little.

"No. I am from Paris," I told him, trying to keep the snap out of my voice. "I've never set foot in South America, but it is quite the popular locale. I've met many men who say they work there, too."

I plunked the glass on the counter.

"Well, there is money to be made," Burée said, completely without guile.

"And how do you make yours?" I asked. "Coffee?"

It is always coffee.

Shaking his head, Pierre drew in a long, slow sip of liquid.

"Bat guano," he said.

Bat shit? I could not have heard him correctly.

"Pardon?" I said, choking out the word.

"Yes," he said and took another sip. "It is a rather lucrative industry."

I knew then that M. Burée was for real. No purported coffee king for this man, and instead bat shit in all its glory.

And so I let Pierre stay on my primary stool, my favorite stool, for the rest of the evening. We are supposed to encourage the men to move on, rotate them quickly through. The more bodies on the seats, the more money everyone makes. But I liked having him near, even if he was a timid drinker and an even more timid conversationalist.

By the end of the night I was seriously considering him for my next romance. There is something gentle and charming about Pierre. You see?

Already I'm calling him by his first name! I even contemplated allowing him to escort me home but decided to remain prudent for now. I promise, this will not be the last I'll see of M. Burée!

On my regrettably companionless walk home I noticed a marked chill in the air. It's difficult to imagine I've been in Paris long enough for the weather to turn from cold to warm and back to cold again. I remain in the same *hôtel* as a year ago, yet I've traveled far. Money is still going out, but now it comes in several times over. Money I've earned, money I did not have to lift from a run-down convent.

And so I've decided. It is time to upgrade my accommodations. I will miss the girls, especially my darling Aimée, but I cannot abide another winter. It's true I have more dresses to pile upon me while I sleep, but I aspire to more than "suffering through." I was born to do more.

Jeanne Hugo may be the envy of Paris, but not for long. One day she'll have to acknowledge me, and my station. A storm of change is coming. When the winds really start to howl, Jeanne will plead for my attentions, to be invited into *my* home. Finally she will understand what it's like to feel spurned, alone, desolate. Madame Daudet will cease to be this city's darling because, at last, the envy of Paris will be me.

Chapitre XXII

She hadn't noticed the man standing over her left shoulder.

" 'You can acquire things from the male species.' Is this true, ma chérie?"

April startled, then scrunched down low as if it were a baseball aimed at her head and not the curious, amused stare of Luc Thébault.

"Madame Vogt? 'Allo? Avril? You are visible, you know. Though the crouching is quite cute. Like a bug."

"Uh, hello there," April said, wriggling herself to an upright position. "I'm surprised you could find me."

April had squirreled herself away in the furthermost corner of the furthermore room, the last several hours spent reclined on a celery-colored tufted velvet chaise severely bleached by the sun. With her back to the doorway and feet propped up against the windowsill, April pored through Marthe's entries. She was hiding from the modern world, a little bit, and hadn't expected a visit from anyone, least of all Luc.

"You are difficult to miss," Luc said.

April turned around and rested both hands, and the journals, on the arm of the chaise.

"I am the only one here," she said.

"Yes. I see that. Is this an invitation or a warning?"

April rolled her eyes, not wanting to give Luc any response he might misinterpret or abuse. Sighing, she placed the papers atop a nearby jaguar-pelt settee as Luc continued to loom above her, both arms crossed over his chest. His wavy hair was still wet from a shower, his stubble thicker than it was the day before.

"Can I assist you with something?" she asked.

"I don't think I've ever seen a person so engrossed."

He smiled wide, perhaps affectionately, treating April to a complete view of his snaggled incisors. Orthodontia was no folly of Luc Thébault's, but his crowded picket-fence teeth were somehow endearing all the same.

"Well, it's an engrossing story," she said.

April flicked her head to the left to remove the strands of hair clinging to her forehead and cheeks. Her hair had always been long, pin straight, and fine, not to mention prone to suffer unduly from static electricity. Five minutes of sitting in that dusty nexus made April's hair look as if it'd spent five years underneath a knit cap.

"I could read these all day."

She jerked her head again, but the action did nothing other than generate a pinched nerve somewhere in the back of her neck.

"Goddammit! Ouch."

"Are you all right, Madame Vogt? You seem to be experiencing physical difficulties. A, what do you call it in English? Saisie?"

"I'm not having a seizure."

April wrapped her hair around the pen she'd been holding, which she swiped from a Dallas Hilton several years before. Large auction, that one. Lots of pieces, all of them wrapped in big Texan grandeur. The seller was 90 percent finished outfitting his twenty-thousand-square-foot tacky Versailles replica when his balance sheet flipped and money ran out.

In came the auction house. April was there because the guy's wife made a job out of importing pieces from France, not due to any affinity for Continental furniture but because the items were exactly that: Continental, from France. Also: expensive. And she could brag about the hundreds of thousands of dollars in shipping fees. The woman never knew what she had. But she had an auction of her very own.

"Luc, I have some bad news," April said.

"Oh no! This sounds dire."

"Well it is to me. There won't be a separate auction after all. The assets from the estate of Marthe de Florian will be placed with other items. I will still establish dates and time periods and artists, but history is now far less important. I'm not even entirely sure I need the rest of the journals. I'd *like* to see them, but it's not absolutely required."

"Interesting. What you just said."

"About the auction? I know. It's hugely disappointing. Marc and Olivier didn't even consult me on the decision. I mean, not that they had to."

"No. Not about the auction. 'Estate of Marthe de Florian.' You meant Madame Quatremer, non?"

"Sure. Of course," April said, though she had meant what she said the first time.

"You are upset," Luc noted as he lowered himself onto the jaguar settee and crossed his legs in the way available only to slender Frenchmen.

"Well, it is their office, their commissions and premiums," April said. "They've determined this is the most economical move so my opinion is somewhat moot. But, yes, I am upset inasmuch as I think she is deserving of her own show."

"What about the painting?" Luc asked. "The one you three grew so excited over? Bolini?"

"Boldini. That will go into an impressionist collection we are debuting in the fall."

April sighed. Loudly.

"Tell me," Luc said, "did you think she should have her own show before you read the journals?"

"Does it matter?" April shrugged. "Anyway, I read the journals pretty early on. It's hard to separate the reading of them from the pieces. Tying it all together is the entire point of my professional existence."

Biting her lip in squelched frustration, April began inspecting a traveling domino set that was on a nearby table. She scribbled "carved ivory games casket" in her notepad while silently willing Luc to leave, even as a small part of her wished that he might stay.

"Olivier and Marc are lucky to have you on their team," Luc said, leaning in toward her.

"You Frenchmen are flatterers. Anyway, don't feel as though you must stick around here. You've been a tremendous help but it seems I won't need the rest of the journals. The pieces shall be fairly easy to describe without them."

April stood, slipped her shoes back on, and pretended to take immediate interest in a wire plant stand. No more daydreaming, she told herself. No more visions of cancan dancers or elephants or nipple chandeliers. April was there for the kingwood and mahogany and all the grand, solid pieces she could sell without someone else's life holding them up.

"Avril," Luc said.

Ignoring him, she continued.

"I could make some big production about how I should still read the journals," April rambled. "And part of me wants to. But you'd see right through it, non? You'd quickly surmise what I was up to."

"Avril," Luc said again.

"So you're off the hook! No more meddlesome furniture specialists hounding you about diaries. Quel soulagement! Anyway, your client should be quite pleased in the end, financially speaking. I've seen hundreds of furniture collections over the years but nothing like this. I hope you're getting a share of the pie or croissant or mousse or whatever colloquialism the French use. Not a single piece of junk in the entire flat."

"Avril," Luc said a third time, but louder now. Firmer. In command. "Stop speaking and listen for a moment."

He reached up and grabbed the hem of her dress. Though he held lightly, April felt as though she couldn't move.

"Did I say loaning the journals was conditional upon the way you planned to conduct the auction?" he asked.

"I'm sure it's not something you contemplated."

"Has anyone ever said you speak at a frustratingly rapid clip?"

"No. Never." She couldn't bear to meet his gaze.

"You may have the journals if you'd like them," Luc said. "You may read the rest."

"Really?" April said, now with eyes wide as she stepped toward him. "But I mean . . . I don't really *need* them."

"Ah, but did you not say you could drum up an excuse? If you really wanted to? I'm sure you'll manage to unearth a tidbit or two to aid with provenance."

"You're right," April said. "It . . . it can only help, yes?"

"Oui."

April put a hand on Luc's shoulder. It was the highest level of effusiveness she felt comfortable offering, yet still left her jittery and careening in her heels for the second time that morning.

"I am truly grateful," she said. "I promise the opportunity will not go to waste."

Maybe she still had a chance. There was plotting to be done, and when it came to furniture April was an exceptional plotter.

"You are very dedicated to the furniture," Luc said, as if reading her mind.

He leaned back onto his elbows, falling farther into the settee. The jaguar. April winced. Please be careful with the jaguar.

"You seem very—how do you say it—googly-eyed when looking at all this?" he said. "Except for now. Now you seem nervous."

"Yes . . . well . . . the settee . . . do you mind?" She winced again. It seemed Luc would do only as he pleased.

"You know, this room, this flat—" Luc made a face. "It all seems a little garish to me. A little gauche."

"Garish? Gauche? Are you joking?"

"I never joke, Avril."

"Well, as they say, there's no accounting for taste. Good grief, Thébault, there's not a garish piece in the entire flat. Look. Here. And there. And over there. There are four François Linke pieces in this room alone. And those are merely the ones I can point to!"

"Linke? Never heard of him. Of course I have not made it my business to keep current with furniture trends."

"François Linke is no trend. His pieces define the Belle Époque! They are gilded and fancy and whimsical and completely aggressive in their optimism."

"Optimistic furniture?"

"Look at this armoire." April reached up and smacked a hand against its side. "The marquetry, the detail on the roses. Does it not say money will always flow? There will be no wars? The good times will last forever? It reflects everything the time period stood for."

"Sadly, it does not say these things to me."

"Let me break it down into terms you can appreciate. A comparable piece went for nearly two million dollars at auction a few years back. This is in similar if not better shape."

"Two million? Why would someone spend two million on an armoire?"

"I guess when you have enough homes and jets, you need to find somewhere else to park your funds."

"It looks like someone painted on it."

"Yes, that's the marquetry." April exhaled loudly, a sound one could rightly confuse with a scoff.

"There is a golden nude atop the dresser," Luc said. "This confuses me."

"Armoire. It's an armoire. And that's not a 'golden nude.' That's Minerva, the goddess of wisdom."

"The goddess of wisdom in the bedroom? How dull."

"Here, I'll bet I can find a piece that might appeal to someone lacking a healthy level of optimism, which seems to be your affliction." April hurdled over several piles of old newspapers. "Yes. Here it is. Even a grouchy solicitor has to appreciate a grandfather clock. He's exquisite, non? What is that face? Who doesn't like a grandfather clock?"

April leaped back over the newspapers and to the opposite corner of the room. She brandished four knives and a pistol, but Luc remained unimpressed—a surprise to April as she assumed every man enjoyed a good display of weaponry.

Beginning to sense a challenge, she flashed a grin, and dashed to another part of the room. April then showed him matching giltwood mirrors ("the mirrors, they don't work so good") and a *bureau de dame* she would've made Troy purchase if she felt assured of their continued cohabitation. The *bureau de dame* elicited some reaction from Luc, at least, inasmuch as he immediately pictured a woman on all fours, a man writing atop her back, an image he found uproariously funny.

Luc stayed the balance of the day and listened as April lectured on the finer points of Madame de Florian's furniture. It was downright invigorating to have someone with whom to share the details of the spoils. Sure Luc checked his mobile on a near-constant basis and rolled his eyes at April's eighty-seventh usage of the word "exquisite," but she didn't mind. Someone was listening. Sometimes that's all a person needed.

Chapitre XXIII

It seemed like minutes, but the hours flew as Luc settled onto the jaguar settee, and occasionally (when it didn't make April flinch) lounging atop Marthe's very bed. Meanwhile, April danced around the master bedroom and into the adjoining chambers, showing off the pieces as she recorded their details into her notebook.

April tried to inject life into the objects, trotting out a story to accompany every engraving, brushstroke, gilding, or gemstone embellishment. Luc caught her eye for brief moments, now and then, but this time hers had the twinkle and energy. He seemed happy to take it all in.

When April's phone rang at ten to five, she had almost forgotten she owned one. With a touch of unexpected spunk (April was hardly ever spunky), she bounded across the room to rescue her BlackBerry from the depths of her purse.

"TV3," the Caller ID told her. It was her husband, Troy Vogt III.

"I, uh—" She stared at the phone. "I guess I can let it go to voice mail?"

"Please, don't ignore your mobile on my account." Luc rose from the settee, the jaguar fur slick and matted from where he'd sat most of the day. "You've not touched your phone once since I've been here. Surely people are trying to reach you."

"Too late," April said and pretended to press the Answer button. "I missed it. He'll call back."

"Ah." Luc smiled. "He. Your husband, I presume?"

April cleared her throat.

"Yes," she said. "That'd be him."

"The famous husband. Troy Vogt."

"Wait. You've heard of him?"

"Indeed. Le grand m'sieu."

"Big shot? I don't know about that."

"The Google says yes."

"I'm sure he'd like to think so, anyway," April mumbled.

"I'm curious," Luc said, smirking—always smirking. "How did a pretty furniture expert meet le grand m'sieu? Do you travel in the same circles?"

"Hardly. We met in Paris, actually."

"Paris? Quel choc! Two Americans find each other in this big city? What are the chances?"

"Pretty decent when you're on the same flight back to the States. All right, so I guess I'll see you tomorrow? Later in the week?"

"Not so fast," he said. "My interest is piqued. Who has secured the heart of a charming Continental furniture expert? How did it happen? Did he approach you? Or vice versa? What am I asking? Of course he approached you. What did he say?"

" 'How's the wine?' Are you done with the questions, Monsieur Thébault? I can arrange a call with my husband if you're interested in getting to know him better."

"Ah, I see. The lady has reached her maximum number of questions. Okey-dokey."

" 'Okey-dokey'? It sounds ridiculous when you say that in your accent."

"Non. You are wrong. Everything sounds better in a French accent." Luc extended a hand. "Not to worry, I am finished with torturing you for the day. We can push discussion of le grand m'sieu to a future time. For now, I thank you for such a fine education. It was a treat."

"Anytime, Monsieur Thébault," April said, reaching toward his outstretched fingers, disappointed he'd not gone for the double-kiss. Maybe all the furniture moving rendered her too gamey for anything more. April covertly sniffed her left armpit as she accepted Luc's hand.

"And now," he said, her palm still resting inside his. "Shall we eat?"

"Pardon?" April pulled her arm back and let if flop against her side. Her face flushed.

"Do you have dinner plans?" he asked.

"Dinner?"

Was he . . . could he be . . . asking her out? No, it was impossible. The man was being friendly, she decided, though friendliness seemed, so far, an uncharacteristic condition of Luc's.

"Dinner," he said.

"Dinner?" April repeated. "Dinner *dinner*?"

"Yes, I think we've established it's dinner I'm referring to. You have to eat, non?"

April spat out a laugh.

"Well, merci beaucoup. It's a lovely offer, but I have a lot of work to tackle. A rain check perhaps?

"Rain check?"

"That means not tonight. Later."

He gave a funny little smile. "Yes, I know what 'rain check' means. Another time, then?"

"Yes, definitely."

"You should probably call your husband back anyway," he said, his tone at once chilled. "You would not want him to worry."

"Ha!" April laughed. "Yes, you're right. He'd never worry but is dying to hear about the master bedroom suite no doubt. Next time, Luc. We'll have dinner the next time."

She turned toward the interior of the apartment, where hours of work did, indeed, wait for her. Before she could even think the word "bureau," April felt two hands clamp down on her shoulders then spin her back around. April found herself staring straight into Luc's linen shirt.

"This is no way to say good-bye," he said, releasing her shoulders. "If Madame does not mind"—Luc swept a deep, comical bow—"a less unceremonious dismissal for the slovenly solicitor who has taken up your day."

"Oh, gosh, hardly," April sputtered, her face reddening by the second. "You are, like, the least slovenly person I know."

"You do flatter me."

Luc rose and leaned in to kiss her once on each cheek.

"Until next time, Avril," he said and winked.

As Luc sauntered away April was surprised to find herself smiling, if not vaguely regretful. Why didn't she accept his dinner invitation? Her trust in Troy might be on shaky ground, but April trusted herself. Dining with a colleague was a common occupational exchange. Why, then, was she suddenly overcome with a fluttering stomach? What, exactly, was she afraid of?

Chapitre XXIV

That she rejected Luc made April feel unexpectedly empty and bereft. Why did she say no? What was the alternative? Another pathetic night in bed getting drunk on burgundy and Vacherin Mont d'Or?

Not that April hadn't fully enjoyed last evening's events, her hangover and cheese bloat a pretty decent indication that all was not lost. Still, this was Paris. You didn't eat in bed when you were in Paris. You got out, you explored, you rolled home at an hour during which you were normally asleep. Usually you did this with someone else and April could've too if she hadn't been so quick to react, so immediately dismissive of the impulse she felt.

Five cafés sat within viewing distance of her front steps. April chose one with an orange awning, no visible name, and a menu posted outside, which was the maximum level of detail she could've provided someone looking for the place. April stepped through the doors a few minutes past seven thirty, shockingly early for a Parisian dinner, but she was hungry and exhaustion was a decent excuse for any kind of culinary transgression.

Her neighborhood café was small, a typical cozy, ten-table joint that could be found in any arrondissement in the city. April approached the hostess and requested a table, party of one. The hostess looked over her left shoulder and sighed heavily, though nine of ten tables were free. April muttered something about eating quickly and the hostess sighed again, grabbed a menu, and clumped off. April followed, but it didn't necessarily feel like the correct response.

The woman sat April directly beside the only other patrons, a late-middle-aged couple whom, though not egregiously touristy, April identified as American after a brief sartorial assessment. Without trying to eavesdrop April learned they'd tottered down from the Opéra and picked this place based on a recommendation from a now-dead friend who'd been there twelve years before. The couple did not stop to contemplate whether it was the same restaurant or a different restaurant in the same location. Either way, Patty Perkins loved the place.

It took the waiter a full ten minutes to acknowledge April's presence in the café. As she waited, April fidgeted and squirmed and tried not to ask her neighbors for a bite of their veal. Were they not even going to finish it?

April checked her phone, scrolling through the day's notes, then reviewed her missed calls. Troy was one of them but April was not ready to call him back. Instead she removed a pile of folders from her tote and set to work.

"Bonjour, Mademoiselle," the waiter said and yawned. "Que voulez-vous?"

"Bonjour," April replied, smiling widely.

"Que voudriez-vous?" he asked again.

"Le filet de boeuf." Beef. Yes. The correct choice. April could already savor the taste on her tongue. "A point, s'il vous plaît."

"Pour commencer?"

"Uh . . . yes. Oui. Le cassolette d'escargots."

"Cassolette d'escargots?" he said and laughed out loud. What was this silly American doing ordering snails? April was not a gastronomical pansy. Yes, she'd eat snails. She'd also eat liver and livestock entrails and anything else the French wished to throw her way.

"Oui," April replied, her smile brightening. "Cassolette d'escargots, s'il vous plait. Also . . . and . . . um . . . Vittel ou Évian. Et . . ." She thought for a minute and then added, quickly: "Et du vin. The, uh, 2007 Georges Duboeuf Côtes du Rhône. Merci beaucoup."

"Très bien." The waiter rolled his eyes, a little bit. "Merci."

He snatched the menu from her hands and toddled toward the kitchen. April sighed and looked at the stack of properties before her, somehow less inviting than they were a few days ago, before she met Marthe. Alas, Marthe's was not the only auction pending, and Birdie was on her to get the Stateside stuff done too. Paris or no, April did have certain obligations, and if she wished to remain in good standing at work she had to get through these by the end of the workday in New York. She could call Troy later.

As the waiter uncorked a bottle of Georges Duboeuf tableside, April reviewed her notes. She scribbled additional comments in the margins and pinged Birdie with requests for follow-up research. Birdie pinged back with results as well as extra tidbits April never thought to ask. When Peter said they needed a dozen lots coming out of her office, it was her full office in play. Birdie did far more work than her pay grade and title indicated.

"Brilliant work," April wrote. "As always. You need a promotion."

"Don't want a promotion," Birdie replied. "Prefer backstage. Plus if we do crappy work only U get fired."

April smiled. She was trying to conjure up a witty reply when another text rang through. This one not from Birdie. April nearly dropped the phone into her plate of snails.

"Hey," it read. "Do you have a minute?"

"Hey?" April barked aloud. "*Hey?*"

Her neighbors were right then extricating themselves from their tight space. They paused and hovered, wondering whether this forsaken and lonesome woman was trying to chat them up, wondering whether they should walk away slowly or cut a zigzag path as one would when escaping an alligator attack. They were from Florida, April learned, therefore probably familiar with trying to avoid long and potentially dangerous creatures.

"Not you," April said to the couple as she pointed at her BlackBerry. "I was talking to my phone."

The Floridians smiled shakily and bolted from the restaurant.

Hey.

Friggin' Troy.

Who was *Hey*, exactly? It wasn't your wife, semiestranged or not. "Hey" was no kind of greeting for someone you pledged to love until death (or environmentalists) did you part. *Hey*. He could shove it right up his *nancy*.

"Hey you," she typed, lit with fury.

"Good. You're there," he fired quickly in response, writing each word out as intended and without abbreviation but sounding snippy all the same. "Do you have a minute?"

April had either a minute or exactly zero time to spare.

"I'm in a restaurant," she wrote, then stopped.

April glanced up to see the waiter walking toward her, plate in hand. Though the *boeuf* was small, no bigger than a box of paper clips, April could smell the meat from several tables away. Her phone vibrated a few times but she did not look down. The waiter set the plate before her and added with a smirk, "Bon appétit!"

"Can't talk now," she typed. "Call later."

April tossed the phone into her purse and set to work immediately on the *boeuf*. The prior night's bed cheese was not so bad, but this—this was worth the trip to Paris. Seared on the outside and perfectly rare inside, it didn't technically need a knife to cut through it. She only barely had to chew. This meat was so good April thought she could rightly consider it dessert. How, exactly, were beef and chocolate not in the same food family? They acted like first cousins, at least.

Lost in her little meat-filled world, April barely noticed when the hour turned over to 9:00, and then leaned toward 9:30. Crowds filtered in now, people who knew the hostess, who knew the owner. At 9:37 the waiter flung her bill onto the table without inquiring as to dessert. April's welcome had been officially overstayed.

After signing her name on the tab, forever befuddled by Continental tipping conventions, April gathered her things and stepped into the brisk spring evening. She inhaled deeply and immediately felt something rise inside her. It was the city's magic hour. Streetlights flickered. The sky above was purple. Couples meandered arm-in-arm.

Though she had no arm through hers, April found herself smiling.

This despite the fact her marriage was in trouble. Despite the fact that her job always felt a little bit in jeopardy, too, whether or not it ever actually was. Then there was April's family back in California, in such a constant state of precariousness there was almost no point in worrying. All these things, yet April wanted to cry out at her own good fortune. She was there. Back in Paris. For a second she could pretend she'd never left.

Chapitre XXV

As she stomped up the stairs to her third-floor flat, still drunk on the city and probably also a little on the food and wine, April's phone rang. Troy, no doubt. She had promised to call him after eating but never really mapped out when or how, or what she might say in response to his text.

Hey. It was hardly the worst missive a husband might send his wife, but it chafed her nonetheless. Was there really so little left between them? Or was it that there was too much—too many things that could set the other one off? Was "hey" their new middle ground? Fortified by the wine and also by her ire, April answered.

"'Allo?" she said, slightly gritting her teeth. "Troy, listen, sorry I haven't—"

"Not Troy!" the voice sang. "Better than that boring husband of yours! It's me!"

"Well, hello you."

April smiled as she unlocked the door to her flat. It was Chelsea, her older stepdaughter, she of the blond hair and blue eyes and freckled nose. Though Chelsea was now sixteen and slathered those freckles with a liberal amount of makeup, April could not stop seeing the seven-year-old she had first met. In addition to a few very valid reasons for not wanting her own children, April also had to wonder if a subsequent batch of Troy's offspring could even compete with the first. After all, they'd be jacking with half the gene pool, and it seemed impossible that April-generated kids could be anything less than watered-down, cliché versions of Chloe and Chelsea.

"I didn't check the Caller ID," April said as she closed the door behind her. "How are you? What's going on in New York?"

"You never check the Caller ID. And anyway—New York? Please! Why are we talking about far-flung provincial outposts when you're in France? Way to rub my nose in it."

"You really were meant to live in Paris, weren't you? Provincial," April said with a snort. "I don't agree, but, like I told your father, if I'm still here when school gets out, you are welcome to leave your far-flung outpost and visit. I'd absolutely love to have you."

"Believe me, I've been working that angle nonstop since Dad mentioned it. But you'd have to convince *Su-s-a-a-a-n-ah*," Chelsea said, drawing out her mother's first name. "And she is having none of it. Apparently I'm 'not going to Paris unchaperoned, Missy!' "

Shaking her head, April kicked off both heels and tossed her tote on the couch.

"I'm fairly certain I could handle the chaperoning requirements," she said, moving through the apartment. April reached for the light switch but pulled back. Her path was clear, illuminated by the city lights twinkling through the windowed wall. "Though if your mother's not comfortable with the arrangement—well, there's not much I can do."

April understood what this was about: The woman's never even had kids! How many times had Susannah said that, behind April's back as well as to her face? Less comely gene pool or no, sometimes April wanted to procreate if only to prove it didn't make Susannah so special. People had babies every day, saintly mothers and meth heads alike. Of course shutting up ex-wives was probably not the best reason to create another living human, but it was tempting at times.

"Can't you talk to her?" Chelsea pleaded. "Or to Dad?"

"I'll try, but—"

"You don't understand! It's even worse than not going to Paris. She's taking us to visit Armand's wretched desert homeland for most of the summer. Old gal's probably gonna rope us into arranged marriages or some shit. And Armand will make us wear burkas."

"Really? He will?"

"I'm assuming." Big sigh. "Never mind. Forget it. There's no way Susannah will cave."

"Well, I'll talk to your father one more time," April said. "Last-ditch effort."

"Good luck with that. He's, like, the last person who can get her to do anything."

"Perhaps we can phrase it differently. Not a vacation. Something meaningful. With your A in AP Art History . . . it's still an A isn't it?"

"Yes! I can't believe you have to ask!"

"With your Art History and interning in my office over spring break, maybe we can convince your mother it's an educational experience. She seems supportive of your interest." Shockingly, April did not add, "I can probably get you into a class or two at the Sorbonne."

"Oh my god!" Chelsea wailed. "That's just mean! Now you're going to make me cry! Go ahead and talk to her, but you know how it is. Susannah doesn't change her mind. About anything."

"No," April agreed. "She does not."

April wanted Chelsea to come, but not enough to battle Susannah over it, not enough to listen to the ex-wife complain for the next ten years that some mean, childless party girl tried to destroy her family's Middle Eastern excursion.

"So, what's up?" April said, anxious to drop Susannah from their conversation. As Chelsea and Chloe morphed from children into teens, it was April's goal to maintain a close connection to the girls without using shared Susannah vexation as a unifying force. Like any proper goal, this oftentimes felt unattainable.

"'What's up'?" Chelsea repeated. Another sigh, this time bored, not exasperated. "Oh, not much."

You dialed me, girlfriend, April wanted to say.

"Um, all right. So did you call for a specific reason or just to chat?"

April paused in the doorway to her bedroom and slipped out of her clothes. This room didn't have the wall of windows, but there was still glass and she was still bare and lit from behind. April contemplated what people might see as she stood in that doorway and found she didn't entirely mind. It was okay to be a little naked all the way over in the Ninth.

"Well, both, I guess," Chelsea said. "But mostly I called for a reason. Three, actually, if you care to hear them."

"Bien sûr!" April said happily. She was already starting to feel seasick from the up-and-down of Chelsea's mood. "Lay them on me."

"Okay, first of all, I got the pictures you texted me. And, holy shit, that portrait?" Chelsea's voice regained its formerly chatty speed. Good grief, the dramatic personality swings with those kids. April tried to remember if she was that all over the place at sixteen. "Marthe de Florian was a beautiful woman."

"I know," April said, smiling from the inside out. "Though it's actually pronounced 'mart.' "

" 'Mart.' Interesting. Well, that painting is to die for."

"He's a master," April agreed.

"I'd heard of Boldini, but only vaguely. I planned to duck into the Met during my free period, but they don't have him on display, which is bullshit."

"Most of his stuff is in private collections."

"So I've gathered. Crap. I have to go in a second. I'm being summoned. Okay. Second question. I have to know, which museum did you go to first? When you got to Paris? Give me the juicy details. But the SparkNotes version because I really have to go . . ."

"Well that will be easy," April said. "Because I've only been to the apartment, which to be honest, is pretty much the best museum I've ever set foot in."

"Jesus. I can't believe you're in Paris looking at these amazing pieces all day, every day, and I have to go to the effing Gaza Strip for summer vacay."

April let a chuckle escape from her lips.

"Jesus," Chelsea said again. "Okay, third and final reason I called, I need you to see a guy about a purse."

"Ah," April said, grinning now. "There it is. Somehow I'm questioning whether you really care about museums."

"No! I do!" Chelsea chirped. "I swear!"

"Uh-huh. So, tell me, what guy and what purse?"

"Well, okay, maybe a couple of guys about a couple of purses. First, Goyard."

"What now?" April said. "How do you spell that?"

"You've never heard of Goyard? Jeez, you need to get out more! Well, not to worry, I already looked the address up for you. It's at 233 rue Saint-Honoré. Are you familiar?"

"I am."

April stepped toward the desk. She picked up a pen. Goy-yar. Or was it actually Goyard and Chelsea got the pronunciation correct? April had been working with both girls on their French, but as with all things said to teens, you never really knew what took.

"Is that 'G-O-Y'—" she started.

"Okay. First, I want the Croisière weekender bag. In, like, a good color, but nothing too crazy. Nothing you've seen in New York. And, gawd, certainly nothing you've ever seen knocked off."

"Not sure I'm the right person to assess what's been seen in New York. I wouldn't want to embarrass you by purchasing a thousand-dollar handbag that someone else might possibly have, or one that, god forbid, has been replicated."

"A thousand dollars!" Chelsea laughed. "You kill me! It's not a thousand dollars!"

The laughing, April suspected, was probably not because she picked too high a price point.

"Then I want the Sardaigne vanity case in gold leather. It has the Goyardine canvas, you know?"

"No."

"You'll figure it out. And I want my initials on both. Whatever color looks best. You decide. Also, if you have time to pop over to Moreau, I would love, love, *love* the Diligence Pochette. In a bright color, like turquoise? I mean, it's a pochette. You're supposed to have fun with it, right?"

While it sounded harmless enough, April knew from experience that a "pochette" as requested by Chelsea could run upwards of three thousand dollars.

"I don't think I got all this," April said, losing track of her notes somewhere around 'weekender bag'.

"I'll text you the details."

"Can't you just do Louis Vuitton or something?"

"Louis Vuitton?" Chelsea made a gagging noise. "That is so prosaic, April."

"See? You can't rely on me to pick out the right handbag."

"Hmm," Chelsea said. "It's true you have a classic style. But your tastes are a bit utilitarian."

"Why, thank you. This is why I need you with me. We could spend all weekend at the Galeries Lafayette—you'd love it there."

"The Galeries? Tourist trap. First place I'd go is L'Éclaireur."

April laughed.

"You know way too much about Parisian shopping for someone who's never been here."

"I know, right? It's like my skills are totally wasted. Effing Susannah. Speaking of, you can't tell her this because she would fuh-reak, but Chloe went on her first date."

"No, really?" In April's head: a girl of six, not fifteen. Scabbed knees. Strawlike hair. What kind of sicko was interested in a little girl? The answer was, of course, any given teenage boy because though Chelsea was more obvious in her beauty, both girls were as pretty as their parents. "I don't know why I'm so surprised."

"Probably because, like me, you thought she was a lesbian."

"Chelsea! I did not!"

"Anyway, awesome big sister that I am, I totally covered for her, because Susannah says *no dates until age sixteen!* Insert finger wagging. Don't worry. It was a totally innocent situation, natch. I mean, I wouldn't let Chloe get up to any shenanigans. I'm looking out for her."

"I'm sure you are," April said, thinking of all the times Chelsea used her sister as an alibi for her own (suspected) misconduct.

"I met him," Chelsea went on. "He's okay . . . dorky-cute. He goes to Poly Prep. In *Brooklyn*. And he's into 'performing arts.' I mean, whatever. It's sort of adorable. But also gross. And—aw shit—hold on a minute."

April waited as she heard shuffling and the cupping of a hand over the phone, which did little to dampen the sound.

"Hel-*l-o-o-o*," Chelsea said in a drawl. "Why are you barging into my room uninvited? You're not allowed to do that. You're supposed to give me privacy now that I'm an insecure teen girl trying to find her way in the world. I might be holding a box of tampons or something. Haven't you listened to a word Susannah's said? No bueno, Padre. No bueno."

"Padre"? April's stomach went squirrelly. She had not expected Chelsea to be at Troy's, though April was only barely cognizant of what day it was and what might be happening back in New York in her absence.

As father and daughter squabbled back and forth, April's finger hovered over the End Call button. Maybe she should go. Maybe it'd be easier for everyone if she ended it there, before anyone else got hurt, or in trouble, or yelled at by Troy.

Eyes clamped shut, April moved her finger ever closer to the button. It would be a relief, she thought, to hang up. Leave him out there, waiting, wondering why she never called back.

Chapitre XXVI

Who are you talking to?" Troy wanted to know.

She had not hung up. Somewhere in the agony and fear, April stayed on. Maybe because she thought of Susannah, a small crumb of her heart softening toward the polished, beautiful, sharp-tongued woman. She'd been in April's place once, not in the exact same manner, but probably also waiting somewhere, wondering how long she'd hold for Troy.

"It's really none of your business," Chelsea snipped.

"It's time to get off. I hear you giggling and swearing in here. You're supposed to be doing your homework. Swear to God, Chelsea. How do you plan to get into college? On your charms and good looks? It doesn't work that way. And I'm not pulling strings. I won't do it!"

"God, Dad, chill. I was only talking to April."

"April?"

Goose bumps ran along her arms.

"But I appreciate the vote of confidence."

The phone swooshed. It smacked into a hand.

"April," he repeated, sounding positively thrilled. April contemplated for a second that he might simply turn off the phone, and she cursed herself for not doing it first. "All right. Go do your physics."

"Yeah. I heard. Bye, April!" she called. "I'll text you about the bags!"

"Bye, Chels," April whispered, a pang shooting through her. If there was a divorce, what were April rights with regard to the girls? Could she reasonably demand visitation? April wondered when she would next see them, if she would see them.

"You were at a dinner?" Troy said into the phone, straight off, no greeting to be had, not even "hey." "Is that why you weren't picking up?"

"Um, yes," April said and burped a little, the taste of the steak and Côtes du Rhône lingering in the back of her throat.

"Long dinner. Next time, a little quicker callback might be in order?"

"Sorry. I didn't realize it was something important."

"I didn't realize I didn't qualify as important."

"That's not what I meant."

"Well, how was your dinner?" His voice was funny, up too high, cracking and uneven. "I thought the grand meals didn't happen until the auction was ready to go."

"It wasn't a dinner *dinner.* Just a meal. At a local bistro."

"Yeah. Who with?"

He zipped something. Was he going somewhere?

And wait a minute. What was he doing home in the first place? It was late afternoon in New York. He only came home before nine o'clock if there was somewhere else he had to go.

"Hold on a second," April said. "What are you doing home right now? And do I hear luggage? Are you traveling somewhere?"

"Yes! That's why I've been trying to call. I have a closing in London. Yesterday the deal was dead but now back, alive. I didn't think the fucker would close but here we are. Don't mess with Troy Vogt, you bastards. I can wait it out all day long."

"London? A closing?"

It was an unexpected announcement, yet also not. If a deal closed in some distant part of the world, Troy showed up to sign the final papers and attend the requisite closing dinner. Stanhope hadn't closed a deal in a while, over three months in fact, so this was good news. Sort of.

April couldn't recall how many deals there'd been in their seven years of marriage, or during the nine years they'd been together. She couldn't remember what percentage required international travel. All she knew was that the last time it happened Troy went to Singapore. And in Singapore he had sex with someone else.

"Yes," Troy said. "A closing. We're acquiring a 90 percent stake in a manufacturer of bearing components. I think I told you about it."

"All right." April paused for several beats. "And you are telling me because—?"

"Well, I thought telling your spouse before you left the country was compulsory. Most wives like that sort of thing."

Was he trying to be rude or funny? Sometimes it was so very hard to tell.

"Only London, or do you have to go further?" she asked.

Having left the desk and her hastily scribbled notes about Goy-something-or-other handbags, April returned to the window. Standing in purple lacy boy shorts and a camisole, she watched the people below her. The friends, the couples, the lovers—people in twos. April thought of her husband, in London by tomorrow, a train ride away. Why don't we meet up for dinner? He might say. A romantic rendezvous on the Continent. But he would not say this tonight. And she would not ask.

"London is close to Paris," April said flatly, attempting to erase the hopefulness from her voice.

He had to make the first move. It wasn't a test or a game, but April couldn't stay in the marriage without some modicum of desire, lust, and/or good old-fashioned effort on his part. And if she suggested they meet, April would never know if he'd acquiesced out of pity or guilt. Troy needed to show her what she meant to him.

To be fair, April could not quite remember if the old Troy would've come to see her in France or just waited until they were both back in New York. For the past few months it hadn't been easy to separate the person April fell in love with from the person she wanted him to be; both impossible standards. Unfortunately and probably also unjustly, it was still too easy to see Troy as a cheating, heartless villain and not a regular person, flawed and prone to mistakes.

"Huh," he said. "I guess you're right. No need to worry about time-zone issues then."

"Yeah. Time-zone benefits." April exhaled. "So. Well, have fun, I guess."

"Do you not want me to go? Is that the problem?"

"Why wouldn't I want you to go? It's fine!"

"Well I haven't been gone overnight since—"

"Yes, I know," April snapped. "And I'm okay with it."

Was she okay with it? Yes, no, not really. What choice did she have? April couldn't tell him not to go. There was a pact, unspoken but a pact all the same. You couldn't keep punishing someone for the same crime no matter how badly you wanted to. Fish or cut bait. April was on the pier, whether she was coming or going she did not yet know.

"In the interest of full disclosure," he said, sounding like the very best or the very worst of deal makers, depending on where at the table you sat. "You should know that Willow Weintraub is traveling with me. She worked on the transaction, too."

April didn't respond. Troy sighed.

"No reaction?" he said. "There's nothing you want to say?"

"Nope. Not really. Other than, you know, maybe avoid sleeping with her this time."

"April, that's not fair."

"You are correct. But, hey, glad she's joining you. I'm sure her presence at the dinner is highly necessary."

"She's in the middle of her engagement. Like it or not, she is part of this team. I would have suggested she not come, that she find other work, but I'd be forced to cancel her contract, and it would require a lot of explaining to my partners and to our portfolio companies who have been working with her. Plus I could get sued. So there's that."

"Forget it," April said. "Just. It's fine."

"I won't cheat on you ever again. I don't know how many more times I have to say it."

"I actually don't want you to say 'ever again' at all." April stepped away from the window and walked toward the bathroom, all too aware of the full backside exhibition she offered the street below. It made her feel good, almost, as if she were punishing Troy. Other people can see me naked, too! Of course Troy would not care an inch.

"Action over words," he said.

"Something like that." April ran her toothbrush beneath the faucet. "People have work dinners. With members of the opposite sex. Attractive ones, even. I get it."

If April wanted to bring up drinks with Luc, now was the time. For a second she considered it, but what was there to say? She didn't want to be spiteful, and, honestly, there was a small amount of joy in keeping the news to herself. Of course this could've been the very thing Troy once thought about Willow.

"Oh," Troy said, sounding hesitant. "Okay. Well, good."

"Good."

"Good."

April wasn't sure what she wanted him to say, but "good" (end of sentence, full stop) was not it.

"I was thinking." Troy's voice was distant, tinny. April turned the phone away from her mouth and started brushing. "Maybe when you get back we should go into counseling."

April spat into the sink.

"You know how I feel about counseling," she said.

"But it can't hurt, right?"

"Can't it?"

"I'm not sure why you're so certain your dad doesn't benefit from the person he sees. It's taken a long time—"

"That's an understatement!"

"But he's gained an entirely new perspective on stuff with your mother."

"First of all, I'm not even going to ask how you know about my father's perspectives, new or otherwise," April said. "Second of all, do not bring up my mother when we're in a middle of a *thing*, okay? It will end badly for you."

"What are you so afraid of?" Troy asked, forever pushing, forever needling the spot that hurt. "You've been though a lot in your life. This stuff with your mom, it's intense. People see a counselor for far lesser reasons. Why are you so averse to the concept?"

"Because therapy doesn't work, and I don't need it. We'll get through this. One way or another, we'll get through this."

In other words April's life might be in shambles but she would not actually die from a broken heart. It was not physically possible. Her father was proof of that.

April moved into the bedroom. She peeled back the comforter and slid between the sheets. Shivering, she looked at the clock, she looked at the lamp, she looked at the worn little nubs on the blanket. Troy said nothing. She couldn't even hear him breathe.

"Sounds like you're on your way out the door," April said as a printer groaned in the background. She heard the clack of his computer and the muffled leather thump of his briefcase on the desk.

"Yes. The car will be downstairs any minute. I love you, April."

"I love you, too."

"And I miss you. Already."

"Then come," she blurted, surprised at herself. Damn wine. "Come to Paris. It's so close. We'll be so close! Even if only for dinner one night. A romantic rendezvous. It actually sounds kind of sexy."

"Sounds wonderful," he said immediately. "But there won't be any time. This is strictly an in-and-out kind of deal."

In-and-out. It was precisely the kind of transaction April feared, in more ways than one. Troy knew she was still upset, still insecure about where they stood with each other, but he didn't even *attempt* to consider making the London-to-Paris trip. April tried to look forward, to envision how she'd feel in hindsight. Would this be the moment when she knew it was over?

"Oh! Car's out front. Okay, I need to go. I'll call you from the road. I love you."

"Maybe I could pop over to London . . ." April started, but he'd already hung up.

Sighing, April reached over and flicked off the lamp. It was too silent. Sad, almost. She threw off the covers and padded in bare feet to the windows, where she stood near-naked in the moonlight for the third time tonight. She bent over to unlock one of the paned frames, letting in the night air.

Once back in bed, April pictured Marthe and Jeanne and bat guano magnates as she waited to be lulled to sleep by the sound of Paris through her open windows. She tried not to hear Troy's words. "There won't be any time." It was the first time he'd rejected her outright. Then again, it was the first time April had given him the opportunity.

Chapitre XXVII

It was Friday.

It was also April's fifth day in Paris and Troy's second in London. He was due home by Monday. As he said, it wasn't a lot of time. Yet when April considered Willow Weintraub and all the things that could happen between now and then, it felt like forever.

She spent the morning inventorying the pieces now transferred to the basement of the auction house. Despite Olivier's initial pessimism, they'd been able to make room. April culled through the assets, inspecting stamps and signatures; tracing her fingers over polished finishes and wondering which items had been reveneered, all the while feeling Troy as if he lingered nearby.

Their conversation left April restless for two straight nights, the rebuffed invitation pulling from her a desire she'd not felt in the last ninety days. She wanted him, goddammit. Every time April turned over in bed she expected to see him beside her. She swore she smelled Troy, that she could hear him, that he was laughing somewhere nearby.

Go away, Troy, April thought. Or, rather, come here.

Working in the basement should've been more productive than in the apartment. It took Marthe mostly out of the picture and thus removed a distraction the size of South America (bat guano, anyone?). There was no way to imagine Marthe in that cinder-block basement with its industrial carpeting and damp smell. Alas, it was still working in a basement—and April thought that perhaps Marthe's presence was simply supplanted by Troy's. Having accomplished little by midafternoon, April decided to call it a day, so disoriented and hunchbacked was she with lack of sleep and sunlight.

Skipping up the stairs and into the building's foyer, April decided that if she couldn't rid herself of Troy's ghost, she might as well seek out the real thing. With an "Au revoir" to the guard, April pulled out her phone and sucked in a gulp of air. "Meet me in Paris," she texted her husband. "Please. I miss you." Send. Before she could reconsider.

Outside the weather was abnormally blustery and stark for that June day. As the wind whipped around her face, April buried both fists deep inside her trench. Halfway to her apartment, the phone buzzed. It buzzed again, each sound piled on top of the last. She hadn't expected him to respond so quickly, much less with a call. Maybe things would work out in the end. April ducked into a patisserie and wiggled her mouth out of her scarf.

"You're coming?" she said, backing into the corner lest someone think she was a customer. "You're coming to Paris. This will be good. We need this."

"Indeed we do! But I didn't know I was invited. When do I leave?"

Birdie. April should've known. Rather, she should've checked Caller ID like a normal person. What was she thinking? It was silly to expect Troy's response in the middle of a European workday. April wondered how she could be so wrong so very much of the time.

"Oh. Hi, Birds," she said. "I thought you were Troy."

"Troy?" Rustling commenced, followed by a shower of swear words. "Crap! I spilled Greek yogurt into my bra."

"That'll smell good later."

"You're telling me," Birdie said. "It's like a hundred and fifty fucking degrees here. With a zillion percent humidity."

"I'm glad you never exaggerate."

"What's this about Troy coming to Paris?" Birdie asked. "He's coming to see you?"

"We talked about it," April said, which was not altogether untrue. "He's actually across the Channel. In London. Closing a deal." She'd only *just* texted him. Plans for a rendezvous could in fact be solidified within the hour. Troy wouldn't say no a second time. He couldn't.

"Wow!" Birdie said. "I'm surprised he can pull himself away from the partying."

"Excuse me?"

April pushed herself further into the corner, unconcerned that she was the only patron rudely jabbering on a mobile.

"My best friend is in London right now too," Birdie said. "You know—Hailey? I think you've met her?"

"Sure." April nodded, though she was not sure at all.

"Hailey is the EA for a bigwig at Carlyle. They closed a deal in London this week too and since they all know each other—heck, half of them have worked at both places—well, anyway, they've all been partying it up. She saw Troy! Although I guess I'm not supposed to mention it . . ."

"Saw Troy doing what?"

All at once the bakery felt too hot. April yanked off her scarf and fanned her face with a napkin.

"Partying," Birdie said. "At the Beauchamp Club. The whole gang of them, Stanhope, Carlyle, everyone in between."

"'Everyone in between,'" April repeated. "In between" meant lawyers. It meant environmental consultants.

"Yeah. Apparently it's all hard core. Up all night, straight to business meetings in the morning. Hailey has mastered going to work while still drunk, and it's all too much for even her."

And all too much for April. There was drinking and so what, it's what these finance guys did to celebrate. Five-thousand-dollar bottles of wine, bar tabs that made international news and incited the outrage of decent hardworking Americans. For April it was not about the excess. It was about where the excess led.

April knew how Troy was when he let himself break from his polished, slick-haired mold. Willow knew too, as evidenced by the Singapore Incident, but April's experience went further back.

He was intimidating at first, this man who would later become her husband. They'd been on four dates, five if you counted the business-class-lounge meet-up and their ensuing delayed flight. But at four-point-five dates in, April wasn't sure how much longer it would last.

They got along. They got along tremendously. This was never in question. Troy was kind and attentive and said the exact right thing 100 percent of the time. It was unnerving, that perfect personality combined with those looks: the flawlessly pressed clothes, his ridiculous jawbone, sandy-colored hair always neatly combed, flecks of gray at the temples. Those early days she watched him, waiting for a misstep.

There was a closing dinner for them, too, in New York. April didn't go of course, she was unconnected to the deal and only barely connected to Troy. But he went and then showed up unannounced at April's apartment. When she opened the door she found Troy leaning against the far wall, hair tousled and lips curled into an easy, slow smile. Shit, April thought then. He was incalculably better-looking when he was a little bit undone.

Troy stayed over that night, and things happened to a degree April had never before experienced despite having a reasonable number of experiences to compare against. It wasn't merely the *deed*. Of course they did plenty of that, but they laughed and talked and relished each other until the sun rose across their city. They couldn't see the sunrise, April's old place not being exactly known for its views. Nonetheless, together they felt the light pour over them. April knew then she was done: There was no going back to a life without him, for a time at least.

The problem with Singapore was that April could not blame Willow, not really. She understood exactly how this went. And she was afraid it'd go that way in London, too.

"April?" Birdie said. "You still there?"

"Yes. Sorry. I'm in a shop—it's a little crowded . . ."

April crammed the scarf into her tote yet continued to feel suffocated, as if it were still wound tightly around her neck. The smell and colors (those *macarons*; pink, orange, yellow, white) began to swirl around her like a bad, sugar-fueled trip. Voices sounded like foghorns, circus-like people bustled past.

"Birdie, I have to go," she said. "I'm not supposed to use a phone in here. I'll call you later."

April turned, disoriented. It took a minute to locate the front door.

"Pardon," April said as she battled her way through the shop. *"Pardonnez-moi."*

Someone called her name. April burst through the door. The bell continued to jangle overhead as she moved down the sidewalk. Trying to catch her breath, she slumped out of view, around the corner from the patisserie's glass-fronted entrance. She slid down the ancient, stone edifice; heaving and gasping but unable to catch her breath, each inhale slipping through her rib cage like water through a sieve.

Chapitre XXVIII

April," said a voice.

She shook her head.

"April!"

Someone pawed her shoulder. April opened her mouth to scream, and hoisted her handbag into the air, hoping to fend off the attacker.

"Avril!"

She stopped abruptly as the purse continued its momentum, ultimately knocking her in the skull.

April recoiled at the hit. She then looked up at the floppy-haired man standing above her. He wore a half-grin she could only barely make out through the hair hanging over her own face, not to mention the shock of almost concussing herself.

"Oh," she said. "Luc. Hi."

"You look flushed. Also, you are seated on the ground. I hate to ask the obvious, but are you all right?"

Was she all right? It was the unanswerable question.

"Bonjour," she said and wiped her nose with the back of her hand. "I'm sorry. I did not see you there. You scared me."

"It appears I do this a lot. Is everything okay? You seem distraught."

"Nope!" she said, voice breaking. "Not distraught! I'm fine! Just fine!"

April attempted to stand as gracefully as one could after being collapsed against a patisserie wielding a quilted Chanel handbag as a weapon.

"If you're sure—"

"Totally! How's it going?"

"It is *going*," he said and smirked. Of course he smirked. "Well, I have to say, I am glad to have bumped into you. I've a bundle of terrific news right here in my bag. I was en route to share it with you when I noticed a strange but lovely woman sprinting out of a shop."

"I wasn't sprinting. It was more of a fast shuffle."

"You have a funny way of viewing things. In any case life is looking up for fair Marthe." Luc pulled a stack of papers from his shoulder bag. "She has a new apartment! No more frozen water basins! These are tied in yellow, which I think connotes positive developments for our Madame de Florian. Or perhaps I'm reading too much into it."

"The diaries?" April laughed, though mostly because it was easier than crying. "You have them for me?"

"Of course. I said you could read them. Did I not make that clear?"

Luc handed her the papers. She clutched them wordlessly.

"In which we meet Boldini," he said, grinning even wider.

April held them to her body, still bewildered by everything that had transpired in the last seven minutes, or what might be transpiring across the Channel. She shook her head, trying to clear it all away.

"Is everything all right?" Luc asked a third time. "You look rather upset."

"I don't know." April sighed. "I truly don't." Her marriage, this man appearing from nowhere, the pressure of trying to do right by Marthe—it was no wonder April needed a wall for support. Part of her wanted to fall back into it. "Well, thanks for the journals. Glad we bumped into each other. It saved you a trip. See you soon."

She turned and commenced speed-walking in the opposite direction. Cognizant of Luc's trailing presence behind her, April used little caution in propelling herself onward, stepping into the street whenever someone blocked her way, even if it put her directly in the path of hell-bent Parisians on motorbikes.

"You're going to be flattened like a pancake," Luc called, exerting minimal effort to match her pace. "Salut! Wait up. Talk to me."

Grabbing her bicep, Luc pulled April off the street and led her between two green iron gates. She blinked. Suddenly the wind was gone, along with the sounds of the motorbikes and people jostling past.

"Where are we?" April asked, letting her arm slacken in Luc's hand.

She looked up at the windows above, their boxes exploding with pinks and reds and oranges. Ivy-covered walls surrounded them. Beneath their feet, a stone path. At the end of the path, a bench. April stalked toward it through the undergrowth.

"A courtyard," Luc said. "A place to rest."

"It's beautiful," April said as she sat down on the bench. Another thing she loved about Paris: The city held immeasurable places for solitude, countless side rooms into which to duck. Paris was a destination, yes, but with a thousand little journeys of its own.

"Indeed," Luc said. "Quite beautiful." He remained standing, almost daring her to get up and refuse the respite he suggested. That would be just like her, non? But his tone was so gentle April found herself glad to relax, happy to take the comfort he offered.

This moment. It was getting too soft.

"Well," April said, trying to muster some grumpiness from the bench. "I hope we're not on someone's private property. I don't want to get arrested."

"We're fine. If anyone asks, we're here to see a dentist who's in that building."

April thought of her own dentist then, with his cheesy furniture and fish tank and fake wood counter. She pictured his narrow hallway and the small metal elevator that worked only on Tuesdays.

"Even going to the dentist is exciting in this city," April said wantonly.

"Long day already, Madame Vogt? You seem beleaguered."

"Merci. 'Beleaguered.' You're too kind. And, yes. Long day. Long week. Long month. Longer even still."

Luc said nothing. April scratched her left arm.

"You don't need to babysit me, you know," she said.

April expected him to sit beside her, and in fact a small part of her wanted him to. But there Luc remained, standing in a well-worn spot on the stone path, hands on his hips, sunlight shooting through his black hair.

"What is so rough about it?" Luc asked. "This day?"

"Just my assistant." April shook her head. "She called. And. She's great. I love her. But sometimes she's a teensy bit of a pain in the ass."

"She must be French."

April snorted. "No. Not French. I'm not being fair. She's a fantastic assistant. It's a long story. And actually not even about her at all. Never mind, it's stupid. All of it."

Luc nodded. He would not push further.

"Do you need a minute alone?" he asked.

"I don't think so. But feel free to go."

He pointed to the journals. "I find if I'm agitated, reading is a good escape."

"Ah, you are very wise. For a Frenchman," April said, trying not to smile. "Now that you mention it, an excellent suggestion."

Suddenly the wind picked up again. Luc's hair flapped against his forehead and the tips of April's ears began to sting. She looped the scarf back around her neck.

"Well, I shall see you soon," Luc said. "Enjoy the journals."

"Thank you, Luc. Again. For everything."

"It is entirely my pleasure. Anything to make a pretty girl smile."

With a little salute, Luc winked, spun around, and walked out of the courtyard, carefree and ever casual, never once turning back toward her.

April watched as he paused at the gate to light a cigarette. The wind pushed the smoke, and the hint of his cologne, back toward April. Though filtered through distance and the remnants of tree blossoms still hanging on the branches, it was almost as though Luc were still there. April shifted on the cracked stone bench and waited for the wind to die back down. While pigeons picked at the seeds by her feet she untied the first stack. She had not yet read a word, but April was already smiling.

Chapitre XXIX

Paris, 15 October 1891

Well, it's done. I've moved on. I've moved up! A new apartment! *Je l'adore!*

If I must: It is small and not so far from the old place, in more ways than one. Yet it is mine and it is warm and there is (nearly) room for all my gowns. Best of all, it is free. Pierre would not hear of me paying for it out of my earnings.

Pierre, ah, Pierre. We had a delightful few weeks tooling around Paris, picking up gifts and jewelry, dining at the finest restaurants. But now he has departed to Argentina to deal with bat guano and ancillary matters. We are to marry when he returns, or so he's decreed. Nothing can keep him from me, he says, except death. I'd never wish death upon the poor man, but I do hope he spends the rest of his days minding the guano.

Don't misunderstand. Pierre is a perfectly lovely individual but not someone I want to wake up beside every morning. I do not want to kiss that big, bumpy nose or touch those furry little ears each night before bed. He is an agreeable chap, but I am not yet eighteen, therefore unready to clamp down and cut off the rest of my life, especially if he's providing the suture.

Alas, I made many promises thus it will be quite the debacle when he returns. I can only hope he won't. Based on what the girls in the old place said, men from South America never did. Of course, unlike theirs, my man was actually in South America in the first place.

The girls from *l'hôtel des femmes* . . . Louise and Gabrielle and Aimée. I thought I would be sad to leave them. I expected to look back on our time with a mixture of smiles and tears. But as I packed my last trunk and slipped on my hat I was positively relieved to abandon that godforsaken place. When the girls gathered to bid me adieu I noticed how weathered they were, how utterly beaten down by this city and their occupations. Aimée in particular always looked beautiful to me. But when she moved into the dim light of the hallway for a final good-bye, the state of her face soured my insides. She looked old, crumpled. Makeup settled into her wrinkles like cracked mud in a dry riverbed.

The old woman was right when she predicted high demand for my room. In the days leading up to my departure she was constantly negotiating with potential occupants, squabbling and squawking like a drunken chicken. I was the first person to leave of my own volition instead of being kicked out or dying some horrible syphilitic death. As a result the old bag was extra grumpy. It gave me great pleasure to sashay past with an "Au 'voir" and an Émilie-patented wink.

I was all the way down the front steps, gone almost forever, when a gravelly little voice piped from beside a gas lamp.

"Jeanne Hugo?" the mouse-woman said.

I almost didn't turn, certain my ears were playing tricks.

"Jeanne Hugo," the voice said again. "Daudet?"

I flipped around, words at the top of my throat ready to fall out in the form of expletives. Then I recognized her, Marguérite, the waif who stood beside me at Jeanne's wedding procession all those months ago. Her battered suitcase told me she was the warm body to fill my cold room.

"Bonjour!" I said and reintroduced myself. "So nice to see you again."

Marguérite curtsied, of all things! Then she beamed up at me with that face—those perfect pink cheeks, her tiny white teeth, the large, wet, brown eyes. Here was a slip of a woman: tiny stature, tiny arms, tiny waist, tiny in every possible way except her bosom, which defied natural order. She looked like someone's child. The rest of the girls looked as though they sprang from the cold, brown earth or were made in a factory under the most penurious of conditions. Marguerite was different. At that moment I felt the need to save her. I did not know I had it in me.

"Have you come for my room?" I asked.

"Yes I have. I was so pleased to find a place," she said, sounding like a little queen and not a bedraggled urchin. "Now I need to find work."

She glanced up the side of the building. My gaze followed and I caught a glimpse of Louise peering out her window. My heart skipped.

"My dear girl," I said, sounding like a mother though I have but a year or two on her. "Are you sure this is what you want? This *hôtel*? These people? I am leaving, you see. There is a reason."

"Am I sure?" She crinkled her face. "Well, my options are not exactly abundant."

"We make our own options," I said and reached into my purse. "I want you to have this."

I pressed money into her hand.

"I can't—"

"You can. Please, before you take a job or mire yourself in the vocations of these girls, consider the type of life you want. I hope this money gives you time to figure it out."

"And what do you do that allows you to hand money over to a stranger?" she asked. "Never mind, I already know!"

"No!" I snapped. "It is not that. Have you heard of the Folies Bergère?"

"The dance hall?" she asked, face springing to life once again. "I've seen the posters. Does it really exist? Are those beautiful girls really inside that building?"

"They are," I said. "Those girls and more. I know because I work there."

"You're a cancan dancer?" Her eyes nearly leaped from their sockets. "How positively thrilling!"

"No, nothing like that. I'm a barmaid!" My voice lifted to the sky. "It is a fantastic job."

"Oh." She was palpably disappointed. Even her bosom dropped. "Well, thanks for the chat."

"Before you dismiss it, let me tell you this. To start, the dress is magnificent. The position pays well and I meet interesting people. Most importantly, it's funding an apartment infinitely superior to this one."

Admittedly the job did not pay for the new apartment per se, but without the Folies Bergère there would be no Pierre and thus no new flat, so in the end it is really all the same.

"Why are you telling me this?" Marguerite asked.

"Perhaps there is a position for you."

The words flew out of my mouth like I'd so often seen mucus shoot out of Pierre's nose when he laughed. I had no authority to offer employment. I barely got the job in the first place! If Marguérite strolled in, Émilie would either laugh furiously or toss me out on my *nancy*.

"Really?" Marguérite said. "Do you think there might be?"

"Of course."

A lie. Utter rubbish. In fact I would have wagered a month's pay it would never prove true. Or it would prove true at my expense. *Bien sûr, mademoiselle!* We have a spot for you. In fact a barmaid has just been let go!

"I am there most nights," I told Marguérite, digging myself deeper but unable to stop. "Please come find me. I'll see what I can do."

If not Émilie, I could count on Gérard, I reasoned. Though he had a tough exterior, he was easier to push over than the sickly cat who mewled at my windowsill each night.

"Thank you," Marguerite said, her eyes rounder and wetter than ever, so engulfing they might swallow the rest of her whole. "I truly appreciate the gesture."

"Please come find me," I reiterated. "I will expect you."

This was three days ago. Each night I move between bar and bottles. I smile and charm. I say the right things and turn the proper angles, forever making sure the light hits me in the ideal manner. While I flirt and pretend all is fine, the eventuality of Marguérite sits at the back of my mind.

I should not have asked her to find me. It's a nice idea that could quickly turn to trouble. I've already supplanted Émilie as the prettiest maid in the Folies. I'm no cancan dancer, but I do have a name, not to mention the ability to decide who gets to see up my skirts.

Marguérite is rough and ragged, but beneath the grime she shines. A visit by a proper coiffeur plus a heavy dose of whitening wash, and young Marguérite might best me. I have come far, but the legs on which I stand remain wobbly. I am climbing but cannot yet see the top. Émilie grouses that I suck up all the attention, that her wages have declined precipitously since my arrival. In a few months I could be saying the same about Marguérite.

But I had to ask. I had to try and carry her along with me to this unknown place I'm trying to reach. It made me ill to think of that bitty mouse joining the ranks of *les filles soumises*. Oh, how that vocation decimates a woman daily, by degrees! Marguérite is so very slight, painfully frayed and thin. The men would wear her away to nothing.

The truth is, from the moment I saw her I felt a kinship with Marguerite, a penchant toward the mothering of her, which, as the good Lord knows, is unexpected indeed. We are but a few years apart, but it's as though someone sent her to me for safekeeping. And while Marguérite will likely prove competition, a girl cannot live on man alone. I want her with me.

I think she feels the same; not about the men, but about the invisible tether, this tie between us. There is a reason she happened upon my room. There is a reason she listened as I told her what to do, and what not to. She will come, of this I'm sure. I've not yet warned Gérard. I can only hope there is room under his wing for the both of us.

Chapitre XXX

Paris, 2 February 1892

I can't remember the last time I saw the sun. It is frigid and bitter, and even the snow is colder than it ought to be. The mere act of stepping out of bed each morning is an exercise in determination. More than once I've contemplated walking to work with hot coals lining my pockets. Even Marguérite keeps the front of her bodice tied all the way up!

It's miserable, this shuffling from apartment to work and back again. The snow sticks on my boots, soaking all the way through to my toes. Somehow more snow ends up inside my shoes than around the edges. My apartment is warm, at least compared to my previous residence, but despite a near-constant shuttling of coal into the stove, it stays just damp enough that I can't claim comfort.

Marguérite and I sock up against each other at night. It is the only way to keep warm. Often, though, I must sleep alone. Marguérite's hours differ from mine, given she is a showgirl and I a lowly barmaid. I smile as I write this, without the jealousy I anticipated when Marguerite announced her ascension to bona fide Folies Bergères act.

As each day moves I am happy to be maiden to the establishment's cancan dancers and contortionists. Marguerite is of the contortionist variety, hired because her bosom looks so fantastical when twisted around and pulled out beneath her armpit. I swear she'll one day get stuck in that position! Alas, I have no special talent and no special bosom, so behind the bar I stay. *Oh bien! Je suis heureux!*

Pierre continues to make threats of his impending return from South America while I continue to discourage him. Who wants to be in Paris in the wintertime? Pure drudgery! This part is no fabrication. I also express how keenly I believe a man should seek comfort when away from his beloved. Rumor has it the hired ladies in South America put the Parisian women to shame. I am waiting to be put to shame! Just waiting!

Speaking of shame (or lack thereof!), I've struck up quite the friendship with Joseph Pujol. Folies Bergère patrons know him as Pétomane, the world's greatest farter. As his poster proclaims, he's the only performer who doesn't pay composers' royalties! When he sidled up to my bar and first told me how he earned a living, I did not believe him. Who would? Then I saw him onstage and, well, he erased my doubts. As well as my olfactory perception!

Joseph is one of our most successful acts. People arrive two hours early lest they miss his performance or are denied a seat (or must take a seat in the front row—a most dangerous proposition!) You've never heard such laughter and applause as when he's onstage. Not even with Marguérite's twisting and salty, irreverent mouth! I guess, in the end, we are all still children at heart.

What I love most about our beloved French flatulist is the company he keeps. I've never seen a greater collection of artists and luminaries as when

Pétomane bends over and spreads his cheeks: Émile Zola and Edgar Degas and Edgar's little Italian friend, the painter Giovanni Boldini. They all adore the man. And that makes him a recipient of the best of gossip.

Joseph says Boldini in particular has taken a liking to me, he wishes to paint my portrait, even! Though Marguérite doubts this claim, instead believing that "Pétomane is farting out both ends, as usual," I can't say I would mind his liking or his artistic rendition, or both. He's an attractive man and quite a reputable portraitist, or so they tell me.

According to Proust (the world's foremost gossip), Boldini came to prominence during the 1889 Exposition Universelle, where he served as commissioner for the Italian section. I was only fifteen at the time, and although Sœur Marie took me to the fair, I only cared about witnessing the new, much-maligned Eiffel Tower. What convent-raised child wouldn't want to see the "Tower of Babel" live and in person? There was such controversy over the damn structure I'm surprised the Italian, Boldini, earned any recognition at all!

As the story goes, at the time of the exposition, Boldini had been in Paris some time, having taken over M. Sargent's studio a few years before. Apparently Boldini was quite famous in London before arriving in our fine city. I have not confirmed the veracity of this gossip, but, truth be known, his association with the beloved farter gives him the most cachet of all!

M. Boldini is a funny little man, nervous and cantankerous. Yet there is something lovely about him, those high cheekbones and forehead, the slender features, and his arresting blue eyes. He is quite a bit older than me, than Pierre even, yet he is somehow youthful. Perhaps it is the tantrums he so loves to throw! So fussy, that man. I swear he yells when he doesn't like the way the wind blows!

Boldini comes around my station at least three times a week. According to Émilie, he often appears when I'm not present, leaving nary a franc for the gal. *C'est la vie!* Instead of patronizing Émilie's station, he loiters for five or ten minutes and leaves without taking a sip of alcohol or a bite of food. "Farting out both ends," Marguérite? I think not.

I must take caution, though, as *M. Merde* is a beloved patron of les Folies. I cannot be sure whether he corresponds with Gérard or the other fellows who so often ask after his well-being. My directive is to flirt with the guests, but Gérard would not want me to betray Pierre. I cannot afford to lose my apartment, or my monthly stipend for that matter, particularly when Boldini's financial picture is so unclear. I'm never sure whether he is flush or completely destitute. He is a difficult person to understand, which, of course makes me want to understand him all the more.

Chapitre XXXI

April hadn't planned to go back to work. But Boldini? The flatulist? Monsieur Shit? April couldn't shove them into her tote, not to be touched again until tomorrow.

Marthe's flat was two blocks from April's. She could stop by. Maybe she'd find something she hadn't noticed before. Maybe she'd see an old piece in a new light. Maybe April would finally do something other than wait for Troy not to call. At almost thirty-five years of age you were supposed to be done waiting for the phone to ring.

So with the journals tucked safely in her bag, she returned to the apartment. Climbing the stairs, April mentally prepared herself for the cluttered, discombobulated mess that somehow surprised her every time. She would begin in the dining room, she decided. There was a stack of mismatched chairs requiring explanation.

The front door was unlocked. When April stepped across the threshold she wondered for a second if she'd walked into the wrong place. The mismatched chairs had disappeared, along with 95 percent of the dining room pieces as well as everything from the antechamber and hallway. April's first thought was to call the gendarmes: They'd been ransacked.

"Olivier?" she said, voice echoing against the emptiness. "Marc? Where are you?"

"Back here!" Olivier called. "In the master!"

April's boots clopped across the floors. She found him, as promised, in Marthe's room. He was carefully trying to peel paper from the walls.

"Bonjour, April," he said. "How are you this afternoon? Sorry it's only me. Marc is at a meeting. You have a funny look on your face. Have you noticed these wall coverings? They're Dufour. We could get one thousand euros a panel if we're meticulous in its removal."

"The apartment!" she yelped. "It's empty!"

"A little easier to make your way through, non? Another truckload is on its way to the warehouse as we speak. Cleared out a mess of things to make room for these properties. Soon we'll be ready for staging and photographs. September will be here before you know it."

April tried not to panic. She'd already made her feelings known. Hired hand that she was, April had no jurisdiction over the manner in which the auction might take place. But this was going too fast. It was all going too fast.

"Before catalog copy is finalized I think the team should read Madame de Florian's journals," April said and touched her bag. She wasn't ready to bring them out of the warm circle created by the knowledge only she and Luc shared. Alas, time was not on April's side. As Marthe herself would and did say: *J'ai d'autres chats à fouetter.* She had other cats to whip. Clandestine reading was not on the docket.

"Ah, the diaries. Didn't we review those already?" Olivier asked.

"Only a few pages. There is so much more and the estate has granted permission to use the information in our catalogs. Luc convinced the family it would help with provenance."

"Luc?" Olivier looked up from his work. "Who is Luc?"

"Monsieur Thébault? The solicitor?"

"Oh, yes. Him. Well, is there anything of cultural significance in the diaries? Or merely some old lady's babbling?"

"Babbling?!" April said. "She wasn't old her entire life, you know. And, yes, there is cultural significance. She talks about Boldini! She talks about Zola and Proust!"

April paused as Olivier reached into his computer bag.

"So do you want them?" she asked.

"The journals?" Olivier pulled out his tablet. He shrugged half-heartedly. "Not especially. I don't really have the time to get bogged down in such minutia."

"Minutia. Olivier. I think we're missing out on a big piece of information here." April patted her purse again. "While I fully appreciate the need for fiscal prudence, we're leaving too much value on the table. I strongly believe this. Failing to add more meat to the sale could well be a poor economic decision in the long run."

Even Troy, even her husband with all his spreadsheets and financial models and focus on equity returns—even *he* would've stopped to consider the journals. Whenever he bought a company, which involved an actual *financial transaction* made from his own proverbial skin (that is, he had personal funds involved), Troy wanted to know more background. He called it due diligence but it was really another way to say provenance.

"Hmm," Olivier said with yet another half-shrug. "Feel free to keep reading the journals. I guess we can revisit when you get through them all. Alas, seems like a lot of work for nothing."

He was placating her and any promise to "revisit" was made only to get April off his back. She would let the matter drop at that moment but would not let it go entirely.

"Merci beaucoup," she grumbled. "Excuse me while I tackle the remnants of the dining room."

Eyes stinging (good grief, this really wasn't her day!) April returned to the dining room. Only a small gaggle of cut-rate objects greeted her, mostly a collection of low-value mirrors with a few feathered hats and one umbrella stand thrown in.

April pulled a mirror from its pile. It looked all right, maybe worth a few hundred, possibly a grand if there was some goddamn provenance involved. She turned the mirror over and ran a hand along its backing. April saw nothing that connoted historical significance. A few hundred only if Marthe had her own auction. Otherwise zero. This wasn't good enough to be filler. It could not stand alone.

As April went to stack it against an empty wall, a corner of white slipped from behind the mirror's backing. With a fingernail she dislodged the paper from its hiding spot. It was small, the size of a business card. April's breath caught as she read the name.

Georges Clemenceau.

Not a business card but a calling card, from the onetime French prime minister.

Suddenly giddy, April checked behind the other mirrors and found ever more cards. The names were instantly familiar: Marcel Proust, Robert de Montesquiou (the pistachio-suited dandy), and at least a half-dozen from Georges Clemenceau. She scrambled into the next room, and every room after that. April inspected the undersides of tables and the loose batting of old chairs. Soon her hands were full, fingers stretched and cramping as she tried to hold them all.

"Olivier!" she yelled, jogging into the kitchen where Olivier now stood. "Have you seen these? I found them hidden in some of the pieces."

She scattered the cards on top of his tablet.

"Ah, yes, the proliferation of calling cards," he said and pushed them aside. "We've found hundreds."

"You have?"

"Oui. When we started moving the pieces they positively rained out from the furniture, even the artwork."

"I can't believe I didn't see any of them."

"No one did. Not until our transport gentleman turned a desk upside down—"

"He turned it *upside down*?"

"Oui. Upside down. When the first one came out, Marc immediately inspected the other pieces. He pulled off sides and false bottoms and found hundreds more."

"Marc pulled sides off the furniture?" April went woozy.

Olivier smiled and shook his head. "Guess the old hag was quite popular."

" 'Old hag,' nothing. She was young once, too," April said, a little addled, as if she'd been the one tossed on end and not Marthe's desks and chairs. "What were you planning to do with the cards?"

"File them, I suppose?" he said. "Though they are fun to read, I'm not sure they're particularly relevant."

"But did you see the names? Georges Clemenceau, for one."

"Yes I saw the names." He looked up from his tablet and chuckled. "I didn't expect you to be so interested in calling cards. Seems Monsieur Thébault was correct."

"Monsieur Thébault?"

"My apologies. *Luc*, as you call him. I mentioned filing them. But he said you'd object, that you'd want to see them first. We thought, no, of course not, what does April want with calling cards? She is a furniture expert. But he was right. 'She will object. She will object mightily and at high volume.'"

"He said that."

"Oui. The cards are right here." He opened a box. "If you'd like the rest. They were monstrous to collect." Olivier slapped the cover of his tablet closed. "I shall return to the office. Do you mind locking up?"

"No, of course not."

"Merci beaucoup. Madame Vogt." He shook her hand formally, no double-cheek Continental kiss with the fellow this time. "Until tomorrow."

Olivier flipped around, coat flying out behind him. April waited, listening as his stride turned from pound to patter and then disappeared completely. A chill ran across her arms.

The place still boomed, though no living thing moved. From the corner a stuffed ostrich's tail feathers waved. In another room, in another apartment, someone played a piano. As April trekked from one room to the next, she continued to shiver. Wind howled through the walls.

"I'm sorry, Marthe," she said, though April wasn't sure for what.

Finally she lumbered into the untouched second bedroom. A dozen pieces, she decided. She would get through a dozen pieces. Assuming she kept distractions to a minimum, April could have the lot descriptions drafted before she left. Work faster, not longer. That was April's motto, her own personal calling card. Then again, when it came to Paris, longer was not necessarily a bad thing.

Chapitre XXXII

'Allo?" April said, phone tucked against her shoulder as she tromped down the stairs of Marthe's apartment.

It was not Troy, she knew this. Neither was it Birdie, who could call back at any time to fulfill a very specific request ("Find two similar pieces sold for vastly different values due to provenance"). No, this caller was not based in New York. This one was local.

"April Vogt à l'appareil."

Was it someone from the Paris office? The management company she was renting the apartment from? Did the bistro find her sunglasses?

"Avril," said the voice, smoky and rich and erasing all questions.

April paused at the second floor landing, heart racing though she was going down the stairs and not up them.

"I'm pleased to have reached you."

Luc. How did Luc have her number? It wasn't unreasonable that she might have offered her business card at some point, but she couldn't recall. It seemed more likely that Olivier played a role, or that his assistant had fallen victim to Luc's smooth charm. Still, it felt intrusive, though not necessarily in a bad way.

"Bonjour, Monsieur Thébault. I'm surprised to hear from you. Thank you again for the journals. Actually, there were some interesting developments in the apartment today." April paused, picturing the calling cards, quickly followed by Olivier's half-shrugs. "I thought so anyway."

"Brilliant. I'd love to hear more. When do you leave work?"

"Now, actually," she said. "I'm done for the day—more or less."

"Already finished? What a surprise. I feel as though I only just left you in the courtyard."

"Are you questioning my work ethic, counselor? Because usually you say I work too hard."

"Not questioning, only concerned you're losing your American industriousness to Parisian sloth. The woman I know is supposed to put in twelve-hour days instead of"—April imagined Luc checking his watch, a big titanium Cartier—"approximately two? Maybe you *are* more fun than your brethren."

"No, I'm not," April said. "Well, I mean, I'm not less fun. Or more. I'm . . . I worked in the office this morning and have more to take back to my apartment tonight. Are you accusing me of slacking off, Monsieur Thébault?"

April's voice echoed against the ancient stone walls. Its levity surprised her, especially given the heaviness April felt most of the day.

"Non!" Luc said. "I'd never accuse you of slacking! But, now, taking work home. That sounds like a genuine, blue-blooded American."

"Red-blooded."

"My apologies. Red-blooded American. The rich ones are the blues. You are the reds."

"I'm neither." She shook her head. "I mean I'm American, but it has nothing to do with blood . . . and . . . anyway . . . You said you were trying to reach me?"

"Yes. Are you at the apartment now?"

"I am." April peeked through the window on the landing as if to be sure. "I'm on my way out, though."

"Excellent," he said. "I'm downstairs. Are you available?"

" 'Available.' What do you mean, exactly?"

"Ah, ma chérie. Don't get excited. Tu viens boire une coupe avec moi?"

"A drink—"

"Oui. At La Terrasse, I'm thinking. It's atop the Galeries Lafayette. Glorious views."

"I don't know," April started. "I have a ton of work to get through tonight."

"A ton? You Americans love your exaggerations. Come. It's nearby, and they close early anyway. You're not obliged to suffer my presence for much time at all."

"All right," April said as she made her way down the last set of stairs. "I suppose I have time for one drink."

"Or three. Ah, I see the top of your head."

April pushed out onto the street, and there he stood, shirt pressed and partially unbuttoned, khaki pants slung low, shoes buffed to their shiniest. She couldn't stop from smiling, mostly because Luc already was.

"Bonjour," she said and found her body trembling in spite of itself.

"Twice in one day. What a treat."

Luc led April down the sidewalk, where they maneuvered their way through people returning from work and those already home, now walking their pets. It was a veritable carnival of desk jockeys, dog walkers, and shoppers out there, more reminiscent of Calcutta than Paris, but April didn't entirely mind the fracas. It meant there was no reasonable manner in which to engage Luc in conversation. Socializing "over drinks" was a stressful enough prospect, and April didn't want to fritter away any of her middling conversational topics while leaping over teeming piles of crap.

She'd been to the Galeries Lafayette many times. A few skips from the famed Opéra de Paris, the Galeries were, at their heart, a department store, which was probably why Chelsea scoffed at the thought. But it was a department store only in that it housed a collection of shops beneath one roof. This was no suburban mall, no Westfield Shopping Town. The Galeries could easily hold court to the Opéra's splendor.

Created in 1893 with much attention to gilt and aesthetic drama, the ten-floor behemoth had at its center a stained-glass-and-steel dome, its waterfall of colors forever dancing on the shoppers below, not unlike the Folies chandelier, April guessed. The Galeries Lafayette was a tourist trap as Chelsea said, but this fact did not make it any less stunning. For April it remained an everyday representation of its era, of Marthe's time, the Belle Époque. Because it was built in the so-called beautiful age, it was much more than a place to buy Louis Vuitton or get ostracized by condescending salesclerks.

For all the splendor of the building, its rooftop deck was surprisingly ordinary. La Terrasse was a simple-enough restaurant, with a smattering of high metal tables and white square umbrellas. But the view easily beat anything golden or flashy on the floors below. From where she and Luc took a seat, April could see most of Paris, including a straight shot to the

Eiffel Tower and a prime look at Sacré-Cœur with its imposing white domes and spires. Inside the church was the largest bell in France, its ceiling mosaic the grandest in the country.

"Have you been here before?" Luc asked as he scooted in his chair. "On the rooftop. Of course you've been to the Galeries."

"Yes," April said, sneaking a glimpse at the menu. "I came to the observation deck a few times when I lived here. I'm not sure better views exist on this planet."

April browsed the menu a second time, trying to appear casual, as if perhaps she *could* eat but she didn't *have to* eat, when have to eat was actually the truth. At that hour it was too late for lunch yet too early for dinner. She'd managed to miss out on a day's worth of food yet again, and didn't think she could hold out until the normal Parisian dining time.

Luc signaled the waiter. He ordered two glasses of champagne. Before he could walk away, April quickly added macaroni au fromage to her order. It was merely a fancy way to say mac and cheese, but April figured if ordered on a rooftop in Paris it could hardly be considered bourgeois.

"Do you need to get that?" Luc asked.

"The macaroni?" April said, blushing again, always blushing when she was around this man. "Um, well, I'm kind of hungry. I'm sorry I don't subscribe to your French sensibilities. You know how we Americans are, gorging ourselves every hour of the day."

"No." Luc snorted. "You should eat. You're rather thin. I'm speaking of your purse." He gestured to the chair between them. "It appears to be ringing."

"Oh. Oh!" April grabbed her bag and fumbled for her phone.

"It's amusing you have a BlackBerry. Everyone else has smartphones, yes?"

"I'm a relic, I suppose."

TV3.

April silenced her phone.

"I can deal with that later," she said, slightly bewildered by her own reaction.

"All right." Luc shrugged.

April reached for her glass, but it was not yet there. When she pulled her hand back April noticed it was shaking.

"So, you had something to discuss?" she said, voice as shivery as her arm.

"Yes. I spoke to Madame Quatremer's heir today," Luc told her. "About the journal entries, the things in the apartment, all your questions. And I have some news."

" 'News'?" April tried not to show her alarm. "What is it? Does she want the journals back?"

"Nothing about the journals," Luc said. "Patience, Madame Vogt. First things first. While we wait for our champagne, I think you should read this."

Chapitre XXXIII

Paris, 12 April 1892

I went to Boldini's studio today and, scandal of scandals, not during the four-to-five!

Every proper society matron (or maiden) knows never to visit a man's home other than during this special hour. To arrive at half past three would be uncouth, nay, salacious. You'd be shunned from society at three forty-five. But at four o'clock, why, saunter right in! Leave again at four thirty, hair a-fuss, dress crumpled. This, an acceptable arrangement.

Truth be told, I do not understand this sixty-minute window, but perhaps the shroud of dusk covers impropriety. More likely it works because everyone's agreed to philander at the same time thus no one gets caught!

I arrived at Boldini's at noon, not even close to the prescribed hour.

Émilie warned if anyone saw me it'd be over, every teaspoon of reputation I'd gained frittered away. And indeed I say we're dealing in teaspoons. I've come far, but a little plus zero is nonetheless still rounded to zero. Her point was well taken, of course: Noon was not the appropriate time to call on a man. Even if he wasn't married, even if the impetus of my visit did not involve corset unstringing. Alas, following my shift at the Folies, I had nowhere else to go.

While I care about social customs and propriety, not everyone is of the same mind. Specifically, a little bird of a contortionist named Marguérite, who has taken up with a cancan dancer. The first time the dancer visited our flat I'd not even said hello before the two ladies promptly commenced their sapphic tryst. They didn't mind my presence, but I certainly minded theirs. I saw too much. It's awful how you cannot unsee things, isn't it?

Today I arrived home from my barmaid shift later than usual due to an early-morning duel and the resultant broken glass and decapitated parakeets littering the main floor. Émilie and I spent the late morning sweeping feathers and mopping up little streaks of blood. I so looked forward to a bath and a nap, but Marguérite had other plans. I'd hardly stepped through the front door when Mlle. Cancan waggled her tail feathers inside. I could not well kick her out. I hate to disappoint Marguérite in any fashion. The women invited me to join in on the festivities. I politely declined and said I had somewhere to be, though I hadn't a clue where I might possibly go.

As I wound through Pigalle, dodging the "ladies" returning home from their employ, Boldini's funny, grumpy face popped into my head. He always expresses all manner of opinions following any duel; surely he'd be in prime form after one with so many feathered casualties.

I stopped by the Folies to check for the man. Émilie had not seen him in a fortnight because the two of us never worked the same shift, though I was "welcome to wait and see if he arrived." As waiting has never been my strong suit, I made the audacious decision to visit Boldini's studio directly. I knew where he lived as he bragged loudly and often of his expropriation of the John Singer Sargent place. Émilie issued her warnings, but I pretended not to hear.

It was a long walk, and by the time I was halfway across the Seine, there was no turning back. Literally. I hoped he'd send me home in his carriage.

After a stroll through the Luxembourg Gardens, Parisian weather cooperating for once, I popped onto his doorstep with a smile (no tail feathers for this girl!). Boldini greeted me with cheerful trepidation. By that I mean his voice sounded happy but his eyes looked scared. Perhaps it's good I did not arrive during the four-to-five. Who knows what kind of entanglement I might've found him in?!

"Marguérite needed some privacy in the apartment," I told him. "So I decided to take a walk and, lo and behold, I somehow ended up at your door!"

"You want to come *in*?" Boldini was incredulous, as though I'd pointed a revolver into his rib cage and demanded his pocket watch.

"Well, yes," I said. "That is typically the outcome one seeks when paying a visit to a friend. I've come a long way and will need a ride home, by the by."

Boldini sighed and reluctantly showed me through the doorway and into the studio.

What to say about the studio? It is as much an undone mess as Boldini himself. As I mentioned, it used to belong to Sargent, who was forced to relinquish it following the Madame Gautreau scandal, or Madame X as they call her now, as if anyone could forget that what is now X was once Gautreau.

As Boldini fussed around his kitchen for a teacup (he never found the tea to put in it), I took a moment to appraise the room, to see if I could feel the power of what happened. I was only eleven when the debacle unfolded, but I was already well into the gossips by then, much to the dismay of the nuns.

Now I stood in the very space where the beautiful Madame Gautreau let her strap fall, a small action that later inflamed all of Europe. Part of me expected to turn around and see the infamous portrait.

The studio itself is not horrible. It has potential if one could get through all the paints and canvases and artistic clutter. The room boasts crown moldings, decorative woodwork, and floors made of the finest oak. Its ceilings are so high they echo every breath. From the main studio one can access any three chambers, which are hidden behind heavy drapes. When I paused by one, my hand on the burgundy velvet, Boldini snapped at me.

"Not for guests," he said.

I had to wonder what kind of untoward activities happened behind the veil!

A long mantel stretches the northernmost wall. On it sits a collection of limp, dirty dolls creepier than the Folies dancer with the glass eye and yellow teeth. According to Boldini they were Sargent's, who never returned to collect them after his move. Boldini doesn't possess the heart to throw them out, and Sargent could still come back. Silly man. It's been seven years and even the most generous of timelines does not allow for it. Either way, these haunted dolls will disappear within the month. I promise you this!

To quell any doubts I had about the prolific nature of his portraiture, Boldini's apartment is positively riotous with canvases, my favorite a half-completed self-portrait. In it he dons a wide black tie and a tan coat and displays his usual grim countenance, the ends of his mustache twisted upward, smiling where he does not. Just looking at it makes my insides flutter. I have a taste for the bitter, it seems, instead of for the sweet.

Beside the picture I found two other canvases, both portraits most of the way completed. A mother and her daughter, Boldini said when he sensed my lingering. Something about the word "daughter" squeezed at my heart. Or perhaps the word was "mother."

"It's Josefina de Alvear de Errázuriz," he said when I refused to move from my spot on the floor. "The next portrait over, that's her daughter, Giovinetta, a veritable squirrel of a child."

"Never heard of her," I said.

"You've never heard of Josefina? The wealthy Chilean expatriate?"

I chuckled. Chilean expatriate? Perhaps she knew the guano magnate of the Southern Hemisphere.

"Sorry," I said. "The only South American I know is Pierre."

"Yes, we all know how well acquainted the two of you are. If there's a South American to know, it is Sir Pierre!"

Was it my imagination or did he sound testy about our relationship? Yes, I thought, he was thorny. This was a happy thing.

"Well," I said. "Whoever this woman is, she is quite beautiful. The painting is magnificent."

"Thank you," he mumbled, blushing hard.

I did not add that Madame de Errázuriz was *so* beautiful that looking at her portrait made me feel as though her very eyes were challenging me with that beauty. The woman, this Josefina, glared at me straight from the canvas, eyebrows lifted, mouth pursed in a self-satisfied smile. Even here, back at my own flat, I can see her dress: thick golden satin, dark green stripes, a matching green sash around her waist. What's more, the golden woman sat atop a golden chaise. Madame de Errázuriz was the very definition of luminosity. I promptly commenced my dislike.

"How fortunate they have such an esteemed portraitist at their disposal," I said, as a buttered-up Boldini is always more tolerable than the usual one. "But what is with the young girl?"

As beautiful as the mother was, the squirrel-like Giovinetta looked downright insolent as she slouched against a purple velveteen settee. And her outfit? I did not understand her outfit. It was not befitting a ten-year-old, though there was no age in particular it did befit! Giovinetta sported a four-year-old's bonnet, a cape straight out of a *grand-mère*'s bureau, and some dandy's umbrella propped against her thigh.

Her thigh! Goodness! I can scarcely speak of it without blushing! In the portrait, long black stockings run the length of her legs, stockings more appropriate for a woman of eighteen and not a girl of ten. But that is the very least of it! Peeking over the top of one stocking is a swath of skin. *Mon dieu!* Boldini will fare worse than Sargent!

"What do you mean?" Boldini asked. "Do you not like the portrait?"

"Technically speaking it is well done. But have you noticed the"—I pointed at the girl's leg—"skin?"

"Well, yes." He smiled. "It is my painting, so indeed I noticed. Do you take issue with it?"

"I don't take issue but fear you are in danger of creating your own scandal . . . your very own Madame Gautreau, *Madame X*, what have you! What new painter will take over the Sargent-cum-Boldini studio when you become a social pariah and can no longer make the rent?"

"Oh, Marthe," he said. "I did not take you for such a delicate woman! You witness much more skin after fifteen minutes behind that bar of yours."

"No one wants to see a child's thigh, Giovanni. That is an entirely different matter!"

My outrage was genuine, as was the fear that this kind of scandal would render my dear Boldini exiled from Paris. Exiled from me!

Boldini only laughed.

Unable to suffer another moment of staring at a partially exposed little girl, I wandered the studio to see what other paintings he had in progress. As I inspected the premises, it was difficult to determine whether I was in the flat of a successful man or a struggling one. I suppose that's the problem with artists. One can never tell if they have money!

The more I perused the apartment, the greater Boldini's level of discomfort. He seemed concerned about my opinions, several times making an excuse for this work or that while occasionally insisting he would paint me and it would prove his greatest work to date. Though the statement thrilled me, I knew Boldini didn't mean it, about my portrait. He merely didn't know what else to say.

"You do not have to make my portrait to make me happy," I said and reached for his hand. I laced my fingers through his.

Boldini jumped.

"I am a gentleman . . . ," he burbled. "I am not sure what . . ."

With my eyes I tried to convey a certain message. Namely that I deemed him a gentleman but he did not have to act like one then. My plan was not to seduce the man, but that day my intentions had other ideas!

Before either one of us could come to our senses I led a quivering Boldini into one of the chambers, hoping there was a place to rest our weary *feet*. We were in luck. Pushed up against the wall was Madame de Errázuriz's yellow chaise.

While Boldini pecked and hemmed, I pulled us both down onto the chair. Something sparked inside him. Within seconds he had my dress and corset undone. I blinked, and his fingers ran over my nipples. I blinked again, and he replaced his fingers with his mouth, his hands suddenly busy in a fiendish manner below my skirt.

Allow me to stop here and simply say Giovanni Boldini is not only a skilled artist but an expert in at least a few other areas as well. The man is widely known as a genius with his hands, but I feel as though those particular appendages are getting an undue share of the glory. Either way, an artist he is!

Chapitre XXXIV

Belle Époque porn." April set the journals on the table. "That's a new one for me."

"Oh, dear," Luc said as they clinked their glasses together and cheered Paris. "If you think that's porn, then perhaps the journal entries are not the only periodicals I should share with you."

"And now the 'sexual badgering' begins." April took a sip to keep herself from grinning too wide. The champagne fizzed in her throat, dry and prickly. "I hadn't known Boldini lived in Sargent's studio. I should've known, but I didn't. The diaries, the Sargent studio, it all feels so fortuitous, as if I was the one who was supposed to read these."

It was more crucial than ever that she make the auction happen. A real one. For Marthe alone. She respected Olivier's views on the matter, but that did not make him right.

"This all sounds very self-important and delusional, I realize," April continued when Luc replied only with a raised and semimocking eyebrow. "But Sargent, he's, like, *my* guy."

"Your guy."

"My hus . . . my friends and family, they accuse me of being a teensy bit obsessed with the artist. Well, *Madame X* in particular. She's at the Met."

"'Madame X'? Is this a porn star of some kind?"

"At the Met?! What is *wrong* with you?" April said, almost laughing despite the chastising tone she'd been going for. "*Madame X*, she was formerly Madame Gautreau." April tapped the journals. "Before they changed the name to protect the innocent. Haven't I told you this? I've told you this. Sometimes I feel like you're not listening to me at all."

April batted his hand playfully. She did not want Luc to believe she was serious, to think she was some near-middle-aged shrew keeping careful inventory of affronts and slights.

"Avril," he said, voice serious and unwavering. "I remember every word you say. Every word."

Luc's face held firm, no smirk to be found. April's own face burned as he locked his eyes tightly to hers.

"Seriously, though," she said, fiddling with all the eating and writing implements within grasp. "I've seen *Madame X* a hundred times, a thousand. It's my favorite in the entire museum. My husband"—April found herself inexplicably blushing at the word—"Troy doesn't understand how I can look at the same damn painting week after week, month after month, year after year. We go to the Met. A lot. His grandmother is some bigwig there. Plus—it's the Met. He always wants to check out the latest collections: Klee, British silver, *Rugs and Ritual in Tibetan Buddhism*, what have you. But I always start with her, *Madame X*."

"Ah," Luc said. "There is something you enjoy more than your tables and bureaus."

"Continental furniture is absolutely my thing, but when I was in grad school *Madame X* almost made me change my mind. Alas, John Singer Sargent would be an impossibly narrow focus. And lord knows I couldn't abide spending large portions of my career looking at François Boucher." April made a face. "Or Jean-Honoré Fragonard. *Blech*."

"Yes. That would be dreadful. Those fellows are the worst."

"Angels and cupids and cherubs. Not my taste at all."

"You are a delightful romantic. In any case, given your astounding endorsement as well as that of Madame de Florian, I'll have to look this painting up on the Internet to see what the fuss is about."

"I cannot believe you don't know her." April thumped her glass on the table. "How is that even possible?"

"Ah, we cannot all live in paintings and furniture." Luc finished off his champagne and signaled the waiter for another. "Now. Do you want the news? Or would you prefer to continue waxing poetic about some other lady from some other painting and not our dear Madame de Florian?"

"No! Of course not! We're here for Marthe. Tell me"—April cringed—"but tell me it's not bad."

"Relax, Avril. This news is good. So nervous you are. Squirrelly! No doubt like the young squirrel Giovinetta Errázuriz from Boldini's painting."

"I know those two paintings, by the way, the ones Marthe writes about. Boldini sold them directly to Baron de Rothschild, who sold them to a private collector probably about twenty years ago, long before I was in the business. But we studied all the big sales in graduate school. The transaction was conducted by, shall we say, a competing house. Clearly Baron de Rothschild was of questionable taste."

"Fascinating," Luc said and rolled his eyes. "One cannot hear enough about the vagaries of auction-house sales. Anyway, she'd like to meet you."

"Who? Giovinetta de Alvear de Errázuriz? I'm pretty sure she's dead."

"No. Not the rodent-child. Agnès Vannier. Madame Quatremer's heir."

April paused. The heir. He'd finally named the beneficiary to Lisette Quatremer's estate.

"Luc," she said, a little out of breath.

The name Agnès Vannier meant exactly nothing to April, at least not in any way related to provenance. Yet Luc could have gifted her something from the apartment itself for the way April reacted. She gawped at him exactly as one would after receiving an unduly extravagant gift, not unlike the first time Troy placed a delicately wrapped box in her hands.

Jewelry seemed sweet at the time, though unnecessary after just two months of dating, but April figured it was not altogether out of line for someone of Troy's ilk. Until she opened the box and found a pair of pearl and diamond earclips from Paris, sold at a recent "Property of a Lady" auction. Sotheby's conducted the sale, so April had seen the catalog. The lady had any number of flashy, diamond-encrusted, rubied-up assets in her property, but Troy selected the exact lot April would've picked for herself. The earrings were simple, though not plain, at least compared with the other pieces. Still, they were unquestionably valuable. April intentionally avoided finding out the hammer price but knew they went for more than she made in a year, two years, perhaps even in three.

At the time April felt bumbling, undeserving, and frankly would've demanded that he return them had it been an option. Instead she was forced to awkwardly accept the earclips, although April said repeatedly she'd be happy to return them to him at some later date. Perhaps he could save the jewels for his daughters to wear in their weddings one day.

That was ancient history, though, and now April was well versed in the process of receiving gifts. One shouldn't try to match her value to the item's price tag, and instead simply say thanks. But while that certainly applied to diamonds and pearls, the gift from Luc meant so much more that April found herself outmatched. It was all she could manage to utter "thank you" and remove the small napkin from beneath her plate of mac and cheese.

"Are you crying?" he asked after her squeak of gratitude.

"Bien sûr que non!" April's voice was high, scratchy, and thin. "That'd be silly. I'm only a little stunned. I thought Madame Vannier"—the name, April had the name—"I thought Madame Vannier wasn't interested in any curious auctioneers."

"A change of heart, I suppose. And you are no ordinary auctioneer. I've assured her of this."

"Who is she?" April asked, blotting the corners of her eyes. "This Agnès Vannier? Is she Lisette's daughter?"

"No, Madame Quatremer never had any children."

"So is Agnès her sister?" April asked. Her purse vibrated. She didn't bother to check the caller. Troy could suck it, she thought. Of course suck it in a figurative and colloquial manner, Willow still fresh in her mind. "A cousin, then? What?"

"It is not for me to explain. She'd like to tell you herself. Isn't it better to hear the provenance straight from the sow's mouth?" Luc winked.

"Yes, of course. I can ask all the relevant details when we meet."

"Let's be clear. If you meet," Luc said. "*If*. Nothing is guaranteed."

"What do you mean 'nothing is guaranteed'? You said she wanted to!"

"Avril—"

"C'est merdique, Luc." April polished off the rest of her champagne. "Supershitty, as a matter of fact. I'm not interested in any of your games. Either she wants to see me or she doesn't. I don't understand why you'd bring it up only to yank it away again. Yes or no, Thébault. These are your choices. It's really quite black-and-white."

"Nothing's ever black-and-white," he said. "And she wants to meet, yes, but in the end it might not be her choice. Though I appreciate your ardent descriptions—'supershitty' indeed—Madame Vannier is younger than Lisette Quatremer was when she died but remains quite old. Eighty, to be exact. She is not of optimum health, and her constitution is in a most delicate state."

"I'm sorry to hear that."

Luc shrugged. "This is how life goes. We're young, we're old, we're weak, we die."

"If we're lucky," April mumbled.

"Madame Vannier was hospitalized last evening," Luc said, dumping half his champagne into April's glass. "When she comes home, *should* she come home—"

"Okay, that sounds a little harsh."

"It is the truth. Not harsh, not soft, only the truth. Nothing more. Should she come home, Madame Vannier would be pleased to see you. After she regains her strength, of course. But only then."

"Why didn't you say that in the first place? Of course we can wait until she's better. I'd not dream of anything else. I have zero interest in stepping inside a hospital. Been there, done that, more times than I'd care to count." April reached for a piece of bread. "In the meantime I'll finish up my research with the journals. My assistant and I have a plan, actually, and I think it's quite genius, if I do say so myself. It's what's known in the finance biz as running comps—no reason we can't do that with Marthe's assets given the journals, our own bit of inside information."

"The journals."

Luc shifted in his seat. He grimaced as if in physical pain. It was the first time April had seen him visibly uncomfortable. It was the first time he did not seem in charge of every aspect of a given situation.

"Oh, god," she said. "What is it . . . ?"

"Ah. Well. The journals. We do need to discuss those. I guess there is a touch of bad news on top of the good. I will try to get you what you want but for the time being I need to . . ."

"No!" April barked. He could not do this. He could not swap one gift for another. "I know what you're going to say, and the answer is no."

The woman wanted her diaries back. April was sure Agnès Vannier was a lovely person and a delightful conversationalist to boot, but this was not a trade she was willing to make.

"Je suis sincèrement désolé, Avril."

"No," April said again. "Absolutely not."

"Sweet Avril, ma chérie. It pains me to ask. As you seemed to have guessed, Madame Vannier would like the journals back. And reclaim them I must. I can only hope one day you'll forgive me."

Chapitre XXXV

The information hit April like a slap, though it was a blow she saw coming. Forgive Luc? Not a chance.

"Avril?" he said. "Ça va? You won't cry again, will you?"

There was a solution to this. There had to be. Small fragments of ideas began to merge in her head.

"Okay." She cleared her throat. "She can have the journals."

"Really? That easily?" Luc's forehead lifted toward the sky. "This is not my Avril."

"I always planned to give them back, bien sûr. She will have them in a few days. Not to worry, I'm a very fast reader."

Luc shook his head sadly.

"I'm sure you read like the wind. Alas Madame Vannier is nearing the end of her life. She wants them before she dies."

"I understand. But, we have some time, yes?"

"We all have time," Luc said. "But Madame Vannier, you, me—none of us really knows how much."

"Yes, yes, we could all be hit by a motorbike tomorrow. But, be honest with me, how close to dead is Madame Vannier? She at least has a little visibility into her demise. The doctors must have some kind of estimate."

"Estimate? How close to dead? Mon dieu, Madame Vogt!"

"That's not what I meant."

"It is very much what you meant."

"Come on, Luc, you can allow me a bit more time with the journals. S'il vous plaît?"

"Madame Vannier is my client. This is her request, pretty auctioneers notwithstanding. She pays me to handle her affairs."

Yet another slap. He was paid to be there, like Marthe with Pierre, though in this instance the person knee-deep in shit was April. Someone was compensating Luc to tolerate April. He did not say this, but April heard it all the same.

"Luc—"

"Avril."

"Fine. Can't we at least make copies?! You have to let me do that!"

"Well, I see you're very concerned for Madame Vannier's welfare. A dying woman's wish." He clucked his tongue. "Goodness!"

"Sorry," April said, properly scolded but not deterred.

She exhaled and fixed her gaze on the horizon, the purple skyline wrapped around the Eiffel Tower. How to sound like a reasonable person, she wondered? One who valued human life over furniture, over the journals of a ghost?

"I sound grossly insensitive," she admitted. "My sincerest apologies. I am sad to hear of your client's ill health."

"Liar," Luc said with a grin. "You are not sad at all. At least not because of her health."

April would copy the journals. That was the solution to dealing with the demands of a near-dead woman. The Paris office had the requisite equipment for scanning old documents. April only had to find a way to justify the exercise.

"Maybe if you could allow me the afternoon—"

"Enough." Luc sighed deeply. "You are relentless. I cannot take this any longer. You may have the journals for the next three days. There are more still, and I will get them to you by nightfall. Then I will collect all of them seventy-two hours hence." He checked his watch. "With the understanding that if Madame Vannier takes a turn for the worse, I may demand them sooner."

April nodded, holding her breath.

"In the meantime, copy them, read them, do what you wish."

"Thank you," she said with another nod. "I'm sorry I was acting so crazy."

"Oh, this is nothing new," Luc said and squeezed her knee. "I am used to it by now. Though I must say, bereavement counseling was your true calling. I don't know why you're mucking around in the furniture business."

"Very funny," April said and tried to smile, the word "furniture" stabbing her between the ribs. She pictured the apartment, its bareness, the bones of Marthe's life mostly gone.

"Ça va?" Luc said, touching her knee a second time.

"Yes, everything's fine," April lied. "I was thinking about the apartment. You wouldn't even recognize the place. It's nearly empty. They've even started stripping the walls. Everything is moving so fast, too fast. Soon I'll be back in New York, the auctions will be over, and it will be on to the next thing."

As if the next thing could even begin to compare. Whatever auction awaited her, however grand the estate, it was guaranteed to be a downgrade.

"I'm confused. Isn't the disappearance of furniture in exchange for money what your job encompasses?" Luc asked. "You perplex me more by the minute."

"Yes, of course it's about the money for the seller, for the house, but really it is about the art. Art is the important thing. It predates money, after all. They had it on cave walls. Art *stays*. But Marthe's assets . . . We're hurrying so quickly through them all, as if her things were cogs or widgets or something." Her voice caught. "I'm sorry. I don't mean to get emotional but these pieces are important."

Luc nodded. "So it seems. Tell me," he said as the waiter delivered two more champagnes, this time without being asked. "Why are you so intent on conducting the auction *your* way? Why do Marthe's things mean so much to you?"

Before responding April took three big gulps. Already her brain hummed. Forever a lightweight, she was surprised that her already borderline-excessive Parisian wine consumption had done little to bolster her tolerance. What good was drinking heavily now if it did not permit you to drink even more later?

"Well," April said, working to keep from slurring her words. "We have the opportunity to do quite well here. Usually the paintings and jewelry make the real money. And contemporary art—that dwarfs all of it for reasons I cannot comprehend. Anyway, my department is not, as they say 'high-grossing.' The sales commissions and buyers' premiums on old furniture and random knickknacks barely pay assistants' salaries. They barely pay for my travel or the fancy catalogs. This could be different, though. These pieces, with Madame de Florian's background, could set records."

"Though you are an auctioneer—"

"Continental furniture expert."

"Though you are an auctioneer, I do not gather the premiums really matter to you."

"Why? Because of Troy? Let me dispel that notion. I keep my own bank account and our prenup is quite onerous from my standpoint. More onerous than I remembered, actually. . . ."

It seemed like a good idea at the time, a declaration of April's commitment. It was a declaration made only to lawyers and various family members she'd not seen since the wedding, but a statement nonetheless. April handed over a balance sheet at the closing dinner, known as the rehearsal dinner to most in the room, and signed a statement saying that upon dissolution of the marriage she'd take only what was on that sheet plus anything she'd managed to accumulate in checking account number 99844201 or brokerage account 5601-4324. A foolhardy endeavor in hindsight, but at least Troy's future third wife couldn't rightly bitch about April taking all his money.

"Who mentioned anything about le grand m'sieu?" Luc said with a scoff. "I am certainly not interested in him. And neither am I concerned about your financial status or the premiums on furniture or how much it costs to produce a catalog. Non. I did not ask about any of it. I don't care why the furniture is meaningful to the auction house or to any one person's bank account. I asked why the items are meaningful to *you*."

He looked at her pointedly, in a manner so intimate it made April squirm in her chair. Some part of her wanted to run away. The other part wished he'd reach out and touch her again.

"To me?" April said, clearing her throat.

"To you." He hadn't even blinked.

April thought for a moment. There were a hundred different ways to answer, but the whole mess could be summarized in a few words. How much to reveal, she wondered, without giving herself away?

"I think the real question"—April said, suppressing a burp—"is not why they mean so much to *me*, but why they didn't mean much to Lisette Quatremer? Why don't they matter to Madame Vannier? These are heirlooms, evidence of a life. It's inconceivable that Lisette locked it all away and that Madame Vannier wants to sell everything, sight unseen. I don't mean to insult your client. I'm sure she has her reasons. But it is hard for me to think of a valid one."

"Maybe these people never cared about the past," Luc said. "Maybe they don't need evidence of anything. Haven't you heard the phrase 'live in the moment'?"

"Bullshit. Everyone cares about the past," April said. "Everyone. Are you getting another glass? I'm almost done with mine. What time is it? Are they about to close? Should we order more just in case?"

"Perhaps you should hold off. Though you are slight, you are a tall woman, and I'm not certain I could carry you home."

Luc gave another one of his sly winks. April again felt her face redden.

He was disturbingly attractive, this man, attractive in a skinny European kind of way, but attractive nonetheless. True, he was a bit smarmy and the amount of chest hair visible over the top of his button-down indicated a need for manscaping. He also had a nasty tobacco habit, replete with vaguely nicotine-stained nails and what had to be a pair of black lungs.

I don't understand the appeal, April told herself. His face—it did belong on a shadowy, black-and-white billboard, perhaps one advertising cologne or condoms or expensive liquor. But Luc was not her type, if she were single enough to have a type. April liked her men one way: big, sandy-haired, and American. Clean nails. Straight teeth, straight hair.

But if semi-dirty Frenchmen weren't her thing, why, then, did April's heart rate kick up every time she saw him? Why was she drinking (too much) champagne with a near-stranger, on a rooftop in Paris, dangerously close to saying things she'd only ever admitted to Troy?

"You think I can't hold my liquor?" April said, attempting to distract herself as another burp sneaked up the back of her throat. "I'd surprise you."

"You already have." Luc reached over and splashed a bit of his champagne into her glass. "Well, what do you have of your past, Madame Vogt? Roomfuls of family heirlooms passed down from older generations?"

"Hardly." She snorted. "After my mom got sick my dad got rid of it all."

"Sick with what?"

"Nice try. We"—April used air quotes—"don't talk about that. And it doesn't matter, really." God, what a lie! Of course it mattered. It mattered in a million small ways, and at least a few large ones. "It went like this. One day she was there. They took her to the hospital. Then she was gone. There was simply nothing left. If I were younger when it happened I'm sure I would've thought a person's belongings were permanently attached to them, that if someone left, all their stuff would go, too."

"What happened to her things?"

"My dad sold them. To pay for the medical expenses, or to rid himself of the memories, or both, probably." April shrugged. "I would've liked something. But it was all gone before I could ask."

"So no heirlooms."

"No heirlooms, no knickknacks, not even costume jewelry. And for all intents and purposes my dad was gone too. At the risk of sounding melodramatic, I pretty much felt like an orphan overnight. Like Marthe de Florian, I was a teenager standing on the sidewalk watching other peoples' families pass by, left wondering how I could have that, too."

"I'm sorry, Avril," Luc said in his honey-thick French accent. He frowned, hard, and did not appear ready with a smirk or vaguely disparaging comment. "That must have been difficult."

"It's totally fucked up," April said and then covered her mouth. "Sorry for the language."

"Ça fait rien. You've already said many expletives tonight."

"I guess you're right." April stabbed her fork into the last remaining pieces of macaroni. They were tepid and gluey, but she needed the food. "It's just . . . when he did that, when he shipped it all away, or sold it in a yard sale, or however the hell he disposed of the pieces, afterward there was nothing tangible left. Only the shell of some life that once was. I wish I had something. Something substantial I could put in my home, a piece I could look at and say, yeah, there's Mom. Furniture is furniture. I get that. But it still has a memory within it. Don't get me wrong. I have an apartment, a beautiful apartment, filled with expensive pieces. Troy was pretty generous."

"*Was?*"

"Is. If something catches my eye in an auction he doesn't usually say no. But most of our stuff? Gorgeous. Outrageously expensive. But manufactured in the last five years and purchased by my husband. Selected by someone I don't even know."

"That's how you feel about your husband? That you don't know him?"

"That's not what I meant!" April snapped, but then wondered. "It was easier for us to hire an interior designer and simply approve of preselected items. My area of expertise isn't really well-suited for our apartment, or our combined tastes. This was a new marriage for Troy and a new life for me after leaving Paris. We were both starting from scratch."

"So the things from your childhood home?" Luc said. "The heirlooms from your mother? I have to wonder. Would they ever really be enough? They are not her."

"Well, of course they're not her. But it would beat the hell out of what I currently have, which is a big fat zero. So I'd take it. I'd take in a heartbeat."

April scraped the last bits of congealed cheese slime from the side of the ramekin and set the fork down, still hungry and hollow. It was like this whenever April thought about her mom. Her stomach turned into a ravenous pit that could never be filled.

"Your father?" Luc asked. "Is he still with us?"

"You mean alive? Yes, yes he is. 'With us,' on the other hand, is debatable."

"So you're not closer now that the tragedy is behind you?"

"I don't know that the tragedy's behind us," April said. "But we talk frequently. He's a champion e-mailer though he keeps me at a distance, has for twenty years. Plus they're in California and I'm in New York. I try to get out every couple months for a visit but my brother is involved much more than I am. It makes me feel bad on the one hand. On the other, who better? Brian handles this all so much better than I do. I'm glad he's the one who stayed in California, not me."

"You have a brother?"

April nodded.

"Brian is great. He's four years younger. Lives in San Francisco and is married to a nurse."

"Is Brian into the furniture as well?"

"Ha! No. He's a programmer with Google." April feigned typing. "It's actually pretty cool, for computer stuff. You know when you're searching something innocuous and an inane suggestion pops up? Say you want to learn more about dinosaurs and you've hardly finished the 'dino' part when Google suggests, 'Dinosaurs are Jesus ponies'?"

"'Dinosaurs are Jesus ponies.'" Luc wrinkled his nose. "I do not understand. Why are they Jesus ponies?"

"They're not. Okay, maybe this anecdote doesn't translate well. The point is that's his job. Well, a small part of it anyway. He is a programmer who creates bizarre phrases to make people laugh when they're searching the Internet."

"So he's funny. A humorist."

"Yes. Very funny. And a little weird too. But extremely funny."

"Like you." Luc grinned.

"I'm not the least bit funny."

"Perhaps I was speaking of the weird part."

"That's such an outlandish statement I can't even be offended. There are few people less weird than me. I am quite possibly the most average person you'll ever meet."

"Ah, so you *are* funny." Luc said and tapped the top of her hand. "Just as I suspected all along."

April smiled and shook her head. The moment had lifted. She'd told him about her mother, more than she should've thanks to the champagne, but sustained no internal injuries in the process. Now they were talking about Jesus ponies and how not funny she was. April felt safe again. Luc heard the summary version but never gleaned how deep the crack went.

"Well, should we get the bill?" April said, reaching down for her purse.

"Again, I'm sorry about your mother. It must've been hard."

"It still is," she admitted.

Luc leaned back in his chair, flagged down the waiter, and asked for an espresso and the check. When April glanced around she noticed they were the only two left in the restaurant.

"Thank you for telling me about her," Luc said. "Your mom. You're an interesting conversationalist when you stop tap-dancing around all my queries."

"Tap-dancing? I'm not sure about that, or about the interesting part. I'm okay, I guess, but I'm no Marthe de Florian."

April had told Luc the bare minimum about her mother, but it was not even close to full disclosure. Marthe probably would've revealed every last sordid detail and twist, with interesting sidebars about contortionists or enemas thrown in.

"Few people could be that fearless," April added.

"One only needs to try." Luc got his credit card back from the waiter.

"By the way, you said I could get this one."

"Next one. Shall we? It's past closing."

"We shall. Thanks for the meal. And the champagne. Both were delicious."

April popped off the chair and hooked her purse over one shoulder while fidgeting with her hair, which was somehow lodged beneath the straps. It was getting too long, out of control, now nearly reaching her bra. It always grew faster in France.

"Shall I walk you to your flat?" Luc asked. "This area is safe, but what kind of gentleman would I be if I did not?"

"Actually," April said quickly. "I'm going to do some browsing in the Galeries. Try to find a few gifts for my stepdaughters. . . ."

Though Chelsea's gift request specifically excluded the Galeries, April found herself suddenly anxious to leave Luc's company, to step out from his prying glare. She'd had a bit to drink and was getting overly forthright, the words (and other things) loosening in her chest. What was the phrase Troy always used when negotiating a deal? Right. She'd opened her robe too wide; given Luc too long a stare.

Plus April could feel her brain and good sense winding away from her. A voice chirped in her head, wondering if Luc's offer to walk her home had an ulterior motive. Something else—not a voice but something deeper, more instinctual—hoped that the motive was not altogether pure. The degree of this want terrified her.

"I can wait," Luc said with a shrug. "Until you are done with your shopping."

"No! No! That's okay. I might be a while," April said, then added hastily, "Thanks though. Very sweet."

"All right then."

Luc leaned toward her and kissed both cheeks, Parisian-style, needing no gimmick to get there this time.

"Au 'voir, Luc," April said, biting the inside of her bottom lip so she would not blurt out something she might regret. "Okay. Bye. Bye."

April floundered off in the opposite direction, her cheeks still burning from the scrape of his stubble. She was gone before he could say good-bye.

Chapitre XXXVI

Paris, 20 July 1892

The heat Paris summer brings! I quite miss the dampness of the convent at times, even if it settled as a low, wet cough at the bottom of my lungs most months of the year. At least in the summertime it was cool.

Though the streets of Paris have emptied out, the privileged absconding to their ancestral homes, the Folies is busy as ever, which for me is a good thing. I need the funds. Pierre remains in South America, sending me ever-decreasing funds and forever threatening to come home for good. And they do feel like threats. He heard from some unnamed source (Hello, Émilie!) that Robert de Montesquiou occupies my stool most nights of the week. Pierre is not pleased. His sources are not incorrect.

Ah, *Le Comte de Montesquiou*, the dandiest of the dandies with his girlish giggles and floral adornments. The pretty little man claims to be a poet, but his real occupation is having been born into wealth. It's true he spends a lot of time at my station, but *M. Le Comte* does not view me as a romantic interest. I am a sounding board off which he bounces his more outlandish exploits. It's not that my jaw on the floor means he will hold back. In fact, it's quite the opposite. The bigger my reaction, the more likely he'll trot the tale out for public consumption.

Truth be told, every so often I *do* contemplate Montesquiou as a romantic partner. He is silly with cash. Gold coins literally fall out of his pockets as he walks. But while Robert could provide a lady with the best adornments and the finest apartment, there is something so depressingly *unselective* about the man. He will have sex with anything, and have sex with anything he does.

It's funny that Pierre is so suspicious of Robert de Montesquiou yet never says a word about Boldini, the one person who should concern him. If I had a way to accurately assess Giovanni's earning potential, it might be out with *M. Merde* altogether! Though, I suppose, it is not that simple. Like his wealth, Boldini's disposition is utterly unpredictable.

He is such a little tempest of a man. Sometimes Boldini is the storm. Other times he is the calm before. He makes me nervous. He catches me unawares. He is impossible! More than once I've sworn him off entirely, so infuriating is he. Yet when we're apart all I can think of is the next time I'll see him, the next time we'll dine together.

Our favorite is Tortoni's, the place where the smart and literary gather. We often sit with Émile Zola. Sometimes Dumas fils joins us. All the good *boulevardiers* are there too, always at the ready with a clever comment, the perfect *mot juste*.

We sip beer or cassis with sparkling water or absinthe. We talk of politics and literature. We mock various Republican officials, unless they are with us, in which case we praise their efforts. I leave these meals feeling cultured and quite unlike the convent girl who came to Paris eighteen months ago. Whenever I grow glum, thinking too little has happened, I stop and remember the woman-child who watched Jeanne Hugo's marital procession. How very far I've come. Alas, for every grand and enlightening meal with Boldini, there are three more that conclude with me vowing to end relations forever!

Two days ago I arrived unannounced at his studio. I never know in what state I might find him when I arrive. This particular afternoon Boldini answered the door in nothing but a nightshirt, seven different colors of paint streaked through his thin and wiry hair.

"Hello, Giovanni," I said and tried to swing past.

He blocked the doorway, eyes unblinking, staring as though he'd never once gazed upon my face.

"Well, are you going to let me in?" I asked. "I walked all this way."

"You cannot come in," he replied gruffly.

It occurred to me that perhaps I'd hit the four-to-five a little too closely.

He had another woman in the studio. I hadn't known him to entertain others and had somehow convinced myself I was the only one who could tolerate his moods. Alas he is a man, and men have their needs, not the least of these variety.

"Oh," I said, biting my tongue to stop from sobbing. "I suppose you are occupied. Well, then, tell whoever it is I say hello."

I turned to go, sniffling.

"The world is ending!" he shouted. "I am a fraud!"

I stopped walking but did not turn back to face him.

"What do you mean, 'a fraud'?"

Was there a wife? A family? A stable of young men? God, the thoughts that assaulted me in those seconds! I should've known better. I should've known it was all about Boldini.

"I can't believe anyone would pay me to paint a portrait," he cried. "I am a hack, a sham, a novelty painter. I do not deserve to work in Sargent's hallowed studio! It is all too much! Are there any barman openings at the Folies? You must get me a position!"

Sighing, I turned back to face him.

"And what is wrong this time?" I asked.

"The Count. He wants me to attempt his portrait again. I cannot do it! I cannot get it right! He hates every version!"

"*Le Comte*? Montesquiou? Good lord, Boldini, that man will never be happy with a portrait of himself because it will never be as beautiful as the vision he has in his mind!"

"No, the problem is not the Count's. It is mine," he moaned, refusing to listen to an ounce of logic, as usual. "It is over, this painting folly. I will become a bad poet! A drunkard! Maybe both!"

"Well, then," I said, never one to participate in his storms of self-doubt. "Let me know if you wish to unload your paints and blank canvases. I'd like to take up portraiture myself. Seems an easy enough *hobby*."

Boldini emitted a long, low growl, grabbed his coat and hat, and announced he was off to the morgue to set his mind straight. Indeed it was the only place that could cheer him up. I thought to remind him he was still in a nightshirt, but decided it was unlikely the dead bodies would mind. Then again, there has been a rash of grisly deaths of late. The lines at the morgue's entrance often extend three blocks or more. Sometimes I wonder if that particular show gets more visitors than the Folies.

Giovanni Boldini. That funny, crazy man. Just writing his name makes me long to see him, to one-better our prior meeting. Perhaps he will stop in at the Folies tonight. Maybe he will saunter cheerily up to my bar, uplifted by the corpses, and announce a congress at Tortoni's. Dead bodies plus a hit of absinthe are really the best cure for that insane little man.

Chapitre XXXVII

April stumbled up the rue de Clichy, her half-crocked gait further compromised by burying her nose in Marthe's writing. Normally she'd reserve all provenance gathering (she was sticking to that story, it seemed) to an office or otherwise professional location. But she was in Paris. You stepped over history and walked past provenance at every turn. Also, she was a teensy bit drunk.

It was a miracle she heard the phone ring, her mind fully occupied by Marthe when it wasn't part of the way asleep, an even further miracle that she hadn't considered the caller.

"Troy?" April said, staring dumbly at the screen.

She'd forgotten that he was a possibility, that Troy was supposed to call and had not. Meet me in Paris. A suggestion to which he'd not replied. April felt the anger and hurt rebuild inside her.

"Troy Edward Vogt the third!" she called into the phone. "Well, well, well, as I live and breathe. It's lovely to hear from you!"

"Hello, I'm trying to reach April Vogt?"

Whether he was going for serious or funny April could not tell, though Troy was not particularly known for his humor or pranks. Birdie once called him the "antifrat guy," and April's mother-in-law said that at the onset of puberty he'd immediately morphed into a forty-three-year-old man.

"Hilarious!" April chirped. "My husband is hilarious. You are my husband, aren't you? I can't really be sure."

April turned a corner and wound around three couples who all looked as though they'd not fought a minute in their lives. Maybe they didn't have to. Maybe they all agreed on the four-to-five, giving one another the latitude to philander but only during prescribed times. If you agreed to misbehave, at least everyone remained on equal footing.

"April? Is that you?" Her husband's voice sounded genuinely concerned, not at all teasing, which confused April for a moment until she remembered this was Troy she was dealing with, not Luc.

"What? Are you expecting one of your *o-o-other* wives?" she asked, drawing out the vowels in an attempt at a British accent, but falling several glasses of champagne short of anything *Masterpiece Theatre*–worthy.

"What is wrong with you?" Troy said. "I've called seven times in the last five hours. You seem to be irritated, but I'm the one whose calls aren't getting returned."

"Well, I've been busy, you see," April said. She bumped into a streetlight, circled around it, and bumped into the next one. Somewhere behind her a group of men tittered.

"Busy doing what?"

"Oh, I'm sorry, is my work not important enough for le grand m'sieu?"

"Please speak English," Troy said.

"Well, you caught me. I was at the morgue. Looking at dead bodies. Some people find it relaxing."

"'*Dead bodies*'? Are you threatening me?"

"It's quite a popular hobby in Paris. You see, 'There has been a rash of grisly deaths of late,'" April said, using Marthe's words, a direct quote. "Corpse viewing is more popular than ever!"

"Are you drunk?"

"Non!" April said just as she realized she'd passed her apartment. She made a U-turn.

"Should I call back? After you sleep this off? Because you're not making sense at all."

"Mais que tu es bête!" April slipped through the front door of her building just as a flock of twenty-somethings stepped out. "No sleep for this girl. Tell me, what have you been up to this fine day? Working hard? No errands of mischief, I presume?"

"Well, no. On both accounts, I guess. I spent all day at a landfill," he said and chuckled. "I guess it was work, technically, though at a dump—"

"I can see why you find this all so amusing." April could not get her key into the lock. Was this even her apartment? She checked the number, then tried a fifth and sixth time. "Nothing like a site visit to a place perfectly well-suited to its visitors. Ha! Bankers, lawyers—and Willow. All standing in a landfill. Perfect. This is just too good. You have to be making it up."

"Not sure why I'd bother making up something about a landfill, but since you seem interested in the topic, our new acquisition gets its carbon offsets from landfill remodeling, so we had to check it out."

"I'm sure you did." April finally jammed the key into the lock and turned it so hard she thought it might snap in half. "By the by, I heard about the big par-tay at the Beauchamp Club. Was this before or after the landfill confab? I don't know how you fit it all in. You are a wonder, Troy Vogt."

"Uh, before, as a matter of fact. Who told you about the party?"

"One of my sources."

"Lemme guess. Birdie, am I right?"

"You've always been against her." April bodychecked the door and found herself at once lying in a pile in the middle of her floor.

"Did you just fall down?"

"Nope. Dropped a piece of Continental furniture. Twentieth century." She stood, brushing off the back of her skirt. "But I get it. You don't like Birdie because she's onto you. She has your number."

"She has nothing. And I don't not like Birdie. Not that I like her, either. In fact, I have exactly zero feelings or viewpoints on Birdie at all. Though it's a little disheartening to know you put greater stock in your assistant's word than in my own."

"Well, yeah."

"So what did she tell you? Specifically?"

"That there was a party, an all-night party. And you were there."

"Score one for the bird dog," Troy said. "Yes there was a party, and I was there. This is a fact. And I now have a Brioni suit that can't be saved thanks to the odor."

"How upsetting for you! So. Curious. Was Willow at this party?"

"It's odd. You say to stop bringing up her name yet you keep doing exactly that—"

"Answer the question, Vogt."

"Yep. She was there. And also at the closing dinner beforehand. We were on the same flight as well. Do you need the full itinerary?"

"Why?" April asked. "Why was she there? You've always said due diligence was her deal, but that happens before all the documents are signed."

"A closing is 1 percent work and 99 percent celebration," Troy said. "You know that. All the major contributors and stakeholders were there. It is absolutely meant to be an atta-boy for all involved. Lawyers. Bankers. Everyone. Why do I feel like I'm being grilled when I did nothing?"

"So the trip to London was, basically, about a dinner."

"Mostly. Yes."

"And a party."

"All right. Sure."

"And then you were at the landfill all day?" April said. "Like *all* day?"

"Yes. Several of us were. Willow was just one of many—"

"Please stop saying that godforsaken name."

"My colleague," he said, sighing loudly.

"I don't know if that's any better."

"Really? Colleague is your problem? You have them, certainly. Marc, Olivier—"

"Luc. You cannot forget Luc all of people. Mon dieu!"

"Who the fuck is Luc?"

"Here's my problem," April said, deflecting. "Since I need to spell it out for you. You spent all night at a party. You spent all day at a landfill. But you couldn't spare an extra six hours to come visit me in Paris. Nor could you spend the six minutes to explain why not. Or a mere six seconds to reply to my text, saying you could not make it."

"I'm sorry, but do you need your hearing checked? I told you this was all part of the closing. Mandatory."

"I'm sorry, but am I your wife?"

"I could pose the same question to you, April," he said. "Why didn't you take six hours out of your, what is it, *month* in Paris to come find me in London?"

"I have to work," she said.

"Exactly."

April slumped toward her bed. She'd hit a wall, an impasse so big there was no way around it. He had a point. She had a bunch of points before that. So many points made by the both of them. Unless you were playing Wimbledon, points seemed an awfully painful way to get out of or stay in a marriage.

"You're running," he said. "You do this when you're done with something and don't want to deal. You ran to New York to get away from your family situation. You ran to Paris when New York was tough. Then you ran back to New York again when Paris didn't work out."

"I lost my *job*. The museum shut down." She stopped short of the bed. "I would've stayed if I could've. Believe me. But the immigration folks don't really like when you overstay your welcome. They're funny like that."

"I can't keep doing this, April. You need to figure out what you want. If you can forgive me. If you can't. I'm guessing you can't. You're not the most forgiving person."

"What's that supposed to mean?"

"Your dad?"

"I forgave my dad. It's not like he intentionally set out to hurt me."

"Right." Troy laughed bitterly. "As opposed to myself. Here's the thing that kills me about your relationship with your father."

"We're doing this right now? Daddy issues?"

"You simultaneously can't get over his crappy handling of your mother's illness, at least according to you, while at the same time you hold me to the impossible standards he set. So devoted, this man. No one can compete with that level of fidelity."

"I wouldn't want you to! Chelsea and Chloe should always come first," April said, and meant it. "Them. Not me. It's never been in question so why you think—"

"This *thing*," Troy said, stomping over her words like the bull he so often was. "It's behind your eyes every time you look at me. It's even in your voice. I'm not going to always be perfect, or always do the right thing, because I'm not a perfect man. I'm sorry that I'm not, but at least I've never claimed to be. You have to understand that."

"I've never asked you to be perfect," April said. "I only asked you to be decent."

He was right, on some level. April had not forgiven him. She wanted to, desperately even. She loved Troy and the girls and their pretty life in New York City. Throughout the entire situation he was honest, forthright, upfront in a very Troy Edward Vogt III kind of way. I cheated on you, I'm not a perfect man, let's move on. It took guts, yes, but April wanted something more than "take it or leave it." She wanted grand gestures and promises made even if he wasn't 100 percent sure he could keep them.

"Can I ask you something?" she said.

It was a question April had been ignoring for a decade, and flat-out squelching for the last ninety days. Now, with the entirety of the night behind her, with Marthe and the champagne and yes, even, Luc, April found herself ready to toss the words into the universe.

"Did you cheat on Susannah?"

One long pause. Two pauses. Several more beats.

"I'm waiting," she said.

"I am surprised you're posing this question," Troy said, slowly, evenly. "Seems this could've been handled in the early stages of our relationship."

"In due diligence. Yeah. I get it. Shame on me, I guess. Answer the question."

"The reason our marriage ended has not changed since the first time we discussed this. Susannah had an affair with my best friend, and neither of them seemed willing to stop. Plus she's challenging to get along with on a daily basis, as you are aware."

"I didn't ask why the marriage ended. I already know that. I asked if you ever cheated on her."

"Yes," he said at last. "I did."

April let out a sob and slid to the ground. She sat there for several moments, unable to speak, her silent heaves vibrating against the centuries-old Parisian flooring. It was a big reaction to someone else's problem but felt almost like another betrayal of *her* marriage, not Susannah's.

"Are you shitting me?" Troy barked. "You're upset about Susannah? Let me remind you that she was cheating on me."

"Did you know that then?" April said. Not that it was an excuse. Retaliatory sex was ill-advised under any circumstance. But better everyone behaving badly and not just the man you were trying to believe.

"I suspected but wasn't sure. We were in a bad place. I shouldn't have done it but you asked and I don't want to lie. This has nothing to do with us. The circumstances were different. The entire marriage was different from the start. I knew it wouldn't work the second she set foot in the aisle. I was immature and stupid and forever doing things to sabotage the relationship."

"Maybe it *was* different, but you're not really inspiring great faith given it happened again, when you were supposedly in a good marriage. It's all semantics. I mean if you rob a credit union or you hold up a savings and loan, it doesn't really fucking matter, you're still a criminal and should be in jail."

"Wow. That's a new one. I didn't realize marital infractions were a sentenceable offense." Troy laughed dryly and then emitted a deep, long, exhausted sigh. "What I did was horrible but you're not being fair. You have a choice. You either can move past it or you can't. Which is it? The decision is yours."

April closed her eyes and lifted herself from the ground, holding tight to the bed frame for support. She understood all at once Troy would not give her what she was looking for. He could not offer the words or gestures or grand pronouncements to fix everything, to absolve him from past crimes. If anything the pronouncements only seemed to make things worse.

No, April had to get the absolution, whatever form it took, from herself. And Troy was right. She probably didn't have it in her.

"April?" Troy said, voice hoarse. "You still there?"

"I don't know, Troy. I truly don't. I have to go."

April had to go.

Her discarded phone hit the mattress moments before she collapsed on top of it. Face buried in the bedding, April dangled her feet over the blue-and-white woven rug. She let her right shoe drop to the floor. Her left shoe slid halfway off but stopped, suspended in midair, hanging several minutes until finally clonking to the floor.

As she succumbed to sleep, April continued to hear the sound of leather hitting wood, as if it reverberated in the apartment and throughout Paris, this, the final moment of letting go. Every girl knew when the last shoe came off her day was done, finished, well and truly over. It had to happen at some point. It all had to end. If you didn't see it coming, you simply weren't looking hard enough.

Chapitre XXXVIII

Paris, 1 July 1893

It is gone! Tortoni's has come to an end just as they said it would. The party, as they say, is over.

I can scarcely believe it, even after months of newspapers predicting its demise. When I rolled over in bed this morning to find Giovanni beside me sketching *Le Comte de Montesquiou* (the city's favorite dandy, this time with parrot). I said good morning. He said, "Tortoni's is no longer."

"You are a horrible liar." I sat up and straightened my nightgown, which had moved up around my hips.

"Check the newspaper." He said, nodding toward the foot of the bed. "It is there in black and white."

For once Giovanni was correct. As excerpted from yesterday's copy of the *Paris Herald*: "Tortoni disappears from Paris to-day. The café at the corner of the boulevard des Italiens and the rue Taitbout, which for a century has been known as one of the favorite resorts of men renowned in literature, the arts and the aristocracy, to-day follows the Restaurant Brébant, and goes the way of all the earth. On Saturday the work of demolition will begin, and another feature of old Paris will have passed away."

"Goes the way of all the earth"! I tear up to think of it.

This feels ominous somehow. It's cast a shadow over my entire mood. "It's only a café," Giovanni says time and again. "You already have Maxim's. No love lost, as far as I can tell."

But Tortoni's is more than just another café! For a girl who never had a Paris debut, it's as though I made mine in that very establishment. Even if it didn't happen at once, even if it occurred while La Belle Otero danced nearby, writhing around our table with sweat pouring down her legs and one breast falling out of her shirt. Sometimes people were maimed by sword or staff but the place was still glorious . . . and it was mine! Oh, Tortoni's, how I will miss you!

Now everyone will scramble to be the next Tortoni's. Since news of management troubles broke, cafés have sprung up around the city, all desperately trying to attract the best *boulevardiers.* Not the least of these is Maxime Gaillard's place, Maxim's, though he is the only one so far succeeding. This is because of his advertising schemes. He has four windows in the front of his restaurant, a ledge in each window, and a beauty atop each ledge! A genius idea, really, though it was I who gave him the notion during all the hours he spent at my bar.

Oh, did I mention? One of the beauties is me!

It's quickly become a position of prestige. A few of our most famous cancan dancers have expressed a desire to display themselves in the windows of Maxim's, but of all the Folies girls, I am the one he pays to perch like a bird (replete with feathers!). It's my face enticing guests through the front doors, my curved figure casting long shadows on the sidewalk outside. Of course it's hard to remain on my perch. I'm positively flocked by all the roosters who tromp in!

"Your *hair*!" they say. "The color of your hair is unrivaled!"

"Your skin! Smoother and whiter than a baby's bottom!"

Yes and thank you to both, due to the wonders of henna and the marvel that is my facial whitening cream. Not that I need it, of course. *Mon dieu!* It's merely a way to enhance that which God gave me. I suppose my parents left me a legacy after all. My mother lived not long but her beauty was legendary.

Although I must be careful not to stay too long beneath the admiring glances of the *boulevardiers.* Sometimes the overextended use of my precious cream tinges my skin almost yellow. Of course, I suppose there is ever-more cream to conceal this indignity! The things the beautiful must do to remain so. Games and trickery, Boldini says, though he could use a little cream and henna himself!

Maxim's is not my sole source of income, though sweet Maxime gives twice my rate at the Folies. Rather, he gives what he *thinks* is twice my rate but is really closer to three times! And while Gérard maintains strict rules about my Folies gown, I have free reign at Maxim's, the only requirement that I dress ravishingly enough to incite the financial ruination of at least three men per week. It's astounding how quickly these so-called gentlemen will turn their pockets inside out to ply me with food and gifts! Each and every man these days—*les paniers percés*. Baskets with holes in them, all of them.

Typically I occupy Maxim's window sporting a chinchilla coat and dining on champagne and caviar and whatever else men wish to send my way. I often wear an *aigrette* atop my head. It is a glorious if highly inconvenient adornment. The blasted white plume is forever in danger of being torched by the overhead light. But never mind all that—the important thing is that it looks spectacular!

So far Maxim's is a bona fide hit (you're welcome, M. Gaillard!) Perhaps it will even replace Tortoni's in stature. The grande dame of all grande dames *does* frequent the establishment. Yes, I'm referring to Jeanne Hugo Daudet. She could stand to spend a little *less* time there, as a matter of fact. Most nights she drinks herself silly. She once jumped atop the platform and began conducting the orchestra with an asparagus stalk.

Proust told me it's because she and her husband are destined for divorce. As delectable a piece of gossip as that is, I have a hard time believing it. Everyone knows Proust is filled with *merde* almost all of the time. Also . . . *divorce*? In *that* family? After the wedding and the presents? How could it all be worth nothing? It'd be silly to throw away so much over an argument or two. Boldini and I squabble on a near-constant basis. *C'est la vie!*

On several occasions I've attempted to approach Jeanne. Based on how zealously she avoids my window, she remembers me, though I've always suspected this was the case. Sometimes I catch her glancing my way, an invitation to come forward. When this happens I first check Maxime's position (he does not like me to leave my display), and if he is occupied I walk in her direction. Then, inevitably, something happens.

Once I managed to make it all the way to *Bonjour* when the Russians pranced in, as they are inclined to do. Jeanne went all bawdy, jumped on the bar, and screamed, "Here come the Cossacks!" How very Jeanne

Hugo Daudet. Ribald. Classless. She relies on her name and does positively nothing to earn it.

On that particular evening, as Jeanne strutted across the bartop, I skulked back into my corner to watch the Russians storm Maxim's, throwing gold coins as they barreled through. I could forgo all manner of men and Maxim's if I scooped up a healthy portion of the *louis d'or* the heathens toss whenever they enter a room. When no one's looking I do swipe a few. I fear I'm going to need them.

You see, just as Tortoni's has closed, gone to make way for something greater, my tenure with Pierre has likewise reached its conclusion. A week ago I received a telegram. Pierre said there will be no funds this month. I do not know if it's because he has no funds to give or whether he simply does not want to give them to me. I'd come to count on these monthly stipends from South America. Despite knowing his patience with me had worn thin, I did not think his largesse would so quickly follow suit.

Don't misunderstand. Maxime and even Gérard, they both pay fairly and I've no complaints as to my wages. But there is keeping a coat on and your chamber warm, which is necessary, and there is wearing chinchilla and feathers, which is also necessary, but in a different way.

So I made one last effort to save my monthly check. This morning, after a long night at Maxim's and then with Giovanni, I came home and dashed off a quick note on my finest pink linen paper. In it I praised Pierre's manhood and his business acumen. Then I dipped my left breast in some whitening powder and made an imprint at the bottom of the letter. I can only hope this reminder of my skin will survive across the oceans and buy me some time.

Chapitre XXXIX

The flat appeared emptier than it had ten hours before.

April assumed she had been the last to leave, but sometime between La Terrasse and this moment, someone had moved at least a dozen things, including poor Mr. Mouse. Mickey was now supine atop a carton of old books, a "return to sender" sticky note slapped haphazardly onto his face.

Stepping over the piles, April teetered forward and reached for the animal.

"Oh, Mickey," she said and pulled the dusty, round-eared critter into her chest. "They're sending you away."

Using the scarf tied to her tote, April gently rubbed the top of his head. Pieces of black fuzz stuck to the navy and gold silk.

"Cripes. Sorry, little guy. You're in bad enough shape as it is."

She brought him to her nose. He smelled, yes, dusty and old, but there was something else. Sweet. Floral. Marthe's perfume, perhaps? Lisette Quatremer's? It comforted April to think that when you were gone people might still recognize glimpses of you. Assuming, of course, someone left a space for you to linger.

April placed the doll on the Napoleon III console table she'd started on the evening before.

"You should see what's happening to your home, Mickey," April said and took out a notepad. "It's a travesty."

She started to write.

Napoleon III giltwood and ebonized mirror and console table. On back: "No 2."

Third quarter nineteenth century?

Mirror with C-scrolls, flowers, and rocaille ornament.

Crescent moon, three stars flanked by a pair of doves.

Rouge royale serpentine marble top, cabriole legs.

April checked the back, which bore a label inscribed: "De la grand antichambre/de Kiosque de Gezira/Console or et ébène." She smiled, astonished. Only Marthe de Florian would own a piece that once lived in a palace in Cairo.

"Grand Antechamber, Gezira Palace," she wrote, and underlined it twice. Hardly fit for lot 379 of a "random European crap" auction.

Suddenly April heard the sound of a key trying the lock. She stepped behind the console and reached for a decorative sword. It wasn't sharp but could do some damage if smashed across an interloper's skull.

"Hello?" she squawked before the door opened. "Bonjour?"

Luc stepped into the hallway.

"Avril?"

"Oh, Jesus." April exhaled. She peered out from her hiding place. "You scared me. Again."

"You have my eternal apologies," Luc said as he set his satchel on the floor. "I did not expect to see anyone on a Saturday. What are you doing here?"

"Catching up on a little work."

Occupying her brain. Trying not to think about the man across the Channel or the woman with him.

"In Paris on a weekend and you only work. How positively dreary."

"You're here as well," April said and stepped around a black dresser. "Thus you are equally dreary."

"Ah, yes, but I've just come to look for a particular painting as directed by Madame Vannier. I will then immediately proceed to my weekend, not a thought of work until Monday."

"If you're here for a painting you're out of luck. All artwork is now offsite. Olivier and Marc can give you access to the warehouse on Monday. I doubt they're around today. Sorry you wasted the trip."

"It's no waste," he said with a shrug and proceeded to rest against a lacquered commode, a Riesener number that was a copy of one of the most famous pieces of French royal furniture. The word "copy" sounded cut-rate until you considered it would sell for three hundred thousand dollars at least.

"Can you not lean against the property?" April asked. "Here. I have something for you. Given your propensity to lounge, I've had some folding chairs brought in specifically for your use." She pointed to the corner. "Do you mind?"

"Ah, our Avril. Forever scheming when it comes to her bureaus and knickknacks."

Trying to act put-upon, Luc grabbed a chair and dragged it against the floor. Within seconds April was on hands and knees, trying to buff out the scratch.

"You may take all the precautions you desire, but it seems I cause damage no matter what I do." Luc said with a grin. "So is it a Linke? This commode? You see, I do listen to your furniture sermons."

"Though not closely enough," April grinned back. "You're about a century and a half off. No, this is a Jean-Henri Riesener. He was the official ébéniste du roi—cabinetmaker to the king. It's a copy of a piece owned by the royal family. See here? Marie Antoinette's monogram is on the front."

Luc lowered onto his chair, squinting, looking vaguely thoughtful if not moderately fatigued.

"Anyway, I'll spare you more of my *sermons*. But have you seen this?" April said and reached behind her for the previously discarded sword. She heaved it upward and swung it around, grossly misjudging its heft and inadvertently thwacking Luc in the knee. He was less than one-half meter from receiving blunt-force trauma to the groin.

"Mon dieu!" he yelped.

"Oops, sorry. Is your knee okay?"

"My knee is not the body part I'm concerned with. A very close call, Avril. My future children thank you."

"Good thing I'm only a little bit clumsy," April said, blushing hard. "Anyway, isn't this sword beautiful? You're a dude. You should like weapons, right?"

"I am in fact a *dude*, though not by the strictest American definition, I suspect."

"You are correct on that count," April said and ran a finger down the sword's blade. "I don't know how we'll value this, or if it has any value at all. I wonder if Marthe used it to scare away her overly pushy paramours. Or a rival!"

April lunged forward and pretended to pierce the gut of Jeanne Hugo, though her imagined fictional violence did not stop at that one person. She wondered if anyone had ever stabbed an environmentalist, a venture-fund impresario.

"Anyway." April placed the sword back in its sheath. "Enough screwing around."

"Avril, why are you frowning?"

"What do you mean, 'frowning'?"

"From the moment I walked in you have shown me a deep scowl." Luc ran a finger between his eyes. "What's wrong? Do we have another furniture crisis on our hands?"

"No, nothing like that."

April pulled out another folding chair and placed it across from Luc's. At once her legs felt weak. She wasn't twenty-five anymore. She couldn't operate in a constant state of medium-to-high-grade stress and then expect to sling a sword around without suffering a few physical effects.

"I've been thinking about Marthe a lot this morning," April said, an accurate statement though not the full story.

"This morning? I was under the impression you thought of Madame de Florian every hour of the day." Luc chuckled. When April didn't respond he gently touched her knee. "I'm only teasing, ma chérie. Tell me, what were you thinking about?"

"The four-to-five," April admitted. "Also known to Marthe and friends as the approved philandering hour."

"Ah, I see, the infidelity offends your puritanical sensibilities."

"No! Not at all," April said, trying to put her thoughts into words that did not say too much. "Actually, there's something to be said for the arrangement. Everyone agrees, so no one must discuss it. No one can get mad. It's not scandalous. It just is. It's like letting your teenager have wine with Sunday dinner. It demystifies everything."

"Are you suggesting a revival of the four-to-five?" Luc asked. "I'd venture to guess you could find widespread support for the idea, though probably only with the men."

"Yeah, the concept probably wouldn't take," April said. "Random question. Would you want to know if your wife was having an affair?"

"I've never had a wife."

"Assume you did. Would you care?"

"As with anything, it would depend on the situation," Luc said. "In general, non. I would not 'care' as you say. It is not the worst thing in the world. Why do I have the feeling this is not a compulsory question?"

April inhaled and studied Luc from the corners of her eyes.

"My husband," she started. "Well, he . . ."

April shook her head.

"He and I have this debate," she added quickly. "A friend of ours, her husband had a one-night stand."

"Your *friend*." Luc nodded with understanding. Of course this *would* be the one American subtlety he was able to interpret.

"Oui." April said but looked away, feeling no need to confirm his sudden mastery of American subtext. "The husband told her about this tryst. To be clear, it was not an affair, only a mistake in judgment."

April could've provided more details of her friend's predicament. She could've said the husband was in Singapore for work. Closing a deal. There was a dinner and too much of some kind of liquor he'd never had. And there was a consultant. The two wound up back in his hotel room. He called his wife ten minutes later and confessed everything. One hundred days later the conversation continued to loop in her brain.

"How big was the mistake?" Luc asked. "According to the couple, whose opinions matter, not according to anyone else."

"There was sex. But it's never only that, right?"

April pictured her husband's hands running over someone else's breasts, along her thighs, beneath her underwear. Troy had his mouth on her nipples. Yet another fact April didn't need to recall or imagine.

"What do you mean, 'it's never only that'?" Luc asked.

"Well, there are many stops on the road to consummation."

"Ah," Luc said. "So, what is the debate then? Between you and your husband? Though it must be said, debating others' marital problems is a bit questionable."

He raised his eyebrows, challenging her.

"Oh, she doesn't mind," April mumbled. "The debate is this: I think he never should've told his wife. Troy thinks it was admirable of the guy to come clean."

"And what does your *friend* believe?"

"She wishes she never knew."

April had toyed with the thought since it happened, but this was the first time she bought it all the way. Though she was not proud of the statement, it felt good to say it out loud instead of think about in the abstract. Luc was not the first person to hear about this fictional friend. April told herself the lie, too.

"Why's that?" Luc asked. "Why wouldn't she want to know?"

"It put her in a bad position. If it wasn't going to happen again, why tell her? To relieve his guilt? Get it off of his chest and onto hers? Who did the admission help other than him?"

"Yes, it mostly helped him, although some might argue 'Truth above all else.' Isn't honesty part of the reason she married her husband?"

"Absolutely. But now she worries, she worries constantly. And the husband. He's almost smug about it, his righteous truth-telling. The forgiving, for him, seems to be a foregone conclusion, an expectation. It's as though, sorry I did this, but I'm not perfect so . . . read between the lines."

"She's anticipating it might happen again."

"Yes," April said. "And the anticipation is almost the worst part. Maybe she should implement Marthe's four-to-five. Somehow get it included with all the other unspoken societal agreements. You open the door for old ladies. You throw out your trash. You are allowed the occasional meaningless tryst as long as it doesn't disrupt your regularly scheduled program. No one is surprised. No one looks stupid."

"You don't really believe this."

"Don't I?"

"Personally, I think it's a fantastic idea," Luc said. "If you want to know the truth—"

Suddenly his phone rang. Luc looked at the Caller ID and grimaced.

"Merde," he said under his breath. "I have to go. Can we continue this conversation later?"

"No. I mean, we can. But it's unnecessary."

"I wholeheartedly disagree." He stood. His knees creaked on the way up. "I'm sorry to dash off like this. I wouldn't unless I absolutely had to. Do you mind that I'm leaving you here alone?"

"Of course not, alone is how I started."

Luc placed his folding chair in the corner, careful not to scrape its metal legs against the floor a second time. Walking back to her, he began with his usual smile, followed by the "au 'voir, Avril" she could nearly hear in her sleep.

"Take care of yourself," he said.

April smiled weakly in return but did not get up. She couldn't do it. Her legs (her body, her mind) lacked the power to stand. Though she now looked forward to their physical farewells April simply couldn't muster the strength.

"Bye, Luc," she said, sounding like Chelsea or Chloe or any given American teenager. "See ya later."

"This will never do. Here." He reached out a hand. "Lève-toi."

"Luc, just go, okay? I'm exhausted. You don't want to be trifling with a grumpy—"

Without warning Luc learned over and pulled April upright and ultimately straight into him. As she stood, fuzzy-brained and eyes blinking, Luc bowed his head and placed a delicate but firm kiss on one cheek: "Take care"—and then the other—"sweet Avril."

He turned and disappeared from the flat. April remained frozen for several minutes, surprised to find she could stand after all.

Part Trois

Chapitre XL

April tried to ignore the quickly flipping calendar as the furniture in Marthe's flat continued to dwindle. On the plus side, each remaining piece required more effort than the last. April saw anomalies. She had questions that required more research. Time. She needed more of it.

Inlaid with boxwood and ebonized lines, the piece has a breakfront demilune red griotte marble top above a paneled frieze. There are three drawers and two hinged side drawers with laurel-leaf decoration and a central tablet inlaid with fleurs-de-lis. Two long paneled drawers are inlaid sans traverse with a marquetry center [repainted?] panel featuring a basket of peaches and flowers, flanked on each side by a hinged door simulated as two short drawers. The commode stands on hairy lion-paw feet and features acanthus legs [refinished?]. Each foot rests on a plinth.

Questions upon questions, ever more excuses to keep working, to stay in Paris. Maybe she could stretch her trip a few days. The best thing about research was it could never be fully exhausted. And, as April told Peter and Olivier and anyone who cared to listen, she was waiting on an interview with Agnès, Madame Vannier, a woman who could well prove the most intriguing research source of all. Thankfully she was not yet dead.

It was a Wednesday afternoon and April sat in one of her folding chairs inspecting a bronze figure by Aimé-Jules Dalou. April had seen his sculptures before, in museums and the Luxembourg Gardens, but she'd never held one in her hand. Usually his works were on a grander scale, standing as monuments and not household decorations. Where did Marthe secure this piece, April wondered? Was it from Boldini or Montesquiou or the shit tycoon? Or did it come from Dalou himself? Marthe had to be the sole woman in history for whom all these possibilities had an equal chance of being true.

This statue, like so many of Dalou's, was a nude, a woman with a rounded back and bottom, both knees tucked up into her chest. She sat on a rock, undressed, resting chin on shoulder and contemplating the stream below. April felt a little like Dalou's nude at that moment: curled into herself, totally exposed but showing nothing, the inevitable dunk into cold, fast water minutes away.

April snapped a picture of the statue with her phone. She had a camera she used for work, but this photograph she would e-mail to Troy along with a breezy comment about how it'd look great in their apartment. Feel free to buy this at auction! Just kidding. (Not really).

But April remembered she could not share this with Troy. Well, she could, but he'd wonder why the hell April was talking home decor when she was supposed to be figuring out whether she wanted to stick around their apartment in the first place.

They hadn't spoken in four days, only e-mailed or texted, throwing out excuses about work and time differences to account for the lack of phone communication. *Je vais tomber dans les vapes!* I'm so tired I could pass out! Both fully comprehended the subterfuge, which left April to question why they bothered at all by now.

"Zut!" April said to the BlackBerry screen. "No Dalou for me."

Like a rattlesnake, the phone buzzed in her hand. April tossed it to the floor as if it might have an actual bite. The BlackBerry rang on. April crouched down to pick it up.

"Oh, Birdie, hi."

Was she relieved? Disappointed? She could describe furniture all day long, but not her own feelings when looking at someone else's phone number.

"Did you get the copy I sent last night?" April asked.

"I did," Birdie said. "Thanks. It's now on Peter's desk. The man is, by the way, annoyingly anxious for your return. He keeps asking when you'll be back."

"How sweet. He misses me. Alas, my flight isn't until July eleven."

"I know, I've told him 51,000 times but somehow he can't remember longer than ten minutes. He, like, cannot function without you or something. It's pathetic. He even asked if you can come back earlier."

"Earlier?" April balked. She thought of Madame Vannier. She thought of Troy. "No, I cannot do earlier."

"Yeah, I know, and I'm stalling like a bastard, but it's not easy. The woman's still alive, right? The heir?"

"Yes. Still alive. For now."

"Good. I have a few interesting comps, like we talked about—properties sold within their own themed auctions versus part of a bigger group. There's not a ton of one-for-one, but maybe it's a start. Anyway, I'll send you what I have."

"Thanks," April said and sighed.

"Chin up! Peter is totally on our side."

"Which is great, but I'm not sure he has much pull over here."

"When is this quote-unquote unreachable woman going to be reachable again?" Birdie asked. "Maybe she can sway the Paris office?"

"That's the hope, but she's a wild card. She's ill and in the hospital. So the timeline is a little hazy."

"What if you don't get to talk to her before you're supposed to leave? Can you, like, call her or something?"

"Oh, I'll talk to her," April said. "I'll stay an extra week. Two weeks. A month. I'll show up at her deathbed if I have to."

She was surprised to hear herself say it out loud. As her upcoming flight loomed (July 11: two weeks), April woke each morning a little queasier, a bit more anxious. The reservation was made to get her home for her birthday. If she stayed in Paris April would spend it alone, though a lonely "celebration" was on the docket in New York, too. Lord knew it was better to be solo in Paris than in your own home. Yes. She would extend the trip. Peter said to take as long as she needed. There was no shortage of need.

"Extend the trip?" Birdie said and laughed. "You've got to be shitting me. Peter's head would explode."

"Wouldn't be the first time."

"Why do I feel as though you're going to stay forever? Like you'll somehow end up working for the Paris office?"

"Sounds delightful, but I do have a job and a life back in New York." Not that "back in New York" wasn't terrifying. Not that April's "back in New York" would look at all the same as when she left it. "I'll need to return at some point."

"As long as you realize that. Because you *will* have to come home." Birdie's voice dropped as if delivering bad news. She added earnestly, "This is your home."

"I know," April said. "Well, let's see how much I get done in the next week or so. Remind Peter about the interview. Tell him I'm still waiting."

There was a slight hesitation, as if Birdie was about to issue her obligatory "sure thing" but decided instead to wait. Maybe she knew what would come next. Maybe she sensed a pause was exactly what April needed. On the other hand, she might've simply choked on some breakfast muffin as she had so many times before.

Whatever the case, Birdie was silent a single moment too long. Enough so that April was able to slip in, before anyone could think better of it, "You know what? Tell Peter tough shit. Extend my return flight. By two weeks. For now."

Chapitre XLI

Paris, 30 November 1893

It's been months since I've written in this journal. So much to tell but so little I can say!

Well it's happened. Yesterday the final letter from Pierre arrived. My guano gent knew the sorts of things I'd been up to and declared he'd no longer fund my exploits. To which *specific* exploits he refers I do not know. He told me not to respond, not to beg or plead or send any more imprints of my flesh. We are done. He paid for the apartment through the end of the year, and then I must find alternate housing. I will have to move! Next month! I cannot afford it. Where has the money gone? Into frocks and shoes and champagne, I suppose. I thought I'd made more!

I went to Boldini. He would save me, I knew. Our relationship has developed into something more than I'd intended at the outset. It is one of kinship, not objects or necessities. Indeed he hasn't bought me one damn thing, and more often than not *I'm* paying for *his* meal at Maxim's!

Over all these months I'd built goodwill. I was less expensive than any other paramour he might have entertained in his lifetime. As such, he should have no problem helping me through this sticky time. Why, I was downright cheery when I marched toward his flat, figures dancing in my brain. Giovanni would come through, I was certain!

He was fresh from the morgue when I swept into his studio. I was glad for the good spirits in which the corpses always put him. It was the perfect confluence of circumstances. For a moment I was glad Pierre cut me off. No more distant noose around my neck! Able to spend time with Boldini, free of any sense of guilt! Not that I experience guilt, as a rule, but sometimes these feelings sneak up and surprise you.

"I have great news!" I told Giovanni as I strode through the door and twirled for his benefit, the skirt of my gown fanning out behind me. "I am in love with you. I have ended my relationship with Pierre so we can be together without reproach, without the gossiping mouths of the dance hall girls and boys!"

"You love me?"

He scrunched his face as if tasting one of Marguérite's dastardly collations. Poor child thinks when she's done with the Folies she will become a chef in the finest restaurants in town. (A female chef!) Her food is dreadful, and the only place she's actually going to wind up is in jail for poisoning guests. That and too fat for contortioning due to oversampling of food!

"You love me," he repeated.

Again with the sour face.

"Indeed!" I danced up to him and wrapped my arms around his neck. "We can be together! Forever! No Pierre to block the way."

Giovanni then looked at me squarely, wiggled his nose, and said, "Marthe, I adore you. But I am not rich enough to love you."

"How could you say that?" I cried. Oh, the heartbreak! The immediate fracture across my chest! "You cannot refuse my love. I want to get married!"

"No you do not," he said. "You are only bored."

"I love you, Boldini, you idiot! With my whole heart!"

I put a hand to my forehead and attempted to pass out. He caught me before I landed.

"I have quite a lot of work to do," he said. "Please take your theatrics elsewhere. I will call on you later."

"You don't have time for love?"

"I have time for love. I said I cannot afford it. What I do not have time for are your variant emotional states, which are another matter entirely. Please. Begone with you. I will see you later."

What could I say? Filled to the hairline with humiliation, I slunk out of his studio. Despite Sœur Marie's long-ago admonishments I allowed my sobs to break loose on the streets, emotionally naked for the world to see.

I then did the only thing I could: I proceeded immediately to Marguérite's new flat. That she has a new flat when I am in such constant straits confounds me. Marguérite has had lovers, lovers aplenty, but they are all women!

At first I thought her penchant for the gentler sex was a ruse, a way to attract a certain kind of male. Yet her dedication remains steadfast. She has no sexual interest in men, she claims. Can you believe such a thing? Counting on women to support you? Honestly! She might as well wait for pixie dust and talking giraffes! I suppose this mythical line of thinking is why Marguérite believes she can cook meals for the great men of literature and arts and actually get paid for it.

When I arrived at Marguérite's mysteriously acquired flat she was contorted into a figure eight. She answered the door this way, her bottom up above her head, debuting like a turkey looking for a mate. Momentarily relieved of my own problems, I asked why she could not greet visitors in a normal fashion. Then I breezed past and into her surprisingly grand parlor. Marguerite followed, waddling across the floorboards, still all tied up in her salacious numeral.

"What's wrong?" she said, her voice twisted and guttural, giving new meaning to the term "talking from one's ass."

"My life is over!" I wailed and fell onto a couch. Unlike Boldini, she did not stop my descent.

As I worked up the best of my sobs, I rubbed the seat with my fingers. It was made of a smooth velvet pattern and far nicer than anything in my flat.

"Where did you get this?" I could not help but ask. I sprang into an upright position and ran my hand along the nailhead detail on the seatback. "This is extraordinary."

"I purchased it. How else? Tell me, Marthe, do you need money, is that why you've come?"

"And why do you assume this?"

"Because the only time you get this emotional is over francs and louis!"

"All right," I said. "You are correct. I am having some financial difficulties. Pierre has cut me off."

"It is only a wonder it took him this long. What happened to your wages?"

"Gone! The necessities in life are dear. I do not make as much as the stage performers, it seems."

"You don't make as much? Ha!" Marguerite snorted and pulled herself to standing. Her boobs dripped down toward her waist. The nipples were brown, fat, and erect. "I've always said you should have the Folies give your wages straight to Maxime and save time!"

"Please, Marguérite, I beg of you, for your oldest friend?"

"All right," she sighed. "I cannot give you much. But I will give you what I can."

"Well, thank you," I said, trying to smile. "I am much obliged."

"Please use it for food and other necessities, not your chinchilla wraps or questionable beauty products."

"Questionable?!"

"Marthe—"

"Très bien," I sniffed. "As you wish."

After taking possession of the funds and watching Marguérite demonstrate her latest contortionist feat, I bade my friend adieu and walked back out onto the street. The sky had grown dark. Black clouds hung low over the city, and the air was damp. As I counted the moneys, panic took hold around my neck. Marguérite's funds would only last a month or two. The time would go fast.

Afraid to return to my flat, to bump into any knowledgeable landlords, I stumbled down to Maxim's for a quick drink. Alas, as often happens, one cocktail turned into three turned into four and more. Before long I was dancing with La Belle Otero in between the tables, her collection of pink rabbits scampering beneath the chairs. I stepped on at least one.

We had a grand evening. For a time. Then, while wrapping a scarf around my head and between my legs at the instruction of La Belle, I looked up and saw her. Jeanne Hugo. She was very obviously watching me. It seemed the optimal time to confront the woman.

After pushing La Belle Otero aside, I marched straight across the restaurant to where Jeanne sat atop a piano, legs crossed, the skirt of her gown draped in a most strategic way. It must be said: she is not the plain toast anymore. For the sake of her reputation, she could afford to be a little *more* plain.

According to Maxime I shoved over not one but two waiters on my way to the piano. When I reached Jeanne, I put one hand on either side of her and brought our noses to touch. She'd been drinking champagne. The smell was on her breath.

"How does it feel?" I asked, tears running down my face. "To be able to sit on some poor sap's piano without a care for tomorrow? Knowing what you know, knowing what you've taken from others?"

"Why do you assume I don't have a care for tomorrow?" she asked and guzzled champagne straight from a bottle. "Perhaps I have a lot of cares. Perhaps even more than you."

"You don't have to worry about feeding yourself, do you? Or where you will live? Or how you will buy the next most fashionable coat or hat? You have everything!"

"Everything is not everything," she said.

Everything was not everything? Everything *was* everything, and it meant so much. It meant my life.

Jeanne never had to be with a man who repulsed her, one who reeked of *merde* from a cave. She didn't need to roost in a goddamn barroom window, back aching, to pay off a dressmaker or two, all the while smiling at a hundred more men who made the bat guano swain look like a prince.

She never worked behind a bar, staring longingly at the stage, wondering how she could get beneath the lights. Nor did she have to borrow money from the very friend she was supposed to be looking after or try to persuade a man to love her in order to pay the rent, when really love was all she felt in the first place. And yet! Yet this was a place I could stand and legitimately say I'd come far. *Mon dieu!* The indignity.

" 'Not everything'?" I said, frenzied past any modicum of decency. The marriage, the presents, the four homes: This was her "not everything." All of it from a stroke of luck and a little bit of wiliness to boot. "I don't know how you can say those words when you're who you are. When you know who I am!"

"You? You are nothing but a crazy lady! Always have been."

Dizzy with rage, I yanked the champagne bottle from her hand and threw it against the wall, narrowly missing Maxime's group of midget friends. The room went dead. The piano player stopped. My breath stopped, too.

"Here come the Cossacks!" someone called. Everyone looked from Jeanne and me toward the door, and there they were, spilling into the room like hens freed from a coop. The Russians.

"The Cossacks!" the room shouted in unison.

"Save yourselves, here come the Cossacks!"

A call back to Waterloo, but a call that all current battles were over. It was time to have another round, to gather gold coins from the floor.

Precisely on cue the pianist started banging on the keys and people cheered. Somehow I got swept up in a crowd moving toward the door and was ultimately deposited outside. I landed on the sidewalk, my dress and spirit torn. Everyone had forgotten me, which was either a relief or the worst feeling in the world.

Tripping down the rue Royale, sobbing against the background cheers of Maxim's revelers, I bumped into an old friend. It was Pujol, our city's beloved flatulist. I never thought a farter could present such a romantic vision, but there he was, dandy and dapper, whistling as he went.

"Joseph!" I cried and threw myself into him. "My world is ending! I cannot go on!"

"Ma chérie," he replied and stroked my hair. "Whatever is the matter?"

I hiccupped and then poured my troubles at his feet. He nodded while I spoke, eyes downcast, the lone person sympathetic to my plight.

"Oh, sweet Marthe, I am sorry you are in such a state," he said. "Are they not paying you enough at the Folies?"

"They are plenty generous," I said and looked up at him, hoping that, despite the tears, he still found me beautiful, that the whitewashes and hair dye achieved their desired effects. "I am in such a bind!"

"Well, let me help you."

"Really?" I blinked hard, trying to make my eyes big and weepy like Marguérite's. "Oh, could you? I would be so grateful! I promise, whatever you want—"

He stepped back.

"Please. You do not need to promise anything. I am happy to help. Though I am a little low on cash myself I will try to come up with something. I might need to find a little creativity, but I will do my best."

Crying big, plump tears of relief, I hugged him again. He offered no figures or guarantees, only a promise, which seemed as valuable as the Cossack gold. I needed only that—a promise of help, undefined, with the possibility to stretch forever.

Chapitre XLII

April?" a gruff, irritated voice snarled into the phone.

More than a week had passed. April thought she was in the clear given her extended ticket and not a peep from anyone back in New York. Usually Peter favored in-the-moment reactive rants, but this was worse. He'd given himself time to stew.

"Peter?" April replied meekly. "How are you?"

"This is unacceptable!"

Phone hot against her ear, April walked to the window. Since the weather had finally warmed, noontime in Marthe's apartment was stifling, the air thick with allergens and smoldering clouds of dust.

"Whatever has riled you up"—she started, despite knowing exactly the whatever—"I'm sure it's not that bad."

"Don't play dumb with me, Vogt. This is about your e-mail and the revised itinerary Birdie printed out and smacked on my desk."

"We made the plans over a week ago."

"*We* made the plans? Ha! That's rich. I don't remember being involved. Who is this 'we' you speak of?"

"Fine. I made the plans. Birdie followed my directive. Regardless, this all happened eight, nine days ago? You're getting upset *now*?"

"It's taken me this long to calm down! I should fire you right now. In fact I think I will."

Peter was like this, bombastic, prone to flying off handles. He threatened to fire April at least once a month even though performance reviews contained only accolades and great long declarations about the extent of April's talent and expertise.

"You're supposed to be in the office on *Monday*," he went on, voice climbing with each word. "We're not exactly sitting around here scratching our asses, wondering what good ol' April is up to. There's work to be done. Other auctions. I had to go look at some house on Long Island *by myself.*"

"How awful," April said. "And I'm sorry I'm not there to help. But I wouldn't have extended the trip if it wasn't completely necessary. You said I could, remember? When you first sent me? You said take as long as I needed. I need longer."

Peter sighed, the fight seeping out of him already.

"Birdie said you were supportive of what we're doing," April reminded him. "And that you were in full agreement. C'mon, Pete. You know I'm right."

He sighed again, loudly, to make sure April heard.

"Do not call me Pete."

"Come on, boss. You know I have to stay."

"You realize this costs us money, don't you?" he said. "And auction season is fast approaching. I need you in New York. Even Karen wants you back. Apparently I'm insufferable when you're gone. My wife does not like being called during the day, it seems, at least not to discuss work. You're making us both miserable! You're wrecking our marriage!"

"Send her my sincerest apologies," April said, stifling a laugh, since he sounded so forlorn. "I so wish I was there to be on the receiving end of your constant work-related stress. But the extra time in Paris will pay for itself in the end. The better the provenance, the higher the sale, the higher the premiums. You taught me that, Peter. It's exactly what you would do yourself. The old Peter. The young and hungry one."

Peter blubbered his lips as April braced herself for a response.

"It would behoove you not to insult my age," he said. "All right. You've got two more weeks."

"*Yay!*" April yelped. "And to be clear, you mean two from today? Because—"

"*Two*. From *today*."

April squeaked again.

"Then that's it," he said. "No more BS extensions."

"Great. Perfect."

"I don't know why I let you get away with these shenanigans," Peter grumbled.

"It will pay for itself in the end!" April said again, happily. "Promise! Okay, I'd better get back to work so I can be ready."

"Yes. You'd better."

The phone went dark.

Breathless with the sweet, glorious thrill of victory, April scrambled around the apartment collecting files and notecards. It was Friday, and Olivier and Marc had left for their country homes the night before. April saw no reason to stick around ingesting dust particles. She would spend the balance of the afternoon working at the place des Vosges, in the sunshine.

At one o'clock the city heat was almost unbearable. After weeks languishing in the drizzly-gray fifties and sixties, the weather had taken a sudden shot upward, landing somewhere in the midnineties and enveloping Paris in a thick, damp blanket of heat. When talking Celsius, which April did for dramatic effect, the temperature nearly tripled in a few days' time.

Straddling the Third and Fourth Arrondissements, the place des Vosges was a bit of a hike from the Ninth, especially when carrying a laptop and sweating profusely, but it was one of April's favorite spots in all of Paris. Her furniture museum had been only a few blocks away, and rare was the day she hadn't walked beneath the arches of the square or stepped out onto its grass.

Many years had passed since she'd last seen the Vosges, but April could still picture the red-brick and white stone buildings, their steep blue slate roofs, and the two-tiered fountain with its water-spitting lions. Henry IV created the place des Vosges as a royal pavilion more than four hundred years before. Now the buildings included shops, restaurants, and upscale Renaissance townhomes. But before all that, and for centuries, it was the preferred location for duels. April wondered if any of Marthe's cohorts ever matched up on the lawns. It was hard to imagine swords or pistols where now lovers, sunbathers, and toddlers littered the grounds.

April found a table beneath one of the arcades. She pulled out her laptop and started to work. Already crowded when she appeared, the park grew ever-more populated with each passing minute. Stylish mothers arrived with their soft-haired tots, seeking shaded sandboxes. Smartly dressed couples strolled by, hand in hand, sometimes speaking animatedly and other times not at all. Tourists and backpackers reclined on the grass.

April wanted to recline on the grass, too. Peter was antsy, but how much work did she really have to finish right then? It was almost the weekend. All good Parisians were already off and enjoying their respite. As the thoughts trickled though her mind, April could almost feel Peter's rage from across the ocean.

The answer was, of course, all of it. She had to do *all* the work, and as quickly as possible.

Gazing with some degree of longing at the backpackers (*Mon dieu*, what a life, no responsibilities to be had!), April picked up her phone. Birdie promised to send over some pictures, groundwork for their grand plans. Though there was no e-mail yet from Birdie, another message awaited. April's heart flinched.

"I have some news about Marthe," Luc had texted some seven or eight minutes before. "Where can I find you today? Are you in the city?"

"Yes!" April wrote back, fingers flying. "I'm at Carette, near place des Vosges. Table outside. Will be here another hour or two."

She figured Luc would've been, like Olivier and Marc, tucked away in an old stone manse by that late time in the week. That he was in Paris, thinking of Marthe (and, okay, maybe even her) made April smile more than was socially acceptable for someone sitting alone. An observer, like the two women in pink seated nearby, might think her half insane. Not that they'd paid a speck of attention to April, or even noticed her at all, but if they knew her, surely they would've thought, oh dear, what happened to our friend April? I think she's losing her mind.

But soon she would not be alone. The manic grinning might continue, but then they would see Luc. And all at once they would understand.

Chapitre XLIII

Luc sat across from her, flashing his wonky-tooth smile.

"Bonjour, Avril," he said. "I came as quickly as I could."

April noticed he hadn't shaved that day, perhaps not even yesterday or the day before. As a result Luc now possessed an almost-beard, which only served to make his aggravating disheveledness all the more appealing. Even the pink-frocked women nearby, previously oblivious, had to sneak a glance.

"You didn't need to hurry," she said, though was glad he had.

Luc shrugged. He reached into his pocket and pulled out a pack of cigarettes. After executing one of those weird palm-tapping maneuvers smokers so enjoyed, Luc slid a cigarette from its box and went to light it.

"I didn't mind the rush," he said. "And thank you for always making yourself easy to find."

As April tried to avoid interpreting that particular comment, Luc cocked his head and looked down at her feet. Then slowly, slyly, he surveyed her legs. Suddenly April remembered she was in little more than a glorified beach cover-up. Not the most professional attire, but it was hot and she was "out of the office." April did not expect to run into anyone who might notice her exposed legs, and definitely no one who would comment on them.

"Cute dress," Luc said with a smirk. "I like it."

"I'm sure you do," she muttered. "Sorry. It's hot. Marthe's flat doesn't have air-conditioning, nor does mine. I didn't think I'd encounter any acquaintances."

"You are so defensive, ma chérie." Luc blew a stream of smoke over his right shoulder. " 'Cute' is a compliment in the English language, non?"

"It is, sometimes. So, did you seek me out to see what I am wearing? Or is there another reason you're here?"

"The clothes are a plenty good excuse." He sneered happily, eyes twinkling like a devil's golden pitchfork. "But alas, non. I have some news. They've released Madame Vannier from the hospital. She is on the pathway to recovery."

"Really?" April popped up off her chair. "That's fantastic news! Such vast improvement in a relatively short amount of time."

"No doubt thanks to your ardent praying over the last few weeks. I know you've been gravely concerned. I'll extend to her your well wishes."

"Please do. And unlike yours, my sentiments are not facetious. So tell me, when can we see her?"

"Not facetious, eh?"

"How about tomorrow? Can we go see Madame Vannier tomorrow? It'd be perfect timing as Olivier is away for the weekend—"

"Tomorrow? I don't know, Avril, should we really wait that long? Perhaps we shall go now! We can beat her home!" Luc stubbed out his cigarette and winked. "A solicitor and an auctioneer, what a spectacular welcome home. It would likely send her right back to the hospital."

"All right, all right, I get it." She rolled her eyes. "For the record, I still don't think this weekend is an unreasonable request, but I will defer to your judgment."

"Ah, my dear Américaine. Always such the eager badger."

"You and your obsession with badgers." April shook her head. "It's a beaver. An eager beaver."

"Beaver. All right. Très bien. I like beavers."

"Oh, good god."

April tried to frown. She stared down at the table, giggles sneaking up her spine.

"Are you feeling ill, Madame Vogt?"

"Yes, quite. Monsieur Thébault, if not this weekend, when do you think we might meet with your client? And this has nothing to do with any beavers," April said before he could interject. "I need to arrange my schedule."

"In a few weeks, perhaps?"

"A few weeks?" April looked up.

"Two, perhaps three. I'm going out of town for a spell—"

"Luc, three weeks doesn't work. I have to go back to New York in two. And that's at the very outside. If I try to extend the trip yet again I will certainly be fired."

"You're leaving?" Luc started. His eyes widened, and he blinked several times. "In two weeks?" The new cigarette he had begun to light now remained frozen in midair. Luc did not care about the potential firing, but this, this seemed to bother the perpetually cool M. Thébault.

"Oui," April said. "Two weeks is the edict. I'm sure you're quite looking forward to the date. No more annoying Américaine hassling you about journals and letters and hospitalized old ladies."

"Yes." Luc cleared his throat once, and then again. He ground out the cigarette he'd never smoked. "Lucky me. Well, then. I suppose we need to work fast."

"It would be much appreciated," she said softly. Was it possible? Did he also view her departure with a discernible level of regret?

Suddenly Luc stood. He looked flustered and rumpled in a way he normally never did. April followed suit, rising to her feet as she straightened her dress. It seemed about a foot shorter than it was when she put it on.

"Well, I'd better be off," April said, with a hopeful brightness, still tugging at the hem of her skirt.

"Off to where?" Luc walked a few steps closer. Some part of his pant leg touched her knee.

"I'm going to lie down for a bit." She nodded toward the lawn. "Find an empty spot, read a few journals, and relax. It is not my forte, relaxing, but the day seems right for it and I don't have many more hours left to lounge in the Parisian sun."

"Indeed you don't." Luc ran both hands through his hair and then hiked up his pants. "Well, allow me to escort you to the lawn."

"Merci."

"Come, my friend. Let's enjoy the light."

Luc wrapped a congenial arm around her. As they walked beneath the arcades, April's first reaction was to shrink, to shake him off. Two steps to the right and she might be out of grabbing distance. But something held April in place.

"Do you come here often?" April asked, wincing, hoping the bad pickup line did not translate.

"On occasion." She felt his body smiling against hers, struggling not to take advantage of her verbal misstep. "And you?"

"I came here all the time when I worked at the museum," she said. "This was my escape."

"It's a lovely space," he said as they hooked left and stepped into the sunshine. "Victor Hugo once had a home on this lawn. Though I'm sure you already knew."

"Really?" April turned toward him, face wide in a smile. "I *didn't* know. *The* Victor Hugo? Grandfather of Jeanne, Marthe's archnemesis?"

Luc laughed and patted her on the head.

"Well, most people know him as one of the greatest writers and humanitarians of all time. But 'grandfather of archnemesis' is, I suppose, an alternate viewpoint." He pointed across the lawn. "He lived in that building. It was once a private residence but now houses a museum dedicated to his honor."

"There's a Victor Hugo museum?"

"You have your Monticello, non? It is quite the same thing."

"Wow! I've probably been here five hundred times. I never had any idea."

April paused on a sunny length of grass that was also shade-adjacent in case she got too warm. With Luc standing so close, she was mostly too warm already.

"All right," she said. "This looks like a good place. What do you think?"

"The best of the Parisian sun, no doubt."

April pulled a shawl from her bag and laid it across the lawn. She did her best to sit down in a ladylike, nonflasher fashion.

"You are welcome to join me," April said and then pulled back. She hadn't meant to say that. "I mean, if you need an afternoon off."

"Need it? Yes. Alas I have an appointment."

"Oh. Okay." April frowned. "I guess some of us have to work. Even on Saturdays. Thank you for helping me find my perfect spot."

"It was my absolute pleasure. Madame Vogt." He gave her a quick little salute. "Au 'voir. Until next time."

Wordlessly and with a slight frown, she watched Luc saunter away. He was distracted, something was not right. Luc never left without a proper good-bye. April touched her face, wondering if she'd done something to put him off.

"Avril?"

She jolted. He had caught her staring and was now walking back her way. What did her face look like? Was her mouth open? Her eyes glazed over? Did she look like a lovesick teenager? Or a serial killer?

"Ça va?" he asked.

"Yes, oui! J'ai la banane!"

Had April learned nothing? *J'ai la banane*. Her regrettable colloquial expression: "I'm fine" and/or "I feel good." Embarrassing literal translation: "I have the banana."

"Super," he said and laughed. "The banana must always be had. I meant to ask. Do you have plans for the Fête Nationale?"

"Bastille Day? Do you mean the actual day? Or the night before?"

Though April knew the holiday itself was on July 14 and most celebrations occurred the previous evening, she did not know why she asked for clarification. Plans weren't abundant on either day, and in fact April didn't have plans at all that week. Or the week before. Or the week after. Her only plans at all in July involved shoring up provenance and boarding a plane into an unknown future.

"Either way," Luc said, shrugging.

"The thirteenth is my birthday," April blurted. "Wait, I mean it's not."

Her face went crimson. Oh, how she wanted to grab the aforementioned banana and shove it into her mouth so she'd stop speaking!

"I'm confused. Is it or is it not your birthday?"

"Fine. Yes." She exhaled. "It is my birthday. I'm turning thirty-five, officially middle-aged, hence my reluctance to cop to it."

"You are only going to live until seventy?"

"If I'm lucky."

"Well, this is perfect. I think you need to experience the quintessential Fête Nationale to celebrate your entrée into 'middle age.' Le bal des pompiers. What do you think?" The twinkle in his eyes was suddenly back.

"Le bal des pompiers? I don't know, Luc."

April had lived in Paris several years, over several Bastille Days, but she'd never been to a fireman's ball. She planned to attend one her last summer in the city, but when her museum closed April was eager to flee all reminders of her failure. She'd meant to come back in a few weeks, after she found a new job and could properly show her face. But April met Troy and plans changed. Then again, when she met Troy it was not merely the plans that changed. It was everything.

"You don't know what?" Luc said. "It would be the ideal way to spend your birthday."

April started to refuse his offer but thought better of it. If there was one thing she needed most right now, it was a bit of dancing and laughter . . . plus, always, champagne.

"You know what?" she said. "I'd love to. Yes. Bal des pompiers. Sounds like a blast."

"A blast?"

"Oui. But you'd better make sure I don't have too much champagne lest I start feeling revolutionary and subject you to random musical numbers. I do a fantastic rendition of 'Lovely Ladies.' "

" 'Lovely Ladies'?"

"You know, from *Les Miz*? Victor Hugo?" She pointed toward the building in which Jeanne's grandfather once lived. "Must I sing a few bars for your edification?"

"I did not realize you were an actress. It is with great difficulty I try to picture you onstage."

"One does not need to be an actress to do a rendition."

"Okey-dokey." He shook his head. Crouching down on her blanket, Luc took one of April's hands in his. She looked down, noticing how smooth and hairless her skin appeared next to his, like a child's. "It is set then, lovely lady. Le bal des pompiers with your solicitor." He kissed her hand, then released it to the ground. "It is . . . what do you call it? 'Booked'?"

"Yes. 'Booked.'" April wasn't sure if the words actually managed to make it all the way out of her mouth.

Luc nodded, that forever-smirk firmly attached to his face. A chunk of black hair fell across his forehead.

"Perfect," he said, brushing his fingers along her arm before pulling away for good. "I look forward to it. Au 'voir once again, ma chérie. We will see each other soon."

Chapitre XLIV

Paris, 10 May 1894

Even so many months later I can hardly step into Maxim's without fear of seeing Joseph Pujol. Oh how quickly our relationship soured. How rapidly he's fallen from the city's graces! The world's most famous farter, once the Moulin Rouge's premiere act and now Paris's social pariah. He blames me, but it was his idea in the first place!

I only asked for help. I did not ask that it take a specific form. I did not ask for an impromptu farting exhibit with the highest fees he'd charged to date. When Pujol announced his plan he never once mentioned it violated his exclusive contract with the Moulin Rouge. He never mentioned they might sue him for damages!

M. Pujol is now in a horrible position. The Moulin Rouge took all they could, and his solicitors grabbed the rest. I gave back what remained of the show proceeds, but I could not very well ask my former landlord for a return of rental payments. He does not care if the money came from bar wages or a whorehouse or an illegal farting show. He received the money and the money he will keep. I'm not even a tenant anymore!

I've tried to rectify the situation. Every day I beg Gérard to give Pujol a show at the Folies. He'd worked there before. But who wants to hire a man known to betray his employer? A man who already left your establishment once in pursuit of higher pay? He already had some of the highest royalties to begin with. It is all so disastrous. I fear Pujol will soon resort to street-corner flatulence. How undignified, and what a fall from grace.

And it gets worse. Boldini is suddenly off my charms. He won't even acknowledge me! I've knocked on his door. No answer. I've left notes asking him to call on me, at home or at the Folies. No response. I've waited in the alley behind his studio, which resulted in him tracking down a *gendarme* to accuse me of assault.

"This lady tried to rob me!" he cried. "She's an opium addict and a thief, and you should incarcerate her immediately!"

Guess which favored barmaid missed her shift at the Folies because she was fermenting in the Paris jail? I should invoice Boldini for lost compensation. At least someone (Boldini, I hope) alerted Montesquiou to my predicament. *Le Comte* loves a girl in trouble, or a boy or goat for that matter, and was all too thrilled to come to my rescue. I could not have made myself more appealing if I'd dipped my body in gold and affixed diamonds to my eyelashes. Paris's favored dandy cheerily paid for my release, sporting his favored pistachio velvet waistcoat, *bien sûr.*

I suppose it is time to accept the truth: This is the end of us. No more

Boldini. No more lazy mornings in his studio. No more evening strolls through his courtyard and out to the Luxembourg Gardens. At least paint-fume headaches and artistic tantrums will also disappear from my daily routine, a bittersweet result to be sure. The love we'd built over the months is now gone, as if it never happened in the first place. Marguérite says I'm being overly theatrical, that it will all work out in the end. But, truly, what other eventuality can one assume when one's lover has her arrested and thrown behind bars?

Already I miss Giovanni's company. I miss his funny, grumpy ways. I feel robbed of a relationship that meant a lot to me. Also, I feel robbed of an explanation. All this robbing . . . perhaps I should call the *gendarmes* on him! Boldini never warned me he was fed up, incensed, ready to part ways. At least Pierre offered that dignity. I asked Giovanni if he was mad about the Pujol farting debacle or whether it had to do with Montesquiou. He refused an answer, saying I shouldn't have to ask. That he could have saved me from either or both situations is entirely lost on him.

Since he does not afford me the luxury of an explanation, I can only assume this is about Montesquiou, the Pujol business being less personal and less involving illicit deeds (farting shows excepted). Boldini is jealous of our relationship but I cannot figure why. I proposed to the silly little portraitist and he would not have me! After his refusals and the Pujol nonsense I really had no choice. It is mostly a business arrangement, and anyway a lady could do worse than hitch herself to *Le Comte*! It is not my fault Boldini has failed so many times to paint him.

"I thought you had standards," Giovanni snarled when he first heard of my situation with M. de Montesquiou. "Have you forgotten the hours we've spent slandering the man?"

"Slandering"? We were not that cruel! Granted, we've exchanged quips at *Le Comte's* expense, but all of it humorous banter on the subject of a man who begs to be talked about. It's true, Robert can be a bit of a dullard and would never love a single soul as much as he loves himself. But he knows all this! He would laugh at the jokes, too. So, then, what's the harm in repeating these things and then proceeding to his bed? This is my survival we're talking about. I wish Giovanni could understand.

Chapitre XLV

Paris, 2 June 1894

Le *Comte* is not so bad.

Boldini: "If you must keep saying he is not so bad then he is quite so." Giovanni is talking to me now, at least, even if it is only to peck at my decisions while offering me no other choice.

We can all agree Montesquiou is a half-baked conversationalist. He strives for literary and artistic achievement, but his grandest contribution to date is what critics called "a ponderous volume of utterly incomprehensible poems." But thank heavens he does have other fine attributes. He knows how to thrill a lady, unsurprising what with all that experience, not to mention the man looks positively exquisite at dinner tables or sitting in the parlors of learned and titled men. He is infinitely more presentable than Giovanni, though that is a low hurdle to be sure.

Montesquiou is a most beautiful specimen, his looks are unassailable. He is wiry and graceful with slick, black, wavy hair and a perfect mustache (not as scratchy as Boldini's!). And *Le Comte's* nose—Giovanni is doubtless envious of his nose. Robert is a finch where Boldini is a parrot. On the other hand, Robert's teeth call to mind birds as well, or rather birdseed, so small and black are they. This is why he smiles only with his lips.

This *Le Comte*–perfected smile was on full display when he signed the documents on my new apartment in the Ninth. It's glorious, this place, all seven rooms of it. I now have both an antechamber *and* a drawing room. Sometimes I worry it is too much space. Of course even too much is never enough. And I will have a grand time filling it up!

Already we've started on this endeavor. Every day new gowns and jewels arrive. Montesquiou sends artwork and vases and the finest bone china, delivering them through the most exclusive dealers and even a suspected smuggler or two. I have tried to pass some of these objects off on Pujol as recompense, but he will accept none of my charity.

According to the gossipmongers, when Boldini heard of the apartment and my benefactor, he took his collection of *Le Comte* portraits-in-progress and impaled them on the statues outside the Opéra. I daresay the decimation of the Robert de Montesquiou works will provide the most satisfaction Giovanni will ever find in painting the man. Oh, such wicked thoughts. Forgive me, Robert! But you can be so difficult when you feel your beauty is not appreciated to its fullest extent!

It's amusing, the beautiful pieces the beautiful Montesquiou sends to my home when his looks as it does! The man is thirty-nine years old and still lives at his parents', in an apartment atop his father's Quai d'Orsay mansion. Though the mansion itself impresses, the rooms above are positively atrocious. Simply to access the flat one must ascend a treacherous staircase and crawl through a tunnel lined with Egyptian tapestries. And that is just the start! At every turn it is a violation of all five senses, six if you include common sense.

Le Comte has a red room and an orange room, a purple one under consideration. When he is of bad *humeur* (not as often as Boldini, thank goodness!) it is to the gray room Robert goes, where he sits on his gray furniture and smells his gray roses, specially bred for him by a farmer in the countryside.

There are polar bear rugs and a Russian sleigh (here come the Cossacks!). One must not forget Montesquiou's pet turtle—a live turtle!—which crawls around the Persian rugs sporting a jewel-encrusted shell and defecating at will.

If a moderately attractive woman enters the premises, *Le Comte* will drag her through his *nuances les plus tendres*, the blasted tie collection, and "entertain" his guest with a story of each. Did you know ties can have stories? If they belong to Montesquiou they have much to say. However, the ties are no match for his photograph collection. There are 199 pictures but only one subject: *Le Comte*.

Sometimes I worry that my apartment displays too much good taste and Robert will come to understand the eyesore in which he lives. I am not, at this juncture, seeking a roommate of any sort and do not wish to host *Le Comte* on a nightly basis! Alas, Montesquiou's apartment is a perfect reflection of his personality, so I should continue to remain unencumbered.

Plus, logistically speaking, Robert uses his quarters to enjoy the comforts of women other than myself. I've seen no evidence but know they exist: American heiresses, actresses from the Folies, the positively antique Sarah Bernhardt, and perhaps the occasional boy to boot. We do not speak of it. Just like a married couple! Sometimes it's nice to know that others share the burden of entertaining him.

Though Robert can be trifling, our time together is not altogether torturous and we share many common interests. For example, we both positively love to parade throughout town in my new carriage! The vehicle is a thing of beauty—an eight-spring landau upholstered in blue satin and pulled by four black horses. It's quite the appropriate carriage given what so many people call my breed, *les demimondaines*: "eight-spring luxury models." "Luxury models," indeed! I would not have it any other way.

On Fridays we grab a friend or two and assemble in the carriage, me in a jaguar-lined coat, my hat trimmed with roses and bird feathers. Montesquiou dons whichever silk suits his mood and off we go to make our appearances at the cafés.

Though I still like Maxim's (even post-Pujol, even if or because we might see Boldini there) Robert prefers Paillard's, the favorite restaurant of the Prince of Wales. That so-called prince is such a wet sally with all his moping. If he forces me to listen to his refrain one more time I might stick hot pokers in my ears.

"Everybody recognizes me and nobody knows me," the prince complains without end.

Yes, that is true. No one cares to know you because you are a bore! You make Montesquiou look like an intellect of the highest order!

I prefer staying above the Seine as opposed to below it. The Folies, Maxim's, the Moulin Rouge . . . what does one need with the Fifth, Sixth, or Seventh when we have it all in the Ninth? This is what I say to Montesquiou anyway.

Sometimes, though, I am forced to venture downward, as *Le Comte* is such a fan of Café Procope. Though it is not my kind of place (the clientele are as dry as Marguérite's *petit poulet en cocotte fermière*), at least it has some history, a cadre of vaunted former guests. Voltaire was a regular some century and a half ago, drinking up to forty cups of coffee a day while openly ridiculing the Catholic Church. Victor Hugo himself spent no small amount of time in the establishment. When I'm there I like to imagine him sitting nearby.

After we pay our social dues at Café Procope and its less illustrious neighbors, Montesquiou and I drive our carriage back up the rue Notre-Dame-des-Champs. It is not the most direct path, and, truth be told, there is no real reason to take this detour. I imagine Robert is doing it for my benefit, but of course it could also be for his.

Regardless, no matter how debauched I am or how very well I feel I've moved on, as the carriage turns on Boldini's street, as I see from afar the tall white brick building and the black iron gates glinting beneath the gaslamps, we pass the studio and I always look for a light. My head stays cocked toward Notre-Dame-des-Champs as we turn onto the boulevard Raspail and then cross over the Pont-Royal back into the Ninth. Montesquiou never says a word, never remarks upon my distraction.

Sometimes I wake up the next morning, groggy, head clogged with the night before, and all I can think of is my grumpy portraitist. I want to see him. I want to laugh at whatever Maxim's mishap occurred nine hours before. I attempt to discuss these things with Robert only to find he's missed the spectacle altogether, so busy was he staring into a mirror or running a comb through his beard.

However, to his credit, when I get a little testy about all he's missed and the scant bit of attention he pays, Montesquiou knows how to set my mood right again. All he must do is open *Le Figaro* to find my name in the fashion pages and somehow, miraculously, it is almost always there. Three years ago I straggled into this city with the earth's shabbiest frock falling off my frame. Now Parisiennes clamor to read about my clothes. They try to emulate my dress! My hair! If feathers seem ubiquitous it's because I wore them first.

According to Montesquiou, I am now more popular than Jeanne Hugo. True or not, he is rather adroit at entertaining my distaste for the woman. Though I suspect he is merely paying homage to my ire. The papers *do* speak more of my gowns, my hair, and my jewels than they do of hers. Although perhaps this is less about me and more about her. Why discuss Jeanne Hugo's frocks when you can talk about her divorce?

Yes, it's true. Jeanne finally left that scoundrel of a husband, Léon Daudet. Too much gambling, too much drinking, too many affairs, to speak nothing of all that time spent criticizing the union. As contemptible a creature as Léon is, I never would've guessed their marriage might end like this. With all the excess and beauty of the day, it's hard to believe it played out in the darkest alleys, in the beds of shabby old hotels, in the most vile and hateful ways imaginable. Some small part of me feels sympathy for Jeanne. Of course, when that happens, I brush it away as quickly as possible.

While we're on the subject of dark alleys, Robert is off to one of his *clubs* tonight. I will spend the evening with Marguérite. Dear Marguérite. I am well on my way to quitting my post as a Folies barwoman, thanks to Montesquiou's generosity, and she would do well to follow my direction. Yet the silly girl insists on loving other female performers, not counts, and no amount of cajoling will convince her otherwise! It is not about the sex, I tell her. It is not about the sex!

Nonetheless Marguérite is doing quite well. Her contortionist act continues to gain notoriety. She's even received a competing offer from the Moulin Rouge! I suppose she's chiseled out a little specialty for herself, a niche. And isn't that exactly how Marguérite is? Always doing things her own way. Of course, this is often much to the detriment of her friends as well as polite society. If she doesn't wish to wear a corset, she won't wear one. If she wants to make poached pigeon she will try to pass it off as pheasant!

My driver is at the door, the horses outside my window clomping their hooves on the cobblestones. I suppose it's time for me to stop writing and depart to Marguérite's to dine badly. I feel glum this evening, not in the mood to converse with the cancan dancers and acrobats. I suppose I should take Robert's view of things. He never contemplates a dinner party without declaring, "The place of honor is where I find myself." Since he is his own favorite company, Montesquiou is always the happiest man in the room. As ridiculous as it seems, I suppose we could all take a lesson from him.

Chapitre XLVI

The kitchen table was stacked with papers awaiting transcription into the auction catalog. April rose and took a quick glance at her phone. It was nearly six o'clock, only fifteen minutes since she'd last checked for a birthday greeting from Troy, which was in turn only fifteen minutes since the prior inspection.

April should've been showered by then, preparing for the birthday Fête with Luc. Instead she stared down at the work in front of her and at the blank phone, and found no reason to celebrate, hirsute, attractive French companion notwithstanding. She was in Paris to work, not attend a fireman's ball with her attorney. A few hours in, and already April sensed thirty-five was going to suck.

She dialed Luc's number.

"Bonjour!"

"Hello. It's me, April."

"'Allo, me Avril. Are you anxious for the Fête Nationale celebration this evening?"

"That's why I'm calling. Listen, I appreciate your generous offer to take me out. Unfortunately I must decline."

"'Decline'? Nonsense!"

"Je suis désolée. I know it's rude to cancel at the last minute, but I just don't have it in me tonight."

A long pause settled on the line. Horns bleated in the background, followed by the roar of motorbikes. Luc did not speak.

"Luc? Are you still there?"

"You don't have it in you?" he said. "What is this expression?"

"It means I don't have the energy." She snorted. "Which makes me sound *very* thirty-five-plus, I realize. Quite geriatric."

"You do not have the energy *now*? This does not make sense. If you stay on your derrière all evening you will definitely lack the energy *then*. You will not have the energy at all."

"Valid point," she conceded. "Okay, maybe it's more about my mood than my flagging energy levels. Honestly, I am a bit glum, a little blue."

"And you aim to cure this glumness by yourself? At home? On your thirty-fifth birthday?" Why was it his logic always sounded more reasonable than hers?

"I have a pile of work to get through," April said, despite knowing he was a little bit right. "After that, perhaps a glass of wine or two, a bit of fromage, and then an early bedtime. Everything always looks fresher in the morning, including thirty-five-year-old auctioneers."

"You will work the night of your birthday?" Luc asked, aghast. "Avril, you can work anytime, but your birthday and the Fête Nationale are now. Don't you want to enjoy today and, for a change, not worry about yesterday or tomorrow?"

"Seriously, Luc. I am not up for it." She did her best to sound firm.

"'Seriously'? You are always too serious. Too seriously." His lips smacked against a cigarette. "Alas, non. You will not decline because, as with any good lawyer, I know what is best for everyone. It is clear we need to start the festivities immediately. This is an emergency, and we cannot wait for the bal des pompiers to commence. We must prepare with joyeux anniversaire cocktails beforehand."

"Cocktails beforehand? In America they call that prepartying. And it's not the best idea when I'm moderately depressed and have a lot of work to do."

"You have no choice in this matter. The moment we hang up I will send you a text with my address. Come over, and we will enjoy some aperitifs before we depart for the bal des pompiers."

"Luc—"

"Do not fret, Madame. I will not force you into my home." He snickered. "We can go to the café below my flat. Revelry in public. No badgers. I promise."

April sighed. She didn't want to go out. It seemed like a lot of effort for an evening that would undoubtedly produce moments of extreme awkwardness followed by a multitude of day-after regrets.

Yet waiting out Troy's belated birthday wishes seemed worse. A gal could only stare at her phone for so long. The idea of wallowing over a good Côtes-du-Rhône was much more romantic in theory than actually finding oneself alone all evening, listening to the sounds of Fête revelers on the streets.

"All right," April said at last. "You've convinced me. I wish you luck. My expectations are high."

"Excellent. I plan to exceed them all."

April laughed in spite of herself.

"When should I come?" she asked. "Nine o'clock? Nine-thirty?"

He chuckled. "Now, of course. You come now."

April looked down at her yoga pants and braless thirty-five-year-old chest. She was a long way from going out Parisian style.

"Let's say between six-thirty and seven," she said, walking toward her bedroom. "I am not exactly presentable."

"I am ready when you are. See you soon, ma petite."

"'Ma petite'? I am hardly young. Au 'voir, Luc."

April turned off her phone and chucked it onto the bed. She immediately dived into the bureau, wondering if she had enough time to swing by the Galeries Lafayette and find something more festive than her boring American shopping-mall clothes. A fireman's ball was basically a trumped-up block party, but it was still a block party in Paris.

After throwing on a sparkly embellished skirt (*Le Comte* would be proud), and dumbing it down with a black tee, April grabbed her purse and headed out onto the street. She decided to hoof it to Luc's although it was faster to Métro or cab. There was something April wanted to see, and it was not just more of Paris.

Chapitre XLVII

April left her building and crossed down into the Eighth Arrondissement, veering toward the Seine.

Her route was deliberate, directed toward the rue Royale, a short blip of a street between the place de la Madeleine and the place de la Concorde, not far from the purveyor of Chelsea's new overpriced handbags. As she approached, April's pace picked up. A smile snuck onto her lips.

She turned a corner and there it was: Maxim's. April stopped and took in its red awning, wood facade, and swirly gold lettering. She imagined Marthe perched inside the window. The Cossacks came in. They spilled out. Then April saw Marthe tripping down the street and into the arms of Pujol.

"I would've given you the money," she said.

A twenty-something Parisian hipster paused, a questioning look on his face. April blushed and waved him by.

Reluctantly pulling herself from the scene of so many of Marthe's epistles, April took another quick turn and made her way through place de la Concorde, the largest square in Paris. A temporary grandstand stood in the middle, built for the Bastille Day festivities and decked out in blue, white, and red awnings. The area around it was calm, almost desolate, and April could not picture the liveliness that would overtake it the next day. There would be tanks, fire engines, helicopters, planes, and marching troops. Cheers and fireworks would ring throughout the city.

April moved slowly along the Seine, watching the barges float by and the Bastille Day flags flap in the breeze. She perused the *bouquinistes*, inspecting novels and pictures she had no intention of purchasing. Time and worry grew faint.

As she meandered, Luc sent a series of texts inquiring as to when she might arrive. At least someone was attempting communication on her birthday. April smirked (he taught her how) and ignored the messages. He could wait.

Flicking through a set of Arc de Triomphe prints in one of the bookstalls, April considered the ways she might later harangue Luc for his impatience. He complained she took life too seriously, yet now he was annoyed with her lollygagging. As April scripted a list of snappy retorts, her fingers hit a six-by-six watercolor wedged between all the eight-by-tens. She lifted it from its bin, expecting another Parisian landmark. Instead it was the New York skyline. April jumped. The painting fell to the ground.

"Qu'est-ce que vous faites?" the vendor bellowed, veins in his neck swelling.

"I live there," April said in plain, ugly English as she bent down to pick it up.

He barked out an expletive or two.

"I live there," she said again, this time to herself. It didn't seem real. The city she loved, her home, felt so far away.

After paying twenty euros, overpriced but April was in no mood to haggle, she rolled up the picture and shoved it into her handbag. April continued onward to Luc's, the awkward bulge of New York pressing against her side.

Luc's apartment was easy to find. Given his occupation and the flat's location in the tony Sixteenth Arrondissement, April imagined an upscale, traditional Haussmann decorated with a tasteful, expensive minimalist bent. When Luc gave her a quick tour, April encountered no surprises save several pieces of midcentury furniture she immediately eyed for auction.

"Êtes-vous prêt?" Luc said after he caught her taking surreptitious pictures of his coffee table. "Or are you going to abscond with some of my furniture?"

"If you ever decide to abandon your apartment for seventy years I hope you keep me in mind as potential heir. Or, at the very least, leave strict instructions for your actual heirs to contact Sotheby's."

"You auctioneers are vultures." Luc chuckled and grabbed his phone. April resisted the urge to check hers. "Allons-y! Off we go!"

After bidding adieu to the glorious coffee table, April followed Luc down the stairs and into the café on the ground floor of his building. Once seated on the terrace next to a low fence overlooking the street, they promptly ordered a bottle of champagne and an assortment of *fromages*.

Sharing, April reminded herself as the cheeses glistened in the fading sunlight. You are sharing this with someone else.

A dozen pieces of cheese and two glasses of champagne later, the million little worry larvae started to leave April's brain. She listened as Luc told her about his childhood in Dijon and boarding school in Lausanne, and time spent in America, at Georgetown for the second of three law degrees. Soon they were bickering about who was more egregiously over-degreed, and April realized she'd gone ninety minutes without once inspecting her BlackBerry.

As Luc settled the check, she reached into her bag, fully expecting a missed call or two. Surely Troy would ring before lunchtime in New York. Alas, April's phone remained unbothered, not an e-mail or text or voice mail to be had.

"I'm sorry, but did you just say the word 'bastard'?" Luc asked, eyebrows raised.

"No, no. Of course not. I didn't say a thing."

April sank her hand deeper into her bag. Her fingers brushed against the Manhattan skyline. She recoiled as if touching an electrical wire.

"Snake in your bag?" Luc asked, snickering.

"Don't even go there." April rolled her eyes. She yanked the painting from her purse. "New York City. I found this among *les bouquinistes*. I hate this picture. I don't even know why I bought it."

"You purchased a painting you do not like?"

"It sounds odd, I know."

"Yes, yes it does."

"But I think I was *supposed* to buy it. It was as if the vendor had it specifically for me. His bins were filled with all the typical Parisian landmarks, but after two seconds standing in his stall I happened upon this."

"Sounds like a coincidence." Luc shrugged.

"I don't know. Of all the stalls I stopped at that one. His paintings were no more attractive than any of the others. Plus, I work at an auction house. Unfortunately I have a high bar for artwork. It's like New York is *following* me."

Luc chuckled. "It is. But not in the form of badly painted watercolors."

He reached for the receipt and wrapped it around his credit card.

"You should've let me pay," April said. "You keep saying 'next time.' "

"It is your birthday. You do not pay. And this is a business expense for me, anyway."

"Business expense?" She tried not to let her disappointment show. "Um, all right."

April pushed back her rattan chair and stood, wobbling on the way up. She reached for a patio heater to steady herself. Luc winked, having caught this vulnerability. She extended a middle finger in his direction.

"That needs no translation," he said and patted her on the back. "Êtes-vous prêt, Mademoiselle?"

"Oui. Grudgingly. Oui."

"Ah, Avril, you make me laugh."

Luc stepped easily over the low iron fence and out onto the sidewalk. Before April had the chance to navigate the stakes (which admittedly would have amused Luc to no end), he simply leaned over and hooked his forearm around April's waist with a firmness that felt like a wall. Luc tucked his other arm under her knees and swiftly lifted her up and over the barrier. She didn't have an opportunity to protest.

"You're stronger than you look," April said as he stooped to let her gain footing on the sidewalk.

"And you, my friend, are lighter than you look," he said, his hand still firmly centered on her lower back. "Much lighter."

"It's a wonder you're not married." April was careful to avoid looking too closely into the eyes that were still mere inches from hers. "You really know how to butter a gal up."

"Merci beaucoup! I do try." He reached out and tweaked her champagne-flushed cheek.

April could not hide her smile. Luc removed his arm and jerked his head toward the nearby crosswalk.

"*Allons-y*," he said.

Off they went.

Chapitre XLVIII

Already the streets teemed with partiers bumping and pushing and yelling. It was chaotic, Las Vegas bachelorette party chaotic. People walked into cars. Mopeds drove onto sidewalks, scantily clad waifs hanging off the back like flags. Without thinking or planning or meaning to, April grabbed onto Luc's arm for anchor. He was two steps ahead but glanced back and smiled, the skin crinkling around his eyes.

They arrived at the designated *caserne* shortly after ten o'clock. Outside firemen stood ready to greet their guests, the *pompiers'* lantern behind them lit red, fire trucks on the street also lit and on display.

Inside the first courtyard a Brazilian brass band in wigs hammered out songs loud enough to make the ground shake. Twinkle lights and flags dangled overhead. Concession stands lined the yard. Even at that early hour the crowd was thick. Couples danced. Single women prowled the food booths, trying to engage the firemen when they weren't too busy slinging hash.

"Wow!" April said, the blood pumping through her veins in time with the music. "I sort of feel like I'm at the world's classiest frat party. Where's the beer garden?"

"There is a champagne bar inside," Luc said.

Because of the noise he had to lean close when he spoke, his hot breath giving April a raging case of goose bumps.

"Champagne," April said, stepping back. "Much better than a beer garden. Show me the way."

Once again taking hold of his arm, April trailed Luc inside to the champagne bar/disco room, the setup not reminiscent of any municipal building April had ever seen. Of course this public building had been erected over four centuries ago, in the greatest city in the world, so they weren't exactly talking DMV or small community town hall. April felt the gravitas then, even with the firemen attendants surrounding her in their skintight shirts.

Champagne in hand, Luc pointed her toward a long, low grill sizzling with row after row of mouthwatering sausages. Equivalent fare could probably be found in any given NFL stadium in the United States, but the building, the meats, the free-flowing champagne—everything about it was dizzying.

"Sausage!" she gasped. "It's like I've never wanted anything more."

Luc turned, eyebrow cocked. "What did you just say?"

"Uh, nothing." She shook her head. "The food looks great."

He grabbed her hand. "Allons manger."

They sidled up to the barbecue, where yet another muscled, chiseled young buck rolled pieces of pork over the coals.

"Un comme ça, s'il vous plait," April said, endeavoring to sound polite and not like the ravenous middle-aged harpy she was.

"Comme vous voulez," the fireman said and pulled one off the grill. He plunked it on a stark white Styrofoam plate and passed it April's way. The poor little dog looked so lonely.

"Also one of those," she added quickly.

"What do they say in America?" Luc grinned, teeth pointier than usual. "Your eyes have grown larger than your stomach?"

April was about to protest when she noticed he had two as well.

"J'ai faim," she said, feeling a little defensive. "Must be all the champagne and walking."

"Ah, yes, the champagne. Of course. Let's go this way," he said. "Looks like the other courtyard might have a place to sit."

April nodded. Champagne glass tucked into the crook of her arm, sausage plate balanced in her right hand, she followed Luc into the adjacent courtyard, all the while thinking there was no better gastro combination than the things she held in her hands.

The second courtyard was at least four times larger than the first and boxed in by stately stone buildings. Blue, white, and red flags surrounded the stage. The dance floor writhed like a box of snakes. A woman in a white feather dress stood at the microphone belting out a bastardized version of an American pop song.

After winding through what was very nearly a mosh pit, they took a seat on a metal bench somewhere near the back. The minute April set her purse on the table, it jolted, from the music or a call, she wasn't sure.

Just in case (would she ever learn?) April extracted her phone while almost jeopardizing the future of her drink and sausages. The music might have helped, but the BlackBerry was ringing too. April sat staring into her palm while the feather-dressed woman announced the band's short break.

"Ça va?" Luc's brow furrowed.

"Oui," April said, still staring. "It's just my father. Finally he calls for my birthday! I was starting to wonder."

She watched the phone belch out its final rings. When it rolled to voice mail April checked and saw she had another missed call, this one from Troy.

"It's about fucking time," she mumbled.

"Do you need to speak with him?" Luc asked.

"Nah. It's pretty loud out here," she said, frowning.

It wasn't loud, not right then. Although someone hooked up an iPod to one of the speakers, most of the dancers scattered to find another courtyard, a different place to gyrate and grind.

"Well, it is up to you," Luc said. "But don't let me stop you."

"I'll catch up with everyone later," April said at last. She turned off her phone. "Don't want to miss anything here!" She lifted her glass. "À ta santé!"

"And cheers to you as well." They tapped plastic glasses and took a sip.

Using the side of her fork, April cut off a generous piece of sausage and then bit in, her teeth cracking through the thick, charred coating to reach the oily goodness inside.

"Oh my god," she said, taking another bite, shamelessly talking with a mouth full of food. "This is ridiculous. Ridiculous!"

"It is rather good. I agree."

Luc continued to take his reasonable, Parisian bites while April gobbled down both sausages and wondered if she should go for a third.

"So, Avril," Luc said as he started on his second. She hated him right then for having more on his plate. April wished they were married, but only because she wanted to reach over and finish the rest of his food. "How does it feel, thirty-five?"

"Great so far!" she sang, not really knowing one way or another, though things were already immeasurably better than they had been a few hours before. "But it does feel like a milestone. Way more than thirty ever did."

"That's because Americans like to make thirty-five scary," Luc said, wiping his mouth. April glanced at her napkin, which she had not yet used. There'd been no time for manners.

"What do you mean 'scary'?" she said. "And what Americans?"

"The doctors. The television programs and newspapers."

"I don't follow."

"Is thirty-five not the time when they demand women cease procreation?"

April laughed. "'*They*,' whoever '*they*' are, don't demand anything. There are women who have babies in their forties! Their fifties, even!"

"But do they not show you lots of terrifying literature about deformed progeny and such? This is what I hear. Pregnancy after thirty-five may only be accomplished via massive doses of drugs that make you fat and crazy."

"I think it's the pregnancy that makes you fat and crazy," April said with a snort. "I'm not really sure how to respond to your . . . suppositions. I should probably be angry because I think you're calling me old even though you have—what? Five years on me? Seven?"

Not that his years mattered, not that age ever did for a man. Luc had a point. For a woman thirty-five was a medical turning point. For men it was simply one more than thirty-four, one less than thirty-six.

"It is not an insult," Luc said, slicing off another piece of sausage. "I think it's atrocious they scare women like this. No more babies! You are too old! My sister had babies into her forties, and no one mentioned a thing."

"There *is* science behind it," April said. "Fertility nosedives at thirty-five and the risk for birth defects goes in the opposite direction. It's a fact."

"Or so they say." Luc rolled his eyes.

"I tend to believe the professionals," she said. "But I'm nutty like that. And anyway, it's a nonissue for me. Yes I'm thirty-five, but I won't be having kids."

"Why's that?"

"Beg pardon? Isn't that question a little personal?"

"It is a question and you are a person, so . . ." He shrugged. "I'm only curious. Why don't you want children?"

"It's not that I don't want them per se—"

"Is it because of your mother?" Luc asked, the words stabbing April in the chest. "Because you lost her so young?"

"Wow, you really know how to make a girl feel giddy on her birthday." April inhaled deeply as Luc cast his eyes downward, in an almost embarrassed fashion. "Is it because we lost her? No. That's not exactly how it's all gone down."

They had no one moment of losing, after all. There was more to it than that.

"It's not that she died. I mean, I *suppose* there's an aspect related to her illness. But, it's simply easier to say kids were never my thing to begin with." April crushed the unused napkin in her fist. "So, the band is getting back onstage. Shall we dance? I am in the mood for dancing."

April was never in the mood for dancing, but it seemed a better option than continuing their current conversation.

"Are you sure?" Luc asked, hovering halfway over the bench, uncertain whether he should really stand.

"Dancing? Are you kidding me? I'm a pro. What about me doesn't shout, 'This girl has moves!'?"

April forced a laugh. Tears threatened to flood her eyes as she tried to smile them away. God, her mom. She missed her so much. Sandra Potter was the most amazing woman, even if she was a perfectly ordinary, traditional kind of mother. In her California beach town it was the hippie burnout parents who were cool, the ones prone to leaving pot brownies unattended on the kitchen counter. Still, despite Sandy Potter's downright anemic coolness, April always liked her mom best.

"I'm sorry," April said, dabbing her eyes with the balled-up napkin. "I always get a little emotional about her around my birthday. I start thinking about the ways I failed her, how I could've been a better daughter. God, I could *still* do better even if she was none the wiser."

"We can leave," Luc said. "We can go somewhere else. Less crowded. We can talk about this. I'm, ah"—he ran all ten fingers through his hair, nails scraping against his scalp—"I am not a very good *talker* but we can go elsewhere. We do not have to stay."

"No," April snapped and stamped a foot for good measure. "I want to dance and enjoy my birthday. You promised you could make it happen, Monsieur Thébault." She lifted an eyebrow as her tears started to dry. "You promised."

"Promise I did."

Luc took her hand and held it firmly, safely in his. As he led her to the dance floor, April did her best to push away all thoughts of her mother, her birthday, parenting, and Troy. Better to let Luc simply pull her along.

Chapitre XLIX

The night slid by in a blur.

They danced, they drank, they consumed ever-more champagne and sausage, April besting Luc in food consumption though both were polite enough to not mention it.

Women batted their eyelashes at Luc as he displayed heroic efforts in pretending to look right through them. Whenever April spent a moment unattended, sleazy men chatted her up, actual sleazy men, not the cute-sleazy she unsuccessfully tried to ascribe to Luc. Ultimately the original supposedly smarmy Frenchman would return from the bathroom or champagne fountain to chastise the badgers for messing with *ma femme*. *Femme* meant "woman" but *ma femme* meant "wife." April appreciated the gesture in a way that had little to do with chasing away strange men.

They talked about Marthe. Luc had read more of the diaries than April might've expected. And, for all his joking about how she thought of little else, he also spent a surprising amount of time thinking about *la demimondaine*.

April told him what she saw in Marthe's words without trying to wrap it all up in the guise of provenance. They speculated on Jeanne Hugo, and also Marguérite. They joked about Montesquiou and his flamboyant ways and tried to spot dance-floor revelers who most matched his description. Indeed the fire station had many *Les Comtes* traipsing around but no reasonable proxy for Boldini.

By the end of the night April wondered how she could ingest so much champagne yet not feel any drunker than when she first walked in and witnessed the scene inside the *caserne de pompiers*. None of the social awkwardness she anticipated came to pass, not a sliver of embarrassment. It was, to sound like a seven-year-old girl, the best birthday ever. And April felt exactly that young and carefree.

When the party was over, after the firemen good-naturedly (though adamantly) pushed the crowd from the dance floors and courtyards, Luc and April stepped out into the cobalt sky of morning. They paused on the sidewalk as Luc checked his watch. It was almost five o'clock. April was not someone who stayed out until five o'clock. She was not someone who stayed out until the next morning at all.

"That was . . ." April started, unable to find words to do the night justice. They walked a few paces before she continued. "Amazing. The best birthday I've ever had. Thank you for forcing me to go."

"I'm glad, in the end, you decided it was fun," Luc said, his pace matching hers. After a full night of dancing it was as though they were now physically in sync. "And as far as Bastille Days have gone, this was my favorite too."

April nodded, heart fluttering in a way she did not appreciate, her entire body weak with equal parts exhilaration and exhaustion. She was shaky, her forehead still damp with sweat. As the cool Parisian air whisked past them, April shivered. They walked a few blocks in companionable silence until the point they had to decide. Luc lived in one direction, April belonged in another.

She cleared her throat.

"All right," she said. "I turn here. Good night. And thanks again. It really was a special night."

"Non. I am going with you."

"Oh, that's silly. Your flat is in the exact opposite direction."

"Non," he said again, this time leaving no room for discussion. "No gentleman lets his date walk home in the dark alone."

"It's almost dawn," April pointed out. "*Date.*" He called her a date. "So it won't be dark much longer. Really, Luc, I don't want to put you out. I am fine on my own. Paris is a big city, but I know it well. It's probably safer than if I were walking home in New York." As she spoke, April volleyed her weight from one foot to the other. Go. Stay. She wasn't sure what she wanted him to do. "Funny, isn't it? New York is home, but Paris is where I feel safe."

"I understand completely." Luc took her hand. "Nonetheless, I will accompany you."

April smiled again. "Thanks."

She decided not to fight it.

The stroll back to the flat was both too fast and yet interminable at the same time. April felt every bone of Luc's hand wrapped around hers. His pulse pounded in her skin. She alternated between enjoying the foreign sensation, that of someone *holding her hand*, and worrying what it all meant, or if it meant nothing, which was maybe the worst option of all.

April was so disoriented by the conundrum of a stranger's fingers that when Luc jumped onto the curb and announced, "Here we are!" she had to peer at the building behind him to be sure.

"Yes," April said, surprised, then added quietly, "I guess we are."

Luc dropped her arm and put both hands on his hips. With one of his wry smiles he winked and hooked a thumb into the smartly frayed waistband of his fitted denim jeans.

"Well, Madame Vogt, tonight was a pleasure indeed."

"It was," April said, her eyes growing hot. "Thank you, Luc. I am not typically a fan of birthdays, but this one did not totally suck."

He grinned. "That is a ringing endorsement. I preferred your previous 'best birthday ever,' though I suppose not totally sucking works too. May I add it to my résumé?"

April paused for thirty seconds, a minute.

"That's it?" she said.

"What's 'it'?" Luc appeared legitimately confused.

"Come on, Thébault! You can do better than that. We both used a variation of the word 'suck.' Where's your off-color comment?"

"I was under the impression you found my off-color comments tiresome."

She could not tell if he was joking. And the truth was she didn't. April didn't find his comments tiresome at all.

"Maybe sometimes," April lied. "But they are so very you, and now the conversation seems naked without them."

"Naked?" He grinned.

"Yes," April said. "Completely bare. Nude. À poil."

She stepped up onto the curb and met him face-to-face, nose-to-nose.

Without thinking, April leaned in and pressed her lips so softly against his they barely touched. She held for only half a second and was the first to pull away.

And in that instant, April understood. She saw how it was so easy for Marthe to flit from patron to patron, to fall easily into long-term flirtations or beds or financial arrangements, while still being able to recognize the real thing when it happened. Boldini was no lark, no dalliance.

It took only that half second for April to feel the sense of love and protection she'd been lacking for so long; and to know how genuine it was. It's what Marthe spent her whole life trying to find, and to reclaim once she found Boldini. And here, in Paris, April had found it, too.

So April kissed him again. This time it was Luc who pulled back.

"You've had too much champagne, non?" Luc said, trying a smile but looking moderately pained and confused. He wobbled as he backed away from her.

"Nope," April said. "I'm feeling quite sober, as a matter of fact. The most clear-headed I've been in months."

He made a sound, like a *hmph*. Luc was trying to walk away but only because he felt he had to.

"You should probably escort me upstairs," she said. "You never know what kind of vagrants and ne'er-do-wells loiter in my hallway."

"April—" he said, voice raspy. "I don't want to get you into any precarious situations."

"Oh, believe me. I don't like 'precarious' either. There isn't a person alive more careful than April Vogt. I get it, now, though. I understand Marthe."

"This is about Marthe?" Luc said, eyes narrowing.

"Yes. No. It is and it isn't. It's just—I finally appreciate that she could never love anyone she had to rely upon. In the years she had patronage from all those other men, she sought out *love* from Boldini; she didn't need his money. She wanted only his affection. Luc, I—"

This was not like April. She'd never been so forward, so flagrant, so boob-print-on-linen-paper. But it felt good. Sometimes being someone else felt right.

"April," Luc said, interrupting her again, using the American name that he so rarely uttered. He took several steps forward, so close April could literally smell him, and closed his hands around hers. April was surprised to find his skin clammy, a little jittery. "I think you've lost your head. Or have you sold the Americans on the four-to-five after all? Technically we are right now sometime after four but before five. Though it *is* morning, and I can't imagine you've accomplished a feat of social upheaval in such a short period of time."

The jokes that normally came so swiftly from Luc's mouth now seemed to stutter and stop.

"We don't need the four-to-five," April said. "It's for people who are being watched, not those free to do what they want."

She slid her hands from Luc's grasp and then wrapped both arms around his waist. They'd been close all night, but April could not believe she was this close now. She half expected him to jump back, in surprise if for no other reason. But he did not. Instead Luc pressed himself closer.

"I thought you were married," he said. There was no smirking this time. "Le grand m'sieu and whatnot."

"No," she said. "There is no grand m'sieu. Not anymore."

Chapitre L

Paris, 3 May 1896

I attended the *Bazar de la Charité* for the first time today.

It is the most fashionable event of the month, perhaps the entire spring! I can only hope I'll get written up tomorrow. I worked hard enough on my dress and baubles . . . I worked hard enough loitering in the general vicinity of the *Figaro* gossips!

I've known of the *Bazar de la Charité* since my days in the convent. It is an annual charity event organized by the Parisian Catholic aristocracy, and given the convent girls and women were both Catholic and in need of charity, it stands to reason we would find it so appealing!

Sœur Marie used to bring me into the city to see the enormous wood-and-canvas structures erected on the Champs-Élyseés. Sometimes she was one of the nuns brought in to bless the proceedings. Either way, after the initial blessing, we stood together in awe of the grandness, the pomp, the red and white banners fluttering in the wind. We used to spend hours on a bench outside watching people come and go, dreaming up stories for each one.

Back then I pledged to enter the tents one day, not as a member of the assisted poor, but as a gracious lady donating time and treasure to the indigent. Sœur Marie said not to set my sights too high. Be happy with your station. Be happy for a warm bed (cough, cough) and regular meals, and make no grand designs on someone else's life. I always gathered Sœur Marie hoped I'd make grand designs on following her life, but joining the convent was never a consideration for me. I wanted the tents, I wanted the salons, I wanted Paris.

For most the *Bazar de la Charité* is an annual event, something that arrives on the calendar along with Christmas and New Year's Day and all the things a person can set her clocks or social calendar by. And maybe one day I will see it the same way. But today. Today. Today after eleven years on the outside (and, really, twenty-two if you think about it), I pushed open the tent. I walked through the turnstiles. I gaped at the hundreds of visitors, the coterie of women standing behind tables hawking novelties, the proceeds of which would go to help little girls like I once was.

"Already I'm bored," Montesquiou said the second we walked in, before I had a chance to catch my breath or assess my surroundings. "Let's find the Hall of Mirrors. I need to practice my technique."

His "technique." *Mon dieu*, his technique! The *Bazar* features not only goods for purchase but also performances such as those put on by ladies not quite ready for the Folies or even the exceedingly second-rate Moulin

Rouge. It's also a chance for members of the highest social stations to act out their theatrical aspirations without fear of disapprobation. It would never do for a baron or count or lady to step onstage and perform, but in the name of charity, *c'est d'autre chose*!

Robert didn't plan to contort or bare a leg—though one couldn't put it past him—but he did have it in his mind to treat visitors to one of his so-called famous mime sequences. The last time he did this the papers referred to him as "*Le Comte,* man of letters and sometimes miming" for months. It was fairly horrifying, but when it comes to Montesquiou there is a spectrum of horrification, and miming is at the very lesser end. His so-called orchestra of odors from two years past was worse. His flatulence is less charming than Pétomane's.

Mime threats aside, Robert mostly behaved, but only because he was trying to impress Proust, his new protégé. Proust claims himself a writer but is little more than the city's smallest rumor mill, and he follows Robert like whores used to follow Georges Hugo. He copies *Le Comte's* every idiom, mannerism, and flourish, even the way Robert giggles like a girl after finishing a story. Then again, Proust acts like a female better than most girls around. He was created with the entirely wrong sexual organs!

I cannot write the term "sexual organs" without mentioning Boldini. The reference is in poor taste, admittedly, but if a woman can't dabble in scandalous talk in her own diaries, where can she? In any case, as we promenaded through the *Bazar* I kept my eyes roaming for a glimpse of Boldini, though it was exactly the kind of place he'd never deign to enter. It's not that I wanted to see him, though it could not hurt to have him see me look so exquisite. But more than that, I had a score to settle. After years of agonizing, after a hundred starts and stops, M. Boldini finally completed his rendition of *Le Comte*. How convenient! Now that I've taken up with the man, Boldini suddenly finds him easy to paint. I guess not all works were impaled on the Opéra spires.

The Affair of the Cane, the papers called this portrait (and still do). According to Montesquiou, Boldini positively insisted on the inclusion of *Le Comte's* beloved turquoise-handled cane in the portrait. He ordered Robert to hold it up near his mouth and gaze at it fondly, as one might an old lover one was glad to see again. Or as the always-naughty Marguérite declared, in the manner Robert usually reserved for admiring his manhood!

"Admit it," Marguérite snickered. "The way he's grasping the neck of that cane in his white gloved hand is exactly as he does to his member in the boudoir!"

"I wouldn't know," I snapped back. "When I'm there he has no need of his hand!"

Marguérite was not the only one who made jokes. Not even close! That damn portrait produced such a slew of jibes I wondered if the hilarity would ever stop. Just where do you plan to put the cane, Monsieur de Montesquiou? Et cetera.

As incensed as I was over the whole thing, Robert merely laughed and said, "It is better to be hated than unknown." I strongly disagree. One must maintain a semblance of respectability because if you don't have a solid reputation, then what do you have?

Though Robert believes Boldini intended no ill will, I am certain the blasted man wanted to show *Le Comte* at his worst: the man's dandy essence magnified tenfold. The situation was exacerbated by the recent eruption of Boldini's popularity. Conventional wisdom now states that anything he creates is both genius and true to life. Ergo, if it appears that the subject longs to shove a cane up his derrière, then it must be the case!

As shameful as the whole experience was, with Robert there will be no hiding. He continues to drag me to Maxim's and the Opéra and even my old place of employ. A chorus of tittering follows our every step! At least *Le Comte* understands that I require recompense for the mortification. Never has he plied me with so many beautiful things. My flat does not seem as large as it once was!

Gifts aside, after one hour in the tents, Montesquiou miming around with that damn cane, it seemed positively crucial to locate Boldini and put him on the receiving end of my wrath. I've tried to fault Robert for the debacle, so stupid was he to let Boldini dictate the props, but he doesn't seem to care.

As we wandered through the *Bazar* I stopped every one of Boldini's associates to inquire after his whereabouts. I asked Gauguin and Bourget and even that midget. They all said he was there, perhaps but not for sure. So single-minded was I that when a harried, haggard woman careened into me I didn't notice her face. At first.

"Please watch your step," I said as she trampled over my shoes. "This place is crowded, and you can't rush through like it's a barn burning."

I thought she was one of the poor, a penniless spinster there to help serve food and count change. But when my eyes finally took hold of the woman's face, I saw it was Jeanne Hugo Daudet herself, standing before me with those ugly little children hanging off her skirt like trained monkeys.

"Watch yourself," she snapped back.

"Oh, Madame Daudet. Bonjour." A certain thrill crawled up my spine. "I did not notice you. It's so very odd that wherever I am you turn up! Really quite peculiar, don't you think, Madame Daudet?"

I used her former surname so as to emphasize Madame Daudet's twice-married status. Marguérite reported that after Jeanne's most recent wedding she showed up at the Folies and plunked down at her brother's former table, now vacated since Georges ran off to Italy with his wife's cousin. After downing two Pernods, Jeanne proceeded to sob into her handkerchief for the duration of the evening. She hated having a second marriage. She hated that she had to wear a suit of brown instead of a dress of white.

Alas, I will allow the woman this: Her new husband, Jean-Baptiste Charcot, seems a decent fellow. For better or worse, he is far more interested in adventures on mountaintops than in bedrooms or bordellos. I'd previously overheard him at the Folies, when I still worked there, and he spoke of little else than what peaks he'd scaled or wanted to scale and what gravity-defying objects he attempted to fly. Though he might fall off a cliff, at least he will not catch the clap.

"I'm not sure why you repeatedly use my former name," Jeanne said, straightening her spine as visitors to the *Bazar* continued to bustle around us. "I'm not sure why you address me at all. I don't believe we've met formally. If we had, you would certainly know my name. Unfortunately I cannot keep track of every impoverished person I've graciously helped along the way."

"You are so amusing," I replied, trying to mask my internal rage. "You should be careful, you know. There are rumors you've remarried. I told people it is not possible, so barely out of wedlock are you from Léon. I am not sure who is spreading such vicious lies, but you should find the source and stop them immediately!"

Jeanne Hugo Daudet Charcot smirked and lifted her eyebrows.

"Actually, I have recently married the most dashing fellow in all of Paris . . . in all of Europe, even! Although you know this, do you not? Your boy dandy worked so very hard to secure himself an invitation to the party." She clicked her tongue. "We were so sad we could only invite the important people of Paris."

I hastened to point out that, despite calling me a stranger mere seconds ago, Jeanne admitted to knowing both *Le Comte* and me. Yet the victory did not seem mine to take.

At that moment Robert marched up. I took the opportunity to "startle" and "accidentally" spill my newly purchased perfume oil across Jeanne's dress. She screamed in horror, shielding her eyes as she fell to the ground, even though the liquid was nowhere near her face. It wasn't even hot.

"Oh, Le Comte! You startled me. I am so very clumsy when alarmed! Poor Madame Hugo-Daudet . . ."

"*Madame Charcot!*" she spat between her teeth. Montesquiou tried to help her to stand, but she pushed him away.

"I'm so sorry to have ruined your gown."

"You are a nasty woman," she sneered, brushing off her backside.

"Well, you would know the species."

"I don't have time to entertain the likes of you!" she cried. "I cannot believe Montesquiou is fooled! He is the stupidest man alive, but even for him this is absurd!"

With that Jeanne lifted her skirts and plodded off in the other direction, those hideous chicken-children clucking behind her. I turned to Robert, at the ready with an excuse. But *Le Comte* was so busy studying his freshly manicured nails he did not have time to contemplate my erratic behavior.

We spent the balance of the afternoon stomping across hay and visiting the ladies selling their geegaws. Sometime after dusk, Robert and I returned to my flat. As he poured a drink I slid out of my shoes and gown. I felt exhausted, tired, and overwrought all at once.

Robert hummed and dripped golden liquid into a crystal glass as I sat contemplating how strange it was we'd been coupled for two years, across one Daudet and at the start of Charcot. It is a long stretch to be with the same person, at least in my world, and though I know *Le Comte* well, I also know him very little. These thoughts bounced around my mind as I watched him pour my drink. It all left me oddly confused. And confused I remain.

For the first time since arriving in Paris, I find my position, my future . . . it all seems so hazy and unclear. I have the apartment now. The gowns. The furnishings and the art. I am not married to Montesquiou, but am I supposed to stay with him forever?

"Drink or sexual congress first?" *Le Comte* asked, waggling his finger through the ice. Nausea crept into my gut.

I'd never not wanted him. Indeed I'm not always primed for his advances and sometimes have to work myself into an amorous condition. But right then the thought of his skin pressing against mine made me ill. It was nonsensical, I told myself, merely a by-product of the *Bazar.* Our surroundings can affect our moods, affect our desires, so much more than we'd like to admit. Truth be told, the whole affair let me down. It's odd how something you've dreamed of half your life looks different once you get inside.

Part Quatre

Chapitre LI

Paris, 9 May 1897

What is it they say? The world can change in an instant? It happened to me. Like a spark to canvas, everything ignited and then burned away, the only thing left standing the structures, the ideas of how things once looked. This is both a metaphor and a strict interpretation of what happened.

Five days ago Paris held its annual *Bazar de la Charité*. As Robert and I departed my flat an intense feeling of déjà vu overtook me. Hadn't we just done this? Hadn't we just left for the *Bazar*? A year had passed, but so little changed. The thought bathed me in an almost crippling sense of immobilization and it took forty-five minutes for Montesquiou to coax me from my home. In many ways it would've been better had we stayed. Then again, I would not have been there for the events that transpired. I needed it all to happen to get where I am now.

This year's *Bazar* was not on the Champs-Elyseés but instead held near the Place des Vosges on the rue Jean-Goujon. As Robert and I walked up to the booming canvas-and-plywood structures something coagulated inside me. One might assume I say this in hindsight, but I felt so out of sorts that Montesquiou asked after my well-being. *Le Comte* concerned with another? It was a first. He once found a man stabbed and bleeding at his feet and turned to me to query whether I liked his suit.

I was not stabbed or bleeding, but one does not speak candidly to Robert, and so I lied and said everything was fine.

Stomach spinning, I followed Robert through the turnstile and out onto the Norwegian pine floors, an upgrade from the prior year's hay and sticks. The decorations were also different. To access the main area each person was required to walk through a maze of badly painted faux-scenery: hills too green, cows resembling spotted hippos, flowers painted colors found only in *Le Comte's* special-breed gardens. The maze was unavoidable; one had to use it both to enter and to exit the *Bazar.* The point was to amuse and divert, and to control the movement of the crowds. I found it cumbersome. Then it got worse.

Once through the maze, guests were herded like swine into various lanes, which in turn shuttled visitors through a low, narrow doorway and out into the exhibit hall. Finally the escape! Thirty booths lined the room. Though the attendance matched the previous year, the main floor did not seem as congested because the majority of guests were crowded into one particular corner: a motion picture exhibit.

The famous George Méliès was there to present his latest film, *The Conjuring of a Lady at Robert-Houdin's Theater.* As expected, *Le Comte* bunched up with the rest of the viewers to snare a closer look. Anything new or different is a magnet to the man. I stood back and inspected the trinkets of a Gypsy lady somewhere near the maze's exit. I was interested in the film, but the ether required to keep the picture machine running made me lightheaded. That is, I suppose, why some people stood near it in the first place.

Shortly after two o'clock, Robert walked over and announced his boredom, right on time. He planned to head to Maxim's. I was busy negotiating a black-pearl acquisition with an old mustachioed woman so told him to go on ahead. I watched him leave. I watched him walk into the maze. I saw him do this! No one believes me. Isn't that how it always is? People want to believe the stories they create themselves.

After approximately ten minutes of haggling, the hirsute woman refusing to budge, the movie machine emitted a loud, clacking sputter. Necklace twisted around my hand and wrist, I looked to where the projector continued to grind.

"And that is why motion pictures will never take off," I said to the woman. "Who can concentrate on the film while being subjected to that ruckus?"

Suddenly a spark flew off the machine and landed on the ether lamp. The lamp exploded off the table and shot across the room. Before anyone could grasp what was happening, the fireball hit one side of the tent and ignited the canvas. Not a single thought passed through my mind. I merely looked down to find my feet already running away from the fire.

I was halfway through the maze by the time the smoke caught up with me. Behind me people screamed. Young men trampled over old ladies. People shoved their way through the narrow passage, gasping for air, pushing for life. I clung to the back of one man's coat, and soon we were released out onto the street, everyone still screaming, everyone running wild like a bunch of *Apaches*. Though not everyone was running. Most were still inside.

All in all, 140 perished, many from the most renowned families in Paris, including the Duchesse d'Alençon. Several people I know died, though no one I hold dear. Still, it feels as though I've lost something.

When I found Montesquiou at Maxim's later that day, tears and soot lined my face. He ridiculed my appearance and asked if I was trying to impersonate an Arab. Even after I told him what had transpired, he continued to make fun. Furious, I left *Le Comte* to his own devices and returned to my flat, where I spent the rest of the night weeping into a pillow.

The old man with the crutches, did he make it out? What about the two precious girls in blue bonnets and silk sashes? The Gypsy woman could not have. She ran toward the flames instead of away from them. When I woke up the next morning, head thick from crying, her pearls were still wrapped around my hand.

Unfortunately for Robert, "the affair of the cane" continues to haunt him, now to a much more damaging degree. The papers are frenzied with accounts of folks behaving badly as the *Bazar* fire roared, each day a new tragedy to tell. As the tales go, it was every man for himself, every woman and child blanketing the way. And no one has suffered more injurious reports than Montesquiou himself.

The reports state that Robert was in the tent when the fire broke out, and that he caned people out of the way so he could get to safety. They say he used the famous cane as a "cudgel for living women and as tongs for dead women," among a dozen other atrocities. The gutter journalist Jean Lorrain started the rumor, he so perpetually bitter at being called "a poor man's Montesquiou" multiple times in the press. The man refers to Montesquiou as "Grotesquiou" in public and in print, lest there be any question of his jealousy.

I've tried to come to *Le Comte's* defense, but no matter how many times I've said he was not there, that he'd departed some time before and didn't even have the cane that day, my protests are viewed as nothing more than a concealment.

Alas the fool did not help his case when he popped by the Palais de l'Industrie to see the bodies, most of which were charred beyond recognition. He lurched and leaped over the corpses, lifting sheets (with his cane!) to peer at the faces of the dead.

What if I had died in the fire? What if I had wasted the last three years of my life with a dandy who doesn't care that all of Paris thinks he is willing to beat cripples and children to save himself? The worst part is that I understand how people could believe the rumor. The assumption is fitting! It is something he would've done. He didn't, but he could have.

Three years with *Le Comte*! Three years with a man newspapers dub "the world's most laborious sayer of nothing." He is extraordinarily generous. Indeed, he's given me an apartment and enough jewels to adorn every member of the French aristocracy. I was able to leave my post at the Folies thanks to him. Nonetheless I feel as though Giovanni gave me more despite never giving me anything at all.

Some say the fire was deserved, a divine wrath being foisted upon the rich. A well-known priest sermonized that the very cause was God's ire at the scientific and social ideas of the new generation. He called the fire an "exterminating angel"—said almost hopefully—and assured everyone that the victims of the fire died in expiation of the nation's sins. I do not subscribe to this line of thought, the deceased children had not a crime to atone for, but the idea of the fire as means to expiate one's sins has somehow stayed with me.

When Montesquiou came to see me this morning, I announced my intent to formally disengage from our most informal contract. There would be no more dinners at Maxim's or nights in my bed. It was a dangerous assertion. Everything I had was his first.

"I understand," Robert said. "I'm surprised we lasted this long."

"I will not relocate," I told him, my voice shaky. I did not want to ask what might happen to the apartment. I did not want to ask what might happen to me.

"Then don't." He shrugged.

"I will try to pay the rent, I—"

"Shush." He placed a finger over my lips. It tasted funny, like burnt salt. I could only hope those particular rumors were true; that he used *only* his cane to poke around the charred corpses. "You shall stay. I have no use for this apartment. We can work out an arrangement suitable to us both."

"But I said no more—"

"I don't mean that kind of arrangement."

"I will try to get my job back with the Folies. Maybe they'll even let me on the stage this time! I've developed a reputation for myself. People might actually pay to see me lift my skirts."

"Only if you want to," he said. "Do not worry about the apartment."

"I have to—"

"Ma chérie," he said and kissed me on the nose. "Don't fret. It is only money, and there is always more of it."

With that, he grabbed his cane, tapped it against the ground two times, and skipped out of my apartment. If I expected disagreement or fight, he gave me neither. Perhaps this was Robert's way. Or perhaps the rumors were true, the rumors of an American heiress coaxing him across the ocean. She wants to get married, they say. And I say good luck to the both of them.

After Montesquiou left, and before I could think better of it, I locked the flat and proceeded to Boldini's. I didn't know why. I didn't know what I might say. I only knew I had to go. As long as he wasn't with another woman I could figure out the right thing to do.

Pausing at the door of his studio, I inhaled deeply, raised my fist, and knocked three times sharply. Footsteps moved across the floor. They were loping, irritated footsteps, and my heart swelled at the sound of Boldini.

He opened the door.

"Giovanni!" I cried. "Please don't lock me out. I cannot bear to be apart from you any longer. I don't know how this all went awry, if it was because of Montesquiou or Pujol. I can't take back what happened with the farting show, but regarding Montesquiou it is over. I'm probably too late by three years, more than a thousand days. But know that all the time I spent gazing at diamonds and furs I was trying not to think of you!"

Boldini did not answer. I sank down to my knees and locked my arms around his calves, sobbing into his trousers. He jostled his legs, trying to rid himself of me. I clung tighter. Finally he pushed down on my head and wrenched himself free. He turned and walked inside.

But he left the door open.

Stunned, I glanced up from my pathetic place on the ground. Boldini went to his canvas. He held tight to his silence. He did not speak as he picked up his brush. He did not offer solace or guarantees. But he let me inside.

Slowly I rose to my feet. I crept across the floor, worried that the open door was an oversight and not an invitation. Boldini was known to leave stoves on, paints dripping, his clothes at the tailors' for twelve months straight.

However, as I glided across the room Giovanni glanced up ever so slightly. I detected the smallest of nods. After planting myself on a settee, I crossed my legs and smoothed my now-crumpled skirt. Boldini continued to paint. He said nothing. I watched, grateful for what felt like a fresh start.

Chapitre LII

When April woke Luc was gone, but there was no confusion. He had been there. There was a note ("Ma chérie, a beautiful time") and a rumpled other side of the bed, not that April needed any evidence of what happened.

She wasn't sure how to feel. April had slept with someone who wasn't Troy. Always unfavorable to betray your marriage vows, but what was their marriage at that point other than a piece of paper? A stack of paper if you counted the prenup, and god knew how much paper after that if they ended up divorcing.

"If they ended up divorcing." She was surprised the word "if" still had a place at the table. More than that, April was surprised she was thinking of it as "divorcing," as a verb instead of the noun she usually pictured.

Legal documents notwithstanding, Troy could say very little about April's Fête Nationale dalliance. He'd cheated before, on her, and on his previous wife, and, no doubt, on whomever he'd dated before Susannah, and further back still.

But that wasn't it, exactly, payback or sexual one-upmanship. There was something more with Luc. April would not call it feelings or even a crush. But her wanting him was at least a little separate from her problems with Troy. Last night didn't happen because Luc was the only person around and sporting the correct sexual organs. She may have been drunk, but it was deliberate. It was Marthe going to Boldini's studio after the fire.

April smiled. "Marthe's back with Boldini," she wanted to text the handsome attorney who'd seen her naked, the very man who'd—oh god!—lived up to every expectation April hadn't known she'd set for him. The only problem was if April told Luc about Boldini she'd have to come up with something to say afterward, and she wasn't quite ready to face that conversational hurdle. So April intentionally left her phone and computer untouched until such a time as she could figure out a smooth *rentrée* into their regularly scheduled relationship, if that even still existed.

Instead April spent most of the next day in bed, reading and working, but mostly sleeping. Whenever she summoned the strength to rise, she pattered about the apartment in bare feet and lingerie, the humid July air blowing through the curtains and chilling her still-warm skin.

Fête Nationale celebrations continued on, the parades and fireworks and throngs of citizens booming throughout Paris. The ruckus made concentration difficult, though whatever noise clogged April's brain was not merely a result of the holiday.

Setting auction estimates, scribbling out last-minute descriptions, none of it got a fair shake with sneaky pieces of Luc popping up and derailing April's good intentions. From his initial eager kisses, gentle at first, then persistent, him muttering, "Putain, c'est pas trop tôt!" as he tried to catch his breath. Literal translation: "Damn, it's not too early!" The French equivalent of "It's about fucking time!"

April felt him pressing into her as they navigated the hallway, their shared giddiness as they tripped up the stairs together, how Luc kept bumping her up against the apartment door as she contended, yet again, with that damned sticky lock. April couldn't wait. She literally did not think she could.

They quickly lost their clothing, all of it damp and sticky from the hours of dancing. April wasn't sure when or how they'd finally made it to the bed, only that they'd arrived. She kept seeing flashes of his smirking face as it closed in on her; kept feeling the terror and ecstasy the night brought her.

And when she woke up—April remembered it now. In her groggy haze she opened her eyes to see Luc leaning over the bed. He kissed her gently on the forehead, the smell of yesterday still on his breath.

April jolted to the present. She glanced toward the window where raindrops tapped on the open panes. Good thing she was leaving soon, April tried to tell herself. It was increasingly difficult to get a damn thing accomplished in this city. This was Paris. There were too many distractions.

Chapitre LIII

April finally left her flat late the next morning. Judging by the piles of trash on the sidewalks and the French flags battered, torn, and tangled up in bushes, the rain had kept very few Parisians away from the party.

April made her way to Café du Mogador, a little place in the Ninth across from the stunning Église de la Sainte-Trinité. The café's red awning called it a "sandwicherie," which sounded perfect until April felt the sense of queasy pseudo-excitement (plus fear) still lingering from the Fête. The idea of food was unsettling.

Still, April had to eat at some point, her last sustenance having been in the form of three pastries snagged from a display near the firehouse exit a day and a half before. She picked the last remaining table (small, round, marble) and was trying to work out how to fit both her laptop and a pen on it when a waiter appeared. After placing a halfhearted order, April set her notecards on the table, a stack of papers on her lap. Computer use would have to wait. It'd been a few days, what was an hour or two more?

Now that provenance was established on the Boldini and other "important" pieces, April was going over final copy and making last-minute changes to the catalogs in which Marthe's assets would sit. There were a few open items, a gaping hole or twelve, which April relied on Birdie to fill. That's what she did—filled in the missing, picked up the slack.

Remembering something Birdie had dug up about a set of woefully hard-to-describe chairs, April went to check her e-mails and was startled to find her phone dead. How long had it been off? Twenty-four hours? Forty-eight? April remembered powering down while at the firehouse. Was it possible she'd never turned it on again?

The phone seemed to take hours to come to life, to scroll through the programs and see what needed updating. Finally the voice mails appeared. Eight, to be exact. Troy would be annoyed. Worse, her father would be panicked. April cringed as she recalled the missed incoming phone calls from the night before last, when she was out with Luc.

"Sorry, Dad," she said aloud, nervous fingers fumbling for the Voice Mail button. "Please don't call the gendarmes quite yet."

Before she had a chance to listen to the messages, April's BlackBerry whirred. She checked the number: It was her brother, unsurprising since she'd inadvertently gone radio-silent.

"Ack, hi, Brian," she said straight off. "Is Dad looking for me? I'm so sorry I've been incommunicado. I didn't even realize my phone was off for two days. Please tell him I haven't been abducted or bombed on the Métro. I feel horrible. I'm the worst daughter in the world."

"April."

Brian's voice was sharp. It was never sharp. Suddenly April understood that something was wrong. She should've guessed it the moment she saw his name. It was almost noon in Paris, which meant six o'clock in New York, which meant three in California. Three o'clock in the morning: the dead part of the night, too late for night owls, too early for early birds. This was when bad stuff happened.

"What time is it?" April's skin went cold. "Why are you calling me this early? What's going on? Are you okay? Is Allie okay?"

"Have you talked to Dad? Tell me you've talked to Dad."

"He called while I was out for my birthday, and I was going to call him back. I didn't mean to scare anyone."

"Tell me you called him back."

"I didn't even realize my phone was off. I'm so sorry. I'll call him right after we hang up."

"Fuck," Brian said once, and then a few more times for good measure. This was not like her brother, the good-natured techie surfer. He rode waves, he did not create them. He didn't worry. He didn't stress out.

"Brian. Please. Tell me everything's okay."

"Ha." He laughed bitterly. "Not okay at all. Shit. Well, I guess I'm going to have to tell you right now, over the phone, which is a motherfucking bitch. What choice do I have?"

"Brian, you are seriously freaking me out."

He inhaled deeply and let out a sad, angry, twisted laugh. Then he spoke.

Chapitre LIV

There are the moments you know you'll remember forever as soon they happen: your engagement, standing at the altar and saying "I do," the news of your spouse cheating, someone saying the words "you're fired." All those beautiful and wretched pieces of news available on your personal movie reel at any second and until the end of time.

Still, April was surprised to find she could not remember this particular moment. Within seconds of Brian spitting out the words, she'd already forgotten how he said them. Of course she recalled the gist of what he told her, the gist of how she felt. But April would only ever remember what she did next.

The minute Brian hung up the phone (did either of them say goodbye?), April dialed Luc's number for a reason she could not comprehend. April only knew she needed someone, and she didn't want to call Troy. In hindsight it was an inappropriate reaction but at the time it seemed like the most natural thing to do.

"Bonjour, Avril!" Luc's voice came over the line. There was a pause as he bumped and shuffled. A door closed. "Have we recovered from the birthday festivities? Did you see the news? One of the firehouses burned down that night. Ironic, non? A firehouse burning down. If only they had some fire trucks in the vicinity."

"One of the firehouses burned down?" April thought of Marthe and the others scrambling out of the *Bazar de la Charité* maze. She could nearly taste the smoke and hear the screams. For a moment she forgot about Brian's news, for a longer moment still her night with Luc. "Is everyone all right? Were people hurt?"

"Everyone escaped unscathed, thank goodness. There was quite a lot of damage but none of the human variety."

"Oh." April said and exhaled. "I'm relieved to hear it. Listen, I really need to talk to you."

"You do?"

"Yes," April said, only barely remembering to be embarrassed by their night together, by the fact he'd touched every inch of her, that she'd wanted him to. He knew her intimately; and not just physically. Perhaps this should've sent her into fits of insecurity, but it seemed silly now, like worrying about your luggage as the flight went down. "I was wondering if I could see you. Is there somewhere we can meet?"

"Avril, you are concerned about the other night, non?"

"Actually, no—"

"Please don't get so serious about it and worry-worry-worry. I know how you are. Enjoy it for what it was. No need of explanations and backtracking . . ."

"No," April said with force. "Not that. *That*. It happened."

"Oh."

"And it was great."

"Yes."

"This—is not about that. It has nothing to do with you, really. I don't know why I dialed your number. It's just . . . I mean—"

"Avril? What is it? Now you have *me* worried, which will never do."

"I can't—I can't—" she stuttered, sobs working their way up her chest but sticking in her throat and making it hard to breathe.

"Is this about Marthe?" he asked. "The flat?"

"This is about me. Present day. Something happened."

"Where are you?" he said. "At your apartment? I will come now."

Her apartment? April blanched. Their night together was, apparently, not as far away as she suspected. The image of him showing up at her doorstep brought instant panic. She thought of her messy living room, the still-rumpled bed, her clothes scattered across the floors, plus about a hundred other clues as to what happened between them. No. There would be no Luc in her apartment today.

"I'm—I'm at a café," she said. "Not at home. Never mind, Luc. I shouldn't have called. It was stupid."

"I'm coming over."

"No. The apartment's a mess and I—"

"Then you come here. Do you still have my address?"

"Your address?" She thought for a moment. It was, of course, still in her phone. Not that April had intentionally saved it, she just wouldn't have permanently deleted a text from Luc. "I think so."

"Excellent," he said. "Where are you now? How far away? In the Ninth?"

"Yes," April said, a little dazed. Was she really going to do this, was she really going to show up at his home and dump her problems at his feet? "Are you sure you want me to come over? I realize this isn't very professional, and I don't want to put you out—"

"Just come. No excuses or apologies. Just come."

"All right," she said, nodding and biting her lip. "À bientôt. I'll see you soon."

Chapitre LV

April's chest quivered as she slipped the phone into her pocket. She wondered how she might stand, how she might get all the way over to the Sixteenth without first shattering into a million pieces.

After dumping a stack of euros on the table at the exact second the waiter delivered her order of Croque Madame, April bolted out of the restaurant and hailed a cab. Leaping into a taxi, she read Luc's address to the driver. She slammed the door and off they puttered toward the Sixteenth.

She had to do something. April needed to fill the space instead of staring out the window letting dark thoughts take residence in her brain. Voice mails. She had to check her voice mails. None of them could be worse than what she'd just heard.

There were eight in total. April was right. None topped Brian's announcement because they were all variations on what he said. The slow build-up, the increasing urgency, the dancing-around-of-what happened. Troy had no messages about her birthday, but even he belted into the phone, "Call me right away! It's urgent!"

April was glad she heard it from her brother first. Brian was the best possible person to deliver bad news. If only Troy had used him as an intermediary those months ago! Then again, that news almost seemed like nothing now, even if Troy's confession was unexpected and what her brother said inevitable, the high-magnitude aftershock April had been bracing herself for.

"Madame?" The cab driver peered over his shoulder.

"Pardon?" April said as she deleted the last voice mail, tears running down her cheeks.

"Nous sommes ici."

"Oh." April looked up. "Indeed we have. Merci beaucoup."

She passed him the money and lunged out of the car with the very distinct knowledge that he was watching her go.

Positively relieved at the sight of Luc's building, and then the feel of his stairs beneath her feet, April sprinted up to his apartment, hiccupping and sweating as she went. At his doorstep she knocked with one hand, the other pressed against the doorjamb to keep her body upright.

"Entre donc!" Luc called. "It's unlocked!"

Shaking, April jiggled the ancient, loose doorknob, fussing and pulling until she was finally able to push through to his living room. She stood in its center with tears trickling down her face and neck, mouth curdled in a sob. She paused to catch her breath.

"Luc?" she said, voice strained. April wiped her eyes with a sleeve. "Are you here?"

He walked through the kitchen door then, hands on his hips. April wondered if Luc knew how often he stood like that.

"You arrived much faster than expected," he said, blinking fast. He looked nervous, which April understood. If not for Brian's news she would've been nervous, too.

"Luc, it's so good to see you," April said, falling against his chest. "I am so sorry for bothering you, but I had to come."

"Au' voir, Luc!" a voice sang from the back bedroom. "À ce soir!"

It was a woman—a woman's voice. Vomit splashed up the back of April's throat as she pulled away from him.

"Who . . . is . . ." April struggled to get the words out as she turned toward the sound.

A woman floated into the room then, a woman dripping in Chanel, Hermès and Parisian litheness. Her hair was long. And straight. And thick. It was the exact color of caramel. Was she a model? A ballerina? She really could've been either.

"Ma belle," Luc said and put an arm around the woman's waist, grimacing the slightest bit. "C'est mon ami, April Vogt."

Luc enunciated her name like he normally never did. *APE-ril*. She felt exactly like a hairy, lumbering primate right then.

"Ah! Avril!" The woman's face lit up. "It ees so *PLAY-zure* to meet you!"

He had a girlfriend. Of course Luc had a girlfriend. It was stupid to care. Shallow. Short-sighted. But care she did. April thought her heart had broken all the way by then, but as it turned out, it had room to crack a little more.

"Bonjour," April said, reeling. She found herself glaring at Luc, though she had no right to.

"Oh!" the woman squealed again. "Très bien! 'Allo! 'Allo!"

April shot Luc another glance.

"Everyone's questioning—" she heard him mumble as she turned her attentions fully toward the woman.

"Everyone's questioning"? Questioning what?

"Ravi de faire votre connaissance," April managed to choke out, graciously, she hoped.

"This is Delphine Vidal," Luc said and gestured toward the woman. "Banker extraordinaire."

"Zee banker gaming . . . what do you call it? 'Hooka'?"

April crinkled her forehead. "Uh, I'm not sure what you mean . . ."

"Hooky," Luc corrected her. " 'A banker playing hooky.' You'll get it right soon, mon amour."

Delphine pretended to pinch his ear.

"Zees man of mine ees trés terreeble." Delphine shook her head and grinned. Her teeth were blindingly white and disturbingly straight, rendering her almost horsey, but in a good way. There were horse people and there were equestrians, and Delphine Vidal was the latter. "So zees ees sweet Avril! I hear very so lots of much about you! "

"I'm surprised Luc has even mentioned me," April stuttered.

"Luc speeeks about you all zee time," Delphine said, still beaming. "Zees is so 'appy to meet!"

"Oh, well, that's very kind," April said, though she was decidedly less " 'appy to meet." She hadn't known English spoken horribly could sound so appealing. "Thank you."

What had she been thinking? Of course Luc had a girlfriend. Why wouldn't he? And what did it matter? Did she really envision herself hooking up with some Frenchman despite one (albeit perfect) night? Did she fancy herself Marthe and him Boldini? That she could walk into his apartment and he'd let her watch him paint until she felt normal again? Maybe next they could head to the morgue.

The woman probably knew about the other night, too. A pity-fuck, no doubt, Delphine offering her paramour for the greater good. She seemed exactly that progressive, and exactly that generous.

"Luc say you are from zee cee-tee of New York?" Delphine said, green eyes twinkling.

"Elle parle français," Luc told his girlfriend as she struggled to form the words. "Ça va?"

"Yes. I 'ope to practice zee English!" Misunderstanding the directive, Delphine grinned ever wider, the ends of her mouth now somewhere near her earlobes.

"Trés bien, mon amour!" Luc smiled in return.

Where he'd been fidgety and anxious ninety seconds ago, the usual Luc was starting to reappear, the man April knew, or imagined she did, anyway. He made a few teasing remarks to Delphine about her English, then squeezed her backside. April snapped her head away so fast she kinked her neck.

Those hands. They'd been on her such a short time ago. April's face blazed in embarrassment and anger.

"I. Have. To. Go," Delphine said, separating each syllable. "Very so much *PLAY-zure* to meet you!"

She leaned in and bestowed upon April the double-cheek kiss.

"The pleasure is mine," April quacked.

"Au 'voir!" Delphine danced away, waving over her shoulder. Platinum-and-diamond bangles twinkled along her arm. "À bientôt!"

As though a desert wind just flashed through the apartment, Delphine Vidal was gone, leaving Luc and April empty and dry-mouthed on his fancy wool and cashmere rug.

"Her English is very poor," Luc said.

"She tried. That's what counts. Is Delphine your girlfriend?"

Luc paused before answering.

"Oui," he said at last. "She is. But understand, you are not the only one—"

"Does she live here?"

"Did you come to ask of my living situation?"

He sounded annoyed, as if April had no basis for the question. On the other hand, maybe she didn't. April shook her head.

"I want to know," she replied sheepishly and turned toward the window. "I need to know."

"No," he said and sighed. "She does not."

"Where was she the night before the Fête Nationale?"

"Working on a transaction in Luxembourg," he said. "Avril, why are you here? You said something was wrong. Let's talk about that instead of my living situation. Although if you wish to continue on this path, indeed I might have a few questions for you as well."

"Point taken," April grumbled.

"Avril?" he said again, this time gently reaching for her arm.

"I dunno, Luc. Maybe I should just leave. It's so long. Sordid."

April inhaled deeply and studied Luc, wondering if she still trusted him enough to share the news. Somehow the answer was yes.

"Tell me," he said.

"Well." She exhaled. "I did come all this way. Bothered you in the middle of the afternoon"—saw things I shouldn't have—"I guess. Well. . . . Remember when we were out the other night and my phone rang? And you said to take the call and I said no?"

"Oui. Your father. Ringing with birthday wishes."

"Yes. Well, sort of. It was my dad, but that's not why he called."

April closed her eyes. She took in several more breaths. Everything inside her body churned.

"Avril." She felt Luc shift on his feet. He brushed his fingers against her arm. "What happened? What is wrong?"

"It's my mother," she said, and her eyes popped back open. "She—well—she died. My mother died."

Chapitre LVI

Once the words were out of her mouth, spilled onto the furniture and across the floor, April sank down onto Luc's couch and buried her face in her hands.

"What do you mean, 'she died'?" Luc asked. "When you were a teenager?"

"No," she said and looked up without caring about her red and mottled face. "She died the night of my birthday, when we were at the firehouse. Although it was technically morning in California. Either way, while we were eating sausage my mother had a fatal stroke."

Luc did not respond. He remained on the other side of the room, an eternity of space between them. It hurt her that he was so far away. It was physically painful.

"I do not understand," he said. "You told me she already died."

"No I didn't. I never said that."

"You did."

"Name one time I said she had died. *One*."

"Well, I can't recall specifically, but surely you must have."

"You misunderstood," April said. "I realize I can be a little cagey about her situation, but obviously I wouldn't have said she died when she was alive. That doesn't even make sense."

"I do not understand," Luc said again, stepping even farther away from her. Soon he would be in the kitchen and April would have to shout. She wanted him to reach for her, to tell her it would all be okay.

"Forget it," April said. "I'm so sorry, Luc. I never should've come. I'm a wreck and with Delphine"—she pointed halfheartedly toward the front door, the imprint of the "banker extraordinaire" still somehow visible—"Just forget it."

April mentally berated herself. She wanted too much from Luc, too much from them, as if there were a *them* to begin with, when their only true connection was a contract signed by Agnès Vannier and Sotheby's, the names Vogt and Thébault not even part of the document.

"Avril," Luc said. "You must explain yourself. Your mother. Gone. Missing. When all this time she was here. You've lied to me."

"I haven't lied!" April snapped. "And she wasn't 'here.' She was absolutely gone before I left for college. Physically, no. There was a body and it was hers. But to all intents and purposes the woman I knew disappeared."

Luc frowned. He was trying to seem stern, angered by her withholding of information. But even from the couch and at that great distance April understood that the true face he was showing was one of concern, of worry.

"My mom has—*had*—early-onset Alzheimer's," April told him at last. "Do you know what that is? Is there a different expression in French?"

"I know what it is," Luc said, his face still grim but starting to soften.

"The symptoms began when she was young," April went on. "Extremely young. I was about fourteen when things started to go awry. Or, at least, I was fourteen when I started to notice. Mom was forty-two."

"What happened?" Luc asked. "When things started to 'go awry'?"

"Oh, ordinary stuff. Losing keys, forgetting to pick us up at school, confusion in grocery stores, not recognizing her own car. All the little things you can write off for a while."

"Until you can't," Luc said, his voice like gravel.

"Right. Until there's that one thing." April slammed a fist into her palm. "Where you have to open it all up and look inside."

"So what happened?" Luc asked again as he took a few steps closer. His feet were now partway onto the rug. "What was the one thing?"

"Do you really want to hear it?" April asked. "Because it's a pretty fucking depressing story."

"Yes. I want to hear it. You have to say it."

April nodded, and for only the third time in her life, she told the story of the zoo.

Chapitre LVII

It was her brother's tenth birthday. Due to their mom's recent bout of forgetfulness, which was attributed to stress and lack of sleep, Dad decided there would be no formal party for Brian. It was too taxing. Instead Mom and her two children would enjoy a day at the zoo.

April was fourteen at the time, thus rather irritated by the endeavor from the onset. It was summertime and school was out. Her friends were at the beach, rubbing baby oil all over their bodies and lying across giant strips of tinfoil. April wanted to be there too, but instead was forced to meander around the hot, hilly zoo, surrounded by the smell of sweaty monkey fur and elephant feces plus one little brother who was hardly any fun at all.

The morning went as expected, namely with an excessive amount of time spent standing in the snake enclosure watching reptiles swallow small white bunnies whole. On the one hand, it was disgusting. On the other, at least the snake pit gave April relief from the heat.

When Brian finally tired of watching the demise of defenseless furry creatures, the three made their way to a hot-dog window. The lines were long, and what started out as treacherous boredom turned into something else entirely. About halfway through the line, their mother started to panic.

"Where are your parents?" she asked April, then Brian. "Are you two here by yourselves?"

"We're with you," Brian answered, confused.

"Mom, what are you talking about?" April looked around to make sure she didn't see anyone she knew.

"There are bad people in the world!" their mother rasped, voice low, as if the "bad people" were listening and waiting to pounce. "Come, come with me!"

"What the hell?" April said as their mom flagged down a groundskeeper and asked for directions to security.

"I'm hungry," Brian whined.

"I'm taking you to the police!" their mother screamed, clutching their wrists and dragging them through the park.

Brian looked over at his big sister and laughed, hoping she might laugh too. This was a joke, he thought, Mom acting silly. April smiled back even though she knew their life had just changed, that nothing would ever look the same again. You could shrug off lost keys and dishwashing detergent accidentally put in the freezer. Forgetting the faces of your children? Not an anecdote for bridge group.

"Hello, ma'am, can I help you?" a guard asked as they stormed the stuffy security trailer.

"Someone left these minors alone at the zoo!" April's mother shouted, flinging the kids forward, their wrists now red and lumpy from her grip. "You have to find their parents! They won't tell me anything!"

"All right." The man finished off his Slurpee and pulled out a notepad. He looked directly at April. "You're hardly a kid. Where are your parents?"

"This is a little hard to explain," April said nervously. Brian stood beside her, alternating between giggles and feeble little cries. "She *is* our mother."

"Uh, beg pardon?" The man swiped a hand over his mustache, then ran a blue tongue over his lips. April would never get over that particular shade of artificial blue.

"This is our mom," she said. "This happens sometimes. She gets confused. Her name is Sandra Grace Potter. She was born on December 2, 1951. We are Brian and April Potter. Our father is Richard. He works at the naval base on Coronado. We live in Coronado, too."

"Oh my god!" their mother shouted, startling everyone in the room. Even the rotating desk fan jumped.

Finally, April thought. She realizes what's going on.

"My purse! Someone stole my purse." She turned to April. "Did you little hooligans take it?"

"Mom—"

"I can't find my purse." She started patting her sides, her stomach, her breasts.

"Don't worry, ma'am," the security officer said. He reached for a walkie-talkie. "I'll put a call out. See if someone found it. What does it look like?"

"Hmmm." Their mom placed a finger to her chin. "You know what's funny? I don't even remember!"

"It's maroon," April said. "Leather. With a drawstring top. There should be keys to an Oldsmobile station wagon inside. And probably a million little bunched-up pieces of scented pink Kleenex. Also black-cherry-flavored ChapStick."

Recounting these things made fourteen-year-old April's eyes water. She couldn't figure out why.

"So you did steal my purse!" their mom screamed.

"Mom, I didn't. Okay, this is so weird."

"April?" Brian whimpered, a corner of his shirt twisted and shoved between his teeth. He was ten but at that moment looked closer to three.

Eyes locked on the maybe-family members, the guard mumbled into his walkie-talkie. He needed help of a kind he could not articulate.

That a good Samaritan found Sandy's purse in the aviary was the lucky break April (and the security guard) needed. They were able to ID the woman as well as her children based on the school pictures in her wallet. By the time their father showed up, Mom had mostly regained her bearings, unaware they'd been at the zoo all day but with a vague recollection of trying to help someone else's kids.

"And so," April said, looking up and catching Luc's gaze for the first time since she started the story. "That was the beginning of the end."

"Wow," he said and rubbed his chin. "That is quite the story."

"Yes. It was awful. What sucks even more is that it happened at the 'World Famous San Diego Zoo,' that whore of a tourist attraction that insists on forty-seven billboards on every highway and nonstop advertising loops on radio and television."

"That is, as you say, *brutal*."

"'*Brutal*' is right. When I moved to New York for college, people always thought I was crazy to leave San Diego. The truth was it would've driven me crazy to stay."

"And then to Paris," he said with a half-smile. "It was even further than that."

"I never really looked at it that way." She shook her head. "Anyway, things sort of went south from there. Or, even more south than they already were. Dad thought he could take care of her, but by my fifteenth birthday she was in a home. There was no sweet-sixteen party and certainly no car. I had to coerce our neighbor into taking me to get my license. My dad was more or less absent from then on. As much as Mom was. More. At least he had a choice. On my fifteenth birthday I felt like I lost both of my parents, even though up until two days ago both were still alive."

April grabbed her purse and pulled out her wallet.

"Here. I'll show you. A picture says a thousand words, right?"

She plunged her fingers into the space behind her credit cards. Tucked amid a checkbook, three business cards, and stamps from some lower price point, was a photograph. April extracted it and passed it Luc's way. Much to her surprise, he was now beside her on the couch. She looked down to see their thighs nearly touching.

"These are your parents," Luc said, studying the photograph, eyes following the curve of the man's sparsely covered head as it leaned over a hospital bed. Beneath him a blank-faced woman reclined against two pillows. His eyes were closed; hers were vacant and staring. They held hands. Or, rather, the man clutched the woman's hands as her fingers sat limply inside his hold.

"It's them," April said with a nod. "Don't even ask when it was taken because I have no idea. He's been in that position for the last nineteen years. Or he was, at least until the other night. Poor guy. What the hell is he going to do with himself now?"

"C'est incroyable," Luc said. "That is true love."

"I suppose that's one way to look at it," April muttered.

"But it is beautiful, non? We all want to feel this way." Luc went to slide his hand around April's waist or touch her back—or something—but then uncharacteristically pulled back. "Most people never get the chance. Too many things—people, life—it all gets in the way."

"I'd never figured you for a romantic," April said, lying in some way. "And while I agree he loved her tremendously, at the risk of sounding like the teenage April, what about *us*? He still had a family to raise but completely forgot about us."

"Somehow I doubt that."

"Troy, my husband, ex, my—"

"Le grand m'sieu," Luc said and tried for a smirk. "Yes, I am familiar."

"Le grand m'sieu thinks I hold *him* to these standards, that my so-called 'trust issues' stem from the fact I don't think Troy could ever display that level of devotion. But I don't want that. He *should* love Chelsea and Chloe more than he loves me. I'd be upset if he didn't! That's where my dad got it wrong. Troy's girls should be number one, the wife a distant second."

"Avril," Luc frowned. "That makes me sad. *You* should be number one. You should also not refer to yourself as 'the wife.' "

"Ha! You've got that second part right."

"That's not what I meant—"

"They're his kids, Luc! They're his forever. I could get sick or just plain leave."

"You could leave," he said. A question? Was it a question or a statement? Or was it simply an echo of April's words?

"My dad knew my mom wasn't going to get better. It wasn't like she could come to her senses, or they could work things out, or she would even know who the fuck he was the next day. Yet all he cared about was spending every waking moment with her, even as she deteriorated. He quit his job. He sold everything, every heirloom and stick of furniture and car to pay for her care, to put food on the table since he bailed on actual employment. He did a few odd handyman jobs around the island, favors offered up by our neighbors, I'm sure, but our life was basically stripped to the bone. Looted."

"The heirlooms," Luc said. "The things in Marthe's apartment. Your job. It all makes sense now."

"It's not that simple," April said. "I didn't want those things, the *stuff*. Lord knows I lack a spacious apartment in the Ninth to keep it all in." April tried a smile, Luc smiled wistfully in return. "I only wanted something to keep, something that was hers, something substantial that would outlast even me."

Luc smiled again, brighter this time. "You have in mind one thing, non?"

"Oui." April nodded. How was it that Luc almost always knew the correct answer? "Mom had this long cherrywood dresser passed down from her grandmother. It was gorgeous. It had that shiny, glistening marquetry. Queen Anne–style but not actual Queen Anne. You know the kind, with the brass pull handles?"

"Not really—"

"Anyway. It was *so* her. I can close my eyes and picture what was in every drawer, even her horrible skin-colored bra and panty collection." April let her lids fall shut. "I can see the doilies on top, the pink and orange perfume bottles sitting on them. I see Mom brushing her hair in the dull mirror, my Girl Scout picture tucked in the corner."

April opened her eyes again. She was surprised to find Luc tearing up.

"I've spent years looking for a replica," she admitted. "We've had a few come through for auction, but nothing exact. I even went to the consignment shop my father took it to in the first place. They sold it to someone named Carol for $125! Can you believe it—$125!? I put an ad in the paper looking for any Carols who bought that dresser, said I'd pay five times what she did. I'd pay fifty times. A hundred times! Anyway, that ad ran for a year. Nothing."

"I'm so sorry, Avril, I don't know what to say."

"That's what bothered me so much about Marthe's apartment. How could her children, whoever they were, and her granddaughter, leave it behind? Didn't they want something to remember her by? And never mind the furniture," April said and laughed dryly. "Never thought I'd say those words. Although the furniture grabbed me first, it's the journals I think about when I go home at night. If I were Lisette I would've kept those above all else. Maybe I don't want the damned dresser after all. Maybe I just want my mom's life, her memories. Of course, given her diagnosis, memories were the very first thing she lost." April shook her head.

"You are an extraordinarily strong woman," Luc said as he moved closer. "I knew that from the onset, I just never realized the extent until now."

Luc inched ever closer. He was still hesitant, a little reticent to make contact, whether due to her story or the night in her apartment or Delphine or some combination of the three April did not know. She smelled his cologne, the cigarettes on his breath, and although he was not yet physically touching her, April felt him as though he was.

"I'm hardly strong," she said, shoulders loosening. "What did I do? I ran. Mom didn't know who I was. My father didn't care. I decided to start fresh somewhere else because I'd lost what I had in California. I still went to visit like a dutiful daughter but I tried to start over. I went to college, and then grad school. And ever-more grad schools until I could grad school no more. I thought my life would reset here in Paris. And it did. Sort of. For a second there everything was perfect."

"Americans and their quest for perfection," Luc said. "One day you will learn it's not achievable. It's not even something you want. So, ma chérie, here is the question I pose to you. What will you do now? You cannot worry about what you didn't do. What will you do going forward? This is the only way to find your answers."

"In the long run? I have no idea. But short-term I'm going back to San Diego," she said. "I'm going home to say good-bye."

Chapitre LVIII

Paris, 17 April 1898

Intentions! Oh, for the devil are they!

You can have them. They can be pure and good. In your mind you will execute them in a very precise manner with the purest of hearts. Then something happens and shoots it all to hell. Does that make a person any less good? I don't think it does.

Since that fire beneath the tents, I have scarcely spent a night away from Boldini, save for his multiweek adventures to Monte Carlo to commit hara-kiri. No matter how he aggravates me I continue to love the bristly, cagey man.

Still, the temperament of our union can be trying. Indeed, he never tries to smooth things over with jewels or furnishings. For now I am able to live off the generosity of *Le Comte,* yet I worry about tomorrow, and the day after that. Heaven knows Boldini cannot be relied upon to contribute. So many years have passed, yet I still do not know if he is a rich man, a poor man, or something in between.

I could not for a third time survive that bone-weakening feeling of near-destitution. There might not be any bat guano kings or famed flatulists or amorous counts to save me the next time. So I've done what I had to. I slunk back to the Folies and asked for my former job. Precious Gérard said that as long I remain beautiful he will always make a spot for me. I cannot guarantee the beauty part, but damned if I won't try. Henna and the latest in enamel whitening masks will continue to be my greatest allies!

The day I reclaimed my position at the Folies was the day after Boldini returned from a six-week trip to Monte Carlo. The minute my shift was up, I scrambled over to his studio, anxious to see him after all this while, anxious share in the good news: Gérard took me back. Boldini no longer had to worry about supporting me. Not that he worried about it in the first place!

When I walked down his street I spied from a distance a gorgeous eight-spring carriage with gold wheels. Out of it stepped a green velvet dress the color of vomit, none other than Jeanne Hugo stuffed inside! That wretched son of hers, the one from her first marriage, was beside her, sulking and pouting all the while.

"Jeanne au pain sec," I gasped. Live and in the flesh.

Then, like she belonged there, the woman tramped right into Boldini's building! My throat closed. No, it could not be. She could not be going to see him. I moved closer toward the studio. That's when the light turned on in his parlor, Jeanne Hugo's horrible high coiffure framed by the window.

The slut! The whore! Only someone of her flimsy morals would bring a child to a tryst. My first thought was to charge the studio, demand an explanation, and perhaps impale the woman with the end of my parasol. Then, for better or for worse, I had a second thought. Off I marched in the opposite direction.

Jeanne's husband was home when I arrived, which was a miracle in itself and only confirmed my idea was a sound one. Though Jean-Baptiste

Charcot is a trained physician, and his father once the most famous neurologist in all of Europe, the man prefers the wide open spaces of glaciers over the confines of a surgical room. After his father passed away and Jean-Baptiste was financially free, he left the profession altogether and bought a bevy of ships with which to sail the world. He is most often found in the Shetland Islands, Iceland, or Greenland, which is why it was so meaningful to find him in Paris at the precise moment I went looking for him.

When met by his servant I introduced myself as (famed Folies dancer—cough!) La Belle Otero and said I needed to see M. Charcot immediately. He'd been quite fond of the lady before his nuptials with Jeanne, so I knew he would agree to see me masquerading as her.

Jean-Baptiste's manservant accepted my lie though he must've seen La Belle a dozen or more times before. It was yet another thing to indicate the universe was on my side. After Jean-Baptiste entered, the servant offered a wink and politely shut the door behind him.

"You are not La Belle," Jean-Baptiste said straight off with a wry smile, though he did not seem displeased.

"Well, you are correct on that account. But lucky for you I am better."

I said this distractedly as I looked around, shocked by the pink damask wallpaper and gilded surfaces enshrining us. Jeanne, that horrible woman, had taste. This was the kind of apartment I should have. Mine, though lovely, was downright drab in comparison.

"Tell me then, Non La Belle, why are you here?" Jean-Baptiste asked.

"Your wife is having an affair with Giovanni Boldini, the painter," I told him.

"Are you quite certain?"

"Yes, quite."

"Hmmm." He looked confused though not necessarily upset. "Well, he is painting her. Perhaps you have mistaken portrait sittings for something more scandalous."

My face blanched in surprise. He was painting her? Giovanni was putting that face to canvas? It was worse than an affair! Bestowing his sex upon her I could handle, but not his talent!

"No," I said. I grabbed for my belly, certain it was about to spew forth my lunch. "That cannot be."

"Yes. She wanted a painting with her son. Tell me, was Charles on the premises when this so-called dalliance occurred?"

"Of course not!" I lied.

Boldini. I could not believe he betrayed me in this manner. He was painting Jeanne Hugo Daudet Charcot–whatever she might call herself next! It was worse than if I found them *in flagrante delicto* on the studio floor. It was worse than if she fell pregnant with a hundred of his babies! Was he trying to hurt me? At that moment it was the only possible explanation.

"I think they're quite in love," I added for good measure.

My scalp felt as though it was on fire. As wonderful as they are, whitening masks do not allow the skin to moisten or release heat, thus everything gets more or less pushed up into the hairline. Sometimes I fear my face will peel away completely. Alas, preserving my beauty is worth every moment of discomfort.

"An affair." Jean-Baptiste nodded earnestly. "Tell me, Non La Belle—"

"I am Marthe. Marthe de Florian."

Jean-Baptiste did not blink at the name. He did not show even the feeblest flicker of recognition. I grew so upset I thought my face might crack right there.

"Tell me, Marthe, do you normally find it your duty to report on the dalliances of Parisian society?"

"No," I said and pursed my lips. "But I thought since you were still newlyweds and your wife one of the prettiest women in all of France"—oh how it hurt me to cough out those words—"I thought you might like to know!"

The man smirked and took a few steps toward me.

"Well," he said and reached for a hand. "She is rather lovely, but I find her beauty no match for yours."

I was a goner after that one! Between the humiliation of Boldini *painting* another woman and the realization my name meant nothing to Jean-Baptiste, to Jeanne, to their household, I readily accepted what he wanted to give me. Namely, the full breadth of his manhood!

We did the deed quick and dirty on the floor of the parlor, me spending more time staring at the ceiling mirrors than into his face. It was not an altogether terrible experience, and there was a pleasant ninety-second slice of time somewhere amongst the grunting. This was the perfect revenge, I decreed: for Boldini, for Jeanne, for anyone who doubted my ability to improve my station in life. There I was, copulating in the parlor of the most famous woman in all of France! With her husband, no less!

Revenge. So many people are looking for it. So many people exact it. Yet no one ever tells you how empty it is. All this time I thought I'd feel better after putting one over on Jeanne. Is it possible I actually feel worse?

Chapitre LIX

Paris, 7 May 1898

There are delicate ways to state things and not-so-delicate ways. It is my journal, so I choose to be indelicate.

I am pregnant.

Even as I write the words, even as I wrote them one hundred times last night to make my brain believe, they still seem foreign. I never intended for this to happen. I never wanted children. Then again, I'd never taken a second to think about it one way or another.

Alas, here I am. Since the day I turned fifteen, my menses have been more regular than the calendar. When I woke up on a Tuesday morning, expecting, and nothing came, I thought perhaps I had my days mixed up. When it didn't arrive the next day, or the day after that, I realized something was amiss. I went to the doctor. The position of my cervix and uterus told the story. I was with child.

Of course I immediately started a course of *emménagogues* to entice my late cycle. The girls at the Folies have myriad suggestions for curing irregular periods, but mine was determined to stay away. I even visited a so-called doctor who worked out of a potions shop in Montmartre. He explained his procedures for encouraging menstrual flow and then showed me the required instruments.

"Do you aim to give me an enema?" I shrieked. "Because that's what it looks like!"

"It requires the same equipment," he said. Then, noticing the stunned looked on my face asked, "Are you all right?"

"I'm not sure," I told him.

"What are you thinking?"

"That I'm going to have this child."

That was that. My fate was sealed.

Dear God, there will be a little person living with me! A helpless person who will require my attentions on a near-constant basis! Rooming with a squalling child cannot be much different than rooming with Marguérite, but there is no chance of this miniature human becoming a contortionist and moving into its own flat!

Marguérite was so thrilled with the news she promised to help in whatever capacity required. Honestly, I think she merely wants a playmate. According to her we can stagger our shifts so someone is always available to care for the baby. Plus we have the baby's father. Men are horrible child minders, but Boldini could do in a pinch, at least according to Marguérite.

What Marguérite doesn't know is I haven't made love to Boldini since I discovered he was painting Jeanne—something to which he has not yet confessed! It was a sexual standoff, a duel. If only I'd relented. If only he had not been so long in Monte Carlo beforehand! Tonight I must rectify the situation. I must lure Boldini into my bed. Even if he is not this baby's father. I would like the chance for it to be so.

Isn't this just my luck? All these years I've been so careful to use *redingotes anglaises*, the so-called English ridingcoats, insisting even when my partner refused. Yet here I am. The one time I eschewed preventive measures I am struck with child!

There is no use wishing for more caution where caution I did not take. It is over! Done with! It happened, and I have the swelling belly (and breasts!) to show for it. Now is the time for practicality, which means first a romp with Boldini. What I ultimately tell him of this baby's parentage remains to be seen. Perhaps I will come clean, explain what happened and why. He knows my disdain for Jeanne. He knows he's kept at least one secret from me! Plus Boldini was away for so long. In all that time I only lay with one other man, and him only once! Frankly, it was quite the heroic effort on my part.

Then again, I do not want to risk Giovanni's spurning me. However angry he was about *Le Comte*, he could be doubly so now that there's a child involved. This is why I must lie with him tonight. Perhaps I will tell him the truth. Perhaps I will not. I only need the chance to say either thing. While the most important thing for a woman to have is money, the second most important is options. A lady must have her options.

Chapitre LX

April didn't sleep on any of her flights despite the fact that Troy insisted on first class and she therefore crossed the Atlantic in an aircraft with fully reclining seats, little cocoon-beds of silence into which everyone but April fell.

Instead she sat upright and sipped wine, read Marthe's journals, and stared blankly out the window at the nothingness below. As she exited the last plane in San Diego a male flight attendant touched her arm and promised it would all be okay.

April trudged down the gangway and out toward airport security, wondering who might greet her on the other side. It wouldn't be Troy. "I'll try to fly in for the funeral but I have a deal to close." It wouldn't be her father. "You know I hate to drive, kiddo." April thought of all the times she returned from college, from living in Paris and in New York, only to muddle through crowds of hugging families on her way out to the taxicab area, where she'd wait in line like a tourist or a business traveler, not someone returning home.

Near the escalators the clamor of travelers intensified. April stopped and peered over the bridge to the "ground transportation" sign below. Around the luggage carousels people huddled as they waited for their bags. They kissed and laughed and a few cried, all of them glad to return to earth and greet the people they loved.

Sighing, April stepped onto the escalator. Then she glanced over and saw, beside baggage claim number two, a lone person. The man wore a T-shirt, board shorts, and a tight smile.

"Brian!" she shouted.

He saluted. April's eyes filled with tears, and she tumbled down the moving steps, shoving at least two kids, one mom, and an oxygen tank out of her way. (Where was Montesquiou's cane?) After landing at the bottom, April threw herself into her brother's arms. He was not a tall man, but Brian felt strong, sturdier than she remembered. He smelled like the ocean.

"Whoa, that is some greeting!" he said, squeezing her tight. This, her little brother. "Either you're psyched to see me or things have really gone to shit."

April pulled back, smiling weakly. "Gone to shit"? Yes, yes they had. She pointed to the black mascara imprints now staining his white T-shirt.

"You're a marked man," she said. "Sorry about the shirt."

"It's cool." He shrugged. "Tears from April Potter. I didn't know you had it in you."

"Ha. They're there, all right. They've always been there."

She rubbed her nose with the corner of her cashmere wrap. Standing across from her brother in his frayed shorts, flipflops, and sunglasses, April suddenly felt ridiculously overdressed. It was a land of bikini tops and surfer shirts, and she showed up with high-heeled boots and a concerted effort at accessorizing.

"You look good," she told him. "Très Californian."

Brian did look good, precisely because he looked the same: tanned, fit, salt from the ocean smudged near his temples.

"Thanks, Sis," he said. "And you look skinny."

"Thank you."

"It wasn't a compliment."

"Oh. Well. Thanks anyway. Not to worry. I've been eating plenty. I've taken more than my fair share. "

April thought of all she consumed at the firehouse. She thought of all she consumed later that night. More than her fair share indeed.

"You are definitely *too* skinny," Brian said. "Emaciated. You have very angular features to begin with, and now you look even taller and sharper and more severe."

"Severe. Thanks. Way to make me feel like a crone." She pictured Delphine Vidal then, a person who did skinniness right. "You know, among Parisians I'm considered a 'bigger girl.' "

"Good thing I've never been to Paris. They wouldn't know what to do with this squatty body," he said and flexed his calf muscle.

"You would love it there," April said. "Though no surf. So, shall we go?"

"Your luggage?" Brian pointed to the nearby carousel where a security guard was trying to dislodge someone's jelly-faced three-year-old from the silver chute before he got pummeled by black wheeled suitcases.

"Luggage? You're looking at it." She tapped the Louis Vuitton duffel dangling at her side. "This and my purse. That's it. I've learned to travel light."

He raised an eyebrow. "I take it you're not planning to stay long?"

"I can't. I have to wrap up in Paris. But I'll be back after that. Promise."

"Whatever you say, April." Brian reached out and grabbed her duffel. "Let's go, Louis Vuitton. It's time to head home."

Chapitre LXI

April followed Brian through the automatic airport doors and out into the California sunshine. The glare hit her retinas, burning April's eyes all the way to the back of her brain. The sun was different here, brighter, more intense.

"Jesus," she muttered, fishing around her purse for a pair of sunglasses. "It's so goddamn sunny here."

"You should work for the Chamber of Commerce," Brian said and laughed. "Come to San Diego. 'It's so goddamn sunny here'!"

"I'm serious. There's something depraved and very deal-with-the-devil about it."

"So says the woman fresh in from Paris."

Paris. Instantly April thought of Luc. Then again, maybe she thought of Luc because they were right then walking by a pack of shame-smokers congregated around a concrete trashcan. Despite the advertised hazards of secondhand smoke, April inhaled as she passed. She missed the familiarity of the smell.

"Good grief, it's so excessively hot!" April said as they made their way into the parking lot, the sun beating down on her head. "How far away did you park?"

"Not far. Wimp."

"Hey, I'm wearing boots. I'm also wearing my hair, in other words, a long, heavy, brown blanket draped over my head. I think I'm getting sunburned. How 'not far' exactly? I don't see Betty's car? You brought the rustmobile, non?"

If in the last twenty years their dad had one thing going for him, it was their neighbors. They paid him to fix things that probably didn't need fixing. They loaned him lawnmowers and hedge trimmers and probably, April feared, also sometimes cash. The first day of junior year April found a sack of clothes sitting on her bed, courtesy of Betty Wedbush who was the most giving of all the givers.

Mrs. Wedbush (it was still so hard to call her Betty) lived across the street. In addition to ensuring that April maintained some semblance of sartorial coolness, she also generously loaned out the decrepit gold-and-rust Cadillac that otherwise resided in her front yard. It was the car April got her license in. It was the car that dropped her off at the airport when she left for college, when she said good-bye almost forever. April always thought Betty was holding out to be a replacement mom. She felt kind of sad that Mrs. Wedbush never had a real shot.

"Non?" Brian said and grinned over his shoulder. "Well, *non* worries, princess. You will not be subjected to the Betty-mobile. We drove. Hope my Subaru is an acceptable mode of transportation."

April should've known he'd bring his own car. The drive down from Northern California was long but had many prime surf breaks. April smiled when she noticed that his was the only car in the lot with a surfboard strapped to the top.

"So where's Allie?" April asked as she stepped inside the wagon. The heat from the black vinyl seats singed her hand. Brian threw her bag on top of a wetsuit April hoped was not actually wet.

"At home with Dad."

"He didn't want to come?"

Brian turned on the car.

"Airports," he said and revved the engine. "Not Dad's style."

Soon they were through the airport gates and cruising along the harbor. The water glittered in the sunlight. In the distance April spotted a cruise ship, an aircraft carrier, and several small fishing vessels. Having grown up a few blocks from the ocean, it was hard to believe she'd spent months without going near the sea. Brian never could've handled it.

As they crossed over the bridge into Coronado, April glanced down at the boats beneath them, then over to the shore and the island's boxed little streets, its boxed little houses. Her childhood home would still be there, same as always: pink, square, and with a patchy yellowed lawn. It was a time capsule compared to the multi-million-dollar, shingled, lot-consuming behemoths constantly popping up around it. The Potter residence remained unchanged in thirty years. Not as long as Marthe's apartment, but the woman had competition.

The car eased down off the bridge and onto Coronado. The place was as utopian-looking ever. The cute houses, the Americana streets, all sequestered from downtown's steel gaze leering from across the bay.

"So how's Allie?" April asked as they stopped at the time-suck of a light at Orange Avenue.

"Great, great. Work is busy, but she loves it. Absolutely loves it."

"I always wondered. Do you find it ironic?" April asked. "That after what Mom went through you married a nurse?"

"No," he snapped. "Why? Do you find it ironic you married someone with an assload of money?"

"What does that have to do with anything?"

"You married someone who could take care of you. Someone who had so much you couldn't lose everything. Again."

April snorted. "Don't confuse wealth with caretaking."

"Looks the same from where I sit. So. I should probably tell you," Brian said and turned to face her. "Speaking of caretaking and of Allie, she's four months pregnant."

"Really?" April's face brightened. For a second her heart shed some of its worry. "Finally some good news! My baby brother is going to be a dad!"

She reached over to hug him, stick shift sticking into her ribs.

"Yeah, it's pretty wild," Brian said, beaming.

"Completely wild." April pulled away and looked at her brother. A dad. He was going to be a father. "But perfect. You'll be fantastic. And Allie will be amazing as always. She's lucky. You're lucky. So's the baby. I'm so incredibly happy for you guys."

"Yeah, we're stoked," he said and turned onto J Avenue, their childhood street.

April held her breath. Every time she visited, her neighborhood shifted a little more. A house was knocked down. A new one sprang up. But through it all the old palm and magnolia trees remained, stalwart against even the most ambitious developers, forever reminding April of how things once looked.

"You're lucky, you know," she said to Brian, her voice quivering. "You ended up on the right side of that particular statistic."

"April—"

"No, seriously, you were the right person to be absolved of the burden. Fifty-fifty, right? Well, you struck zero. You won't end up in a bed for twenty years, not knowing the name of anything or anyone around you. You can't pass it on to your kids."

Their mom might've had Alzheimer's, but Brian would not. Thankfully, not Brian, not the man meant to be a dad, a grandfather. And because of this his children, April's future nieces and/or nephews, wouldn't have it either. Maybe the universe knew what it was doing after all.

"I know you took the test forever ago," April went on. "But each time I think about it, it's such a relief. Like I'm hearing the news over again. You're officially out of the woods."

The car rolled to a stop. They were beside her house.

"Think of how relieved you'd feel, then," Brian said. "If the person out of the woods was you."

He was staring at her pointedly. The house was staring at her too.

"Yeah, well," April mumbled, trying to avoid looking any way but down. "Or I could end up very much in the woods. It could literally go either way."

"You need to get some balls and take the goddamned test. It's hanging over your head."

"'Hanging over my head'?" April met his gaze. The house stood behind her, watching, staring, looming. "Fifty-fifty for this crazy fucked-up gene, Brian. You're the zero so chances are I'm the hundred."

"I know numbers were never your strong point, but it is possible to flip a coin and get heads twice in a row."

"Why risk it?" she said. "I never wanted kids, so why take the test? So I can find out whether I have some horrible disease for which there's no cure?"

"Maybe you'll change your mind," he said. "About the kids. You're still young. Kind of."

"Very funny. And there will be no kids." Even if she wanted to take the risk, who was going to be the other party to the transaction? Not Troy. She could also say "not certain other people with a French accent," but not even April was ridiculous enough to give credence to that possibility. "There is zero chance."

"Come on, my kid needs a cousin. I thought you guys left the possibility open?"

"The possibility is now closed. I don't even need a medical diagnosis to tell me that."

"April," Brian said. "What's going on with you and Troy? Sorry, I hate being nosy but I have to ask. What's wrong?"

"That's a strange question." She'd said nothing to her brother or her father. Not a single damn thing. "Why would something be wrong with Troy?"

"He's been calling a lot, for one. Asking after you. It's weird. Very un-Troy-like."

April said nothing while she played with the zipper on her tote. Brian shifted in his seat. His keys clinked as he slipped them into his pocket.

"He cheated on me," April said at last. And then: "I can't believe I just admitted that."

"Fuck. Are you serious?"

"Yes. As hilarious a joke as that would be, it is in fact the truth."

"Fuck," he said again. "Are you sure?"

"Uh, yeah. This wasn't a guess on my part. Troy admitted it. One-night stand, won't happen again, et cetera."

"Shit. I'm so sorry, April. That completely blows."

"Blows it does. While he is sufficiently contrite, I wish he hadn't told me. It changed everything. If it wasn't going to happen again, then why confess? It seems self-serving somehow. Now I'm paranoid, waiting for more bad news. I feel like my entire adult life has been spent waiting for more bad news."

"Like Mom. Like a genetic disease that can't be cured."

"Precisely. One more piece of shit to add to the pile."

"I'm sorry," Brian said. "That is so jacked. Do you want me to beat him up?"

"Funny. And kind of sweet. But no. I'm good. Thanks, though. It's the thought that counts."

"All right, lemme know if you change your mind." Brian paused for a minute. He twisted the frayed pieces at the bottom of his shorts. "Let me ask you something. Is it really true you never wanted kids? Or were you afraid to want them?"

April shrugged. "Does it matter? I'd rather not want kids than take a test that tells me I can't have them, or shouldn't have them lest I pass along some very fucked-up genes. And never mind the kid factor, I can't live with the knowledge that I will end up disoriented and bedridden."

"But—"

"I get it. You were in the same place. But you're a surfer-Zen-it's-all-good type. You make the very best of everything and I definitely don't need a test to tell me I'm lacking *that* particular gene." April sighed. "I just can't do it. I can't live with that kind of fear, forever waiting for the other shoe to drop."

Brian grunted and shook his head.

"I hate to be the bearer of ever-more bad news," he said and pushed the car door open with his foot. "But you're already living that way."

Brian grabbed her bag and started walking up to the house. April remained in place, staring at the grains of sand lodged in the stick shift, wondering if she had the strength to go inside.

At last April turned to the pink house, which was now dulled to salmon from the sun and the salt. Twenty years of unchecked emotions filled her body. April wondered for a second if she was dying, because her life started to flash before her eyes.

Her mother tending to the camellias (now gone) in the flower beds.

Her brother toddling through the yard (now dirt) in nothing but a diaper and a sunburn.

Her father marching through the gate (now chain-link) with a pipe in his mouth and a *San Diego Tribune* tucked beneath his arm.

April lining up her Little People on the front walk (now cracked), putting them through an extensive reprisal of *Grease: The Musical*.

It was all still there, not only the house but the life she once had. She might not have the furniture or the *stuff* but April had the memories, the mental diaries she could read at any time. Granted there were no professional farters or nipple chandeliers, but that did not make it any less special. And there was no reason she couldn't write it all down.

Smiling the slightest bit, April popped open the door and went inside.

Chapitre LXII

The next morning April found her father in the kitchen thumbing through a newspaper. Forever an early riser, he must've been up three hours by that point, probably even four. No doubt he'd memorized the newspaper front to back while waiting for her, the detail of every inning of the Padres game now typed into his brain and ready to be regurgitated later in place of conversation. It was sad. Now that her mom was gone he had nothing to do.

"Hey, Dad," April said and kissed the top of his mostly bald and freckled head. "How'd the Padres do last night?"

"All-Star break," he grumbled. "Which means they didn't play. Which is a good day for a Padres fan."

April smiled with some effort. His feebleness shocked her when she first walked through the door. He was not young and had just lost his wife, but April did not expect him to be so spare and hunched and grim. In her head he was still the thick-set, strong naval officer from her childhood. Now Richard Potter was an old man by any account, the kind you worried about walking up half a flight of stairs. He was only sixty-three but looked closer to ninety.

"So my dear," he said and lurched to standing. "Can I get you some coffee?"

As much as she needed some, coffee in that house consisted of Sanka and powdered nondairy creamer placed in their cabinet by Betty Wedbush some ten years before. A steep downgrade from Paris to be sure, not that April could drink it before she lived in Paris either.

"No thanks," April said. "I'm good. And Dad, please sit, I can get whatever I need."

"All right." He frowned and lowered himself back onto the chair, a metal thing with plastic straps that belonged on someone's patio in 1978.

"So, where's Brian?" April asked, backing up against the orange-tiled counter. "Let me guess, surfing."

"Of course. Where else?"

"And Allie?"

"She went to watch."

April chuckled. She tried to imagine herself voluntarily watching Troy play golf or racquetball. The thought never occurred to her, even the time he paid a hundred grand to play a round with Tiger Woods in some charity pro-am.

"Sweet Allie," April said and shook her head. "They're cute like that."

She turned and searched the cabinets for a cup but found only a commemorative Dairy Queen glass circa 1980-something. She remembered ingesting copious amounts of milk and Hershey's syrup from it as a kid. They'd had several similar glasses, half a dozen at least, but this was the only one to survive.

"Is the tap okay to drink?" she asked.

"Yes. Why wouldn't it be? Sorry, no bottled water in this house."

"Just asking . . ." April flipped on the faucet, half-expecting a stream of rust-colored water to flow from the tap.

"So, how long you staying?" her father said.

"Oh, uh—" April took three long gulps of water. It tasted like pennies but she was dry-mouthed and parched so took three more. "Until the service, I guess?"

Her father said nothing. He only frowned. Or maybe it was his regular face. April could not recall.

"I'll come back later," she added quickly. "Once I've finished my project in Paris and am back in the States."

"Whatever you think is best," her father said. "Don't feel obligated to return."

April nodded, unsure how to respond, which was par for the course when dealing with Richard Potter. It was hard to determine what was more awkward, the quiet or whatever stilted conversation they might engage in. They spoke often but didn't know each other at all.

"So," she said. "This is hard."

Stating the obvious, it was one of April's finer skills.

"I loved your mother very much," her dad said, blue eyes veined and watering. "I hope you understand that."

"God, Dad. Yes. Of course I understand that. Everyone that's ever met you knows that. You loved her more than anything on this planet."

"Yes, I did," he said. "Her and my children."

April resisted the urge to scoff.

"Mom was lucky to have you," she said instead. "She may not have *known* it, but she *felt* it. I have no doubt. She *felt* it."

"Did I tell you that sometimes she would still recognize me?"

April blinked. She *did*? Her mom possessed some cognitive function at the end? April hadn't known there were any glimpses at all of Sandy Potter during those twenty years. If she had, would April have treated her differently? Spoken to her in some different way?

"Really?" she said. "I had no idea."

"Yes. Every once in a long while, mind you. But it happened. I'd walk in, and she'd say my name with that big grin and those dimples. Of course I hoped for it every time."

"That must've been so difficult," April said and sat down across from him. She placed both hands on top of his. His fingers felt cold, chafed, and dry.

"It wasn't supposed to happen like this," he said, tears brimming. "I thought it was temporary. Your mom's situation. To the very last second.

I keep thinking, even now, Wait, how can she be dead? You were supposed to fix her!"

"But Dad." It was laughable, almost. Fix her? Fix Alzheimer's? April bit the inside of her cheek as a group of kids walked past their fence, boogie boards slung over their shoulders. "You knew there was no fixing, no cure."

"Intellectually, yes," he said. "And I know it sounds crazy. But right up until the end I thought it could be fixed. That they could *do* something. Doctors. Science. Whomever. When your mother went into care, AIDS was a death sentence, and now it's not."

"Okay, but she didn't have AIDS. Unfortunately? That doesn't sound like the right word. This was her *brain*, Dad—"

"I get it," he snapped, then pulled back. He went to pat her hands but did not actually make contact, instead tapping at the air. "I get it, okay? At the last minute and way too late to do anyone any good. But I get it. I was in denial about so many things. Now that she's gone, and you're gone too, and also Brian, though not as much, I realize all those years, they fell through my hands so quickly, like sand. I always thought tomorrow would be okay. But time marches on. Tomorrow doesn't care about me."

"Yeah, that's what stinks about time." April ran a finger around the edge of her glass. "It flies."

"I'm sorry, April. I'm sorry I wasn't there for you. It's amazing who you've become, the both of you, basically on your own."

"It wasn't on my own. And don't apologize. What you did for Mom was amazing. Most people couldn't—or wouldn't—do the same. It was a true love story," April said, thinking of Luc's words. "Everyone should be so lucky."

"What I did for your mom?" her dad said, nose crinkled. "No, April. That's where you're wrong. Everything I did was for you. And your brother. I did it for the two of you."

April didn't know how to respond. She could point out that neglecting one's children wasn't the most selfless parenting act around. She might say that from the moment her mother was hospitalized, April did not spend one second feeling wanted or loved or important. But she would say none of these things because this man was still, and always would be, her father.

"Thanks, Dad," April managed to sputter. "I know you had our best interests at heart."

"No. You don't think that." He shook his head. "Please don't lie to me. You don't think that, and I understand why you've distanced yourself."

"I haven't distanced myself. I've tried to come back as much as possible. I call you multiple times a week! I'd talk to Mom on the phone, even, which was just about the fucking worst—"

"April—"

"Just about the gosh-darn hardest thing in the world to do."

"And so you have done these things," he said and cocked an eyebrow. "But what does any of it have to do with distance? What makes you happy, April? What makes you sad? These are the things that keep me up at night."

"Jeez, Dad, why are you even worrying about me right now? I'm fine."

"Fine. Of course. You've put yourself in a happy, shiny shell where everything is *fine*. You ask a million questions but answer none yourself. That's what you do all day at work, right? Ask questions? But never any providence on yourself."

"Provenance," she said. "I'm sorry, Dad. I really am. I didn't mean to give the impression—"

"Don't apologize. I'm apologizing. I understand why you did it. It's my fault. Looking back there were many things I didn't do right."

"No one does everything right. Not you, not Brian, and certainly not me. We're people. We screw up. That's what we do."

"I thought I was doing what was best," he said, nose starting to run, snot collecting on his upper lip.

"Oh, god, Dad, don't cry. I can't take it."

"The worst thing for kids is to lose a mom, right? She was here for you every day. You both worshipped her. I thought if I loved her enough, waited it out, she would come back. While she was in the hospital they cloned a goddamn sheep." He shook his head. "But no cure for Alzheimer's."

"Hey, technology and progress are awesome. Our phones are so cute and small now!"

Her dad smiled: a rarity. Certainly the first smile since April walked through his clunky aluminum door.

"I thought I'd wait it out," he said again. "Plus I wanted you both to understand that it would be the four of us, forever, no matter what. She was my wife, and this was our family. That was the message I tried to send while I waited for the doctors to work their magic."

April tried not to smirk. Wait for the doctors to work their magic. This was Richard Potter's entire game plan. It seemed naïve to a twenty-first-century brain, but her father was still of the generation who thought doctors were infallible. It was not like the people April's age, all those moms eschewing vaccinations, the breast cancer patients favoring holistic treatments in Mexico instead of radiation at the Mayo Clinic.

"Oh, Dad," April said and sighed, the weight of nineteen years beginning to slide off her shoulders. "All this time I felt—"

April stopped herself. All this time she felt—*what*? Abandoned. Yes, abandoned and alone. But that didn't matter anymore.

"You felt what, April?"

"I felt you were trying your best." April didn't believe it until that very second, but it was progress. She never imagined she'd feel that way at all. "You were doing what you thought was the best for your family."

She said it a second time, more to herself than to her father. Remember this, April. Remember this feeling. April wasn't sure if she'd ever fully shed the decades of resentment but for the first time she saw a way out. She understood why her father acted as he had. April's only wish was that she'd gotten there sooner.

"I understand, Dad," April said. She took hold of his hands again. "One hundred percent. You were there for Mom, which meant you were there for us. You continued to love her in a way no one else could. I'm glad she was married to you."

Her father smiled again. He was almost downright giddy, on a Richard Potter scale anyway. April couldn't wait to tell Brian. And a little part of her couldn't wait to tell Troy. He would be amazed—by the conversation, her father's smiles, all of it.

April scooted the chair closer to her dad and looped both arms around his shoulders. His bones felt poky and brittle beneath her hold. Still, he smelled like himself. A million memories piled on her at once, some happy, some sad, but altogether they reminded April she was home. She could go to New York or Paris, but she would always be from right there.

"I love you," April said when she was finally strong enough to pull away. "And thank you. For this." She pointed around the kitchen, though it was not the house she meant. "For everything."

"Yes. Well." Richard blushed, having achieved his maximum level of emotional output. He plucked an old, yellowed handkerchief from his chest pocket and passed it April's way. "Now that we're being open and forthright, perhaps you can answer a question for me. Sweetheart. Why don't you care for my coffee selection?"

"What?" April said, spitting out a laugh. "No, it's fine, I just—"

"April."

"Okay, fine. You know what? How could I care for your coffee selection when you don't even have one? Seriously, Dad. Sanka? I can get better coffee at an airport."

"Well la-de-da, my high-falutin' daughter." He winked. "Well, there is a Starbucks within walking distance. Shall we go? Will it suffice for the fancy Parisian?"

"Good grief," she said and stood. "You sound like Brian."

"Lucky kid. Come on." He jerked his head toward the door.

"Let me grab some money."

April walked over to her tote bag, which sat atop an oven burner that hadn't been used in twenty years. She pushed aside a folder filled with Marthe's entries to find her wallet.

Then she stopped.

"Actually, Dad." Instead of her wallet, April lifted the journals from her purse. "Before we go I want to show you something I've been working on. I mean, if you're interested."

"Of course I'm interested! You rarely say a peep about your job even though it's one of the most fascinating out there. I'm so proud of you, April. So extremely proud."

"Thanks. Though, really, it's just any old job most of the time. But this Paris project is different. The story has completely enraptured me." April pulled out the first set of entries. "This woman, she kind of looks like Mom, actually. Fair warning—she's a tad bawdy at times, but"— April grinned wide, as if smiling with her entire body—"I know you're going to love her, too."

Chapitre LXIII

Paris, 31 December 1898

It's the end of a year when much has gone wrong, yet it all ended up right.

When I informed Boldini he was going to be a father he unraveled. He threw things and cursed. He said I tricked him into parenthood. I stood there, smiling meekly, trying not to cry, while he threatened to decimate the portrait he'd completed of me. Naturally, when I told him I approved of its disposal (that dress! The god-awful dress!), he immediately made plans for a public exhibition.

Alas, I could not have all the flames thrown my way without shooting a few back in return. So I confronted him about Jeanne. I told him I knew he betrayed me by painting my one true enemy. He never asked permission. He never told me the truth!

Boldini was, to put it mildly, unmoved by my cries. Instead of rushing to my side and begging forgiveness, he sniffed, rubbed a hand over his wiry, skewed hair, and asked a question.

"Whom did I paint yesterday?"

"However should I know?" I replied, gripping my belly, pretending to grow woozy for theatrical effect.

"Whom did I paint today? Whom will I paint tomorrow?"

"I am not your appointment keeper! Truly, Boldini, it would serve you to be more organized. You might find life a little easier—"

"Do I inform you of every commission I take? Do you know which people in this city, in London, have paid my bills?"

"Well, no—"

"Then why on earth should you know I painted Jeanne Hugo? She is just another commission. Nothing more, nothing less."

"That's not the point!" I shouted. "That is clearly not the point! Jeanne Hugo Daudet Charcot is not merely another commission, and you know it. It is an entirely different story."

"Marthe, you have so many different stories not even you can keep track of them all." He turned toward his easel.

Without thinking, I picked up a pencil and flung it at the back of his head.

"Please leave," he said without turning around. "I have many things to consider with this news. I must do it in private."

Humiliated and close to tears, I shuffled toward the front door. I should tell him about Jean-Baptiste, I thought then. His reaction to that news could not have been worse. I paused in the doorway for a second and opened my mouth, ready to take it all back.

"Boldini," I said, my tongue and throat dry. "About the baby."

"Just go," he said. "I don't want another word from you."

So I went. In the end, it was good I left. I am back in his graces (for now!—it's always for now!) More important, he is intent on being a respectable father for my new baby girl, our sweet Béatrice!

Oh my Béa . . . where do I start? Bringing her into the world was traumatic. I never thought I could write about it, or address it in any form. But, here I sit, able to put words to page. It is only because the girl is such a muffin. She is so sweet and perfect it erases most of the treachery I went through when she arrived.

Born just a week ago, on Christmas Eve, Béa came crashing into this world in a most unceremonious fashion. It is truly a miracle she is with us now. After all those days of *emménagogues*, of trying to bleed away the hint of her, when they told me I would lose her at delivery I truly thought I would die too.

Two days before Christmas Eve the contractions began. If the buildup was supposed to be slow, if it was supposed to start weak and rise to a crescendo of agony, it did not happen that way for me. The agony arrived straightaway. The contractions came with the force of a train, ripping through my gut and up my spine, each one a jolt of feverish pain.

Marguérite said I was being a weakling. She'd attended many a birth and in the last few years had somehow transformed into the de facto midwife of the Folies set. According to her, she'd never heard such screams, such dirty words from a lady. Now that it's over I think she'd never heard such screams because she'd never been with a person in such pain.

I labored for the better part of two days in Boldini's studio, the man fretting and pacing around me. Before long, neither one of us could stand it. Marguérite banished him to another room.

Dr. Pozzi arrived sometime during the second day. By then, time was lost for me. When he inspected the baby's position a grim look passed over his face. This was a double footling breech, he told us. It was why my contractions were so difficult, why the baby could not get out.

The pain intensified. They fed me morphine to calm my frayed nerves. Marguérite said it instantly relaxed me but I did not feel a change. The contractions failed to lessen. It did not get any easier for Dr. Pozzi to extract the baby.

When it came time, I hardly had the strength to push. Even though Marguérite and Boldini stood over my shoulder, coaxing me on, I weakened and grew disoriented. Dr. Pozzi instructed me to bear down. I tried, but my muscles slackened. I felt nothing.

"I'm going to have to pull this baby out," Pozzi announced. "The mother is spent. She's lost too much blood."

"Do whatever you need to," Boldini said.

I promised to try harder. Marguérite fed me more morphine. The pain finally left me. All I felt was pressure, the pushing and pulling beneath me, as though my loins were taffy. My head was so light I thought it might float right off my neck. At one point Marguerite carried dirty sheets into the other room. I was surprised to see them soaked red with blood.

Somewhere in the haze, Dr. Pozzi's voice rang through.

"It's the baby or the mother," he said. "We can only save one."

"The mother!" Boldini shouted.

"Yes!" Marguérite agreed. "Of course you always save the mother! What is wrong with you? Every doctor knows this. There will always be more babies."

I screamed.

"Save the baby!" I screeched. "Only save the baby!"

Pozzi put a cloth soaked with ether over my face while I struggled and squirmed beneath his hand.

"We need to knock her out," he said to someone. "I cannot have her causing this distraction."

Instantly I faded away, only to wake up in time to see Pozzi pull a limp, blue baby girl from my body. I thought she was dead. I knew she was dead. I wailed in horror.

"No!" I cried. "Not my baby girl! Please, not my baby girl."

Then, there was movement.

The baby wiggled a toe or bent her knee. She did something to indicate all was not lost. Suddenly a commotion erupted. Pozzi, Boldini, and Marguérite spoke at once. People shouted, then came the sound of skin on skin. Someone placed a baby on my chest. A live baby. She looked up at me. She blinked her eyes.

Oh, I am sobbing now just to think of it!

This was my Béatrice, survivor of death. It was a miracle of God, though the good doctor played no small role. If it wasn't for Pozzi slapping the life back into her, Béa wouldn't be here. I am so grateful to him for saving both the baby and the mother to enjoy her.

It took several days for us all to recover, even Boldini! He spent many long hours at the morgue, inspecting the bodies, trying to lift his spirits. I wonder what might've happened had Béa not survived. Could Boldini still tolerate this pastime of his? I would like to think the answer is no.

Béa is such a sweet child. The perfect baby, really! She hardly ever cries, and her appetite is not so voracious as to completely abuse my nipples. The little girl knows me. She knows I am her *maman* and loves to look up at me, staring intently with her dark brown eyes. It's funny. They say all babies are born with blue eyes. Not my girl, not my Béa.

I cannot believe how scared I was to become a mother, to make this large jump into another life. Now that she's here everything is different. I love her, Boldini loves her, and we adore each other. What began as an imaginable fiasco turned into something grand. As I look ahead into the new year, one that will close out a century, I feel optimistic for the first time in a long, long while. I have a lot to learn about children. Needless to say, so does Boldini! Alas, I think we will all get along just fine.

Chapitre LXIV

Paris, 1 July 1900

They say Jean-Baptiste Charcot has been busy sailing the Indian Ocean for the last year and that he's due home any day. If this is true, I daresay he won't recognize his city. Paris has been overtaken by the Exposition Universelle. I hardly recognize it myself!

Naturally, like the dutiful Parisians we are, we attempted to beat the prior world's fair, the 1889 version which gave us the dubious La Tour Eiffel, that hideous iron lady. It is now 1900—a new century! What better place to display every modernization known to man than at L'Exposition? And I do mean *every*. If there is an advancement or experiment you wish to see, it can be found at the fair! There are X-ray machines and wireless telegraphy and even films with sound (no ether firebombs this time), plus automobile exhibits galore.

Naturally, for every salient, important exhibition sure to change the world, there are five completely inane. Of the hundred thousand demonstrations, at least half should've stayed inside the brain of the demonstrator! Surely the "Exhibit of American Negroes" did not need to come to fruition. And those silly "flying machines"? Really!

Paris doesn't even look like Paris but instead a lady heavy-handed with makeup. The powers that be couldn't let our lovely buildings stand for themselves. Oh, poor Haussmann! All that architectural genius only to have his work covered by facades! We look like a fat, overly made-up, overblown Venice. *Le Comte* took me to Venice twice, and it's nothing spectacular.

The committee spent years determining this exposition's *clou*, its signature building to compete with the La Tour Eiffel. Some even wanted to transform *la tour* itself. One faction suggested turning it into a 325-meter-tall woman with searchlights for eyes. During the fair, beams would shoot from her head and scan the crowds. In the end the committee came to its senses, slapped on a fresh coat of gold paint, and went to work constructing new buildings and bridges and palaces.

Today Béa and I attended the festivities with my dear friend Léon Blum. Boldini refused to go. He is interested only in the Olympic Games. It is, I suppose, preferable to corpse-viewing, although not by much. He says they will allow women to compete this year. Who has heard of such a thing? These are supposed to be athletic endeavors! Boldini's favorite sport to watch is the ladies' tug of war. For the men he prefers tennis.

Because he knew of Boldini's exposition obstinacy, Léon Blum offered to escort Béa and me. Though I was pleased to be accompanied by such a learned and lettered man, going anywhere with M. Blum tends to feel like a statement. He is a Jew and a Socialist and about as pro-Dreyfusard as they come. It's not that I outright disagree with Dreyfusard leanings. Indeed I was quite moved by Zola's letter to the president. Poor M. Dreyfus! Jailed unjustly because he was a Jew! They are known to be a lying sort, but in this case the reputation did not seem to fit.

It is not that I care if I am mistaken for a pro-Dreyfusard. I merely do not want to be mistaken for one thing or another! In my line of work I must take caution when it comes to political stances. I cannot alienate my patrons. Nonetheless Blum is a dear man and was willing to take me where Boldini would not, which is all I ever really look for in another man. Aha!

Though Béa is now eighteen months old, she still has not learned to walk. A perfect reflection of her sweet disposition! She is contented to stay in one place and stare at the people around her. I am content to stare right back! She is so very beautiful. So serene! We are blessed to have a child who never cries. Boldini worries that she does not yet talk. I say, look at her father! He can go two weeks without saying a word to either of us. Sometimes I forget he is not her father by blood, so alike are they.

So on this day, my arm looped through Blum's and Mademoiselle Béa in her carriage, we went through the turnstiles and out onto the main grounds to see what Paris had on display. The papers did not exaggerate the crowds, the chaos, the performances. An entire section of the city was devoted to reenacting Victor Hugo's works.

The largest crowd was at the "Human Zoo." Why the exposition needed two Negro displays was beyond me. The spectacle immediately disturbed Léon, of course. He is a kindhearted sort and created no small scene, shouting about the mistreatment of the "animals." I glanced around sheepishly, not sure if I wanted to stand solidly by his side or sneak off in another direction.

That's when I saw her across the way: Jeanne Hugo Daudet Charcot. The last of her last names sent goose bumps along my skin. I looked down at Béa and back up at Jeanne.

"I'll be right back," I said to Léon, who was not listening to me at all. Off I wheeled us toward Jeanne.

"Ah, Madame Charcot!" I said as I accidentally bumped into her shoe with the wheels of Béa's carriage. "I thought you would be viewing the Victor Hugo exhibit."

"I lived with Victor Hugo," she said, staring ahead and refusing to make eye contact. "I've read his works a hundred times."

"Well, how special for you. I guess it's good you were orphaned and had such an amazing grandfather to raise you."

"It was special for me. Quite special."

This sent a fire through my veins the kind of which I'd not yet felt. Normally Jeanne snubbed me or pretended she didn't recognize my face. Now she goaded. The woman was goading me!

"So, how is that husband of yours?" I asked. "I hear he hasn't been in Paris for about two years and some change."

I rammed the carriage into her boot again, forcing her to look down.

"I hope he is well," I continued. "The last I saw him was . . . let me think . . . my daughter was born in December. So, about March of that year? April? It was around the time M. Boldini was making your portrait. You were away from your apartment often. And a lovely apartment it is! The parlor especially. The rugs are quite soft."

Jeanne turned toward me, eyes alight with flames and nostrils flaring.

"Is that your baby?" she asked.

"Yes, it is my baby," I said as my heart filled with pride.

For a second it was not about flaunting our connection, the tentacles I now had into Jeanne's life and home. Béa is a beautiful, precious child and not a pawn. Her paternity is of exactly no concern to me. As such I contemplated whether I should not have come over. Marguérite says I've been reckless lately, forgetful, unthinking. I'd dismissed her comments, as always, but now I had to wonder.

"I should have guessed," Jeanne said. "That is some baby, sans doute."

"You're correct. She is 'some baby.' The most beautiful baby in all of Paris."

"I saw you walk up with Léon Blum." A wide, wicked smile broke out across Jeanne's face. "It's a shame your child has inherited his features. Those dark eyes, the nose, the general dirtiness that bespeaks a Jewish lineage."

My mouth fell open. I did not know which insult hurt worst.

"This baby is beautiful," I said again. "And she is not M. Blum's. Though a woman could certainly fare worse!"

"Of course she is Blum's. Why, just look at her! She has 'Jew' written all over her face. You can always tell a Jew by its face!"

I didn't pause. I didn't think. Instead I reached out and shoved Jeanne Hugo Daudet Charcot into the Madagascar pit, a muddy, man-made swamp where Negroes sat naked, chained to trees and gnawing on prey.

Bedlam erupted. Jeanne screamed and called for the police. Ten more people fell into the pit while trying to pull her out. I sprinted in the opposite direction.

After grabbing Léon's hand, I hurried him and my daughter down the sidewalk and out of L'Exposition, Blum pontificating about the lack of humanity as we went. It was not until we were fully outside the gates that he realized there was no one left to hear.

As I caught my breath on the sidewalk, Béa peered up at me, squinting, smiling slightly at the fun and speedy ride. Léon was squinting, too, but from confusion.

"Madame de Florian," he said. "Why all the commotion? The fast getaway?"

"I pushed Jeanne Hugo into the 'Human Zoo.' "

Léon laughed.

"Well," he said. "That seems a good place for her. But may I ask why?"

"I hate the woman. I truly hate her. She ruined my life before it began."

I paused, sizing him up. If anyone might understand my plight it would be Léon Blum. Boldini had heard the story. He didn't believe me. I told *Le Comte*, and he thought it was a joke. Marguérite knew and never expressed an opinion one way or another. And the nuns knew. Of course they knew. They were the ones who told me in the first place.

"Victor Hugo was my father," I said.

He chuckled. Of all things, Léon chuckled.

"Do you find this amusing?" I asked and poked at his foot with my parasol. "Because it is the truth."

"Forgive me, Madame de Florian, but I thought you were orphaned and raised in a convent?"

"Yes, orphaned, like Jeanne Hugo. The only difference was that Victor Hugo could only take one of us in. He chose her."

I told him the story. I told him about the serving wench, my mother, who worked at Hugo's estate on Guernsey. She was beautiful, with dark brown hair and even darker eyes. The moment Victor Hugo saw her step into the sunlight he fell instantly in love. It took almost a year for him to work up the courage to speak with her. He was so very good with words on paper, but those relayed face-to-face were another affair entirely.

Overtaken by his love for her, Victor finally wrangled the gumption to engage her in conversation. It was some trivial matter: a question about the weather or the price of butter. My mother found him endearing and a relationship was born. Though he was rumored to have a long-term mistress, the truth was Hugo had not smiled since his wife, Adèle, died, but now he smiled only for my mother. They were friends for a long, long time, several years in fact, before they consummated their romance in the usual fashion. It was so spectacular a moment that my mother had known instantly she was with child.

Despite the improper nature of the situation, both were happy at the news. They planned to marry once Victor had certain proprieties worked out. He was in a rather sad position following his wife's untimely death. His beloved daughter—another Adèle—was relegated to an insane asylum. Both sons had recently died, and as a result his grandchildren were now living with him. It would not look very well for France's favorite son to celebrate a marriage amidst all this. Plus there was the matter of the grandchildren. They needed time to adjust to the situation.

While Victor went to Paris to right these family constraints, my mother and her new baby remained behind. Unfortunately the longer Victor stayed in Paris, the more complex his situation, and the greater delay in his return to the island on which he was once exiled. Not the least of these complexities was his granddaughter Jeanne, then a most difficult and petulant toddler.

Soon my mother, Victor's love, fell ill with tuberculosis. At Hugo's behest the estate brought in every doctor available on the island. Alas, this was not Paris, and the medical community was therefore substandard. My mother passed away, leaving me alone with the other servants.

Hugo planned to fetch me from Guernsey and raise me as his own in Paris. Yet Jeanne forever got in his way, this granddaughter who was already two armfuls of trouble and then some. Before long Victor had a stroke. Destroyed by destiny, he had one burden too many, and, being the illegitimate child, I was the easiest to cast off. Not to mention that I served as a constant reminder of my mother, whom he missed to the point of pain.

To Paris I eventually went. But instead of taking me to the Hugo estate, Victor deposited me at the convent in which his mother had once sought solace. He did this even though he'd spoken out publicly against the Catholic Church. I suppose when you're desperate you go back to what your mother first taught you. I wish I had that luxury.

Victor Hugo left me with the nuns and the nuns with enough money to care for me. He promised to return when I was older, when he had the situation with his granddaughter ameliorated. Jeanne was a treacherous young soul, an utter brat, who, when told of my existence, ran away from home and refused to come back until he promised she would never have to lay eyes on my face. Victor promised, but he thought it was temporary. He would get her to come around eventually.

Alas, he never had the chance. Hugo died but a handful of years later.

"And that," I said, my cheeks flushed, voice stuck in my throat, "Is the story of my origins."

"Well, that is an amazing tale." Blum removed a silk square from his pocket and wiped his brow. "I always knew you were something special, Marthe, and now I know why."

"Oh, Léon!" I cried, so grateful was I to have someone who didn't laugh at the notion. "Thank you for your words!"

I flung myself at him and fell into his arms. He petted and kissed my hair.

"There, there," he said over and over again. "There, there."

When I finally glanced up, Léon took my hand and gently brushed his lips against my knuckles.

"Hugo would be so proud of you," he said. "You've come so far. You are a beautiful person, your face and soul."

"Oh, Léon, thank you! That means so much."

Suddenly I felt *something* look at me from across the way, the sting of someone else's gaze on my face. I glanced up to see Jeanne, muddied yet still smug, standing a few meters behind Léon. She'd watched the entire scene. What she heard or didn't hear, I could not ascertain. All I knew was that she was smiling slyly, the corners of her mouth curled up like the devil's horns.

Chapitre LXV

Sandra Potter's memorial service was lovely, but only inasmuch as these things were supposed to be exactly that: lovely, tepid, unobtrusive. It included the usual funeral trappings like flowers, weeping, and much talk of Jesus calling his lambs home.

The day was drizzly. A fine mist settled across a city that was usually "so goddamn sunny." April went through the motions, muddling through the service and all the things she was supposed to do and say. At some point she delivered a eulogy without once looking up from her notes.

After it was over, April stood outside the church with her father and brother, making nice with the nurses and doctors who came to pay their respects. She mumbled robotic platitudes as people scooted through the receiving line. Smiling tightly and hugging strangers or people she'd only met once, April thought of Marthe. At least April knew her mother. She knew her father. She had thousands of minutes with them, minutes to hold on to until long after both were gone.

Jeanne Hugo. What a jerk.

April felt a little guilty. Of all the now-deceased women she might possibly think of on that day, Marthe and Jeanne were not the most logical.

But ruminating on the Exposition Universelle kept April from contemplating other things. Namely, what might be in the silvery-white casket at the front of the church. With the "Human Zoo" in mind, April didn't have to think about mothers. She didn't have to think about daughters. She did not have to consider why reading about Béa's birth reached inside her, grabbing at new depths of pain.

Most important, April did not have to ask why her husband was the one mourner who failed to show. They were done, it seemed, the ifs all gone. April had been so angry for so long she did not expect it to hurt like that.

The line seemed to last forever, a never-ending trickle of well-wishers offering only the flimsiest condolences. April grew increasingly annoyed as each successive person told her what a nice patient her mother was, how sweet and docile. Well, of course she was docile! Sandy Potter's disease turned her mind from adult to infant. She spent her final days in a bed, being fed by someone else, causing no problems, an altogether sweet and pliant being not unlike Marthe's own Béa.

As the last of the mourners petered out, the haze started to lift from the sky. Brian checked his watch. Even he was weary. Time was short but the afternoon was long. The surf grew choppy as the tide continued to rise. He would not have much time to make something out of that day.

"So, what next?" April said when the line died once and for all. "Dad doesn't want to go to the cemetery. Tell me what we should do now."

"Hell if I know," Brian said. "I guess we go to the luncheon. We all need to eat something."

"I can't imagine being hungry ever again."

April pulled her cardigan tighter, goose bumps spilling over her skin. The casket was now on her periphery. Skinny, sweaty men loaded it into a hearse.

"The ceremony was nice and everything," April said. "But it all feels so empty and useless. You know what I mean?"

"April—"

"Okay, maybe that sounds a little heartless. I guess I'm the one who feels empty and useless."

"Hey, April—"

"It's like . . . what are we supposed do to now? I don't mean the luncheon. Mom's illness has been the background, the white noise in our lives for the last twenty years. Where do we go from here?"

Brian frowned and clapped a hand on her shoulder.

"I don't think we're quite done," he said and then pointed behind her. "We've got a few more guests."

April turned, ready with her now-perfected sad smile. Oh, hello, doctor, thank you for taking care of my mother sometime during the spring of 2003.

But behind her April did not see yet another medical professional coaxed into being there by his boss. She saw Troy Edward Vogt III, live and in the flesh, flanked by his daughters. She almost didn't believe it was him and had to look to Brian for confirmation. Her brother nodded, then smiled in a way that said, I've always believed in Troy. I've always believed in the two of you. Brian was like that. He always saw the best.

Mouth open, April stayed rooted in place. Brian pushed at her back. She wobbled forward. He continued to push until April found herself pressed into Troy's chest, greasy face marring his two-thousand-dollar suit.

"Chloe and Chelsea," April sniffled as she broke free. The girls. She'd start there. It was somehow less difficult than addressing their dad. "Thank you so much for coming. I know you both had to travel far to get here."

Troy kept one hand on the edge of her sweater, holding loosely.

"We wouldn't miss it," Chelsea said, as always speaking for both sisters. Chloe was only partway paying attention and instead watching Brian, as young women were apt to do. "We love you, April."

As Chelsea hugged her, April felt a thump against her side. When she realized the cause she smiled.

"I recognize the purse," she said. "Looks great on you."

"Everyone is superjealous! I've worn it every day since it arrived!" Chelsea beamed, then frowned. "I guess I shouldn't be talking about purses at a funeral."

"Duh," Chloe said, her complete and total offering to the conversation. Nonetheless April hugged her, too.

"Thanks for coming, guys," she said. "It means a lot to have you here."

"Hey, bro, what's up?" Brian said. April saw nothing but Troy's strong hand clutching Brian's. "Glad you could make it."

"I'm so sorry, Brian. This is a rough, rough deal."

April listened to the sound of man-hugs behind her, the echo of back-slapping.

"Thanks, Troy." Brian stepped back into view and shot April a look she could not interpret. "So, hey, I'm going to see where Allie and Dad ran off to. Chelsea and Chloe, want to come with me?"

The girls nodded in unison, one reluctantly, one with a little more oomph.

"All right," Brian said. "Troy. April. We'll catch up with you guys later. See you at the restaurant."

April stood still, listening to the chipmunk chatter of Chloe and Chelsea grow faint, one accusing the other of scuffing her "favorite shoes." She closed her eyes and focused on breathing. In and out. In and out. It was simple as that.

"Do you plan to make eye contact?" Troy asked sometime around breath number ten. "Or are you going to keep your back turned on me? I can wait it out. I'll wait forever."

It sounded like a challenge, but then April thought of her mom. She thought of her dad and all the sand that fell so quickly through his fingers. Sure, April could refuse to move. But what exactly would that get her?

With eyes squeezed shut, April took in a gigantic gulp of air, pivoted on her heel, and turned to face her husband.

Chapitre LXVI

"Come on," Troy said. "Let's walk."

"Um, what?"

April expected a little more tenderness, at least a condolence or two.

"Move. Now."

Without checking to see if she followed, Troy started off down the sidewalk, west, toward the Hotel del Coronado, its red cone roofs looming above the nearby buildings. If Coronado was anything, it was that hotel. The Hotel Del was the landmark, the favorite child, its personality so big it was hard for the rest of the island to shine.

"Coming?" Troy called over his shoulder.

April looked at the church. She looked at her husband's back. She looked at the church again, and then, as if her feet were acting of their own accord, she scrambled after her husband.

"So how was the flight?" she asked, stepping in line with him.

"Peachy," he grumbled, quickening his pace. When they reached the street, Troy punched the crosswalk button. April waited for him to grab her hand. He did not.

"Why are you acting so testy when you're the one who—"

"Yes, cheated on you. I know. I couldn't forget if I tried."

April stopped on the corner. The green man appeared across the street, blinking, encouraging them on. A group of tourists passed, trying not to look but ears perked by the brewing argument. That right there was an adulterer. An adulterer in a suit when everyone else wore flip-flops. Typical.

"Troy!" she yelped "Stop! Don't walk away from me!"

He was already halfway across the street.

April was running after him now, breaking into a near-sprint as her heels clicked on the asphalt. When she reached Troy's side he was standing at the edge of the beach watching the dreary gray surf lap at the sand.

April thought of her brother then. The waves were small, angry, unsurfable. Brian would achieve no solace that day.

"Why are you being so short with me?" April asked. "You're the one who flew out. I didn't ask you to come. I didn't even think you would."

"Once again the faith you have in me is inspiring. You didn't think I'd come to the funeral? I'd hope, whatever the circumstances, if roles were reversed, you'd come to my mother's funeral."

"Sure. Yes. Of course," April said, vaguely confused. It never dawned on her that Troy's mother, the lizard queen of Westchester County, could die. She was a cockroach. She survived seven husbands and the nuclear winterizing of her soul. "But you said you'd *try* to come, so naturally I—"

"I need to hear it from you, April," Troy said as he slid out of his Gucci loafers and dropped them a few feet from a homeless guy. "I need you to tell me we're getting divorced."

"I didn't realize we decided anything. But if that's what you want, I'm not sure why you're asking me to say it."

"It's *not* what I want!" he said, shouting up at the sky. "It is *so* not what I want."

"I feel like you're trying to make me the bad guy."

Troy laughed, hard and sharp.

"No, I think I have that role all locked up," he said. "What am I supposed to think? I told you to make a choice. Move past what happened or don't. And since I haven't heard from you in—what? A couple of weeks?"

"It hasn't been that long."

"For a married couple it might as well be years. I kind of thought if our marriage ended you'd give me the benefit of a little notice instead of making me figure it out via your lack of communication and propensity to hide out in foreign countries."

Troy stepped onto the sand and began plodding across the beach. April glanced down at her own fancy shoes and then over to the homeless guy. With a few curses, she kicked off her heels and trekked across the sand toward her husband, almost ex.

"Real nice," April said when she finally caught up. Troy was seated, face toward the sea. "You're talking divorce one hour after my mother's funeral. Thanks a fucking lot for making this a banner day."

"I'm only talking divorce because you started the conversation. In your April sort of way. And your mom? Don't act as if this is a huge shock. You've treated her as dead since the day I met you. That she was actually alive and not long since expired of some unnamed illness was the biggest revelation I've ever heard on a fifth date."

"You're not being fair," April said. Then she thought of Luc's words. "You told me she already died." Maybe Troy was right. Maybe both of them were.

"I don't disagree," he said. "On some level I'm not being fair. But neither are you."

Troy shook his head as April continued to stand above him, wind tossing her hair, arms wrapped tightly around her waist.

"What am I supposed to think?" she said. "First you cheated. Then you act like you're a superswell guy for admitting it. Then you were in London, a train ride away, with the mistress in question at your side—"

"She was hardly a mistress."

"Sex buddy. Whatever. You were with her in London and refused to come see me. How else would a reasonable person interpret the situation?"

"I didn't make an effort. I can't dispute that. But what about when you were a breakfast table away? A couch away? In the same bed? You refused to see me in New York, too. You were right there, but you might as well have been in Paris."

"What did you expect? You made this huge confession that left me questioning whether I knew you at all. Because *my* husband is sweet and loyal and would never do anything like that. You didn't even tell me in person. You picked up the phone and started firing away, emptying your chamber before I had a chance to catch my breath."

"Fair enough. It would've been better in person—"

"Yes." Or better still not at all. "And on top of this you later admit, whoops, I also cheated on my first wife! Which, I get it, has nothing to do with me. Except everything. Because now it's a pattern of behavior. And patterns are what make the person."

"I never should've told you about Susannah."

"No shit," April mumbled, the surf and sky burying her words.

"But you did ask. And you can't compare the two relationships. My first marriage was over before it started. I remember standing at the altar, sweat pouring off my face, thinking, all right, exactly how quickly would Susannah's mob-adjacent family have me murdered if I bailed? You know my entire marriage to Susannah was shorter than the length of time you and I dated, right?"

"Really?" April said as she dug her toes into the cold, damp sand. "I don't think I ever knew that."

"Susannah and I were married exactly long enough to produce two daughters fifteen months apart. The first time Susannah served me with divorce papers, the first of four total instances, she was seven months pregnant with Chelsea. She pulled the papers each time, but doubtless there would've been a fifth process server tracking me down had I not grown the balls to end it myself."

"She filed when she was pregnant? With Chelsea?"

"Yes. And again with Chloe. So you can't even talk patterns. It's not the same thing. With you, with what happened, I was so goddamned lonely. And make no mistake, I'm not blaming you. But you'd gotten back from that big auction in Texas. Something happened with your mom, or your dad. Or something. You wouldn't tell me. You came home sullen and sad but with the insistence that everything was fine! You were so far away from me."

"Texas?" April thought for a minute. Yes, there was Texas, but Texas was nothing. Had she come back that distraught?

"It'd been building," he said. "Your distance. I guess that happens in marriages longer than two years, but what did I know about that? You don't have to explain yourself, all right? Relationships go through cycles. I get that now. Marriages shift. They are happy or sad or neither. They have high tides and low tides."

"Which is which?" April asked. "Is high tide good or is it low? Because I could argue for either."

Growing up three blocks from the Pacific, they planned their days around the tide cycles. When you walked, when you surfed, when you sunbathed, when you watched the sunset while slugging beer stolen from the Qwik-e-mart. At high tide the water was closer, bigger, more majestic. But at low tide you had the space to run, to walk, to explore the wide expanse of beach.

"Actually," Troy said and chuckled a little. "I don't know. I don't even understand my own analogy."

"Nothing happened in Texas," April said. "Not really. There was a piece in that auction I thought was a replica of an old dresser of my mom's. Anyway, it wasn't the same. The dates were all wrong. Then my dad called, said it was urgent. I flew out to see him, as you probably remember. Turned out there was no actual alarm. So when I said everything was fine I meant it. Everything was as it had been, nothing had changed. Funny how nothing can be such a blow."

Troy nodded.

"So," April said. "If I seemed remote, I'm sorry. But your response was disproportionate to the infraction."

Not that lonely sex was unheard of. Not that April hadn't done the same.

"Absolutely," Troy said. "I'm only trying to explain where I was coming from, which is not the same as an excuse. Bottom line, it felt like a rejection. Then I went to Singapore, and there she was, a female, open and listening."

"They always are."

"And it was horrible. When I cheated on Susannah I felt nothing. Nothing. When I cheated on you I instantly felt like the biggest piece of shit alive."

"Good."

"Well. As long as we're on the same page."

"I wish you never told me," April blurted.

"Excuse me?"

"About Singapore. Why did you tell me if it was a onetime thing? So different from what happened with Susannah the two couldn't possibly be linked?"

"Because I believe in honesty in a marriage," Troy said. "I'm kind of alarmed you don't."

"But it assuaged your guilt and did nothing to help me. Nothing. It only left me sitting around wondering when you were going to announce the next piece of bad news."

"You've got to be kidding—"

"I know it's an unpopular opinion, okay? But there it is. I'm angrier that you dragged me into it than I am it happened in the first place, assuming the first would be the only place. Spouses don't have to know everything about each other. What happened did not affect us at all until you decided that it should."

"Fuck," Troy said and rested his head on his forearms. "I never thought of it like that. I believe in complete and total honesty in a marriage, especially in our marriage because my parents never had that, and I certainly didn't in my first. I wanted us to be different because we were. We were—*are*—different. But fuck. I don't necessarily agree, but I get where you're coming from. I really do."

April spent months questioning whether she really knew this man after seven years of marriage. But suddenly and at once she realized that Troy's immediate revelation of the misdeed was exactly in line with everything she knew of her husband. Troy was black-and-white, a rule follower, and because no one was perfect all the time, if a rule was broken he rectified it immediately, regardless of collateral damage.

"And I understand why you told me," she said. "At all, and in the manner you did. I've been mad about it, but that's not fair. I never told you how I felt, probably because I didn't know myself. But it's like when something bad happens, a path is clear, inviting in ever-more crap. You realize what worst-case-scenario looks like and can picture it fully formed and in color."

Worst case wasn't even that your husband cheated on you once. You could probably get through that. But could you really survive a second time, three times, or more? Would he have a one-night stand and then an affair and then some family sequestered in Connecticut? To April infidelity felt like a permanent and long-term diagnosis, one that would eventually result in death.

"I've been waiting twenty years for my mom to die," April said. "Everything—my life—was going along fine, and then suddenly we found out she was sick, and that the sickness would only get worse. It would gnaw away at her brain, they told us, eventually turning it to Swiss cheese and then to nothing. I'd been waiting, waiting for the eventuality of her illness. I'm sorry if I did that to you, too. I'm sorry if I kept expecting the worst."

"God, April," Troy said and looked up, a red circle on his forehead from his watch. "You can't think like that. You can't live life waiting for something bad to happen. That's miserable."

April shrugged. Troy was right. It was miserable.

"There's more," April said with a sigh. "Remember a couple of years ago? It was right around our fifth anniversary. I was on the phone with my brother, in the closet—"

"You were crying." Troy squinted toward the ocean, remembering. "Wearing a cocktail dress, diamonds, and crying. Sort of yelling, too. You're always so calm. I'd never heard you yell before, especially at the magnificent Brian Potter, doer of no wrong."

He looked toward April and winked, the sibling bond a source of teasing between them. What kind of brother-sister duo was so respectful of one another, so never-complaining? It was downright unnatural.

"Yes," April said. "I was yelling at him. Sort of.

"I can't do it, Brian. I'm glad you're stronger than I am. But I can't and I won't.

"Brian had taken a test," she went on. "To indicate whether he had the gene my mother did. It's genetic. I'm not sure I exactly ever mentioned that."

"You never did," Troy said. "I always wondered—but you never said—I figured—"

"Dad had only just told us. Brian marched right out to get the test. And me? Well, I simply didn't want to learn exactly how shitty my provenance, as we say in the biz. In layman's terms, how damaged my goods."

"And Brian?" he said. "His goods?"

"Perfectly undamaged."

"What about you? Are you ever going to find out? Wait. I think I already know the answer." He smiled wanly.

"I thought 'no way,' but now I'm not so sure. Sometimes waiting to see if there will be bad news is worse than finding out one way or another. The mental torture I've put myself through over the last few months was several times worse than the shock of finding out what happened in the first place. Likewise waiting for my mom to die was weirdly more painful than the death itself. So. Maybe. Maybe I will find out."

And there was another thing, unspoken. Back in the glory days of their marriage, before its longevity was in question, April always said she married up. Troy claimed he felt the same, her brother insisting that the best marriages were like theirs, ones where both parties thought they were getting the better end of the deal.

But Troy would not claim a better deal if April was guaranteed to end up bedridden and incoherent. He would not think he married up if such a shitty provenance were discovered. Now it didn't matter so much. Nothing was signed, filed, or otherwise legally recognized, but it remained unlikely he'd be the one manning any future bedsides.

"I won't tell you what I think you should do," Troy said. "But to be clear, you know I don't give a shit about that, right? Whether you have the gene or you don't? You're probably thinking about the dreaded provenance and crap—"

April smiled, surprised he could still read her so well.

"Bottom line, I don't care what disease you end up with," he said.

"Uh, thanks." Her smile spread wider. "That's an interesting way to put it."

"We'll deal with whatever happens, that or some other thing. And by 'we' I mean exactly that. You told me to say I wanted a divorce, but I won't say it because it's not true."

Troy's voice, which was always strong, flat, unwavering, started to quiver. April was taken aback. She'd never seen him this upset, so vulnerable, even when he told her about Willow. That was over the phone, which probably had something to do with it, but in none of their subsequent conversations did he once show such a crack. Troy was perpetually understated, yes, and not a soul on the beach would mistake this for a bona fide scene. But for Troy this was a demonstration, and a large one at that.

"Thank you," April said. "Thank you for saying so."

I don't want a divorce either.

The words were there, but she could not say them. Did she mean it? Or was it merely a reflexive response? Your husband tells you something, you respond in kind.

When she didn't respond, Troy nodded, biting his bottom lip, eyes watering.

"Shall we go?" he said and jerked his head toward the road. "The conversation's not over, but I'm sort of out of things to say."

April nodded in return. She was almost done as well, but there was one last question she had to pose. Troy respected her point of view on the Willow admission. April had to respect his, too.

"I have to ask you something," she said as they made their way to the street. "I'm not trying to bring up old wounds, I'm really not. But I have to ask."

"Uh, okay." He laughed nervously. "I can only imagine what kind of trouble I'm about to get myself into this time."

"No trouble. Promise." April took a deep breath. "What if I slept with someone, too? A one-night stand. Would you want to know?"

"What kind of question is that? Of course—" Troy stopped. He looked at her and tilted his head slightly to the left.

"Think before you respond," April said, holding his gaze in hers.

"Of course— "

"Think."

"Of course it would depend on the situation," he finally said.

"What if you flew home tonight—"

"I'm not flying home tonight."

"What if you flew home tonight and I went out drinking with my brother and hooked up with some guy I went to high school with?"

"A guy you went to high school with?" Troy looked wary, a little off-balance.

"Like, I don't know, Miguel Guttierez. He was a really good soccer player."

"Uh, is there something I should know about this Miguel person?"

"No! Not at all. Haven't talked to the guy in fifteen years. Never even kissed him. Just picking someone random."

"And foreign," Troy noted.

"Yes."

"And your liaison tonight. It will happen because you are sad and lonely and maybe still quite pissed at me? And Miguel is charming and interesting and perhaps also hot?"

"Something like that."

He sighed.

"No," he said. "I agree with what you said before. I'm a little surprised to hear myself say it, but I agree. I would not want to know. You can keep that to yourself."

April thought, though she wasn't sure, but she thought that Troy understood all she said with her question. April would not bring it up again.

"So I'm almost done with Paris," she said as they found their discarded shoes, thankfully not hocked for malt liquor by any transients. "I should be home within a week."

"Home." His voice was craggy. "Are you planning to come back to the apartment?"

"Yes." April tried to stop her words from weaving. "For now. I mean, if I'm welcome."

Troy bobbed his head in a way that was neither nod nor shake. Together they wiped sand from the bottoms of their feet. After slipping back into her heels April glanced up to find Troy staring at her with an expression she could not name.

"Is this decision," he said. "Is it a *decision*? Or only the first step of many?"

"The first step. I don't know what will happen but it's something."

"Odds, Vogt. Give me odds."

"Probably about fifty-fifty," she said and winked. April was kidding, mostly, but she suspected fifty-fifty was not too far from the truth. The odds sucked, but April still liked her chances.

"Wow, you're killing me," Troy said and smiled in return. "A coin flip."

"Right? What a noncommittal jerk of a statistic."

Troy's face broke into a full-blown grin.

"Well," he said. "At least I know where we stand. For now."

He reached out. April took his hand.

Fingers laced together, they stepped into the crosswalk. April felt lighter somehow, hopeful. It was an odd reaction given she stood at the edge of her marriage after having just watched her mother's life fall away. Although that was the thing about low points: The only place to look was up.

Chapitre LXVII

April returned to Paris raw, her nerves fried. She could hardly step outside the flat without the smells and noises of the city overpowering her. Had the scooters always been that obnoxious? The scent of warm chicken outside her building so pronounced?

Her flight left in three days, and the clock in April's head clicked loudly. Each second was one step closer to the end, the end of her Paris trip at a minimum, her efforts to do something with Marthe's legacy still wildly unhinged. April could not picture what the catalog might look like, whether it'd contain the words "private collection" or Marthe's full name. Never mind the catalog, April could not picture what her *life* might look after she touched down. New York had seemed so distant but was now hurtling toward her at breakneck speed.

April was surprised when Luc called on a Saturday. Since her return from San Diego they'd exchanged passing hellos in meetings and at Marthe's flat. All transactions were of a strictly professional nature, though, and April did not expect to hear from him outside of this, a realization that left her more than a little melancholy and nostalgic.

Despite Luc's downright aggressively appropriate interactions (where were the sexual innuendos?), picking up the phone now felt like a betrayal. They had sex and she didn't tell Troy (outright, anyway), and this was wrong by most any definition. Answering seemed sneaky and underhanded, complicit even absent any direct foul. Alas, April had no illusion that Luc saw her as anything other than a colleague. It was an unwelcome thought, and her reaction to it more bothersome than how to handle the call in the first place.

"Monsieur Thébault," April said, unexpectedly thrilled to hear his voice, as if she were speaking to a long-lost and dear friend. Though his friendship was not long, Luc was certainly lost and dear, in his very singular Thébault kind of way. This was her closest friend in Paris, the man who helped her find Marthe, the man who helped her find so much.

"I have *une plainte*," Luc announced, his customary playfulness returned and dancing around his words.

"A complaint? Oh, jeez, well, get in line."

"We've had absolutely no fun since you got back from California. It's all work. I feel as though you're trying to coerce me into your aggressive Americanism."

April's heart pounded against her rib cage. What was she supposed to say to him? Was she supposed to explain? Not much had changed with Troy despite a bit of mutual understanding gained and an agreement that maybe things could work out, though not necessarily. Then, of course, there was Delphine Vidal. What had Luc been doing mucking around with her when Delphine existed? April had so much to say it was probably best to say nothing at all.

" 'Americanism'? I'd do nothing of the sort," April insisted. "I know you're set in your Parisian ways."

"Hmmm. I think I've disproved that, non? Tell me, Avril, have you ever been to La Guillotine?"

April laughed nervously. "Not literally, no. But I kind of feel as though I've spent some time in a figurative guillotine lately."

"It is a jazz club," he said. "In the Fifth. There is a band playing tonight. I have determined we shall go."

"You've determined."

"It is a perfect idea, your last chance to enjoy the benefits of this city. You leave on Monday, non?"

"Good memory."

"Only"—he said—"for certain things. We shall go. Tonight. I will not accept your declination."

April paused and took a sip of coffee. She wanted to visit the Guillotine, yes, but the things left unspoken between them were shouting quite loudly right then. And the last time Luc "forced" her into a night out it resulted in sex.

"I don't know—" April said finally. Though she'd instigated the Bastille Day dalliance, April had to make clear this would not happen again, and she needed to do this without spelling it out and while still clinging to the last shreds of her dignity. "I guess we can. As long as you understand it's *only* the club—"

"Bien sûr! I would never assume otherwise."

"All right, I guess that sounds fun," April said, wondering if for Luc this was no big deal. He probably had arrangements and noncommittal flings every night of the week. It explained all the smirking, at least. Not to mention his prowess in the boudoir.

"I'll arrive at your flat at ten o'clock," he said. "Wear good walking shoes."

With that he hung up.

April spent the rest of the morning halfheartedly tidying up catalog copy. For lunch she visited the neighborhood *fromagerie*, purchased the biggest, stinkiest piece of cheese possible, and washed it down with a glass of Pouilly-Fumé. It was the perfect meal, even if April continued to burp up its taste several hours later.

Luc arrived at her door fifteen minutes late according to the clock, but thirty minutes early based on his usual schedule. As he stood in the hallway in black jeans, a floppy sweater, and his curly, in-need-of-a-trim moptop, April again felt nostalgic. He reminded her of the goofy boys she dated in college, the ones who were privileged but never understood it. The ones who made April believe she had a big, huge lifetime ahead of her no matter what side of fifty-fifty she might fall on.

"Bonjour," April said and smiled. She felt the inexplicable urge to pat him on the head.

"Tu es belle."

"Merci." April fake-curtsied. It was funny, this language. In America you told someone they *looked* pretty. In France you told them they *were* pretty, straight up. No looking, no appearing, no temporary condition.

"Tu es prêt?" Luc held out an arm.

"*Oui*." April grinned and slipped hers through.

They walked out onto the street and down toward the First Arrondissement. As they went, Luc asked about the funeral, about her father, and about Brian. April found herself able to answer his questions without pretending it had been anything less than torturous. She surprised even herself.

"Ah, so you see," Luc said when April finished. "I was right. It was a love story. Between your parents, and your parents and their children. What a lucky family you've had."

"'Lucky' is not quite the word to pair with Alzheimer's. But we had . . . we have . . . something special. And I'm proud of what my dad did for her."

April stopped walking for a second. "Can you believe it?" She pointed to the building before them, to the iconic pyramid lit for the night. "Can you believe I haven't spent one second in there this trip?"

"Mon dieu! What good are you as a tourist if you don't visit the Louvre? It is time to revoke your passport. I am ashamed on behalf of your entire nation."

"You should be ashamed on behalf of my multiple art-history-related degrees. I went constantly when I used to live here. At least a few times a week. It was practically part of my routine. And this time? Not once."

"Well, you've been a little preoccupied," Luc said. "Anyway the best thing to do in Paris is things you haven't before."

"Well, then consider this trip a success. I've done many things I haven't before," April said, then blushed madly. Yes, she had done many things in

Paris, not the least of which was Luc. "Anyway! No Louvre tonight. Instead to the guillotine, Monsieur! Off with her head!"

April whipped an arm around her head and marched forward. Luc rolled his eyes, laughed, and followed her down toward the Seine.

As April stepped onto the Pont du Carrousel, she paused to say something to Luc but found he was not behind her.

"Luc!" she called, spotting him strolling along the Seine on the port du Louvre. "Where are you going? We need to cross here."

"Ah, but we do not. There are better ways to travel."

"This is the better way," April grumbled, the soles of her feet already blistered and bruised. She jogged to catch up. "Le port du Louvre is lovely and super-Parisian and all, but is it really the most efficient path?"

"'*Efficient*'? Le Port du Louvre is a means to an end, ma chérie. There is another bridge, a better bridge to cross the waters. Le Pont des Arts. Do you know it?"

"*Bien sûr!* Who doesn't?"

Le Pont des Arts was a footbridge connecting the Louvre to the French Institute over the Seine. Though the planks underfoot were wooden, its sides were made of iron, like a taller, more visually pleasing chain-link fence. The bridge was famous for its amazing river views as well as its artistic and romantic flair. It was painted by Renoir and now painted upon on a near-constant basis. During the day you couldn't walk two meters without tripping on an easel.

But perhaps above all else, the Pont des Arts was known for the locks decorating its ironwork sides. In a long-standing tradition, couples hooked these "lovelocks" around the fence links as a symbol of their enduring bond. Some were gigantic padlocks or combination locks like those seen on school gym lockers. Others were painted or inscribed with poetry. Sometimes the fence even contained a lock of hair.

"Glad you are familiar with it," Luc said as they stepped onto the bridge. "Otherwise this could be rather embarassant. Madame Vogt, I have something for you."

He stopped and pulled from his pocket one lock, golden in color.

"A lovelock?" April said, heart racing. This was more traitorous than sex.

"Technically," Luc said. "But not in the way one might assume. This does not have to be a romantic gesture, you see. It can be, but does not have to."

He dropped the lock into her slightly quivering palm.

"I've written your initials on it," he said. "Only yours. Remember, I am no sexual badger."

April tried to laugh, but the sound remained stuck somewhere in her throat.

"You will go back to New York," he said. "And your relationship with le grand m'sieu will resume. You will be happy. Happier than you were before."

"I wouldn't be too sure about that," April muttered.

"The trip to California. You came back and told me you will be happy. You didn't say a word about it, but you told me nonetheless." He smiled wistfully, wrinkles gathering around his eyes. "Don't look sad, ma belle! This is a good thing. Not everyone ends up where they truly want to be."

"I'm not sad," April said. "I'm just . . . I can't explain it."

"You don't need to. I understand. I understand completely." He placed a palm over the lock. "I got this for you, a reminder. Although you will go back to New York, to your home, Paris will be a part of you forever." He latched the lock onto the fence. "And you will forever be a part of Paris."

"That is incredibly kind." April said. She was so stopped up with emotion the only thing she could do next was make a joke. "Except you know city workers cut these down on a regular basis, right? I'll only be part of Paris for approximately ten days."

Luc threw his head back and laughed.

"Always so practical, Madame Vogt. Alas, does it matter? This is life, ephemeral, transient. Just because it's gone doesn't mean it didn't happen."

"Thank you, Luc." April smiled and leaned in for a hug and a double-cheek kiss. "This means a lot to me."

"And you have meant a lot to me."

April didn't know what to say. She stood in place watching the lock wink in the streetlight. Luc nudged her in the ribs to get her going again.

Still in a stupor, April trailed him off the bridge and down into the Fifth, to La Guillotine and ultimately Le Caveau des Oubliettes, the Cave of the Forgotten, though nothing that happened in that city, or with Luc, would ever be.

Chapitre LXVIII

Here we are," Luc said as they walked through the front door of the club. "La Guillotine."

"It's cute. Very pubby."

"Ah, but we are not staying aboveground." He nodded toward the back. "Le Caveau des Oubliettes. Down we go. Into the Cave of the Forgotten."

Together they lurched down a dank, tight, dimly lit set of stairs decorated with rusted handcuffs and chains. They then stepped into a room that was one dirt floor shy of being an actual cave. According to Luc, it once housed prisoners awaiting execution, thus the name was almost literal. April could almost smell the impending death. It was a bit like urine and vomit, non?

The cave fit only twelve tables, most of which were already full. April picked a seat as Luc fetched two glasses of wine. He sat down and scooted his chair close. April wondered briefly about her stinky cheese lunch.

"So," he said as the musicians set up on stage. "Before the band begins and we are therefore prohibited from hearing one another, I have some favorable news to share. Agnès Vannier is ready."

"What do you mean 'ready'?" April said evenly. Not this time. She wasn't going to get ahead of herself. "Ready for a nap? Death? Ready to dance?"

"Dance? De quoi parles tu? I mean 'ready.' We can go see her at any time."

April laughed, but in a laughing-crying-borderline-hysterical manner. Now that she was one foot out of town, of course the woman was ready to chat. Luc called it "favorable news," and it would've been had the matter not become so painfully moot. There was no way April could stay in Paris a second longer. Plus the inevitability of the "Private Collection" label meant that Madame Vannier's take on Marthe and her assets was nothing more than old-lady scuttlebutt.

"Ça va? You look as though you've developed a case of l'hystérie."

"It's just my luck. I have to leave and now she's ready. And no jokes about my lack of concern for Madame Vannier's welfare, please. I get that I'm a single-minded and cruel-hearted auctioneer."

"Je ne comprends pas? I feel you're not listening to me. We can go see her. We. You and I."

"But I leave in three days." April looked at her watch. "Two days."

"I know. And so we see her before then."

"Is that even possible?" she squinted at him. "It's the weekend. I leave Monday. Early."

"I said we can see her, more times than I should've, given your cognitive ability."

" 'We can see her,' " April repeated.

"Oui."

"Really?"

"Oui."

"Really, really?"

"Oui, oui. Are you hard of hearing? I am really growing quite concerned."

April let the news sink in. Madame Vannier. They were going to see Madame Vannier, Lisette's heir, overseer of all physical evidence of Marthe's life. April would finally have her answers. The answers might not matter to Sotheby's or to a single bidder, but they mattered to her.

"I can't . . ." she said, feeling at once giddy and drunk. "I don't know what to say. I'd given up. I figured it wouldn't happen."

"Given your timeline, I did have to press Madame Vannier a bit on the matter," Luc said. "She was quite amused by your interest in the cause."

"Oh, I'll bet she was amused." April rolled her eyes. "She probably thinks I'm a nut job of the highest order. I don't even care, though. This is what I've been waiting for."

"You have been rather single-minded in your pursuits," Luc said, grinning.

"My mind was on a few other things," April said and smiled in return. "But Madame Vannier is up there. Full disclosure, though—this is probably not going to help the auction. Despite my efforts, the house won't budge and at this point it's futile to keep pressing. So I can sit here and crow about provenance but it'd be merde. I'm doing this not for Sotheby's but for myself."

"So you won't keep pressing on the auction? On getting Marthe her own affair?"

"Nope." April took a gulp of wine. "I've given up."

" 'Given up'? That does not sound like my favorite American."

"Eh." April shrugged. A man onstage played a few notes on his saxophone. "I tried but I'm stuck. You can only bang your head against a wall for so long."

"What if there is no more wall? What if someone else already went through it? "

"I think you're screwing up your idioms again."

"I'm not trying to use any idioms. I'm trying to tell you some news, some news about the head-banging auction."

"For the record, a head-banging auction would probably involve music albums and cans of hairspray. But, do tell, which auction are you referring to? One of Marthe's?"

"In a manner of speaking, yes."

"Which one? Furniture or paintings or the ever-exciting silver, gold boxes, and vertu?"

"None of those. The one auction. In October. For all of Madame de Florian's estate."

"What are you talking about—"

"She will have her own auction, Avril. Just as you wished."

April stared at Luc's face, waiting for a smirk or a wink or some other expression indicating he was full of shit. He had to be full of shit. Full of shit was his thing.

"Not funny," she said.

"I'm not trying to be funny."

An instrument squeaked. April shook her head as if trying to clear her brain.

"A few weeks ago a birdie told me—" Luc began.

"No more of your lame attempts at American idioms, please. What 'little birdie'? Who told you and what did they say?"

"Birdie," he said again. "This is not an idiom, I don't think?" He tightened his lips in concentration. "She said Birdie was her name. At least I think that's what she said."

"Birdie!" April gasped. Could it be? Did Luc know what he was talking about? "My assistant! Is that who you spoke to?"

"Yes, yes. She said she was your assistant."

"When? Why? What happened? How did she even—"

"You sent her Marthe's journals, non?" Luc asked with a touch of disapproval. "I was not aware you shared them."

"Yes." April cleared her throat. "I did. But for our records. And for research. Birdie is my research assistant. Provenance."

"That again?"

"And, not to worry, I used the proper procedures for scanning old documents."

"Avril."

"Okay, fine. I sent them to her. *Copies* of them. It was for our files, yes, but also my own prurient interest. I also showed them to my dad and my brother and one of my stepdaughters, and I don't regret it. Sorry, but I don't."

"Well," Luc said and took a sip of wine. "It's a good thing you have such a big mouth."

"I see the Luc Thébault charm is in full effect—"

"I am being serious. You shared these with your assistant and it seems this assistant shared your same viewpoint, about the auctions."

"Bien sûr! Of course! She has a brain in her head. But I still don't understand why she spoke to you."

He shrugged. "She rang. Told me what I needed to do."

"What do you mean?"

"One has a lot of sway when one threatens to take his business elsewhere. One can get the exact kind of auction he desires."

"You threatened to take the auction to another house?" April said, starting to laugh again.

"Per Birdie's advice, yes I did. She gave me an indication of the value of the estate, and I made sure to equate this into commissions and premiums that would be lost if this auction did not stand alone. The Boldini, of course, was the linchpin. Maybe I'd let Olivier have a little vertu, but not the Boldini."

"That was a dangerous game. But, my god, a brilliant one."

April let the air run out from her lungs. She had that weird feeling, the one you got after narrowly avoiding a car crash or almost getting run over by a cab.

"Madame Vannier was very grateful," Luc said. "When Birdie explained how much more the estate would generate with the items grouped together. And the journals, they gave provenance, non? Just as you said. Because we learned these things were owned by Victor Hugo's heretofore unknown daughter."

"It's true," April said, nodding earnestly. "I know you thought provenance was an excuse, and on some level it was, but there's nothing more important in an auction. And Marthe de Florian has the most fascinating provenance I've ever seen in my job."

"If not for your efforts, your dogged pursuit of provenance, there'd be no separate auction." Luc smiled. "As a small token of her thanks, Madame Vannier said I could give you this."

Luc reached into his leather satchel as April tried to fully process the information. An auction for Marthe: the attention, the press, the private views. All the frenzy she deserved.

"This is for you," Luc said and plopped Mickey Mouse on the table.

April's mouth dropped open.

"It was once a present from Boldini to Lisette Quatremer. Madame Vannier wanted you to have it."

Before she could think, April reached out, snatched the mouse, and held it to her chest. Though he still smelled of dust and old people, Mickey was perfect.

"Are you sure?" April asked. "This is a relic, an heirloom, potentially worth many thousands of dollars to the right collector."

"What's an heirloom unless it means something to the person who has it?"

April's eyes watered. It was a long time before she could bring herself to release the animal. Even as a man stepped onstage and welcomed the crowd, April could not let go.

As the instruments started to ting, Luc scooted his chair closer and placed a hand on April's thigh. She reached down and wrapped her fingers around his. The gesture was congenial, mostly, but with the full weight of what happened behind them. At once April remembered the first time she saw Luc, smoking that cigarette in the dust-ridden flat as she wondered how the hell she could comb through the clutter, the mess in the apartment and in her life.

April thought of their first meal together, at the Café Zephyr, when she nearly toppled over the low-lying fence. She thought of the rooftop deck at the Galeries Lafayette, the moment when April finally understood Luc was not just a smirky, salty lawyer with an inflated sense of self. There were more restaurants, more chats, all the hours spent in Marthe's home explaining to Luc exactly how special each piece was. And, of course, there was Bastille Day, the firehouse, her bedroom—a mistake to be sure, but one April didn't altogether regret making.

She leaned toward Luc. It was nearly too loud to speak.

"Thank you," she said. "For everything. For every big and little thing."

"Ah, I've done nothing," he said. "We've had fun, haven't we?"

April nodded, biting her lip, tears running down her face.

"Ah, sweet *Avril*. No tears. It's not over. It will never be over. And tomorrow is the best part." He paused and gripped her hand tighter. "Tomorrow . . . tomorrow we see Agnès."

Chapitre LXIX

New York Times
MME. CHARCOT SEEKS DIVORCE
Granddaughter of Victor Hugo
Charges Her Husband with Desertion

PARIS, Feb. 15 – Jeanne Charcot, née Hugo, granddaughter of Victor Hugo, has filed a petition for divorce in the Paris courts against her husband, Dr. Jean Charcot, son of the famous nerve specialist, and head of the French Antarctic Expedition, on the grounds of desertion.

The petition creates the liveliest interest in Parisian circles where both parties are prominent.

Madame Charcot had been divorced previously, having been, before her marriage to Dr. Charcot, the wife of Léon Daudet, eldest son of the late Alphonse Daudet. Shortly after she was married to Charcot the latter had a dispute in a theatre with Léon Daudet, and a duel was fought, in which Charcot was slightly wounded.

Charcot left France over a year ago in an attempt to reach the South Pole. Fears have recently been expressed that his expedition has met with disaster. A relief expedition is now proposed.

Chapitre LXX

Paris, 4 June 1905

Dear God, how did everything get to this state? I did a horrible thing today, truly horrible. I don't know that I can ever forgive myself.

It started with Boldini and one of his sour moods. Is that not always the case? My stomach hurts just to transcribe the scene, but transcribe it I must. My brain is moving too fast, the words are spilling out of me. I must find somewhere to put them.

How to explain this particular sour mood? You see, Parisians seem to be off the great Giovanni Boldini, Master of Swish. Like sheep in a herd they follow the whims of American collectors, a laughable situation to start. I cannot fathom from the bowels of which of Satan's henchmen the idea that Americans have taste originally sprung. And "bowels" is the exact right word. Their discernment is for shit. Alas, some American or another woke up one morning and decided Boldini was entirely out of fashion. Before, you were not anyone unless Boldini painted you. Now there is not anyone who wants to be painted by him.

These cretins are all enamored of Pablo Picasso, the crazy stupid Spaniard who somehow coerced the American Gertrude Stein into purchasing his works. The man has more names than Jeanne Hugo Daudet Charcot, even if you include the extra one she will add following her divorce from Jean-Baptiste and her inevitable marriage to the next poor fool who happens upon her doorstep, or her bedchamber.

For his part, M. Picasso is legally known as: Pablo Diego José Francisco de Paula Juan Nepomuceno María de los Remedios Cipriano de la Santísima Trinidad Ruiz y Picasso.

That alone says all we need to know of the man! Insane and overdone.

Not only does he have a benefactor in Mademoiselle Stein, a fortune never bestowed upon Boldini, who required no ugly American to make his mark, but M. Picasso employs a publicist! It is only that coxcomb Apollinaire, the one with the curly hair and a ruby on his pinky finger, but a publicist he has. Everyone thinks Apollinaire is so cultured and wealthy. He only looks this way because his mother dresses him. I know this for a fact!

Last night Boldini came to my flat to dine. He was too distraught to eat in his studio surrounded by paintings, by all the things once beautiful that suddenly felt like failures. Knowing the depths to which his foul moods could sink, I'd dismissed the cook for the evening once she finished preparing the meal. I would straighten up myself. I hate to clean, and with the recent odd numbness in my wrists and forearms it's more difficult than ever, but this was the least of my worries. I let her go, knowing full well I'd have more than dishes to clean that night.

Boldini sat at my table and refused supper, all peevish like a billy goat with the flu. I told him to buck up, stop complaining, and devise a solution. Maybe he could alter his painting style. Maybe he should go to London to work a few commissions. Lord knows it will take the English at least a decade to catch on to his nonsense, at which time the tide of favor will shift back to Boldini here in Paris!

Well, he continued to grumble and drink more wine. Béatrice sat in the adjoining room trying to work a puzzle to little success. In between grunts and complaints, Boldini cast sidelong glances her way. I knew what would happen before it actually did.

"She has never gotten any better," he said, finishing off the last bottle of wine in the home, which is a testament to his inebriation as I am always well-stocked.

"Whatever do you mean?" I blotted my mouth with a napkin.

"You said she would walk later and talk later and read later. She is six and a half and 'later' has yet to happen. She looks like a young girl but remains an infant!"

"Boldini!" I snapped. "Keep your voice down! Béa may be simple, but she is the sweetest cookie of a child. I am blessed to have her as my own. *We* are blessed."

"You only say that because she is pliant and does whatever you order. She thinks you're perfect. I guess you *are* very fortunate, then. She will never know the real you."

"That is quite enough!" I snapped and threw a fork down on to my plate, with less force than I'd intended, given the peculiarities with my hands and joints. "I will not entertain this mean-spirited conversation."

"Tell me, Marthe, why is she slow?"

"She had a difficult birth," I said, voice quivering. "You were there."

"Yes, her birth was difficult, wasn't it? It was very odd."

"She was a double footling breech. I don't know why you're haranguing me about this."

But I did know. I knew exactly why.

"Yes, but you'd think that no matter the position, a premature baby would not be so difficult to deliver."

"Well, I am not a doctor," I said and stood, gathering up our plates. "And neither are you."

"Ah, yes, but Dr. Pozzi is and he told me Béatrice was awfully large for a baby born at her supposed gestation."

I glanced away. My lip was trembling.

"She is not my child, is she, Marthe?"

Without answer, I tramped off into the kitchen and busied myself with the cleanup. I scraped and scrubbed while Boldini continued to yell, "She is not mine!" He grew so boisterous that even Béa started crying. She ran into her bedroom and slammed the door.

"Are you happy now?" I screamed, marching back into the dining room. "You have upset the one person in the world who never gets upset!"

"Tell me the truth, Marthe! I only want the truth."

"Fine!" I said, surprised by the word. I did not mean to confess. "You are not the one who impregnated me. But make no mistake, you *are* her father."

"Not anymore!"

Boldini pushed back his chair, which then toppled over and landed with a thud against the wall. He grabbed for his coat and made a fast path to the front door.

I tried to chase after him, but he shook me off. He said we were done and he would support us no longer. It took years, and then it took Béatrice, to persuade Boldini to throw a few francs our way. The man is not our sole source of income. There are a few other contributors, not the least of whom is Clem, the statesman known as "the Walrus." Nevertheless, the financial hole into which Boldini flung us is deep indeed, to speak nothing of the emotional one. I slept not once last night as I scrambled to devise a plan.

I could locate Jean-Baptiste, I reasoned, and threaten to go public with Béatrice's parentage, which was no kind of solution at all. First I would have to find him. The world-famous "Polar Gentleman" spent the last two years in Antarctica and is allegedly missing at sea. Even if he weren't missing, he would have to care. His divorce with Jeanne is to be finalized any day. He is a beloved adventurer, and citizens forgive him any indiscretion. Therefore, when it comes to my accusations he has very little to lose. I suppose that's what happens when you live on a boat.

Utterly distraught by the time dawn came, I did the only thing I could. Oh, God, I hate to think of it now! I packed Béatrice's pink suitcase with her favorite frocks and dolls, hired a hack, and together we took the long, bumpy road out of town.

We arrived at the Home for Idiots and Imbeciles shortly before one o'clock. My face was wet with tears, little rivulets cutting through my whitening mask, and I could not speak through the sobs. Béa, blessed Béa, simply looked up at me with those dark eyes, clear and trusting. She smiled and squeezed my hand.

"Darling," I said before we exited the coach. "This is a wonderful school. Maman will miss you terribly but you will learn so much! Here they will train and educate you to speak and, eventually, teach you a trade. Perhaps shoemaking or carpentry or gardening. When you're grown you can return to Paris with your maman and take up a post as a clerk or laborer. We'll live together for the rest of our days. What do you think, my love?"

She blinked at me happily like she always did. Oh, my heart!

We got out of the cab and walked into the main office, where I filled out scores of forms. The director showed me the living quarters. My eyes stung with the bleakness, the metal, the urine-stained mattress. Already my resolve dwindled.

The last stop was the playground. Here was the place I would let go of Béa's hand and send her into the world without me. It was supposed to give me comfort, all these smiling, happy, giggling children playing in the sunshine. Instead it nearly made me vomit.

Kids climbed amongst the equipment, tripping over their own feet, drool spilling from the sides of their mouths. They might try the same thing once, twice, thrice, or more, always failing, always failing, never getting it right. Not a single person stepped forward to help them.

It was too much to take.

"All right, Madame de Florian," the director said. "It is time to let your daughter go. Allow her to be free and learn amongst others like her."

I loosened my grip for half a second.

Then I closed it tight again.

Sweeping Béa up into my arms, I turned and ran to the coach, leaving everyone and everything behind, even her pink suitcase. The truth was I could not have kept it. Every time I saw it I would've hated myself.

We returned to Paris by nightfall, me hugging my girl for the entire trip, over every bump, around every turn. I didn't know what we would do then, I certainly don't know now. I only know I need Béatrice by my side. The rest I can figure out in time.

Chapitre LXXI

Paris, 14 August 1914

It is as though all the pressure built over the past few months, the past year even, has finally released in a pop heard around the world. Yes the pop is messy and loud and a bit terrifying, but throughout Paris there is an enormous sense of relief.

Germany has finally declared war. This is good news because the war, we knew, was coming. German troops already invaded French territory twice. As the papers say, the declaration forced them to take a formal stance of aggression. This will not be looked kindly upon by our neighboring countries or even those across the seas.

More than this, hope comes in the form of retribution. We might finally avenge the Franco-Prussian War! The minute the news hit the wires people were dancing in the streets. Parties erupted in every café, every dance hall, and nearly every public square. The crowds were enormous. People rode in carriages and atop white horses. They wept for joy. People kissed strangers or family members to whom they were not speaking. Flowers were sold on every street corner. It was a wedding party in which we were all the brides.

Caught up in this sweep of good feelings is Giovanni Boldini himself. When not toiling away at portraiture, including way too many of the rich Italian Donna Franca Florio, he comes to see us. No matter how many times he's renounced Béatrice he cannot keep himself away more than a few weeks at a time. In our years together as (almost) husband and wife he grew quite fond of the girl.

At least Boldini outright admits he misses Béatrice. However he cannot extend the same platitude my way. I suppose there are too many things between us. What can I do about it now? Though I apologize for everything, I am sorry for nothing.

My Béatrice, she is such a lovely young lady. She has recently taught herself to read and to write! An amazing feat! Her musings do read more like those of a girl of six than a woman approaching sixteen, but I truly never thought we would get to this point. Though she will never be a scholar she will remain, forever, my Béatrice.

There is more I want to write, but I cannot remember the words I'd come to tell. Plus, my hands! My hands are worse than ever, and the deadening is now starting to travel to my face. A so-called doctor diagnosed me with Phossy jaw, a condition of the factory girls. As I never had to resort to such occupational measures, the only reasonable conclusion is that the doctor is a quack.

According to Boldini, the numbness at times extends to my mind. Two weeks ago he slashed his latest round of Donna Franca Florio portraits in a fit of self-loathing, but blamed it on me. I broke into his flat, he said, and went mad, claiming they were portraits of Jeanne Hugo. The gall of the accusation! As if I would do that! As if I could even confuse the two women! They look nothing alike. Perhaps Boldini has Phossy *brain* from those paints he uses.

Nonetheless I feel the years encroaching. I am not old, though not young either (ha!). But as I turned forty this year it's time to increase the henna and facial whitening agents. There are still men to charm and bills to pay. It all makes me so very tired sometimes, so very, very tired.

Chapitre LXXII

Paris, 10 February 1919

The weather is cold and damp. I could not afford to put coal in my fire today, to heat this apartment filled with my things. My hand cramps as I scratch out these words. I fear my fingers might stick to the pen.

This city is dead. The trees, the animals, even the war that once looked so promising is done, thousands of bodies still being shipped home, families hoping for this one last glimpse of loved ones, even if all they get is a corpse. What happened to the Paris I once loved? The one filled with gilt and satin? As much as Paris is dead, its soul is gone too.

And so is my own heart, my daughter, my Béatrice. She is also dead. It is either ironic or fitting or completely unfair that a girl who struggled through childbirth to enter the world left it in the exact same fashion. There was blood, so much blood, and in the end they could not save her. If only Dr. Pozzi were still alive perhaps my Béatrice, my soul, would still be here. Instead she is gone, and I am left with a different baby girl, Elisabetta. Lisette is what Béa wanted to call her when she was sure—so sure!—this baby she carried was a girl.

I raised my child. I am not prepared to be a mother again. I do not have the means or a way to get them. As much as this world is crumbling my looks are, too. I will have to lower my standards or begin selling off the beautiful pieces given to me by Clemenceau, by *Le Comte*, by Giovanni Boldini.

Boldini. I can hardly write his name. This, the man I loved for most of my life, the man who reentered the fairy world created by Béatrice and me. He saved my life once only to ruin it later. I thought when Giovanni came back it was for the both of us. Alas, Giovanni didn't miss me but Béa, and he missed her in the most inappropriate manner. Boldini got her pregnant. He killed her.

He said it was a misunderstanding. Marguérite says I've concocted something out of thin air. But what is there to possibly misunderstand? To make up? Nothing he can say will make it right. He tried to make amends by giving me the portrait he painted of me all those years (decades!) ago. It was his final parting gift, which I promptly attempted to sell to the French government. They would give me nothing for it. That's how unimportant the man has become.

In sum, the wretch left me with three things: a useless painting, a dead daughter, and a baby I do not want and cannot take care of. Thus I must do what I couldn't before. Tomorrow it is off to the idiot's home. It may be a harsh sentence for this young child, but I cannot keep her. My feelings are something lower and darker than indifference. It is not her fault but, like Boldini, she killed my Béa.

The director of the asylum, if he's still there, was a kind man. They teach their students trades, ways to become productive members of society. It is more than I could give her. After all, if I'd left Béa there she would still be alive.

As I pack Lisette's few things for the journey, the tears come hard. No, I tell them, stay away. This is not the moment for regrets. Marguérite is on her way. She will join me on the journey. With her help I will be brave enough to leave the child. This time I will not look back.

Chapitre LXXIII

They traveled the long road to Sarlat-la-Canéda, the windows of Luc's BMW M6 down, the wind pitching April's hair into hedgelike proportions. She thought more than once the distance was long enough that, had they been in the United States, she would've insisted on flying. Yet somehow April was glad of the length of the trip.

Lisette's desertion of the flat finally made sense. If April's own grandmother had ditched her at the local Home for Idiots, she would've eschewed the woman's knickknacks and paintings too. Still, as brutal as the action was, April felt sorry for Marthe. She was so full of love for her daughter that it must've taken the severest kind of depression to force her to abandon Lisette. The one man Marthe trusted betrayed her in a most egregious fashion, her favorite person dead at his hand.

"Even in an automobile you work furiously," Luc noted as they eased off the highway and onto a twisted road surrounded by purples, surrounded by yellows, surrounded by greens, all of it beneath a turquoise sky. Even compared to California the effect was almost too much for April's eyes.

"I'm trying to write interview questions," April said. "But failing miserably."

"Why don't you—how do you call it? Float by the seat of your pants?"

"Fly. It's 'fly.' And considering I hounded the ailing woman into seeing us I need to be prepared. I don't really know where to start. At first I only cared about the furniture, the paintings, all the amazing pieces in the apartment. I wanted to find out why Madame Quatremer would leave it all behind. Now it doesn't seem to matter."

She patted the stack of journals on her lap.

"This is what I care about," she said. "The rest of Marthe's story. The journals told me so much, but they're incredibly sparse at the end, such massive gaps of time. I need the filler, the in-between. I'm hoping Madame Vannier has it."

"Well," Luc said and smiled. "As always, I hope you get what you want."

As they twisted deeper into the countryside, April closed her eyes and leaned back into the seat. Like a crooked country road, her mind started to turn and wander. She found herself thinking about her mom. April pictured her face: those green eyes, the wide, flat nose, and the sprinkle of freckles across her cheeks. By the time she died those freckles were long gone, institutional fluorescents a sad downgrade from California sunshine.

April very nearly nodded off to sleep.

"You're smiling," Luc said suddenly. He reached over and patted April's arm, interrupting her waking dream. "What is so amusing to you?"

"Not amusing." April rolled her head to the side. She gave a tired little smile. "I was thinking—dreaming? About my mom."

"What about your mom?"

"I was thinking about animals."

"Animals? Why? Did you have a lot of pets growing up?"

"No, the Potter household was no-feather, no-fur. No-fin, even! Brian once brought a goldfish home from the county fair, and Mom made him take it back. To the fair! You know you're in a sorry state if carnies think you're weird." April laughed. "Yet my mom *loved* animals. If there was a crippled dog or cat in the neighborhood she'd fix it right up. I've seen her tape a cat's tail and create a makeshift brace on a dog's leg using hacked-up rulers and duct tape. Once she tried to administer CPR to a bird that flew into the living-room window."

"Did it work?"

"I think she blew up its lungs. I remember sobbing at the screen door."

"Poor little Avril," Luc said.

"Poor April is right! She was blunt too, to an almost indecorous extent. A woman in the neighborhood had a miscarriage, and my mother proceeded to tell us, at Sunday dinner, that the neighbor gave birth not to a baby but to a giant hairball with teeth. I thought my father was going to pass out."

"Sounds like an entertaining woman. Maybe I would've enjoyed her almost as much as I enjoy you." He winked.

"I've been writing it all down, these stories, our memories. I'd forgotten how great she was. She was stuck in my head as this stern, teetotaling, rule-following kind of housewife, but now I wonder. Had she been born a little later perhaps she would've ended up one of those free-spirited hippie types. Or maybe if she hadn't married a naval officer."

"And what if you'd not married a financier?" Luc said.

"I was long since me when he came along. Moving on! Doesn't this car have a radio? An iPod?"

April reached down and turned whichever knob her hand first found.

"That is the air-conditioning," Luc noted as a blast of air shot her in the face.

"Make yourself useful and put on some music." April leaned back into the headrest and closed her eyes. "I need to think."

Within seconds April fell into that slip of space between dream and reality, where the outside mixes with the inside. April smelled Luc's cigarette at the same time she saw her mother, at the same time Marthe slid absinthe down the bar toward a man who looked like Troy.

When April next opened her eyes, thinking she took a ten-minute nap, the clock told her it was closer to an hour. Luc was jiggling her leg.

"We're in Sarlat," he said. "In case you want to freshen up before we arrive."

"Why?" April scooted into an upright position. Her mouth felt tacky. "Do I need to freshen up?"

April flipped down the visor and searched her purse for something that qualified as "makeup." Unless Marthe time-traveled and swapped handbags, there was zero chance of finding anything capable of freshening up in that particular pit of loose paper and excess pens.

"Ah! Eight-year-old lip gloss from some unnamed source!" April announced, producing a mangled pink and sparkly tube. "Fingers crossed whoever dropped it in here didn't have herpes."

"Did you just say the word '*herpes*'?!"

Before April devised an appropriate retort she was struck by the view outside.

"Wow! This is Sarlat?" she said. "Is this place for real?"

It was amazing, this village. A time capsule, perfectly medieval with its yellow sandstone buildings, steeply pitched roofs, and cobblestone streets. It was almost offensive in its quaintness, like it belonged in an amusement park.

"Did they rebuild it or something?" April asked, still stunned. "Or has it been this way all along?"

"All along, I suppose."

Luc swung around a corner and proceeded down an alley that looked better suited for a secondhand *moto*. April gripped the sides of the car as Luc deftly navigated trash cans and people and goats.

Soon they shot through one last alley-street and out onto a dirt road. The path was long and straight, surrounded by green fields. At the end of the road stood a square stone house. April let out a small gasp. It had to be Agnès Vannier's. There was no other place for the road to go.

Chapitre LXXIV

Even though it was warm outside, Agnès Vannier sat before a crackling fireplace with a velvet blanket draped over her lap. A large upholstered box was at her feet.

There was no questioning the woman's age and recent ill health. Her shoulders were slight, bones poking through her sweater like fingers, wispy arms folded like grasshopper legs. She had a fluff of white-blond hair through which April could see her pink-marbled scalp. Her eyes were ice blue, the color of a glacier, almost transparent.

"Welcome to my home," she said in French after a maid or household assistant of some sort let them through.

"Thank you for having us," April replied, unsure whether to approach the woman in the rosewood chair or remain several yards back. "It is a pleasure to be here."

Madame Vannier looked her squarely in the face.

"I will not speak any English," she said.

"Ce n'est pas un problème." April inched herself closer to Luc, suddenly seized by the urge to grab on to some part of him: his sleeve, his belt, the outer edge of his right pocket. She felt loose, unsecured.

"May we sit down?" Luc asked in French and pointed to a narrow white-upholstered loveseat made in the days when people were not quite so large.

"Please do." Agnès tilted her head as a small smile formed at the corners of her mouth.

"Again, we appreciate you taking the time to speak with us," April said, reminding herself to talk slowly, to count the breaths between her words. When it came to speaking French in nervous fashion, April had to be sure she kept inhaling. "My name is April Vogt, and of course you know Monsieur Thébault."

"Yes, Luc." She touched the small sapphire pendant that sat in the pool of gaunt space beneath her neck. "The handsome solicitor. So, Madame Vogt, why you have come all this way?"

"To begin." April cleared her throat. She extracted the diary pages from her bag. "I wanted to return these in person. Thank you for loaning them to our auction house. They were of great assistance in determining provenance."

April handed the papers to Madame Vannier, who then threw them onto the coffee table and chuckled. The sound came not from her throat but somewhere deeper, moister, perhaps a pair of lungs besieged by pleurisy.

"Luc told me you would say this," Madame Vannier said. "About the provenance."

"Yes, well." April brushed a piece of hair from her face. "It is true. So thank you, again."

"You have said 'thank you' quite a lot." She lightly touched her temples. "Please stop."

"Yes, ma'am, I only wanted to express—"

"What did you think of the journals?"

"I, uh, well . . . I loved them," April said. "I absolutely loved them. I wished there were more entries. Marthe de Florian was a fascinating person."

"'Fascinating.' That is one word to use." Madame Vannier chuckled again. The sound made April tremble. She moved closer to the fire. "I do not have much time, today or on this earth. So let's get to it, shall we? What is it you would like to know? So you can determine your . . . provenance."

April dived back into her purse to locate a pen. She tested three on her yellow legal pad before finally finding one that worked.

"My questions are many," April said and looked to Luc for help. He shrugged. This was her show, he seemed to say. He only bought her the ticket. "But the first is how you fit into the story."

"Madame Vogt, did you come to ask about me? Or would you like to know about Marthe and Lisette?"

"I came to learn about all of it, really."

"We'll get to me. I do not feel like answering this. Not yet."

"Um, all right," April said, momentarily reverting to English while her brain spun. What was it April *really* wanted to ask? Did she even know?

"Madame Vogt?"

"I'm sorry," she said. "Trying to formulate my thoughts. You see, I understand quite a bit thanks to the journals." She nodded toward the table. "I suppose I'm trying to fill in the missing pieces."

Luc coughed. April snapped her head in his direction. Was he issuing a warning? Or suffering the ill effects of his tobacco habit?

"I'm curious," Madame Vannier said. "What is it you think you understand?"

"Not everything, of course, but I do have better comprehension of the personal relationships, of Marthe's love of Giovanni Boldini and why she was so angry with Jeanne Hugo. I also now see why Lisette—sorry, Madame Quatremer—left the apartment behind."

"And why was that?" Madame Vannier asked.

"Well, despite everything, despite how very much Marthe loved Béatrice, I am sure Madame Quatremer felt a certain sense of disconnection since she was put up for adoption at such a young age."

Put up for adoption. It sounded so much better than abandoned at a home for idiots and imbeciles. But at least, in the end, Marthe considered Lisette part of her family. She felt some duty toward her. Otherwise Marthe never would've left Lisette Quatremer the apartment and its treasures.

"'Put up for adoption'?" Madame Vannier said. "This is not true."

"But the journals—" April pointed to the table. She glanced toward Luc. He shrugged again. She looked back at Madame Vannier, who continued to bore into her with that eerie fluorescent stare. "Marthe said she was taking her granddaughter to a home. She couldn't care for her on her own."

"Well, that second part is certainly true," Madame Vannier said with a little snicker. "But no, she never took her to the home in the end. She planned to but her good friend convinced her otherwise."

" 'Good friend'? Do you mean Marguérite?"

Madame Vannier nodded, and a wide grin erupted across April's face.

"Well, of course Marguérite would step in," April said, goofy with the thought of it. Leave it to Marguérite to help Marthe do the right thing.

"So you've come to appreciate dear Marguérite."

"Yes! Absolutely. She was a great friend, wasn't she?"

"Indeed. Frankly I don't know why she put up with the illustrious Madame de Florian," Madame Vannier said, rolling her tongue theatrically. "Luckily for Béa, luckily for Lisette, Marguérite made it her personal mission to look after her."

"Look after whom? Lisette? Or Béa?"

"Both in their way. But I was referring to Marthe."

"What do you mean, 'Marthe'? No one looked after her. Of course, yes, she had 'clients' and they provided material things, but Marthe was remarkably self-sufficient, don't you think? She came to Paris without a dime, without knowing a soul, and made a life for herself. Just look at all the items in her apartment! It was a rich woman's flat. She did quite well, don't you think?"

April glanced toward Luc for what felt like the tenth time. How many times would she say the words "don't you think" until someone finally agreed with her?

"If one can judge a life by personal possessions then I suppose you are right," Madame Vannier said at last. "I care to judge it in another manner. Marthe was a terrible mother, utterly selfish."

"Excuse me?" A flash of heat rose to April's cheeks. "Don't you think that's a little harsh?"

"Or not harsh enough. By today's standards she would be considered abusive, neglectful at the very least. Especially by your American standards."

"You're wrong!" April cried and leaped from the couch.

Luc tried to grab her arm but missed completely. She snatched the journals from the table.

"I read these," she said, shaking the papers. "Not all the days, not even all the years were here, but I know this woman. It may sound crazy but I feel as though I know her."

"Do you?" Madame Vannier's voice was rough, like sandpaper. April felt like a scolded child. "Tell me, why do you think only some journal entries were found in the apartment? What happened to the rest?"

April shrugged. "I suppose the same thing that's happened to most documents from a hundred years ago. They were lost or destroyed or thrown away."

A devilish smile slithered across Madame Vannier's face.

"Destroyed, yes. They were destroyed. By Lisette. After Marthe died."

"What do you mean?" April asked, almost coughing out the words. "I thought she'd not been to the apartment in seventy years?"

"She hadn't. Marthe de Florian died in 1935. Lisette left Paris in 1940. In between were enough years to go through the woman's things, to rid of herself of that which she did not want to see. You think these letters and words were important to you? Well, they were everything to Lisette. Like you, she was trying to piece together a story, to understand things she could not."

"Wasn't she there? She had all these people around—her grandmother, Marguérite. Didn't she already know the story?"

"Oh, Madame Vogt," Agnès said and started to laugh.

The laugh turned into a cough that morphed into a hack that brought four previously unseen household workers running. Someone prepared honey tea. April sat frozen as Luc rubbed her back. People fussed and swirled around the old woman.

"Pardon me," Madame Vannier said once the commotion died down and her assistants disappeared into the woodwork from which they'd come. "I am quite on my last legs. Where were we?"

"I said something that sent you into a fit of hysterics. But if you can't continue, I understand."

"Ah. Yes. 'Hysterics.' Madame Vogt, surely you know there is always more to a person than what you see, or what they decide to show you."

"But—"

"Shush. Enough. You came to find the missing pieces? Well, the missing piece was Lisette. Did you not figure? She has a story, too."

Chapitre LXXV

Agnès Vannier, Prewar Paris

Elisabetta de Florian looked exactly like her grandmother. They shared similar dark, curled hair, matching black eyes, and the same long, proud nose. Lisette hated it.

She did not want to be like the woman who raised her, all wild-eyed and desperate. *Grand-mère* was frightening, unpredictable, a kitten one second, a ferocious wildcat the next. More than her moods, Lisette feared the endless stream of men who pounded into and out of their flat. These so-called gentlemen were usually rude and often violent and almost always drunk. Whenever one came to call while *Grand-mère* was out, Lisette hid the calling card behind a painting or tucked it up inside a bureau.

"Did anyone stop by while I was away?" *Grand-mère* might ask.

"No," Lisette would tell her. "It was quiet as a morgue."

There was never much to eat. *Grand-mère* would dine at restaurants with the men, these interlopers, and come home smelling of chicken grease and something more acrid. As the years moved on, *Grand-mère's* belly went from flat to puffy to distended. It took her longer to get dressed in the mornings as she attempted to wheedle her sausage arms into dresses that went out of style years before.

"I am rather hungry," Lisette often told her.

"I'll see what I can do," *Grand-mère* always replied. "But money is hard to come by these days. We must do our best with what little we have and continue to prepare for the worst."

Whenever *Grand-mère* was absent from the flat, Lisette would look around at her grandmother's things. She studied them, envying their solidarity, their permanent place in the world. There were vases and chandeliers and paintings, a million relics collected and accumulated and piled up. They called to mind excess, thus made young Lisette wonder why they could not afford to eat.

Once, after *Grand-mère* went missing for several days, Lisette took a candelabrum to the corner pawnbroker and sold it for a pittance. She knew it was worth at least five times what the oily little man paid for it, but at that moment a full stomach was worth more.

When *Grand-mère* returned home and passed by the pawnbroker's window she recognized the piece as something from her flat. How she distinguished it from the forty others exactly like it Lisette would never know. After assaulting the owner with a walking cane (once the prime minister's, now hers) and accusing him of being a thief and a "dirty, filthy Jew," *Grand-mère* learned it was her own granddaughter who sold the piece.

Grand-mère stormed into the flat, shouting for the head of Lisette. Lisette, knowing her grandmother had trouble moving about, barricaded herself behind several pieces of furniture. It was one benefit of their cramped, crowded apartment: There were many places to hide.

"Things will get much worse before it's over with!" *Grand-mère* shouted. "We need to save our pennies! We need to prepare for the worst! The worst will come!"

Lisette never understood. Her grandmother was saving these objects for a rainy day, yet it was already pouring outside.

As the years went on *Grand-mère*'s compassion and mental clarity continued to decline. Often she screamed at Lisette for no reason, claiming the girl had said something she hadn't or lain with someone she'd never met. Despite her grandmother's profession, when accused of sex Lisette had no earthly idea what Marthe meant. She only knew it was something she'd never done.

The screaming always commenced at high pitch, and Lisette learned to hide behind a dresser or an armoire and wait for the storm to pass. After bellowing on for many minutes, *Grand-mère* would stop suddenly, in mid-sentence, as if her vocal cords had been pulled from her neck. Her face would freeze on one side, the other half drooping and dripping like candle wax.

By the time she was ten, Lisette knew there were only two people in her life to count on: *Grand-mère*'s old friend Giovanni Boldini, and her even older friend Marguérite. *Grand-mère* refused to speak to Boldini, the war between them having gone on for years, but Marguérite took her to see the man. She told Lisette that whenever she needed someone there was always her, Marguérite, and this man, the painter Boldini. In the years that followed, whether hungry or lonely or sad, Lisette went to see one of these two people. She spent many nights sleeping in their guest quarters, many happy, full hours dining at their tables.

Boldini passed away when Lisette was twelve, but Marguérite remained in her life. It was Marguérite who fed Lisette when she was hungry, who mended her dresses, who taught her how to read. It was also Marguérite who taught Lisette to be herself instead of what she thought other people wanted to see. It was a lesson never learned by *Grand-mère*.

When her grandmother died in 1935, it was almost a relief. Lisette was no longer subject to her rants and now had free reign over the things inside the apartment. Lisette was not the most worldly when it came to the appraisal of furniture, but she understood the items' true value, which was freedom.

Within months of *Grand-Mère*'s passing, Lisette began weeding through the mess, sorting the items by potential value and ease of transport. Marguérite told her of a local auction house: Sotheby's. This house would take Marthe's things and sell them on the block for a hefty price. All Lisette had to do was prepare the objects for sale. It sounded easy enough, but Lisette never got quite that far.

She started with the heaviest armoire in the flat. Lisette spent so much time hiding behind it she figured it would be the easiest to let go. That is, until she opened its doors and found her grandmother's journals inside. There were dozens of diaries, perhaps a hundred or more, all filled front to back, bound with colored ribbons, and completely intact. At least for a while.

The woman who wrote the journals was not the *Grand-mère* Lisette knew. There was a liveliness to her, especially in the early years, a brightness Lisette had not expected. Marthe was not all outbursts or teary, garbled missives. *Grand-mère* did know how to love. She loved Boldini. She loved Marguérite. She loved Béatrice. She even loved Lisette.

As she went through the diaries, more than a little teary and garbled herself, Lisette pulled each page from its binding. She kept the entries that made her smile, or made her understand, and threw the rest into the fire, where they sparked and crackled and ultimately turned to ash.

Lisette always intended to get through the remainder of *Grand-mère*'s things tomorrow. She would auction them tomorrow. It's funny how quickly tomorrow becomes yesterday and then last week and then you run out of time. Before long tomorrow was 1940 and twenty-one-year-old Lisette was no closer to ridding herself of Marthe's excess than she had been five years before. Like the rest of the nation, she had bigger things to worry about than Louis XVI armchairs.

In that year the Nazis poured into France. The blitzkrieg began in May, and Paris toppled thereafter. Newspapers soon snapped photographs of Hitler posing jauntily before the Eiffel Tower as if on holiday. On June 14, Lisette stood on a sidewalk with her fellow countrymen and watched as German troops marched into her city. People stood in stunned horror. Others cried. Everyone wondered what would become of their country, what would become of their families.

It was only by chance that Lisette found herself beside an older woman in a long black mink coat. And it was only by chance that she turned toward this woman and recognized her as Jeanne Hugo. The sight of her face jolted Lisette. *Grand-mère* had no fewer than one hundred pictures of Jeanne in her apartment. What was once flat suddenly came to life.

"Excuse me," Lisette said to Jeanne Hugo. She was not a forward person but the war, having just started, already began to change her. "I hate to bother you at such a momentous time, but I suppose that is the very best time to say this. You and I, we are related."

Jeanne turned, eyes large, forehead lined with a million wrinkles.

"Beg your pardon?"

"Yes, well you see, I recently discovered that my great-grandfather was Victor Hugo, your grandfather! Yet, here we stand, side by side."

Lisette did not mention that her own grandfather was Jeanne's former husband. She suspected it was a revelation that might not be taken well.

Alas, if Lisette anticipated a smile or a pleasant acknowledgment of any kind, she was gravely mistaken.

"I thought you were dead!" the minked lady screamed. Several people stared, including two German soldiers smoking beside a lamppost.

"What's that?" Lisette tried to step back, but with the thick crowd there was nowhere to go. "Dead? Whatever do you mean?"

"You are that Folies whore! Marthe de Florian! Sold your soul to the devil for your youth!"

As wild as *Grand-mère*'s eyes were at times, Jeanne's made hers look as calm as a pool on a summer's day. The whites were red, the pupils so large that staring into them was like falling into a dark hole.

"Oh, I'm sorry," Lisette said and laughed nervously. "No, I am not Marthe de Florian, I am her granddaughter. Giovanni Boldini was my father." She'd learned this some three years before but still loved the way the words bounced off her tongue, the whole of it still fresh and new. "I believe he painted you and your son at one time? My grandfather was someone you knew as well—"

"Of course I knew your grandfather!" she screeched. "He was Léon Blum! A Jew! A sour, arrogant, malicious, untidy, unwholesome, blundering Jew!"

While Lisette remained in place, aghast, Jeanne did the unthinkable.

She ran over to the two Germans who were standing nearby smoking and enjoying the march.

"This girl over here, she is a Jew! And she's stolen something from me! I am Victor Hugo's granddaughter. I demand you incarcerate her immediately!"

Though it's unlikely the two cared about her relation to Victor Hugo—indeed they'd probably only vaguely heard of him to begin with—they stepped down from their post and approached Lisette cautiously, curiously. Whether they planned to speak with her or incarcerate her or do something else entirely (she'd heard rumors—God, she'd heard rumors), Lisette didn't wait to find out.

Using a burst of heretofore unknown strength, Lisette pushed and wormed her way amongst the crowd and then darted out into a backstreet not yet jammed by the spectacle. After kicking off her shoes, Lisette sprinted through the alleyways and sneaked between buildings until she made her way home, never once turning back to see if they followed.

Her chest heaving, Lisette stood against her locked apartment door and reminded herself she was safe. When a knock didn't follow in five minutes, in ten, in twenty, she tried to settle her breath, for a moment anyway, as in the long term the breath would never quiet. Lisette knew that staying there, in Paris, would mean a million long-drawn-out seconds waiting for someone to knock. She would not live like *Grand-mère*, always fearful, waiting for the worst to come.

Grabbing one small satchel of things, Lisette went first to my home, and together with my mother we went to Marguérite's. Since my father's death we were struggling too. Prospects in Paris did not look good. We heard people were fleeing to the countryside and thought perhaps we should do the same.

Marguérite saved us as she saved Marthe so many times. She spirited us away to her family home in the South of France. You see, she was not the urchin Marthe thought she met at Jeanne's wedding processional. No, she was simply a small girl from a wealthy family who wanted to be her own person.

Less than a week later, France signed an armistice with Germany in the same railway carriage in which Germany had surrendered in 1918. It took only six weeks for the country to collapse. We planned to stay in Marguérite's home a few months, a year at the most. Yet we stayed forever. Lisette could never bring herself to go back. She never needed Marthe's things after all.

Did you notice the plaque on the door? The one that said "Quatremer"? That was Marguérite's family name, and Lisette took it as her own. She told us it was because of her fear that someone might again accuse her of being a Jew. According to pamphlets distributed throughout Paris, Lisette's features matched the offending ones.

Really, though, we all understood the truth. Lisette took her name because Marguérite was the closest thing to a mother she ever had. But more than that, Lisette took her name because Marguérite was the only other person who knew what it was like to love the barkeep from the Folies, the difficult, the wonderful *Grand-mère*.

Chapitre LXXVI

Luc and April hadn't brought sleepwear or toothbrushes. They expressly planned to leave before nightfall but never counted on the sheer emotional weight of Madame Vannier's story. They did not figure the telling of it would so exhaust the woman she would have to retire to bed before a further question was asked.

So April and her solicitor spent the evening fully clothed, lying side by side on a mattress that felt more like a pallet of bricks. April kept both hands folded on her chest as Luc snored softly beside her. She counted each minute, each hour, constantly checking her phone, desperate for the time they might rejoin Madame Vannier.

The moment the first light of dawn broke across the bed April was up on her feet. She jostled her companion awake. He greeted her groggily and inquired as to the time. April reminded him one of the best features of the elderly was their up-with-the-roosters morning spryness.

Though it was barely six o'clock when April and Luc lumbered out into the kitchen, Madame Vannier already waited for her guests at a round, red table.

"Bonjour," April said and was surprised to find her voice jagged like glass.

"How are we this morning?" Madame Vannier asked, dipping a tea bag into her cup. "Would you like some tea or coffee?"

"Coffee would be lovely," April said. "I can make it."

"I've got it," said a voice from behind her.

April jumped. It was yet another of Madame Vannier's assistants, standing at the ready beside the coffeepot. April looked over at Luc, who stood in the doorway rubbing his eyes, his hair sticking up in a thousand directions.

"Merci," April said and sat her nervy self down. She noticed then the box that was at Madame Vannier's feet the night before was now on the table.

"Are all your questions answered?" Madame Vannier asked with a small chortle. "Now that I've told you Lisette's side?"

"No, I only have more."

"I thought as much."

Luc slid a chair between them. He went to light a cigarette. April reached out and wrapped her hand around it.

"You can't smoke that in here!" she said.

"I'm having flashbacks."

"It is fine." Madame Vannier cackled. "Americans, non?"

"Oui. Americans." Luc shook his head. April nudged him under the table with the top of her foot.

"Do tell me, Madame Vogt, what other questions do you have?" The woman took a sip of her tea. It went down her throat with the sound of water rushing through a pipe.

"Actually, I want to know more about Marthe's mental state prior to her death."

April thought of her mother and the ways Sandy Potter might've been misunderstood if she'd been in that apartment in that year and not in San Diego at some later time with a husband who supported her.

"I know Lisette had mixed feelings about her," April continued. "Which is wholly understandable given her tumultuous childhood. But I have to wonder. When I read the journals Marthe seemed so different, especially in the earlier years, from what you've described. But some of the later entries—let's just say I now see things I didn't before. I guess Boldini was right, her mind was slipping. I was thinking—wondering—do you think it is possible Marthe had Alzheimer's?"

" 'Alzheimer's'?" Every feature on Madame Vannier's face pinched into a tight bunch.

"My mother had it," April explained. "Actually, when I first saw Marthe's portrait she reminded me of my mom, and now I'm reminded again. She never experienced any violent mood swings, at least none that I saw, but it can really affect a person's mental well-being, their sense of orientation. I think it's probable she had—"

"She did not have Alzheimer's," Madame Vannier said as if she was a doctor or had personally performed the autopsy.

"It might be difficult to see that side of it, but it is really quite possible—"

Agnès reached into the box and pulled out a small white canister, the kind that might contain three ounces of two-hundred-dollar face cream. Except this one was old, tinny, and had a thick film of white around the edges, like plaster. Madame Vannier passed it her way.

"What is this?" April asked, turning it over in her hand.

"Marthe's famous face cream."

"Ah, the whitening mask." April smiled. "I would've loved to see it in action. It must've looked ridiculous, especially as she got older. She spared no caution in lathering it on her skin."

"Read the back."

"Excuse me?"

"The ingredients. On the back."

April turned it over. She read the first one and did not need to go further. *De plomb.*

"Lead? She put lead cream on her face?"

"Yes, every day. Multiple times a day. It's what eventually killed her. First her face became paralyzed, and her mind soon followed. Lead poisoning for the sake of beauty. Factory girls got lead poisoning from their working conditions. One could argue that Marthe did, too."

"Wow." April dropped the jar onto the table and wiped both hands on her jeans. "Poor Marthe."

"Poor everyone," Madame Vannier said with a sigh. Luc continued to sit between them puffing on a cigarette and looking like the wrong side of a hangover. He was not, April guessed, a morning person.

"Did Lisette ever reconnect with the Hugo family?" April asked. "Once the war was over?"

"Well, Jeanne Hugo passed in 1941."

"What about the others? They were technically her family. It is an important heritage, I would think. At least it was important to Marthe."

"When Lisette left Paris she *left* Paris. It did not matter to her what happened in an orphanage sixty years earlier. And given her encounter with Jeanne, she did not have high hopes for a future with the extended Hugo family."

"I can't blame her for that," April said. "The nuns almost did Marthe a disservice by revealing her lineage, telling her what she could never have. It drove Marthe to the point of obsession."

"Lineage is a double-edged sword, non? Sometimes it tells you too much. Your so-called provenance is not always good. I've learned this firsthand many times over the years."

"With the Hugos?"

"With my own background."

"I'm sorry." April said, squinting, confused. "I'm not familiar with the name Vannier."

"There is no reason for you to be. It was my mother's maiden name and should mean nothing to plucky little auction-house historians." Madame Vannier smirked. "It was her married name you might recognize. You recall the painting you found? In the apartment? The one you believe is so valuable?"

"Oh, god, don't tell me it's not a Boldini!" April said and thumped her head on the table. "I cannot take this."

"It's a Boldini, all right," Madame Vannier said and once again emitted one of her hyenalike chuckles. "Come now, Madame Vogt, don't you want to face me when you ask these questions?"

April lifted her head from the table.

"Thank god," April said, a little breathless. "You would've caused a whole mountain of problems for me if you'd said otherwise."

"Well, goodness!" Madame Vannier said and slapped her chest. "I certainly wouldn't want to cause any problems for *you*. Not to worry, ma chérie. It is a Boldini. I say this with authority because I am a Boldini, too."

Chapitre LXXVII

The Boldini revelation brought an added heaviness to Madame Vannier's breathing, which in turn drew an entirely new batch of home health aides to the kitchen. This time they came with hard-core pieces of medical equipment, including a portable oxygen tank. Watching Madame Vannier take gulps of air from the mask made April want a hit, too. Her breathing was also labored after what she just heard.

Madame Vannier was Boldini's daughter, his legitimate daughter. At age eighty-seven, the ever-crotchety Boldini decided to settle down once and for all. He wanted a wife and a family despite the advanced date on the calendar. At his wedding luncheon Boldini apologized for his geriatric state and famously announced, "It is not my fault if I am so old, it's something which has happened to me all at once." The Master of Swish was able to sire one more child before he died of pneumonia less than eighteen months after the wedding.

"Can we get you anything?" April asked after a Latin-looking man wheeled away the oxygen. "Some water? Should we step outside?"

"No, I am fine," Madame Vannier said and settled back into her chair. She had a new teacup in hand and offered her icy cool smile as if nothing happened. "So now you know my part in this story, how I fit into the picture."

"It is an amazing legacy," April said. "You must feel very proud of your father."

"I never knew him." Madame Vannier shrugged. "He died when I was so young, and as a girl I did not much care for his artistic pursuits. Like most children, I did not understand them. So perhaps 'pride' is not the correct word. I've come to appreciate him, however. I must confess I get a certain satisfaction when one of his paintings sells for a high price at auction. According to my mother, bless her soul, to be adored for his talent was all he ever wanted in life."

"Your mother," April started, remembering what Marc and Olivier told her. "She wrote about the painting in the flat, correct?"

"Yes." Madame Vannier nodded. "It helped with your provenance, non?"

"Regarding the Boldini it *was* our provenance," April said.

"She would've been pleased to help. Mother loved that man, despite his surly personality."

"He had a heart," April said. "He probably would've been thrilled to know his daughters lived beneath the same roof and took care of each other for so many years. His blood, his brood, carrying on without him."

Madame Vannier smiled. It was not one of her condescending, smug grins but a tight, small, lipless one. It was a smile of sadness and regret.

"He may have loved us both," she said. "But only one of us was blood."

"You said he was your father."

"Indeed I did."

"Oh." The words hit April like kick to the middle. "You think . . . do you think Lisette was not his daughter? I thought you were sisters? Half sisters? It's why you were so close."

"We were sisters," Madame Vannier said with a nod. "But not by blood."

She sighed deeply. One tear spilled from the corner of her eye. It stayed atop her cheek like a raindrop on a pink rose petal.

"Why did Marthe say he was her father, then?" April asked.

"I don't know where the idea originated," Madame Vannier said. "But she believed it entirely. Even Lisette was convinced after reading *Grand-mère*'s journals. It was why she came to our house when it was time to escape Paris. I was much younger, you see. Lisette thought it her duty to look after me, just as Marthe thought it was her duty to look after Marguérite. And Marguérite's to look after Marthe. In the end I am glad she believed this. I am glad delusions of family brought her to me."

Madame Vannier turned her head and gazed out the window, her long, flat face reflecting against the long, flat pane. April fiddled with a worn spot on her jeans. As she had so many times since arriving, April waited for Madame Vannier to gather the strength to continue.

"Lisette wanted to believe, I think," Agnès said, still staring through the window. "Like Marthe, she wanted a family, a history. Don't we all? Alas, a DNA test was conducted postmortem. I should've left it alone." Madame Vannier sniffed. A few more tears dribbled onto her cheeks. "My mother always insisted it wasn't true, that my father swore he never so much as touched the girl. Béatrice."

"Who was Lisette's father?" April asked. "If not Boldini, then who?"

"Béatrice was raised in the Folies. She played with her toys beneath the bar counter. Later, when she was older, she tried out makeup and hairstyles in the dressing rooms of the dancers. Lisette's father could've been anyone. And I mean that quite literally. A beautiful girl, in a dance hall, with only half a mind? I ask you, how many scenarios could there be?"

"A lot." April's chin dropped into her chest. "A lot."

"Now, if you'll excuse me," Madame Vannier said suddenly. She crept up from the table. "I must take a break. This has all been rather exhausting."

Without a good-bye or any indication if she might return, Madame Vannier dumped her teacup in the sink and limped down the hallway.

"That was quite a lot of information," Luc said once the slow pad of the old woman's feet dissipated. "Quite a lot."

April grunted in acknowledgment, her brain and guts knotted. Madame Vannier gave her what she asked for, but it was not what April wanted at all.

"I can't believe Marthe ended up as she did," April said. "She was surrounded by so many people but then she died insane, and in complete obscurity."

"We all die in obscurity," Luc said. "We all go alone. Tell me, Avril, what was it you thought you'd find here?"

"I don't even know. Closure?"

"Closure for you or for Marthe? Ça fait rien. Either way, there is no such thing. Life moves on, the world moves on, the seeds we plant continue to grow. But Marthe de Florian is quite fortunate, non? Despite the crazy. Not many of us have pretty scholars caring about our personal exploits a century in arrears. Marthe will have her big auction. Her portrait will sell to some rich old fop for a million euros or more. The way I see it, she ended up better than most."

Luc stubbed out his cigarette.

"Please refrain from throwing out any seven-figure numbers," April grumbled. "I don't know what I'll do if that painting doesn't go for what it should."

"Provenance, ma belle. Provenance."

Someone shuffled into the kitchen then, an Asian woman in a kimono. She told them Madame Vannier had retired for the day. She trusted they could see their way out and back to Paris, extra emphasis on "back to Paris."

"That's quite the unceremonious dismissal," April murmured once the woman spun back out of the room. "Don't let the door hit your ass on the way out."

" 'Don't let the door hit your ass.' I like it. Into my collection of American idioms it goes!"

They stood. April stole one last glance at Madame Vannier's kitchen (Lisette's kitchen, Marguérite's kitchen) before tiptoeing out into the hallway.

"It's probably best we go now anyway," Luc said once they were in the foyer. He swung open the thick oak door and paused at the top step. The morning sunlight shot through his hair. It turned his brown eyes almost green. "We are nearly out of time. Are you ready to leave Sarlat?"

"Never mind Sarlat." April lifted her tote and flung it over her right shoulder. "My flight departs in twelve hours. I have to be ready to leave Paris."

"Not to worry. You'll be back."

April smiled and shuffled down the steps. Her bag was lighter now without the perpetual existence of Marthe's journals inside. It was odd to think of it as empty. It was odd to think her job was done and in twenty-four hours she would be back in the United States.

April tried to imagine herself driving away from Madame Vannier's home. She pictured arriving in Paris and Luc standing on the corner hailing her a taxi. April would sit in the backseat while the driver wound out of the city, Paris dropping farther and farther behind her.

She could hear the sound of the jet's engines and feel the cardboard-like airplane floor beneath her feet. Taste of stale air in her nose and mouth, April would take a seat by the window, always by the window. The engines would rev and they'd fly back out over Paris, a million lights twinkling below.

Eventually the aircraft would touch down in New York. It seemed far-fetched even if landing was goal number one. April tried to feel herself exiting the plane and swimming through the melee of travelers. She imagined the long and winding customs line. Then what?

If he kept his promise, Troy would be waiting outside security. If he was there, he might grab April's bag (this time she'd let him) and put an arm around her shoulders. Together they'd find a way to navigate their new old relationship.

"Fifty-fifty chance," they said on the beach in Coronado. It was not a sure thing but much better odds than April had given herself. Best of all, for two people who made their livings estimating value, in finance or in furniture, what might be a low number to most was understood by both to be something more. It was not a crapshoot but fifty hard-fought points, worthy of the effort and a very solid start.

April remembered her hesitation when she first stepped into Marthe's apartment and saw the dust-caked furniture clumped in groups and shrouded from the outside. Assessing so many pieces seemed dauntingly hopeless at the time, never mind the matter of how to make sense of the assets' meaning and value. Still, April dug in and ultimately found what she needed. Provenance mattered. History mattered. But it could not guarantee what might happen next.

Her marriage was no less overwhelmed, no less cluttered. This time, though, April knew what kind of courage would be required, the honesty it would take, to root around until her hands cracked and fingernails bled. After tackling Marthe's chaos, her own did not appear quite so bad. There was value there. And unlike with Madame de Florian, there were only two people who needed to see it.

Chapitre LXXVIII

PROPERTY FROM THE
MADAME DE FLORIAN COLLECTION
Important Continental Furniture,
Fine & Decorative Art

MARTHE DE FLORIAN: An Appreciation

Her apartment was shuttered for seventy years, since before World War II and indeed before this auctioneer and many of our bidders were born.

Last spring, when I stepped inside the former 9e flat of Marthe de Florian, I was taken aback by the sheer magnitude and beauty of the pieces before me. Every major period from George II and Louis VXI onward was represented, not a category of Continental furniture or fine art overlooked. It was and remains the single largest and most valuable group of assets belonging to one family that I have seen.

All these months later, I still find myself wondering if I really did see the apartment and its exquisite pieces, all of them entirely fresh to market. My first glance around the home revealed a pink and gilded fairy world, the spoils and their stories all the more bewitching as I delved deeper. Our team encountered an unending supply of treasures, all given life by the diaries left behind, photographic excerpts of which can be found in this catalogue.

Her name might not be familiar to bidders, but the apartment's former occupant and author of the journals, Madame de Florian, was a Parisian courtesan who died in 1935. In her tenure as one of the most famous *demimondaines* of the Belle Époque she entertained the likes of statesman Georges Clemenceau, Count Robert de Montesquiou, and portraitist Giovanni Boldini, who has a very important piece in this auction.

Madame de Florian willed the home's contents to her granddaughter, Elisabetta Quatremer. When the Nazis descended upon Paris in 1940, Madame Quatremer locked the apartment, fled the city, and never returned, though she continued paying rent on the flat for the next seventy years.

Madame Quatremer died earlier this year in Sarlat, and it was the woman raised as her sister who contacted Sotheby's to conduct the sale of the Madame de Florian Collection. We are incredibly honored to oversee this auction. I've gone to great lengths to capture the magic of the lots, and I hope Madame de Florian would be proud.

Some of my most cherished pieces include a pair of painted ostrich eggs, a Napoleon III giltwood looking glass and console originally from a palace in Cairo, and a set of two George III mahogany serpentine commodes in condition so excellent they should really be considered new. That is, if they weren't more than two hundred years old.

Though I should not pick a favorite, I will, and therefore must admit it is the portrait of Madame de Florian painted by Giovanni Boldini. Any moderately well-versed collector understands the significance of a Boldini in its own right, but this work is important for reasons beyond the person who created it. Not only is it the first time this painting has been on the market, a heady-enough claim, but it is also the first time the art world has known of its existence.

Let that sink in for a moment. A Giovanni Boldini: he, the greatest portraitist of the Belle Époque, and a piece unknown to the world, unknown to those who are paid to know everything when it comes to this.

Beyond the Boldini, the quality of the collection defies description, each lot a piece that seduces, each asset untouched since before the Second World War. Prepare to be charmed and dazzled by the oak and giltwood and silver, but mostly by Marthe de Florian herself. Though don't let yourself fall too far under her spell, as competition abounds. You don't want to be caught daydreaming when the final hammer is thrown.

April Vogt
Senior Vice President
French & Continental Furniture

EPILOGUE

April held the book in her hands: three thousand lots, six pounds of finely glossed paper, one woman's estate. The Madame de Florian Collection was finally ready for the auction floor.

Because of the size, they'd broken the auction into sixteen sessions held over one week's time. In the days leading up to opening night, dealers and collectors from around the world descended on Paris to participate in the private views, VIP dinners, and all the ancillary schmoozing required for an event of this size. Heavyweights mingled as the big-breasted client-service specialists tottered around in their red-soled heels.

Opening night was the most important, featuring the biggest of the big-ticket items. The first few properties set the tone for the rest of the auctions. They had to create a buzz loud enough to bring more players to the table. So while there were three thousand lots, the success of the entire auction hinged on the first, the most important, the Boldini. The estimate in the catalog was one million euros. To consider it a success Marthe de Florian had to go for at least one-point-two.

April fretted in one of the VIP skyboxes as she watched Olivier do his sound check. Various worker bees crept along the floor using rulers to properly space the distance between chairs. The people manning the phone banks checked dial tones and cords, sometimes crawling beneath desks in tuxedos and ball gowns to inspect faulty connections. Soon the doors would open and one thousand people would filter in.

Unable to sit, April paced by the front windows, fussing with the curtains as she went. Behind her sat Peter. Beside Peter sat Troy, thumbing through the catalog, frowning at the high prices. Really? Fifty thousand euros for an old chair? It produces no revenue, no EBITDA! As if earnings before interest, taxes, depreciation, and amortization meant anything. His models would've had Marthe's entire apartment fully depreciated, and therefore worthless. She'd quell that deal mind of his yet.

Two rows back sat Birdie, and beside her a woman April considered the most Important Person of all the Very ones in attendance, at least in terms of the auction. It was Agnès Vannier, accompanied by her velvet blanket, home health aides, and a fiendish half-smile.

April was anxious for the bidding to start. Through the windows she watched the press swarm below. Eventually representatives herded the reporters to the standing-room-only section and cordoned them off with a red rope. Bidders started to fill the room.

Once seated, the bidders flicked through the catalog. From her perch April studied the crowd, with particular focus on those in the front seats, the ones most likely to spring for the high-ticket items. She knew to look for that nervous, squirmy energy bidders exhibited moments before lifting a paddle. A lot of people were fidgeting in that room, not only those in the premium seats.

At seven o'clock Olivier took the podium. He could not see her through the double-paned glass, but April gave a thumbs-up nonetheless, though the action was really more for her than it was for him.

"Good evening, ladies and gentlemen," he said. "Welcome to Sotheby's, and to this evening's sale of the Madame de Florian Collection. I think you'll find this collection as remarkable as we have. A few reminders before we begin."

The crowd's twitchiness intensified as Olivier read the bidding rules as well as the conditions of the sale. Finally (finally!) after the taxes-commissions-premiums rigmarole, he gestured toward Marthe, who sat propped up on the rotating stage, bathed in light and shining in her pink-dressed glory. If only she could've seen the cameras, felt the fervor, heard the eruption of cheers. Not even the grandest show at the Folies could've compared.

"Lot one," Olivier called out and banged the gavel.

Then he started. Marthe de Florian was on her way.

"At five hundred thousand euros?" he said. "Do I hear five hundred thousand euros? Who will bid in at half a million?"

The room remained still. April's heart scrambled up into her throat. She held her breath while glaring at the former fidgeters, willing them to bid in.

"Five hundred thousand euros," Olivier said again. "Do I hear five hundred thousand?"

Something creaked behind her. April turned around to see Luc Thébault slip through the door. He planted himself beside Madame Vannier. April smiled. She hadn't been sure he would make it.

"Half a million here," Olivier said as a paddle went up. April exhaled in relief and felt Luc nodding behind her. "Six hundred thousand euros? Do I hear six hundred thousand?"

The excitement started then. All the parties and receptions and even those topheavy women did what they were supposed to. They created hysteria. Paddles shot up.

"Seven hundred fifty thousand euros. Here."

"Eight hundred thousand. Here."

"Nine hundred. Here."

"One million. Here."

They hit the estimate. April exhaled again and closed her eyes. This, a painting not even the French government would take.

Tonight you are the most famous woman in all of Paris, Marthe. Enjoy it.

The numbers continued to climb. One-point-one million euros. A paddle went up for one-point-two million, the magic number at which April considered the sale a success. Perhaps Marthe's newfound fame might last longer than one night.

Olivier's mouth moved faster. Paddles shot up with more frequency. People dialed into the phone banks, the operators scrambling to keep up. The crowd rumbled with excitement.

When the number jumped above one-point-five-million April clapped. She looked over to find Troy on his feet, standing beside her cheering as though he were at a sporting event and not watching fine art.

The number hit two million euros. April yelped, her pulse racing, her brain light. She turned to Madame Vannier, who sat in a wheelchair smiling in satisfaction.

"At two-point-one million euro. Are we finished? Fair warning. Last chance at two-point-one million euro," Olivier said. Then, as the entire room held its breath, "Sold! Two-point-one million euros. To bidder number three-three-four."

April thought she might pass out. She truly thought she might.

The floor broke out in applause. People leapt to their feet and Marthe received a standing ovation lasting two minutes, three minutes, four minutes, more. April attended a Super Bowl once. The excitement and cheers did not come close to what was happening now. Two-point-one million euros, nearly three million U.S. dollars.

"You did it!" Troy said and wrapped April in a hug. "Damn, that was exciting! You did it!"

"No. It wasn't me." April stepped back. "It was Marthe, all Marthe. And this is just the start. There are thousands more lots. I can't believe it. I really can't believe it."

At the podium Olivier called out for lot number two. Legs weak, April slumped into her seat. Troy whooped one more time and sat beside her. He kissed her cheek.

"Brilliant work, babe," he said. "Brilliant."

The remaining properties continued on at the same rapid clip, the excitement escalating and reverberating through the walls and into the skyboxes. Paddles popped up like fireworks. The price board flickered. Numbers and currencies scattered down the board as April made notes, her mouth open in shock. By the end of the night 150 assets had been sold.

Though the prices, as expected, never matched the Boldini, they were all elevated by Marthe's portrait, and maybe also a little by the journal entries interspersed throughout the book.

In the end April did not have to write "Passed" on a single item. The collection was 100 percent sold. The best April had ever done in a single night was 91 percent. But tonight it was 100 percent .

When the final gavel of the night hit the podium, April sprang from her chair. Hugs were exchanged all around. She didn't have the data in front of her, but April knew this would be the most successful auction her small department had ever done. Though perhaps Sotheby's would not consider it small anymore.

"Madame Vannier," April said, when she finally managed to catch her breath, when all hugs and kisses were distributed and most of the skybox emptied. "These numbers, they are unprecedented!"

"It was very exciting," she agreed. "I did not expect to have such fun."

"Well, I'm glad you could come," April said as two men helped Madame Vannier up from her wheelchair.

Upon standing Madame Vannier smoothed the skirt of her iridescent navy gown and then fiddled with the sapphire-and-diamond earrings pulling down her lobes. She smiled, her face suddenly a decade, two decades younger. Her white hair glittered beneath the chandelier.

"I must confess," she said. "It was rather exhilarating. I can see why you have such enthusiasm for your work. It's nice to know my father's paintings weren't so worthless, so out of style. I think he would've been pleased."

" 'Worthless'? Not a chance! Based on the purchase price, few artists are worth more. Your father, he set records tonight. He set a record for his own works. This I know."

Madame Vannier blinked. Hard. Her eyes turned wet as April's gut clenched. She knew better than to personalize the item, to make the seller regret putting it on the floor.

"Your father"—April started, the words gummed up in her mouth—"it's obviously a bit late, but you know we could've arranged for you to keep it? You did not have to sell the painting. There are plenty of other items, as you can see. I'm concerned this wasn't made clear."

She was not supposed to say that, or anything like it. Had Peter still been in the room he would've tried to push her through the plate-glass window.

"No, Madame Vogt," Agnès said with a chuckle. "I did not want that particular painting. It was the money I was after. I needed the money."

April glanced over at Luc, the man forever her Parisian barometer, and noted the smile he was very carefully trying to keep off his face. The woman wanted money, but April couldn't point out the obvious, namely that the auction would generate more than Madame Vannier could spend in the balance of her lifetime.

"I know what you are thinking," Madame Vannier said and laughed again. "That I am too old to need all this money, non? I will die soon. What a waste!"

"Of course not! You're not old at all!"

"That is not true in the least. I am excessively ancient. Alas, I do not want the money for jewels or fancy shoes." She snickered and pointed to the silk slippers on her feet. "The painting, your Boldini, no one knew of its existence before, *non*?"

"Correct," April said. "It was a shock to everyone."

"Giovanni Boldini has another covert painting, ma chérie. It is owned by a private investor and has never once passed through an auction house."

"That's actually rather common. Many of Boldini's works are owned by individuals."

"Yes, but only a few people know of this one's existence. Andreas!" Madame Vannier snapped. "Where is my coat? I am ready to leave. I would like my coat applied to my body this instant!"

"Which painting?" April asked. "I am quite familiar with the full spectrum of his works."

"You don't know this one," Madame Vannier said and wiggled into her jacket, a deep brown mink. "It is a painting of my mother. She is nursing me."

"Another unknown Boldini?"

"Oui. And now I finally have the funds to purchase it from the private investor."

April laughed, out of shock and nervousness and some other feeling she could not articulate. There was another Giovanni Boldini in the world, and Agnès Vannier planned to get her hands on it.

"I suppose I don't need to tell you but this price point will not help your negotiations," April said, still laughing.

"Perhaps you are right," Agnès said with sparks in her eyes. "Mine also has—what do you call it? Ah, yes, this painting has quite the fascinating provenance."

After wrapping a scarf around her neck, Madame Vannier grabbed hold of one of her two helpers and doddered out of the room, leaving April dumbfounded and Luc, forever, smirking.

"I see what you're devising," Luc said, the first words he'd spoken to her that night. "You hope to get the premium on that sale."

"That is not true one bit. I also want the commission."

Troy appeared behind him then, chuckling and shaking his head.

"Monsieur, you know my wife quite well. Can you believe this racket? Charging the sellers and the buyers?" He extended his hand. "Troy Vogt. I don't believe we've met."

"So this is le grand m'sieu. It's a pleasure. Luc Thébault."

" 'Le grand m'sieu.' At some point one of you will really have to tell me what that means. Anyway, thank you for ensuring my wife didn't get into any trouble this summer. It is much appreciated."

"Ce n'est pas un problème. I did what I could. It's a shame you were never able to make a visit."

"Well, that should be rectified soon," Troy said. "Did she tell you? We'll be moving to Paris in the new year."

"Paris?" Luc said, a funny look skittering across his face. He gave April a quick glance from beneath his eyelashes. "This is fantastic news, but it is the first I'm hearing of it. Regardless, bravo! I know your wife is happiest here."

"That's the plan," Troy said. "To make her the happiest."

"Avril!" Luc almost sang. "Such news you've kept from me!"

"Well, nothing's set in stone. We're still waiting for the final okay from the Paris office . . ." April let her words trail off. "So, where's . . . ? I'm surprised you didn't bring a date . . . I mean, how come Delphine's not here?" April turned to Troy. "You should meet his girlfriend. She works in finance too, and is about as stunning a creature as you could imagine."

"Oh! Great! I'd love to meet her!" Troy said a little too enthusiastically, clearly glad this Frenchman had romantic interests aside from his wife.

"Alas," Luc said and smiled sadly. "Delphine is no longer. Or no longer in my world in any case." He shrugged before either could express condolences. "C'est la vie. Sometimes things do not work out as you'd like."

Suddenly the phone rang. It was Olivier, dialing up from one of the operator's phones below. The first night was over. April should come down. This was her show, and he wanted her to share in the glory. Furthermore, if her transfer to the Paris office was going to work out, April needed to meet the European players.

"Olivier wants me on the floor," April said, heart still pounding, adrenaline pulsing through her veins.

"All right," Luc replied. "I will see you tomorrow."

"Yes, tomorrow."

"Nice to meet you, buddy," her big, handsome American husband said.

"Yes, okay, right, buddy."

Smiling, April reached for her bag. She peeked inside to make sure they were there: a new set of letters and documents. These were not as old as Marthe's, a few decades compared to a hundred years, but they were more valuable, at least to April.

The papers were not from some stranger's estate but from her father. April's parents had been packrats after all, at least when it came to letters posted to and from Vietnam. There was even a journal. For so many years April asked about furniture and knickknacks. She never thought to ask for letters.

They walked down the stairs, April grinning as if she might never stop. Troy paused. He leaned into April's ear, and a chill ran along her skin.

"When we move, am I going to have to get chest-hair implants? Because, looking around, I question whether I have the ability to blend in."

"If everything goes the way it should, lack of chest hair will be the least of your problems."

"You're telling me." He rolled his eyes and pretended to groan. "Up to my neck in furniture and Frenchies all damned day."

April laughed.

"You could do worse."

She stepped around him and out into the thick din of voices on the floor. People closed in on her from all sides. As well-wishers kissed April and shook her hand, Troy kept a palm at the small of her back. She wanted to turn around, ask that he bear with her for the remainder of the night. Ask that he stay. Then April remembered. She didn't need to ask. There was no reason to think he wouldn't.

Hugo Extended Family

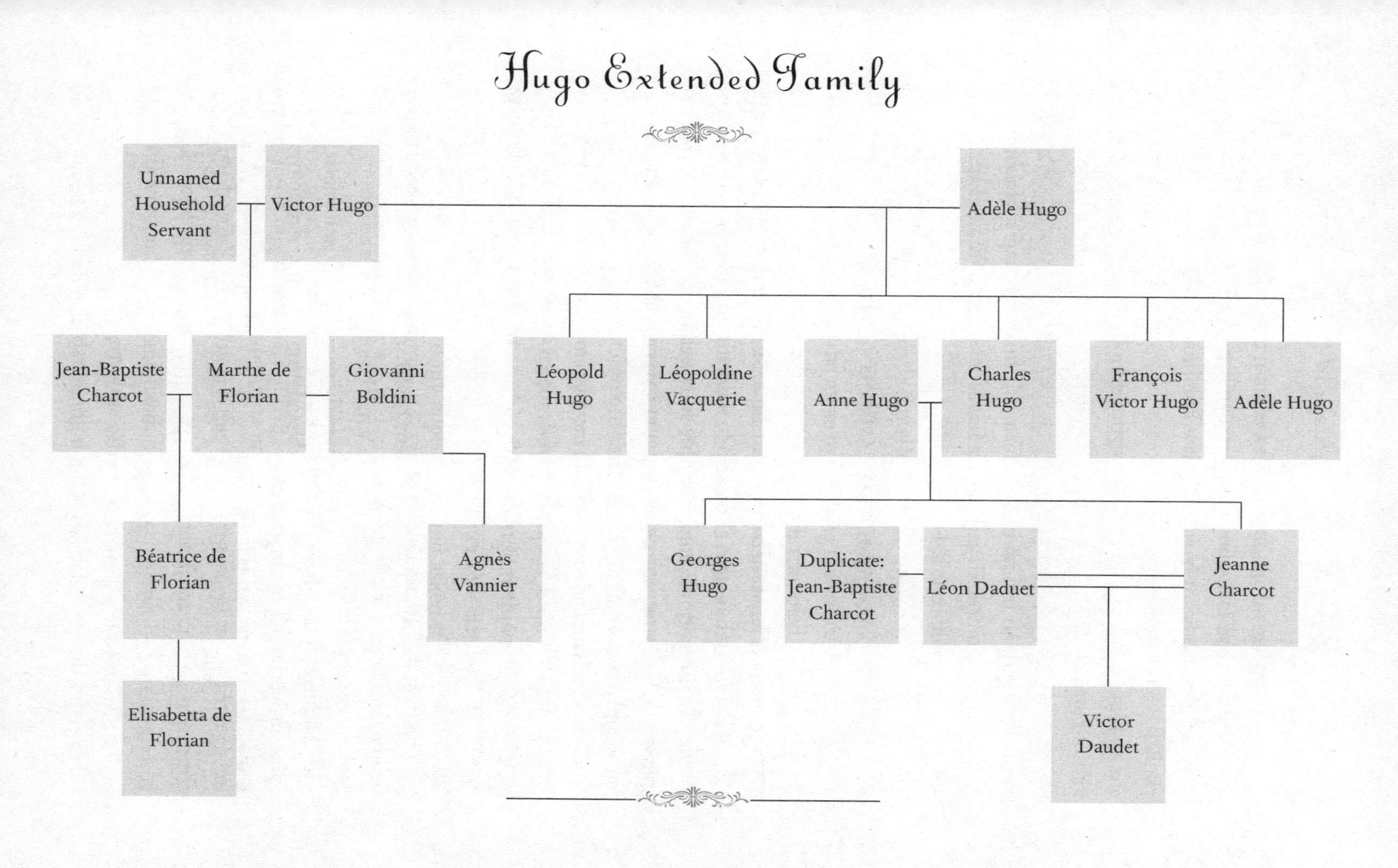

Acknowledgments

There would be no acknowledgments to write, indeed no book at all, if not for the tireless, impossible, and crafty machinations of Barbara Poelle. Thank you, Barbara, not only for sending me the article that inspired this book, but for believing in my voice, sticking with the turbulence, and always making me feel like the only client you have.

To my brilliant and savvy editor, Katie Gilligan, who understood where I was going with April Vogt before I did. I appreciate your enthusiasm, keen insight, and ability to push me in ways I never conceived. I will gladly share a bottle of wine (or two) with you (and Barbara) any day of the week . . . whole pig and all.

The crew at Thomas Dunne Books/St. Martin's Press worked tirelessly behind the scenes to make good on a tight timeline. Thank you to those I've spoken with, those I haven't, and specifically to Sally Richardson for her early backing and to Melanie Fried for keeping me and this project on track (plus answering all manner of befuddled newbie questions). My publicist Katie Bassel ran with this book the minute it landed on her desk. Thank you for your talent, smarts, and so deftly handling late-breaking changes and dramatics. A huge heap of credit goes also to copyeditor Sue Llewellyn. It's like you were born to edit this manuscript.

Thank you to Jeb Spencer, Sig Anderman, Jonathan Corr, and especially Ed Luce for the best "day job" (and night and weekend job) a person could have. I think most would be surprised how engaging and inspiring the corporate world can be.

Inspiration is a writer's greatest asset and no three authors have inspired me more than Tammy Greenwood, Allison Winn Scotch, and Amy Hatvany. Thank you for the continued advice, encouragement, and support.

I can't mention the word support without also thanking my friend of nearly thirty years, Karen Freeman Landers. Thank you for being a sounding board and sharing in the excitement (and attending any and all Chargers games). I am so lucky to have you in my corner.

I must also mention Jen McGlothlin (aka Jenny Walker), my very first "writing partner" and coauthor of myriad Sweet Valley High ripoffs. How did those not take off, I wonder? Thank you also to Aileen Dowd Brill for your advice and for reading many a manuscript along the way.

So many friends have championed this book and the process to get here. Offline and online . . . from book club (Michelle Campbell, Denisia Chatfield, Leesa Davis, Lisa Gal, Kerri Merson, Suzanne Miller, Heather Olson, Sabrina Parr, Kat Peppers, Kerry Rooney, Jenna Scarafone, Dede Watson), to my William & Mary crew (special shout out to Jes Singer), to Facebook groups, to the amazing community of Cardiff-by-the-Sea—thank you, thank you, thank you. I've always been reticent to share "writing stuff" but the reception has made me wish I'd started sharing sooner. I am overwhelmed with gratitude.

As much as I've hit the friend lottery, even more so the family one. To my father, Tom Gable, the first writer I ever admired, thank you for passing along your gifts, encouraging me to write from a young age, and, of course, being a humorous and complex character in your own right.

Thank you also to my mom, Laura Gable, though a mere thanks feels insufficient. The support you've given is unparalleled. I rely on you as much now as when I was a child, though in different ways. You are, in a word, the best.

I'm also fortunate to have two smart and quick-witted siblings to make every family meal entertaining and provide no shortage of material. To my brother, Brian Gable, thank you for lending your persona to the "Brian" character in this novel. I hope you find him sufficiently likable. And to my sister, Lisa Gable Wheatley, for your support and inspiring ambition and for reading several early stories.

Special recognition goes to the extended Gable clan, from California to Oklahoma to New York and everywhere in between. The world is livelier with you guys in it. And a thousand thank-yous to my mother- and father-in-law, Pat and Tony Bilski. You are the most supportive and nonjudgmental people I know, even when my work involves a prostitute. (Sorry!) Finally, to my beloved aunt Janet Yergler Rickerson. I am in awe of your strength and the faith and inspiration you've brought to so many.

And to my girls . . . where would I be without you both? Paige, my silly, sweet, smart firstborn. Thank you for being my reading buddy and for making motherhood easy. I'm sorry you can't read this book quite yet. I'll write something for you soon.

To my spunky Georgia peach, only seven years old and these aren't even the first acknowledgments you've been in. Thanks for lighting up (and amusing) this world on a daily basis, and for your endless social media–worthy comments and observations. You are a force. I wouldn't have it any other way.

My husband's name is at the start of this book, which is appropriate because of all the wonderful things in my life, they all start with him. DB, thank you for making me laugh, picking up my slack, and rolling your eyes only some of the time. I'm sorry the husbands in my stories are always such jerks. I promise you a good-looking, wry, super-nice-guy accountant one day.

And, finally, to the readers, to those who have read this book and those who will not. Thank you for finding and sharing new worlds. Thank you for the discussions had and the connections made. Wishing you many more journeys and a short path to your next favorite book.